"I'm do— — — —very penny I made. I don't care." Blythe smiled. "I have a job as of today. I don't need more than that."

Logan liked her attitude. He just wasn't sure he believed she could go from being rich and famous to being poor and unknown.

"Anyway, it probably doesn't matter," she added with a toss of her head.

"What do you mean, it probably doesn't matter?"

Again she looked away. He reached over to turn her to face him again. "What aren't you telling me? What was the real reason you ran away with me?"

"I told you. It was my girlhood fantasy to run away with a cowboy," she said.

He shook his head. "The truth, Blythe."

She swallowed, her throat working for a moment, then she sat up a little straighter as if steeling herself. "I think someone has been trying to kill me."

CORRALLED

BY
USA TODAY BESTSELLING AUTHOR
BJ DANIELS

First published in Great Britain 2012
by Mills & Boon, an imprint of Harlequin (UK) Limited,
Eton House, 18-24 Paradise Road, Richmond, Surrey TW9 1SR

© Barbara Heinlein 2012

ISBN: 978 0 263 89542 1
ebook ISBN: 978 1 408 97240 3

46-0712

Harlequin (UK) policy is to use papers that are natural, renewable and recyclable products and made from wood grown in sustainable forests. The logging and manufacturing processes conform to the legal environmental regulations of the country of origin.

Printed and bound in Spain
by Blackprint CPI, Barcelona

USA TODAY bestselling author **BJ Daniels** wrote her first book after a career as an award-winning newspaper journalist and author of thirty-seven published short stories. That first book, *Odd Man Out,* received a four-and-a-half-star review from *RT Book Reviews* and went on to be nominated for Best Intrigue that year. Since then she has won numerous awards, including a career achievement award for romantic suspense and many nominations and awards for best book.

Daniels lives in Montana with her husband, Parker, and two springer spaniels, Spot and Jem. When she isn't writing, she snowboards, camps, boats and plays tennis. Daniels is a member of Mystery Writers of America, Sisters in Crime, International Thriller Writers, Kiss of Death and Romance Writers of America.

To contact her, write to BJ Daniels, PO Box 1173, Malta, MT 59538, USA or e-mail her at bjdaniels@mtintouch.net. Check out her website at www.bjdaniels.com.

This is for my little brother, Charles Allen Johnson who, like the rest of the Johnson family, has always given me something to write about.

Chapter One

As he heard the music, he slowed his Harley, the throb of the engine catching the beat coming from the out-of-the-way country-western bar.

His kind of place.

He had been headed back to his hotel before that. But drawn to the music, he parked his motorcycle out front and pushed through the door into the dimly lit room. A clamor of glass and conversation competed with the band onstage.

Like him, most everyone inside was dressed in jeans and boots. The dance floor was packed, the air scented with beer and perfume as he stepped up to the bar and ordered a cold one.

Later he would recall sensing her presence even before he turned, a draft beer in hand, and first laid eyes on her.

He shoved back his Stetson, leaning against the bar, as she made her way through the crowd on the dance floor as if heading for the door. Her tight jeans hugged her hips as they swayed to the music, her full breasts pressing into the fabric of her Western shirt.

His gaze went to her boots, a pair of fancy Tony

Lama's so fresh out of the box that he could almost smell the new leather. That alone would have made him steer clear. Then he saw her face. It wasn't classically beautiful or even unusual enough to hold most men's attention.

No, but her expression of total bliss caught him like a well-thrown lasso. She stopped him in his tracks as he watched her. She was clearly lost in the music and he couldn't take his eyes off her.

When she finally looked up, her gaze locked with his. Her eyes were the color of worn jeans, her lashes dark and thick like her hair cascading from beneath her straw cowboy hat. She'd tied her hair back with a red ribbon, but loose tendrils had escaped and now framed her face.

As she started past him, impulsively he stepped in front of her. "I think you owe me a dance."

Her lips turned up in an amused smile. "Is that right?"

He nodded and, leaving his leather jacket on the bar stool, took her hand. She didn't put up a fight as he led her out onto the dance floor as one song ended. If anything, she seemed curious.

"You sure you can keep up with me?" she said challengingly as a fast song began.

He grinned, thinking the woman had no idea who she was dealing with. He was Montana born, raised on country music and cowboy jitterbug. But to his surprise, she had no trouble staying with him, giving back everything she got. He loved the way she moved with the music, all grace and sexy swing.

Everything about her surprised and thrilled him, especially the way they moved together. It was as if they were one of those older couples he'd seen in Montana bars who had danced together for years.

When the song ended and a slow dance began, she started to draw away, but he dragged her back and into his arms. She looked at him, that challenge still lighting those washed-out blue eyes of hers.

"What makes you think I don't have friends I need to get back to?" she asked as he pulled her closer, the two moving as one to the sweet sounds coming off the guitar player's strings.

"Why would you want to go back to them—if there really are people waiting for you—when you can dance with me?"

She laughed. It had a musical quality that pulled at him just as he'd been drawn to the bar band earlier.

"You are quite full of yourself," she said as if not minding it all that much.

He shook his head. "I just know there is nothing I want to do tonight but dance with you," he said honestly.

She grew serious as the song ended and another boot-stomping tune began. Her gaze locked with his as he let go of her.

"Up to you," he said quietly. Her answering smile was all invitation.

He took her hand and whirled her across the middle of the dance floor as the music throbbed, the beat matching that of his heart as he lost himself in the warm spring night, the music and this woman.

He made only one mistake as the band took a break not long before closing. He offered to buy her a drink, and when he turned back, she was gone.

As he stepped to the front door of the saloon, he was in time to see her pull away in an expensive silver convertible sports car, the top down. She glanced over at him as she left and he saw something in her expression that made him mentally kick himself for not getting her number. Or at least her name.

As she sped off, he walked back to the bar to finish his drink. He told himself that even if he had gotten her number or her name, he was only in Bigfork until tomorrow. He had to get back home to the ranch and work. But damned if he wouldn't have liked to have seen her again.

When he pulled on his leather jacket, he felt something in the pocket that hadn't been there earlier. Reaching his hand in, he pulled out a key. It wasn't like any he'd ever seen before. It was large and faux gold and had some kind of emblem on it. He couldn't make it out in the dim light of the bar, but he had a pretty good idea who'd put it in his jacket.

Finishing his beer, he pocketed the key again and left. As he climbed onto his bike, all he could think about was the woman. He couldn't remember a night when he'd had more fun or been more intrigued. Did she expect him to know what the key went to or how to find her? She expected a lot from this country boy, he thought with a smile.

He was still smiling as he cruised back to his hotel. The key was a challenge, and Logan Chisholm liked nothing better than a challenge. But if she was waiting for him tonight, she'd have a long wait.

THE NEXT MORNING LOGAN woke to see the key lying on the nightstand next to his bed. He'd tossed it there last night after taking a good look at it. He'd had no more idea what it went to than he had at the bar.

Now, though, he picked it up and ran his fingers over the raised emblem as he thought about the woman from the bar. He needed to get back to Whitehorse, back to work on his family's ranch, Chisholm Cattle Company. The last thing he needed was to go chasing after a woman he'd met on a country-western bar's dance floor miles from home.

But damned if he could leave the Flathead without finding her.

"Have you ever seen one of these?" Logan asked the hotel clerk downstairs.

"I'm sorry, Mr. Chisholm, I—"

"Isn't that a key to the Grizzly Club?" asked another clerk who'd been standing nearby. "Sorry to interrupt," he said. "But I have a friend who stayed out there once."

"The Grizzly Club?" Logan asked.

"It's an exclusive gated community south of here," the clerk said. "Very elite. You have to have five million dollars to even apply for a home site inside the development. A lot of famous people prefer that kind of privacy. There are only a few of these gated communities in Montana."

Logan knew about the one down by Big Sky. He thought about the woman at the bar last night. He couldn't see her living there, but he supposed it was possible she'd hooked up with some rich dude who'd invented computer chips or made a bundle as a famous news broadcaster. Or hell, maybe she invented the chip.

It wasn't like he really knew her after only a few dances on a spring Friday night at a country-western bar, was it?

He thought it more likely that she was a guest at the club. At least he liked that better than the other possibilities. "So you're saying this key will get me into the place?"

The clerk shook his head. "That key is to the amenities once you get inside. You don't need a key to get in the gate. There is a guard at the front gate. If someone lost their key, the guard might be able to tell you who it belongs to. I noticed it did have a number on it."

Logan didn't like the sound of a guard, but what did he have to lose? "How do I get there?"

Outside, he swung onto his bike and headed down Highway 35 south along the east side of Flathead Lake. The road was narrow, one side bordering the lake, the other rising steeply into the Mission Mountain Range. Flathead was the largest freshwater lake in the western United States, just slightly larger than Lake Tahoe. This morning it was a beautiful turquoise blue. Around the lake were hundreds of orchards making this part of Montana famous for its Flathead cherries.

The Grizzly Club sign was so small and tasteful that he almost missed the turn. The freshly paved road curled up into the mountains through dense, tall, dark pines. Logan always felt closed in by country like this because it was so different from where he lived. The Chisholm Cattle Company ranch sat in the middle of rolling Montana prairie where a man could see forever.

At home, the closest mountains were the Little Rockies, and those only a purple outline in the distance. Trees, other than cottonwoods along the Milk River and creeks, were few and far between. He loved the wide-open spaces, liked being able to see to the horizon, so he was glad when the trees finally opened up a little.

He slowed as he came to a manned gate. Beyond it, he could make out a couple of mansions set back in the trees. Was it possible one of them was owned by the woman he'd met last night? That could explain the new boots, since few people in this kind of neighborhood were from here—let alone lived here year-around.

He tried to imagine her living behind these gates even for a few weeks out of the year and decided she had to be visiting someone. A woman like that couldn't stand being locked up for long, he told himself.

The guard was on the phone and motioned for him to wait. Logan stared through the ornate iron gate and realized that the woman he was looking for could work here. And that expensive sports car convertible she was driving? She could have borrowed her boss's car last night.

He smiled. And like Cinderella, she'd had to get the car back before morning or suffer the consequences. Now that seemed more like the woman he'd met last night, he thought with a chuckle.

The guard finished his conversation and turning, perused Logan's leathers and the Harley motorcycle. He

instantly looked wary. Logan realized this had been a
mistake. No way was this man going to let him in or
give him the name of the woman connected to the key.
More than likely, the guard would call security. The
best he could see coming out of this was being turned
away—but only after he'd made a fool of himself.

Fortunately, he didn't get the chance. From the other
side of the gate, he saw the flash of a small silver sports
car convertible coming through the trees. The top was
still down. He caught a glimpse of the driver.

She'd done away with her cowboy attire, including
the hat. Her hair blew free, forming a wave like a ra-
ven's wing behind her as she sped toward the gate. She
wore large sunglasses that hid most of her face, but
there was no denying it was the woman from the bar.

"Never mind," Logan said to the guard and swung
his bike around as the gate automatically opened on the
other side of the guardhouse and the sports car roared
out.

Logan went after her.

He couldn't believe how fast she was driving, taking
the curves with abandon. He saw her glance in her rearview mirror and speed up. Logan did the same, the two
of them racing down out of the mountains and onto the
narrow road along the lake.

This woman is crazy, Logan thought when she hit
the narrow two-lane highway and didn't slow down.
She wanted to race? Then they would race.

He stayed right with her, roaring up beside her when
there was no traffic. She would glance at him, then gun

it, forcing him to fall behind her when an oncoming car appeared.

They were almost to the town of Bigfork when she suddenly hit the brakes and whipped off the road onto a wide spot overlooking the lake. She'd barely gotten the car stopped at the edge of the rocky cliff, the water lapping at the shore twenty feet below.

Logan skidded to a stop next to her car as she jumped out and, without a word, climbed onto the back of his bike. Wrapping her arms around his waist, she leaned into him and whispered, "Get me out of here."

After that exhilarating race, she didn't need to ask twice. He was all the more intrigued by this woman. He roared back onto the highway headed north toward Glacier National Park. As she pressed her body against his, he heard her let out a sigh, and wondered where they were headed both literally and figuratively.

Caught up in the moment, he breathed in the cool mountain air. It smelled of spring and new beginnings. He loved this time of year. Just as he loved the feel of the woman on the bike behind him.

The sun was warm as it scaled the back of the Mission Mountains and splashed down over Flathead Lake. At the north end of the lake, Logan pulled into a small out-of-the-way café that he knew catered to fishermen. "Hungry?"

She hesitated only a moment, then nodded, smiling, as she followed him into the café. He ordered them both the breakfast special, trout, hash browns, eggs and toast with coffee and watched her doctor her coffee with both sugar and cream.

"Are you at least going to tell me your name?" he asked as they waited for their order.

She studied him. "That depends. Do you live around here?"

He shook his head. "East of here, outside of a town called Whitehorse." He could tell she'd never heard of it. "It's in the middle of nowhere, a part of Montana most tourists never see."

"You think I'm a tourist?" She smiled at that.

"Aren't you?" He still couldn't decide if she was visiting the Grizzly Club or lived there with her rich husband. But given the way she'd left that expensive sports car beside the lake, he thought his present-day Cinderella theory might not be that far off base.

Maybe he just didn't want to believe it, but he was convinced she wasn't married to some tycoon. She hadn't been wearing a wedding ring last night or today. Not only that, she didn't act married—or in a committed relationship. Not that he hadn't been wrong about that before.

"Don't you think you should at least tell me your name?" he asked.

She looked around the café for a moment as if considering telling him her name. When those pale blue eyes came back to him, she said, "Blythe. That's my name."

"Nice to meet you, Blythe." He reached across the table extending his hand. "Logan. You have a last name?"

Her hand felt small and warm in his. She didn't clean houses at the Grizzly Club, that was definite, he thought, as he felt her silky-smooth palm. Several silver bracelets jingled lightly on her slim tanned wrist. But she could still be a car thief.

"Blythe is good enough for now, don't you think?"

"I guess it depends on what happens next."

She grinned. "What would you like to happen next?"

"I'm afraid I have to head back home today, otherwise I might have had numerous suggestions."

"Back to Whitehorse," she said studying him. "Someone waiting for you back there?"

"Nope." He could have told her about his five brothers and his father and stepmother back at the ranch, but he knew that wasn't what she'd meant. He'd also learned the hard way not to mention Chisholm Cattle Company. He'd seen too many dollar signs appear in some women's eyes. There was a price to be paid when you were the son of one of the largest ranch owners in the state.

"Someone waiting for *you* back at the Grizzly Club?" he asked.

"Nope."

Their food arrived then and she dived into hers as if she hadn't eaten in a week. She might not have, he realized. He had no idea who this woman was or what was going to happen next, but he didn't care. He liked her, liked watching her eat. She did it with the same kind of passion and abandon she'd shown dancing and driving.

"I've never seen that part of Montana," she said as they were finishing. She wiped her expressive mouth and tossed down her napkin. "Show me."

He raised a brow. "It's a five-hour drive from here."

When she didn't respond, he asked, "What about your car?"

"It's a rental. I'll call and have the agency collect it."

He considered her for a moment. "You don't want to pick up anything from your house?"

"It's not my house, and I like to travel light."

Logan still wasn't sure she was serious about going with him, but serious or not, he was willing to take her up on whatever she was offering. He liked that he had no idea who she was, what she wanted or what she would do next. It had been too long since a woman had captivated him to the point that he was willing to throw caution to the wind.

"Let's ride then." As they left the café, he couldn't help but notice the way she looked around as if afraid of who might be waiting for her outside. He was reminded of how she'd come flying out of the Grizzly Club. Maybe she really had stolen that car she'd been driving and now he was harboring a criminal.

He laughed to himself. He was considered the rebel Chisholm brother. The one who'd always been up for any adventure, whether it was on horseback or a Harley. But as they walked to his motorcycle, he had a bad feeling that he might be getting into more than even he could handle.

Chapter Two

Sheriff Buford Olson hitched up his pants over his expanding belly, reached back into his patrol car for his Stetson and, closing the door, tilted his head back to look up at the hotel-size building called the Main Lodge.

Buford hated getting calls to come out to the Grizzly Club. It wasn't that he disliked the rich, although he did find them demanding and damned irritating.

It was their private security force, a bunch of punk kids, who made his teeth ache. Buford considered anyone under thirty-five to be a kid. The "club" had given these kids a uniform and a gun and turned them into smart-ass, dangerous punks who knew diddly-squat about law enforcement.

Buford always wondered why the club had to call him in if their security force was so capable. It was no secret that the club liked to handle its own problems. The people who owned homes inside the gates didn't want anyone outside them knowing their business. So the whole idea was to sweep whatever trouble the club had under one of their expensive Persian rugs.

Worse, the folks who owned the club didn't want to

upset the residents—or jeopardize new clientele—so they wanted everyone to believe that once they were behind these gates they were safe and nothing bad could happen.

Buford snorted at the thought, recalling how the general manager had asked him to park in the back of the main lodge so he wouldn't upset anyone. The guard at the gate had said, "Sheriff Buford, right? I heard you were here for a complimentary visit."

A complimentary visit. That had made him contrary enough that he'd parked right out front of "the Main Lodge." Now, though, as he started up the wide flagstone steps, he wished he hadn't been so obstinate. He felt his arthritis bothering him and, worse, his stomach roiling against the breakfast his wife had cooked him.

Clara had read in one of her magazines that if you ate a lot of hot peppers it would make you lose weight. She'd been putting hot chile peppers in everything they ate—and playing hell with his stomach.

The general manager he'd spoken to earlier spotted him and came rushing toward him. The diminutive man, whose name Buford couldn't recall at first, was painfully thin with skin that hadn't seen sunlight and piercing blue eyes that never settled more than a second.

"I thought I told you to park in the back."

Buford shrugged. "So what's the problem?" he asked as he looked around the huge reception area. All the leather, antler lamps and chandeliers, thick rugs and gleaming wood floors reminded him of Clara's designer magazines.

Montana style, they called it. The Lodge Look. Buford was old enough to remember when a lot of places looked like this, only they'd been the real McCoy—not this forced Montana style.

"In here," the general manager ordered, drawing him into a small, claustrophobic office with only one window that looked out on the dense forest. The name on the desk read Kevin Andrews, General Manager.

Kevin closed the door and for the first time, Buford noticed how nervous the man appeared. The last time Buford had been called here was for a robbery inside the gates. That time he'd thought Kevin was going to have a heart attack, he'd been so upset. But once the missing jewelry, which turned out only to have been misplaced, was found, all was well and quickly forgotten.

Buford guessed though that it had taken ten years off Kevin's life from the looks of him. "So what's up? More missing jewelry?"

"This is a very delicate matter. I need you to handle it with the utmost care. Do I have your word?"

Buford felt his stomach roil again. He was in no mood for this. "Just tell me what's happened."

The general manager rose from his chair with a brisk "come with me."

Buford followed him out to a golf cart. Resigned that he had no choice but to ride along, he climbed on. Kevin drove them through the ritzy residence via the narrow paved roads that had been hacked out of the pines.

The hotel-size houses were all set back from the

road, each occupying at least ten acres from Buford's estimation since the buildings had to take up three of those acres with guest houses of another half acre. Each log, stone and glass structure was surrounded by pine trees so he only caught glimpses of the exclusive houses as Kevin whipped along the main road.

Finally he pulled down one of the long driveways, coming to a stop in front of a stone monstrosity with two wide wooden doors. Like the others, the house was all rock and logs with massive windows that looked out over the pines on the mountainside and Flathead Lake far below.

Buford saw with a curse that two of the security force's golf carts were parked out front. One of the garage doors was open. A big, black SUV hunkered in one of the three stalls. The others were empty.

Getting off the golf cart, he let Kevin lead him up to the front door. Bears had been carved into the huge wooden doors, and not by some roadside chainsaw artist. Without knocking, Kevin opened the door and Buford followed him inside.

He was hit at once with a familiar smell and felt his stomach clutch. This was no missing jewelry case.

With dread, he moved across the marble floor to where the walls opened into a football field–size living room with much the same furnishings as the club's main lodge. The two security guards were standing at the edge of the room. They had been visiting, but when they saw Kevin, they tried to act professional.

Buford looked past them to the dead man sprawled beside the hearth of the towering rock fireplace. The deceased was wearing a white, blood-soaked velour robe and a pair of leather slippers on his feet. Apparently nothing else.

"Get them out of here," Buford ordered, pointing at the two security guards. He could only guess at how many people had already tromped through here contaminating the scene. "Stay back and make sure no one else comes traipsing through here."

He swore under his breath as he worked his way across the room to the fireplace and the dead man. The victim looked to be in his late fifties, but could have been older because, from the tightness of his facial skin, he'd had some work done. His hair was dark with distinguishing gray at the temples, a handsome man even in death.

It appeared he'd been shot in the heart at point-blank range. An expensive handgun lay on the floor next to the body in a pool of drying blood. Clearly the man had been dead for hours. Buford swore again. He'd bet that Kevin had contacted the Grizzly Club board before he'd called the sheriff's department.

Around the dead man were two different distinct prints left in his blood. One was a man-size dress shoe sole. The other a cowboy boot—small enough that Buford would guess it was a woman's. It was her prints that held his attention. The woman hadn't walked away—she'd run—straight for the front door.

AT THE MOTORCYCLE, BLYTHE tied up her hair and climbed on behind the cowboy. She didn't think about what she was doing as she wrapped her arms around him. All she knew was that she had to escape, and wherever Logan was headed was fine with her. Even better, this Whitehorse place sounded like the end of the earth. With luck, no one would find her there.

She reminded herself that she'd thought this part of Montana would be far from the life she wanted so desperately to leave behind. But she'd been wrong.

Running didn't come easy to her. She'd always been a fighter. But not today. Today she only wanted to forget everything, hang on to this good-looking cowboy on the back of his motorcycle, feel the wind in her face and put her old life as far behind her as possible.

An image flashed in her mind, making her shudder, and she glanced down at her cowboy boots. She quickly wiped away a streak of dark red along the sole as Logan turned the key and brought the Harley to life.

She felt the throb of the engine and closed her eyes and her mind the way she used to tune out her mother when she was a girl. Back then it was to close out the sound of her mother and her latest boyfriend arguing in the adjacent room of the small, old trailer house. She had learned to go somewhere else, be *someone* else, always dreaming of a fantasy life far away.

With a smile, she remembered that one of her daydreams had been to run away with a cowboy. The thought made her hold on to Logan tighter as he shifted and tore out of the café parking lot in a shower of gravel.

Last night dancing with Logan she'd thought she was finally free. It was the best she'd felt in years. Now she pressed her cheek into the soft warmth of his leather jacket, lulled by the pulse of the motorcycle, the feel of the wind in her hair. She couldn't believe that he'd found her.

What had she been thinking giving him that damned key? She'd taken a terrible risk, but then she'd never dreamed he would come looking for her. What if he had gotten into the Grizzly Club this morning before she'd gotten out of there?

She shook off the thought and watched the countryside blur past, first forest-covered mountains, then wide-open spaces as they raced along the two-lane highway that cut east across the state.

She'd gotten away. No one knew where she was. But still she had to look back. The past had been chasing her for so long, she didn't kid herself that it wasn't close behind.

There were no cars close behind them, but that didn't mean that they wouldn't be looking for her.

For a moment, she considered what she'd done. She didn't know this cowboy, didn't know where he was taking her or what would happen when they got there.

This is so like you. Leaping before you look. Not thinking about the consequences of your actions. As if you weren't in enough trouble already.

Her mother's words rang in her ears. The only difference this time was that she wasn't that fourteen-year-old girl with eleven dollars in the pocket of her worn jean jacket and her only possession a beat-up guitar one of her mother's boyfriend's had left behind.

She'd escaped both times. That time from one of her

mother's amorous boyfriends and with her virginity. This time with her life. At least so far.

That reckless spirit is going to get you into trouble one day. You mark my words, girl.

Wouldn't her mama love to hear that she'd been right. But mama was long dead and Jennifer Blythe James was still alive. If anything, that girl and the woman she'd become was a survivor. She'd gotten out of that dirty desert trailer park where she'd started life. She would get out of this.

"Who's the victim?" Sheriff Buford Olson asked, sensing the Grizzly Club general manager hovering somewhere at a discreet distance behind him.

"Martin Sanderson," Kevin said. "It's his house."

Buford studied the larger bloody footprint next to the body. At a glance, he could see that it didn't match the soles of the two security guards or the general manager's, and unlike the other smaller print, this one headed not for the door, but in the opposite direction.

As he let his gaze follow the path the bloody prints had taken, Buford noted that the man had tried to wipe his shoe clean of the blood on an expensive-looking rug between the deceased and the bar where he was now lounging.

Buford was startled to see the man making himself at home at the bar with a drink in his hand. How many people had those dumb security guards let in?

"What the hell?" the sheriff demanded as he pushed himself up from where he'd been squatting beside the body. The "club" gave him a royal pain. He moved toward the bar, being careful not to step on the bloody footprints the man had left behind.

Buford didn't need to ask the man's name. He recognized Jett Akins only because his fourteen-year-old granddaughter Amy had a poster of the man on her bedroom wall. On the poster, Jett had been wearing all black—just as he was this morning—and clutching a fancy electric guitar. Now he clutched a tumbler, the dark contents only half full.

The one time his granddaughter had played a Jett Atkin's song for him, Buford had done his best not to show his true feelings. The so-called song had made him dearly miss the 1960s. Seemed to him there hadn't been any good music since then, other than country-western, of course.

"Mr. Atkins found the body," Kevin said from the entryway.

Jett Atkins looked pale and shaken. He downed the rest of his drink as the sheriff came toward him. Buford would guess it wasn't his first.

"You found the body?" he asked Jett, who looked older than he had on his poster. He had dark hair and eyes and a large spider tattoo on his neck and more tattoos on the back of his hands—all that was showing since the black shirt he wore was long-sleeved.

"I flew in this morning and took a taxi here. When I saw Martin, I called the club's emergency number." His voice died off as he looked again at the dead man by the fireplace and poured himself another drink.

Buford wanted to ask why the hell he hadn't called 911 instead of calling the club's emergency number. Isn't that what a normal person would do when he found a dead body?

He turned to Kevin again. "How many people were in this house?"

"Mr. Sanderson had left the names of six approved guests at the gate with the guard, along with special keys for admittance to all the amenities on the grounds," Kevin said in his annoyingly official tone. "All of those keys have been picked up."

"*Six* people? So where are they?" the sheriff demanded. "And I am going to need a list of their names." Before he could finish, Kevin withdrew a folded sheet of paper from his pocket and stepped around the sunken living room to hand it to him.

"These are the names of the guests Mr. Sanderson approved."

Buford read off the names. "JJ, Caro, Luca, Bets, T-Top and Jett. Those aren't *names*." He had almost forgotten about Jett until he spoke.

"They're stage names," he said. "Caro, Luca, T-Top, and Bets. It's from when they were in a band together."

Stage names? "Are they actors?" Buford asked, thinking things couldn't get any worse.

"Musicians," Jett said.

He was wrong about things not getting worse. He couldn't tell the difference between women's or men's names and said as much.

"They were an all-girl band back in the nineties called Tough as Nails," Jett said, making it sound as if the nineties were the Stone Age.

"You don't know their *real* names?" Buford asked.

"They are the only names required for our guards to admit them," Kevin said. "Here at the Grizzly Club we respect the privacy of our residents."

Swearing, Buford wrote down: Caro, Luca, T-Top and Bets in his notebook.

"What about this JJ?" he asked. "You said he picked up his key yesterday?"

"She."

Buford turned to look at Jett. "She?" he asked thinking one of these women account for the woman's cowboy-boot print in the dead man's blood.

"JJ. She was also in the band, the lead singer," Jett said.

The sheriff turned to the club manager again. "I need full legal names for these guests and I need to know where they are."

"Only Mr. Sanderson would have that information and he… All I can tell you is that the five approved guests picked up their amenities keys yesterday. This gentleman picked his up at the gate today at 1:16 p.m.," he said, indicating Jett.

"Which means the others are all here inside the gates?" Buford asked.

Kevin checked the second sheet of paper he'd taken from a separate pocket. "All except JJ. She left this morning at 10:16 a.m."

Buford glanced over at the body. 10:16 a.m. That had to be close to the time of the murder, since the dead man's blood was still wet when a woman wearing cowboy boots appeared to have knelt by the body, then sprinted for the front door.

* * *

Blythe pressed her cheek against Logan's broad back and breathed in the rich scents on the cool spring air. The highway rolled past in a blur, the hours slipping by until they were cruising along the Rocky Mountain front, the high mountain peaks snow-capped and beautiful.

The farther Blythe and Logan traveled, the fewer vehicles they saw. When they stopped at a café in the small western town of Cut Bank along what Logan said was called the Hi-Line, she was ravenous again.

"Not many people live up here, huh," she said as she climbed off the bike. A fan pumped the smell of grease out the side of the café. She smiled to herself as she realized how much she'd missed fried food. All those years of dieting seemed such a waste right now.

"You think *this* is isolated?" Logan said with a chuckle. "Wait until you see where we're headed. They say there are only .03 people per square mile. I suspect it's less."

She smiled, shaking her head as she tried to imagine such wide-open spaces. Even when she'd lived in the desert there had been a large town closeby. Since then she'd lived in congested cities. The thought of so few people seemed like heaven.

Blythe could tell Logan wanted to ask where she was from, but she didn't give him a chance as she turned and headed for the café door. She'd seen a few pickups parked out front, but when she pushed open the door, she was surprised to find the café packed.

One of the waitresses spotted her, started to come

over, then did a double take. She burst into a smile. "I know you. You're—"

"Mistaken," Blythe said, cutting the girl off, sensing Logan right behind her.

The girl looked confused and embarrassed. "I don't have a table ready. But you look so much like—"

Blythe hated being rude, but she turned around and took Logan's arm. "I'm too hungry to wait," she said as she pulled him back through the door outside again.

"Did you know that waitress?" Logan asked, clearly taken aback by the way she'd handled it. "She seemed to know you."

She shook her head. "I must have one of those faces or that waitress has been on her feet too long. I didn't mean to be abrupt with her. I get cranky when I'm hungry. Can we go back to that barbecue place we passed?" She turned and headed for the bike before he could press the subject.

"You sure you've never been to this town before?" he asked as he swung onto the bike.

"Positive," she said as she climbed on behind him. It wasn't until he started the bike that she let herself glance toward the front windows of the café. The young waitress was standing on the other side of the glass.

Blythe looked away, promising herself that she would make it up to her one day. *If she was still alive.*

She shoved that thought away, realizing she should have known someone would recognize her even though she looked different now. It was the eyes, she thought, and closed them as Logan drove back to the barbecue joint.

It wasn't until later, after they'd settled into a booth and ordered, that she tried to smooth things over with Logan. She could tell he was even more curious about her. And suspicious, as well.

"When I was a little girl I used to watch old Westerns on television," she said, hoping to lighten both of their moods. "I always wanted to run away with a cowboy."

"So you're a romantic."

She laughed softly as she looked across the table at him. There were worry lines between the brows of his handsome face.

"Or was it the running away part that appealed to you?" he asked.

"That could definitely be part of it. Haven't you ever wanted to run away?"

"Sure." His Montana blue-sky eyes bore into her. "Most people don't have the luxury of actually doing it though."

"Good thing we aren't most people," she said, giving him a flirtatious smile.

"Oh? You think we're that much alike? So tell me what *you're* like and I'll tell you whether or not you're right about me."

"No big mystery. I like to dance, drive fast, have a good time and I'm always up for an adventure. How else could I have ended up living that little-girl fantasy of running away with a cowboy?"

"How else indeed," Logan said, but he was smiling.

"HAS ANYONE LOOKED IN this house for the four approved guests who are unaccounted for?" the sheriff demanded.

Kevin was reaching for his phone to check with his security personnel when Buford caught a glint out of the corner of his eye. Turning toward Sanderson's body, he saw something glittering on the lapel of the dead man's robe that he hadn't noticed before.

Stepping over to the body again, he crouched down next to Sanderson and inspected the lapel. Someone had attached a safety pin to the left-hand lapel of the dead man's robe. As Buford looked closer, he found a tiny piece of yellow paper still attached to it.

The killer had left a note? Or was it possible that Sanderson had left a suicide note?

The thought took him by surprise. He'd been treating this like a homicide. But what if it had been a suicide, complete with note?

If so, then why would anyone take it? To protect Sanderson? To purposely make it appear to be a homicide?

A history buff, Buford thought of a famous death that perplexed historians still. Captain Meriwether Lewis of the famed Lewis and Clark Expedition through Montana had suffered from depression that was thought to be the cause of his apparent suicide. But there were still those who believed he'd been murdered.

Very perplexing, Buford thought as he moved to a small desk in the kitchen. On it was a yellow sticky note pad. The top sheet had been torn in half horizontally, leaving the glued piece and a ragged edge. The paper was the same color as the tiny scrap still caught on the safety pin.

A blue pen lay beside the pad. Unfortunately there

was no slight indentation on the pad. Whoever had written the note had ripped the scrap of paper off first before writing the note.

"Did anyone remove something that had been pinned to the deceased's robe?" he asked. Both Kevin, the two guards and Jett swore they hadn't. From their surprise at the question, Buford suspected they were telling the truth.

But *someone* had taken the note.

Chapter Three

"So tell me about your life in this isolated place where you live," Blythe said, steering the conversation away from her as they waited for their barbecue sandwiches.

Clearly Logan was itching to know who he'd let climb onto the back of his bike. Not that she could blame him. But she wasn't ready to tell him—if she ever did. Better to split before that.

"Not much to tell," he said, as if being as evasive as she was. "I spend most days with cows. Seems I'm either chasing them, feeding them, branding them, birthing them, inoculating them or mending the fence to keep them in."

"Sounds wonderful."

He laughed. "You obviously haven't worked on a ranch."

The waitress brought their orders and Blythe dived into hers. As she stole a look across the table at him, she thought about how he'd come looking for her at the Grizzly Club, how he hadn't batted an eyelash when she'd suggested going with him, how he hadn't really asked anything of her—not even what the devil she was doing taking off across Montana with a stranger. He probably thought she did this kind of thing all the time.

A thought chilled her to her bones. What if it was no coincidence that he'd come into her life last night?

No, she thought as she studied him. The cowboy had no idea who she was or what he was getting himself into.

She jumped as her cell phone blurted out a song she'd come to hate. Worse, she hadn't even realized she still had the phone in her jacket pocket. She'd thought she'd left it along with her purse and the keys in the car.

Logan was looking at her expectantly. "Aren't you going to take that?"

She had no choice. She reached into her pocket. As she pulled out the phone, the scrap of wadded up yellow note paper fell out. It tumbled under the booth.

The first few refrains of the song began again. She hurriedly turned the phone off without even bothering to check who was calling. She had a pretty good idea, not that it mattered.

The song died off, the silence in the café almost painful, but she saw a girl at the counter looking at her frowning slightly as if trying to either place the song— or her. The girl, Blythe had noticed earlier, had been visiting with the cook.

"What if that was important?" Logan asked.

"It wasn't."

She picked up her fork and began eating again, even though she'd lost her appetite. She could feel his gaze on her. She thought about the scrap of notepaper she'd dropped and what had been written on it. She had shoved it into her pocket earlier and forgotten about it.

"Won't someone miss you?"

"I really doubt it." She moved her food around her plate, pretending to still be interested in eating, and fortunately he let the subject drop. As soon as she could, she excused herself to go to the bathroom. When she returned, Logan was up at the counter paying for their meal.

The girl at the counter was staring at her again as if it wouldn't take much to place where she knew her from. She had to get that stupid song off her phone.

Blythe glanced toward the booth. She couldn't see the scrap of notepaper. Nor could she get down on her hands and knees to look for it without raising all kinds of questions.

Not to worry, she assured herself. The note would get swept out with the garbage tonight. What had she been thinking hanging on to it anyway?

That was just it. She hadn't been thinking. She'd just been running for her life.

BUFORD CAUGHT JETT MAKING a call on his cell. "Hey, I don't know who you're trying to call, but don't. You'll get a chance to call your lawyer, if I decide to arrest you."

"Arrest me?" Jett said pocketing his phone. "*I* didn't kill him."

Buford heard a noise from down a long hallway toward the back of the house. He turned to see three women headed toward the sunken living room—and the murder scene.

He moved quickly to cut them off as the tall blonde in front glanced at his uniform and asked, "What's going on?"

"I'm Sheriff Buford Olson," he said introducing himself and shielding the woman from Martin Sanderson's body. "Where did the three of you come from?"

"The guesthouse out back," the blonde said frowning. "Where's Martin?"

"I need to speak to each of you." Buford turned to the club's general manager, amazed Kevin and his security force hadn't thought to search the house, let alone the guesthouse out back. "Kevin, can you suggest a place I can speak with these women?"

"Mr. Sanderson's library. Or perhaps his office?"

The sheriff motioned for Kevin to lead the way. They backtracked down the hallway toward the back of the huge house, the same way the women had come. Buford left the general manager in the plush library with instructions to say nothing to the other two women, while he took the blonde across the hall to Sanderson's office.

"What is this about?" she wanted to know.

"If you would have a seat," he said. "I need to ask you a few questions, beginning with your name."

She sat down reluctantly and looked around as if searching for something. At his puzzled frown, she said, "I was hoping there would be an ashtray in here." She pulled out a pack of cigarettes, seemed to think better of it and put them back into her jacket pocket.

Buford studied her as she did so. She said her name

was Loretta Danvers, aka T-Top because of a hairdo she'd had ten years ago when she played in the band Tough as Nails. She was thirty-something, tall, thin and bleached blond. In her face was etched the story of a hard life.

"So what's this about?" she asked again.

"Martin Sanderson is dead," he said and watched her reaction.

She laughed. "Isn't that the way my luck goes? So the reunion tour is off? Or was it ever really on?"

"The reunion tour?"

"He was putting our old band together for a reunion tour. At least that's what he said." She pulled out her cigarettes, shook one out and lit it with a cheap lighter. "Guess he won't care if I smoke then, will he." She took a drag, held it in her lungs for a long moment and then released a cloud of smoke out of the corner of her mouth away from him. "With JJ onboard, we could have finally made some money. I knew it was too good to be true. So who killed him?"

"Do you know someone who wanted him dead?"

She laughed again. "Who *didn't* want him dead?"

You, apparently, Buford thought, since with Sanderson gone, so apparently was any chance of a reunion tour.

LOGAN DIDN'T START HAVING real misgivings until after Blythe's phone call. He hadn't even realized that she'd brought her cell phone until it had gone off. It wasn't until then that he'd recalled that she'd said she would have someone pick up the car she'd left beside Flathead

Lake, but he hadn't seen her call anyone. In fact, he'd gotten the impression when the phone began to play that song that she hadn't even remembered that she had the phone with her.

Who had been calling? Someone she hadn't been interested in talking to. Even the ring tone with that pop-rock-sounding song didn't seem like her. Was it even her phone?

He'd realized then too that Blythe hadn't only left an expensive sports car convertible behind. She'd apparently left her purse, as well. What woman left behind her purse in a convertible beside the road? Or had she left it at the Grizzly Club?

After recalling the way she'd come flying out of club, he couldn't shake the feeling that maybe she wasn't as freewheeling as he'd originally thought—and instead was running from something serious. What did he really know about this woman he was taking back to Whitehorse with him?

Every time he'd started to ask her anything personal, she'd avoided answering one way or another. When he'd seen her reach for her cell phone, he'd noticed that she'd dropped something under the booth. He saw her look for it, then, as if changing her mind, go to the restroom. He had waited until the door closed behind her before he'd retrieved what she'd dropped.

It was nothing more than a crumpled scrap of paper from a yellow sticky notepad. He felt foolish for picking it up from under the booth and, as the waitress came by to clear the table, he'd hastily pocketed it without even looking to see if anything was written on it.

He'd been at the counter paying for the meal when Blythe had come out of the restroom. He saw her glance toward the booth. No, glance down as if looking under the booth to see what she'd dropped? Or hoping to retrieve it?

The woman intrigued him. Not a bad thing, he told himself as they left the café and climbed back on his motorcycle. He'd take her to Whitehorse and, if he had to, he'd buy her a bus ticket to wherever she needed to go. All his instincts told him that she needed to get away from something and he was happy to oblige. Chisholm men were suckers for women in trouble.

As she wrapped her arms around him and leaned into his back, he started the motor and took off. He tried to relax as the country opened. He felt as if he could breathe again. Whatever was up with this woman, he would deal with it when the time came.

A few hours later when he crossed into Whitehorse County, he'd forgotten about the scrap of paper in his pocket. He was too busy breathing a sigh of relief. He liked leaving, but there was nothing like coming home.

He breezed into the small Western town, thinking it would be a mistake to take her out to the house until they'd talked. At the very least, shouldn't he know her last name? He had always preferred not to take a woman to his house. Actually, he'd never met one he liked well enough to take home.

It didn't take but a few minutes to cruise down the main drag of Whitehorse. The town had been built up along the railroad line more than a hundred years ago. He waved at a few people he knew, the late afternoon sun throwing dark shadows across the buildings. He pulled into a space in front of the Whitehorse Bar and cut the engine.

"Could we just go to your house?" she asked without getting off the bike.

He looked at her over his shoulder. She had the palest blue eyes he'd ever seen. There was something vast about them. But it was the pain he saw just below the cool blue surface that took hold of him and wouldn't let go.

"You sure about this?" he asked.

She held his gaze and nodded. "Haven't you ever just needed to step out of your life for a while and take a chance?"

He smiled at that. Born a cowboy, riding a horse before he could walk, and now astride a Harley with a woman he probably shouldn't have been with. "Yeah, I get that."

She smiled back. "I had a feeling you might."

All his plans to get the truth out of her evaporated like a warm summer rain on hot pavement. He started the bike, flipped a U-turn in the middle of the street and headed out of town, hoping he wasn't making his worst mistake yet.

BUFORD ASKED FORMER DRUMMER Loretta Danvers to return to the guesthouse for the time being until he could talk to the others. Then he called in the next woman.

"Which one are you?" he asked the plump redhead.

Bets turned out to be Betsy Harper. He quickly

found out that she'd played the keyboard in the former all-girl band and hadn't been that sorry when the band broke up. Now, the married mother of three said she played the organ at church and kept busy with her sons' many activities.

She looked relieved more than surprised when he told her that Martin Sanderson was dead.

"Then there isn't going to be a reunion tour," she said nodding. "I can't say I'm sorry about that. I was dreading being away from my family."

Both women had mentioned the tour. "You don't seem upset by Mr. Sanderson's death," Buford said, surprised since of the three, Betsy Harper had a more caring look about her.

"I feel terrible about that," she said. "But Martin wasn't a nice man."

She didn't ask how he'd died, nor did she offer any suggestions on who would want him dead. Her only question was when she would be able to return to her husband and kids.

Buford sent her back to the guesthouse and brought in Karen "Caro" Chandler, former guitarist and singer.

She was a slim brunette with large soft brown eyes. She was the only one who looked upset when he told her that Martin Sanderson was dead.

"How did he die?" she asked, sounding worried.

"He was shot."

She shuddered. "Do you know who...?"

"Not yet. It's possible he killed himself."

She looked so relieved he questioned her about it. "I

was just worried that JJ might have…done something to him."

The elusive JJ. "Why would you say that?" he asked.

"Everyone in the business knew she was trying to get out of her contract."

The business being the music business, he guessed.

"Then there were those accidents onstage during her most recent road tour," Karen said. "Martin made it all sound like it was a publicity stunt, but I saw JJ interviewed on television. She looked genuinely scared. I was worried about her."

"You kept in touch with her over the ten years since the band broke up?"

"No," she said quickly with a shake of her head. "I'm sure the others told you that we didn't part on the best of terms. The band broke up shortly after JJ left. She was obviously the talent behind it."

Both Loretta and Betsy had made it clear they hadn't been in contact with JJ since the breakup, either.

"Not that I blamed JJ," she said quickly. "Who wouldn't have jumped at an opportunity like that if Martin Sanderson had offered it to them?"

BUFORD SENT KAREN TO THE guesthouse after the interview. All three had claimed the same thing. They'd all arrived by taxi together and had been together the entire time—except for when they'd gone into separate rooms in the guesthouse to sleep.

They said Martin had told them to relax and take advantage of the club's facilities. He would meet with them the next afternoon at two. He had said he had other business to take care of this morning and didn't wish to be disturbed.

All said they had come to Montana because Martin Sanderson was paying their expenses and promising them a reunion tour of their former band.

"What about this morning?" the sheriff had asked each of them. They had gone to bed early, had breakfast in the guest quarters and hadn't heard a sound coming from the main house.

The blonde, Loretta, said she'd been the first one down to breakfast but that she'd heard the showers running in both rooms as she'd passed. The other two, Betsy and Karen, had come down shortly thereafter.

The three hadn't been apart except to go to the bathroom since then.

Buford figured any one of them could have sneaked out to go to the main house and wasn't ruling any of them out if Martin Sanderson's death was found to be a homicide.

"Where is the other member of your former band?" Buford asked and checked his list. "Luca."

"Dead," the blonde said. "Talk about bad luck. Stepped out in front of a bus."

"How does Jett fit in?" he'd asked Betsy.

"Didn't he tell you? He used to hang around the band, flirting with all of us, but in the end, he left with JJ when she left the band. As far as I know, they're still together. At least according to the tabloids I see at the grocery checkout. I don't read them, mind you."

All of them swore they hadn't seen JJ and claimed they weren't even aware that she had arrived yet. When he'd checked the other rooms of the house, he found a guest room at the far end of the house where someone had obviously spent the night. The room was far enough away from the living room that Buford suspected a gun-shot couldn't be heard.

He waited until the coroner and crime scene techs took over before he interviewed Jett Atkins. By then, Jett had had enough to drink that he was feeling no pain.

"So did one of them confess?" he asked with a laugh. "I didn't think so. They know who killed Martin. JJ."

"Why do you say that?"

Jett looked shocked. "It's been in all the trades for months. JJ wanted out of her contract. Martin refused. We all knew it was coming to a head. Why else would he threaten to put her old band back together?"

"*Threaten?* I thought he flew everyone up here to make arrangements for the tour," the sheriff said.

Jett howled with laughter. "There is no way JJ would ever have agreed to that. No, he was just trying to bring her back in line. Those women hate JJ. She not only broke up the band, she also became successful. I would imagine JJ went ballistic when Martin told her that either she played ball or he would force her into doing a reunion tour with women who would have stabbed her in the back just as quickly as looked at her."

"Martin Sanderson could make her do that?"

"He *owned* her. He could do anything he wanted. The only way she could get out of that contract was to die. Or," Jett added with a grin. "Kill Martin."

"Do you think this JJ knew that Martin had already

flown the band members to Montana?" Buford asked. All except Luca, whoever she had been.

"Doubt it, since apparently he had them staying in a separate guest house," Jett said. "I can't say I blame JJ for killing him. He really was a bastard."

"What about you?" Buford asked.

"What about me?"

"What are you doing here?"

"Martin invited me." He grinned. "More leverage. I'm sure he planned to leak it to the press. He wanted it to look like JJ and I were back together."

"You weren't?"

He shook his head. "It was just a publicity stunt. Martin loved doing them. But JJ and I would have had to go along with it, since he held our contracts."

"So you were signed with him, as well. How does his death affect that?"

Jett smiled widely. "Freedom. With Martin dead, JJ and I are both free. Well, at least I am. I owe her a great debt of gratitude."

When Buford was finished interviewing all of them, he asked them not to leave town. Betsy called for a taxi and the four of them left together, but the sheriff could feel the tension between them.

As he watched them leave, he wondered where the missing JJ was and why they all seemed to think she had killed Martin Sanderson.

BLYTHE KNEW SHE WAS TAKING a chance going home with this cowboy. But that's how she'd always lived her life. She was convinced that if she hadn't, she'd still be living in her mother's trailer in the middle of the desert with some abusive drunk like her mother had.

She had learned to take care of herself. She'd had to even before she'd left home at fourteen. There'd been too many nights when her mother would pass out and Blythe would hear the heavy footsteps of whatever boyfriend her mother had brought home from the bar coming down the hallway toward her room.

She'd been eleven when she started keeping a butcher knife under her pillow. She'd only had to use it once.

Blythe shoved that memory away as she watched the small Western town disappear behind them. The air was cooler now as Logan sped along the blacktop of a two-lane. The houses, she noted, were few and far between, and the farther they went, the less she saw of anything but open country.

The land ran green in rolling hills broken only occasionally by a tree or a rocky point. In one such tree, a bald eagle watched them pass. Several antelope stood silhouetted against a lush hillside. Further down, a handful of deer grazed on the new green grass. One lifted his head at the sound of the motorcycle. His ears were huge, reminding her of Mickey Mouse ears at Disney World.

Blythe stared at all the wild things they passed, having never seen them before except in magazines or on television.

As Logan turned onto a gravel road, slowing down a little, she saw cattle in the distance, dark against the horizon. Closer, a couple of horses loped along in the breeze.

When she looked up the road, she saw where the road ended. She really was out in the middle of nowhere. Alone with a man she'd didn't know. For all she knew, he could be more dangerous than what she'd left behind.

She could hear her mother's slurred words, the words she'd grown up with all those years ago.

"You think you're better than me?" The harsh cigarettes-and-booze laugh. "I can see your future, little girl. No matter how you try to fight it, you're headed for a bad end."

She *had* tried to fight it, and at one point, she'd actually thought she'd beaten her mother's prediction. But by then her mother was long dead and buried and there was no one there to hear her say, "See Mama, you were wrong. Look at your little girl now."

Blythe laughed softly. Wouldn't her mother love to be here now to see that all her predictions had come true. She would have been the first to tell her daughter that if you flew too high, too fast, you were headed for a fall.

Clearly, she'd proven that she had too much of her mother's blood in her. She'd flown high all right, but ultimately, it had caught up with her. She was now in free fall. And the worst part was, she knew she deserved it.

As Logan turned down an even smaller road, she stared at the stark landscape and wondered what she'd gotten herself into this time. Logan, she thought, must be thinking the same thing.

Maybe they were more alike than he thought.

The last of the day's sun had slipped below the horizon but not before painting the spring green rolling hills with gold. The sky, larger than any she'd ever seen, had turned to cobalt blue. Not even a cloud hung on the horizon.

At the end of the road, she caught a glimpse of an old farmhouse. Past it were an older barn and some horses in a pasture.

The house, she saw as they drew closer, had seen better days but she could tell it had recently been given a fresh coat of white paint. There was a porch with a couple of wooden chairs and curtains at the windows.

"It's not much," Logan said as he parked the motorcycle out front and they climbed off.

"It's great," she said meaning it. She couldn't see another house within miles. She'd never been in such an isolated place. Here she could pretend that she'd escaped her old life. At least for a little while.

As he opened the door, she noticed that he hadn't bothered to lock the house when he'd left. Trusting soul. She smiled at the thought. The kind of man who brought home a perfect stranger. Well, not perfect, far from it. But still a stranger.

BUFORD WAS GLAD TO HAVE turned the case over to the state crime techs. This would be a high-profile case and while he would still be involved, it was no longer solely on his shoulders.

It would be getting dark soon and he was anxious to get home for supper. He just hoped Clara would lay off the hot peppers. The woman was killing him.

Unfortunately, he couldn't quit thinking about the case, especially what might have been pinned to the man's robe. Too bad someone had taken the note.

He told himself the crime techs would be especially thorough on this one, since clearly Martin Sanderson was somebody. Not only did he own a place in the Grizzly Club, he was apparently some hotshot music producer from Los Angeles.

The club liked to play down the identities of their owners, how much money they had and how they made it. No need to announce it anyway, since the residents probably all knew much more about each other than any of the staff or people outside the club ever could. After all, if they had the dough to buy a place behind the gate, then they were instantly part of the club, weren't they? Clearly Kevin was merely staff.

Buford stopped at the guardhouse to ask about the woman visitor who'd at least said she was JJ when she'd picked up her key. He found it irritating that the residents who left the names of their guests didn't even want the guards to know exactly who was coming for a visit.

"These are people who have to be very careful," Kevin had said when Buford had questioned why they needed so much secrecy. "They worry that they could be kidnapped or their children kidnapped. They aren't like you and me."

"They die when they're shot in the heart just like you

and me," Buford pointed out and warranted himself a scowl from Kevin.

At the gate, the guard was more than glad to talk to the local sheriff about the guest allegedly known as JJ. He described a dark-haired good-looking woman. "She left in a hurry, I can tell you that. She barely waited for the gate to open."

"What was she driving?"

The guard described a silver sports car convertible. "I can give you her license plate number. We take those down on anyone coming or going."

Buford thanked him as he glanced at the plate number the guard gave him. It began with a 7, which meant a local Montana Lake County plate, probably a rental. "How did the woman seem to you when she left?"

"I didn't speak to her, barely got a glimpse of her."

"She was going *that* fast?" he asked in surprise since there were speed bumps near the gate.

"Well, she was moving at a good clip, but I was also about to check the guy on the motorcycle who was coming in just then."

"A club resident?"

He shook his head. "Not one I'd ever seen. But I didn't get a chance to talk to him. As I started toward him, he swung around and took off after the woman in the sports car."

"He *followed* her?"

The guard hesitated. "I saw him look at her as she left and then he seemed to go after her."

"He *knew* her?" Buford asked.

"I got the feeling he did."

"You didn't happen to get the plate on the motorcycle, did you?"

"No, but I'm sure our cameras caught it."

Buford waited. It didn't take long before the guard produced the bike plate number. He pocketed both, anxious to run them. But as he left the guard station his radio went off, alerting him of an accident on the road back to town.

A car had left the highway and crashed in the rocks at the edge of the lake. Firefighters and emergency medical services were on their way to the scene.

Buford turned on his flashing lights and siren. It was going to be a long night the way things were going.

As BLYTHE STEPPED INTO Logan's farmhouse, she wasn't sure what she would find. She half expected a woman's touch. She'd taken him for being about her own age, early thirties, which meant he could have been married at least once or at least lived with someone. But she was pleased to see that there was no sign that a woman had ever lived here.

"Like I said, basic," he noted almost apologetically.

"I like it. Simple is good." He had no idea how she'd been living.

She walked around, taking it in. The place was furnished with apparently the only thought to being practical and comfortable. There was an old leather couch in front of a small brick fireplace, an even older recliner next to it and a rug in front of the couch on the worn wooden floor. The kitchen had a 1950s metal and

Formica top table and four chairs. Through a door she spotted a bathroom and stairs that led up to the second floor, where she figured there would be bedrooms.

"Why don't I show you up to your room in case you want to freshen up," Logan said, shrugging out of his leather jacket.

She couldn't help noticing his broad shoulders, the well-formed chest, the slim hips, the incredibly long legs. It brought back the memory of being in his arms on the dance floor and sent a frisson of desire through her.

Logan headed up the stairs and she followed. Just as she'd figured, there were two bedrooms, one with a double bed, one with no furniture at all, and another bathroom, this one with a huge clawfoot tub.

One bed. She realized she hadn't thought out this part of her great escape. That was so like her. Not that the idea of sharing his bed hadn't crossed her mind. After all, she was the one who'd wanted to run away with him. What did she expect was going to happen?

He must have seen her expression. "You can have this room," he said motioning to the bed. "I'll take the couch."

"I don't want to take your bed."

He didn't give her a chance to argue the point. "I'll see what's in the fridge. Are you hungry? You didn't eat much at the last place we stopped. I could fry up some elk steaks."

She smiled, giving herself away. She couldn't explain this ravenous hunger she had except that maybe she was just tired of going to bed hungry and for all the wrong reasons.

"You've never had elk, right?"

"How did you know?" she said with a laugh.

"You're going to love it."

"I thought you raised *beef*," she said.

"I try to kill an elk every year or so. A little variety, you know?"

She thought she did know.

"There are towels in the cabinet in the bathroom. I just put clean sheets on the bed before I left. Holler if there is anything else you need," he said, and tromped back down the stairs, leaving her standing in his bedroom.

She glanced at the bed, tempted to lie down for a while. The ride here had taken five hours, which wasn't bad, but she hadn't slept well last night and for some time now she'd been running on fear-induced adrenaline.

The memory of what she had to fear sent a shaft of ice up her spine. She shivered even in the warm bedroom. The weight of her life choices pressed down on her chest and she had to struggle to breathe. Did she really think that she could escape the past—even in this remote part of Montana, even with this trusting cowboy?

"There's a price that comes with the life you've lived." Not her mother's voice this time. Martin Sanderson's. "And sweetheart, your bill has come due."

Chapter Four

The ambulance was there by the time Sheriff Buford Olson reached the accident scene. He parked along the edge of the narrow road where a highway patrolman was directing traffic. A wrecker was in the process of pulling the blackened car up from the rocky shore where it had landed, but he could still smell smoke.

As Buford walked to the edge of the road, he could see where the car had gone off, dropped over the steep edge of the road to tumble down the rocks before coming to a stop at the edge of the lake.

He noticed no skid marks on the pavement or in the dirt at the shoulder of the road. The driver hadn't even tried to brake before going off the road and over the rocky precipice?

"The passengers?" he asked as he spotted one of the ambulance drivers.

"Just one." The man shook his head.

Buford walked over to one of the highway patrolmen at the scene and asked if there was anything he could do to help.

"Pretty well have it covered," the officer said. "Looks like the driver was traveling at a high rate of speed when she missed the curve, plummeting over the edge of the road and rolling several times on the rocks before the car exploded."

Buford turned to watch the wrecker pull the car up from the edge of the lake, then asked to see the patrolman's report. He did a double take when he saw the license plate number the highway patrolman had put down.

He hurriedly pulled the slip of paper the security guard at the Grizzly Club had given him. It matched the sports car the woman guest had been driving earlier that morning.

"You get an ID when you ran the plate?" he asked the patrolman.

"The car was a rental. Rented under the name of Jennifer James yesterday."

JJ? Had to be, since the license plate was the same one the guard had given him.

As Buford left the scene, he couldn't help thinking how coincidental it was that one of Martin Sanderson's guests was now also dead. Of course, it could be that the woman had been killed because she was driving too fast away from the murder scene. That would have made a great theory if it hadn't been hours since she'd left the Grizzly Club driving too fast then too—before she'd apparently gone off the road and died at the edge of the lake.

So where had she been during those missing hours? The crash had occurred only miles from the Grizzly Club turnoff. And why hadn't she tried to brake?

Martin Sanderson had approved six guests. Jett

Atkins was accounted for and possibly JJ, along with three members of the all-girl band. Luca was apparently dead.

But it was the elusive JJ who captured his thoughts. That and the safety pin and missing note on Sanderson's robe.

Unfortunately, the woman who'd been driving this car was now on her way to the morgue and she might have been the only other person in the world who knew what that note said and why Martin Sanderson was dead.

LOGAN WENT DOWNSTAIRS AND dug some steaks out of the freezer. He had no idea what Blythe was doing here or what she was thinking. Or what she might be running from, but she was sure as the devil running from something.

He told himself it didn't matter, although he feared he could be wrong about that. Apparently the woman wanted a break from whatever life she'd been living. He didn't even know what that life had been or if he should be worried about it. But she triggered a powerful protective instinct in him that had made him throw caution to the wind.

Too bad she didn't trust him enough to tell him what was going on, he thought, then remembered the scrap of yellow paper he'd retrieved from under the booth table back at the café. He quickly reached into his pocket.

"Logan?"

He started at the sound of her voice directly behind him. It was the first time she'd said his name. It was like music off her tongue. His hand froze in his pocket as he turned.

"Would you mind if I took a bath?"

He withdrew his hand from his pocket sans the note and smiled. He'd seen the gleam in her eye when she'd spotted his big clawfoot tub. "You're in luck. There's even some bubble bath up there. A joke housewarming gift from my brothers."

"You have brothers?"

"Five."

She raised a brow. "Wow. Sisters?"

He shook his head. "Take as long as you want. I have steaks thawing for steak sandwiches later."

"Thanks." She started to turn away. "And thanks for bringing me here." With that she ran upstairs. A moment later he heard the water come on in the bathroom.

Thinking of her, he told himself there was something strong and carefree about this woman he'd brought home and, at the same time, vulnerable and almost fragile. Whatever she wanted or needed from him, he'd do his damnedest to give to her. Right now, though, it was just the use of his tub, he thought smiling, and tried not to imagine Blythe with her slim yet lush body up to her neck in bubbles.

He waited to make sure she didn't come back down before he withdrew the scrap of paper and pressed it open to see what was on it.

Logan wasn't sure what he'd expected to find on the piece of notepaper—if anything. He'd hoped it would be a clue to this woman.

He was disappointed.

There were only two words on the yellow note paper, both written in blue pen. *You're Next*.

He stared at them for a moment. Next for what? He had no idea. The words didn't offer any clue to Blythe, that was for sure. He wadded up the scrap of paper and tossed it into the garbage, pushing it down where it couldn't be seen. He felt foolish for retrieving it, worse for thinking it might be important.

CHARLIE BAKER LET OUT A STRING of profanity when he saw all the flashing lights on the highway ahead. Cops. The stupid woman had gotten pulled over for speeding.

He swore again as his line of traffic came to a dead stop and he saw a highway patrolman walking down the line of cars toward him. Realizing regrettably that he had no way of getting out of the traffic, he quickly checked himself in his rearview mirror.

Charlie and his girlfriend had been on the road from Arizona for four days. He knew he looked rough. Hopefully not so rough that the officer would run the plates on this stolen pickup, especially with a warrant already out on him.

As the cop neared, Charlie put his window down, wishing he hadn't listened to Susie. Earlier he'd stopped to take a leak beside the road. It had been her idea to take that sports car after she'd found the keys on the floorboard—and the purse lying on the passenger seat.

He had looked around, pretty sure that whoever it

belonged to had walked down to the lake and would be coming back any minute. They'd argued about taking the car, but Susie said the owner deserved to have it stolen—hell, was *asking* to have it stolen.

Once she opened the glove box and realized it was a rental, there had been no more argument. "I'm taking it. It might be my only chance to drive a car like this and it sure as hell beats that old pickup you *borrowed*."

She'd been bitching about the vehicle he'd stolen since they left Arizona and he'd been getting real tired of it.

"We can dump the pickup," she'd said. "It's probably going to break down soon anyway."

"We'll talk about it away from here," he'd said. There was something about this that made him uneasy. Who just left such an expensive car beside the road with the keys and a purse in it?

But there was no arguing with Susie. She got in the car and started it up, revving the engine too loud.

Charlie hadn't wanted to be around when whoever had rented the car came racing up and found Susie behind the wheel. He'd taken off in the pickup, yelling at her that he'd meet her down the road at the camp-ground where they'd spent last night.

Only she hadn't shown. Back at the camp, he'd fallen asleep and lost track of time. Susie should have shown hours ago. He figured she'd probably taken off in that convertible and left him high and dry. But he'd decided he'd better go look for her, since if she was in trouble, he knew she'd rat him out in a heartbeat, and now here he was with a cop heading for him.

The officer stepped to his window. "There's been an accident. It could be a little bit before we get the road cleared."

That damned Susie had gone on a joyride and left him. Or, he realized, she could be caught in the traffic on the other side of the wreck just like he was. "What kind of accident, officer?"

"A car went off the road." He was already walking away.

Charlie watched him head down the highway to tell the other drivers of cars piling up behind him. Or, he thought, Susie might have wrecked that convertible. With a curse, he waited a minute before he got out of the pickup and worked his way along the edge of the trees to where a few people had gathered on the side of the road.

It was almost too dark to see what was going on, but as he drew closer, he smelled smoke. Joining the others gawking at the scene, he saw what was left of the pretty silver sports car convertible that Susie just had to drive being lifted up onto the back of a wrecker's flatbed.

"Did the driver get out?" he asked the man standing next to him.

"Trapped in the car. I heard the EMT say she was burned beyond recognition."

As Charlie turned to walk back to his pickup, he took an inventory of his emotions, surprised how little he felt other than anger. He should have known Susie wouldn't know how to drive a car like that. *He* should have driven it. Served her right.

But he knew if he had taken the car, he wouldn't have met Susie at the campground. He would have just kept going, leaving her and the stolen pickup behind. Susie probably knew that, he thought as he climbed into the truck and waited for the highway to clear so he could get the hell out of this state.

He had been getting real tired of Susie anyway. Fortunately, he'd insisted on taking everything from the purse she'd found in that expensive convertible. The cash and credit cards were going to come in handy.

Charlie smiled to himself. He'd never had good luck, but sometimes things had a way of working out for the best, didn't they.

BUFORD HAD TO STOP BY HIS office on the way home and was shocked that he had a half-dozen calls from reporters. As tight-lipped as the Grizzly Club was, he couldn't believe word had gotten out this quickly. But people liked to talk—especially when it was something juicy like the death of a wealthy man from the Grizzly Club. And he'd already caught Jett on his phone.

He decided to see how bad it was. He picked up one of the messages and dialed the number.

"Is it true that JJ was killed tonight on the road just outside of Big Fork?" the reporter asked.

Not about Martin Sanderson? "I'm sorry but I can't…" He realized she'd called the victim JJ. "The accident is under investigation." He hung up frowning.

Who would have given a reporter that information? No one at the scene, even if they'd overheard that the car had been rented to a Jennifer James. Who knew that Jennifer James was known as JJ?

Jett, he'd bet on it. Buford had insisted on the cell phone numbers of Jett and the three members of the former band in case he needed to ask them any more questions. He'd warned all of them not to leave town until the investigation was complete.

None of them had been happy about the prospect of staying around, since they couldn't stay at the Grizzly Club and had been forced to take a cheap motel instead. Betsy had called him to tell him where they were staying, as per his request.

As he grabbed his phone to call, Buford felt his stomach rumble. He was starved. He'd picked up a couple of cheeseburgers at a fast-food restaurant on his way back to his office. Clara would kill him. He was supposed to be on a diet. But she was killing him anyway with those darned chili peppers. He'd prefer to drop dead after eating a cheeseburger any day than keep living with his belly on fire.

He dialed the cell phone number Jett had given him. Jett answered on the third ring and didn't sound all that happy about hearing from him so soon.

"I just had a reporter call me," Buford said. "You didn't happen to—"

"I haven't talked to anyone."

Maybe. Maybe not. From what he'd seen of his granddaughter's rock 'n' roll idol, Jett liked publicity and he didn't seem to care if it was good or bad. He'd talk to anyone, even the tabloids, and he'd admitted that he let Martin use him and JJ for publicity stunts.

"What about the others?"

"Nope," Jett said after getting confirmation from the three women. Buford could hear the background noises. Apparently they were all in a restaurant together.

"Not even about the accident?" Buford said.

"*Accident?* Is that what you're calling it?" Jett snapped. "I should have known JJ would get away with this. She's always gotten away with whatever she did. Have you found her? Is that what she claims? That she *accidentally* killed Martin?"

So he didn't know about the car wreck. Which meant neither did the others, and they couldn't have called the press. But they were certainly quick to blame JJ for murder even before all the facts were in.

Buford decided to let Jett and the women read about the wreck in the morning papers. "I'll let you finish your supper then. Wait, one more question. Why did JJ want out of her contract?"

Jett sighed. "You really don't know much about the music business, do you? Martin discovered JJ, took over her career, made her a star. She wanted more control over her career and her life, but she was making him a ton of money. He would never have let her go though. She knew that."

"Does she also go by the name of Jennifer James?" He asked the real question he had wanted to ask, hoping to confirm what he *did* know.

"*Yes,*" Jett said impatiently, as if everyone knew that. "Is that all?"

"For now," he said and hung up.

He started to call it a night. But then he remembered

the man on the motorcycle that the guard thought had chased after the infamous JJ.

When he ran the number, Buford got a surprise.

LOGAN HAD THE STEAKS COOKED and everything ready for a late supper when Blythe came down wearing his robe and smelling of lilac bubble bath. Her wet, long, dark hair was pulled up on top of her head and he was struck by how beautiful she looked. Everything about her took his breath away. As little as he knew about her, he felt they were kindred souls somehow.

"Tell me about this part of Montana," she said as they ate. It was dark outside, the sky filled with millions of sparkling stars and a sliver of silver moon. A breeze stirred the curtains at the kitchen window. The house felt almost cozy.

He told her about the outlaw era that brought such infamous luminaries as Kid Curry, Butch Cassidy and the Sundance Kid to the area. "It was the last lawless place in Montana."

He told her how the railroad had come through and brought settlers who were given land and a time limit on improving the acres if they wanted to keep it.

"It was a hard place to survive. Not many of them made it. You had to be hardy."

"Like your family?" she asked.

He smiled at that. "Chisholm roots run deep, that's for sure." He didn't tell her how his ancestors had brought up a herd of cattle from Texas and each generation had helped build up Chisholm Cattle Company to what it was today.

Longhorns hadn't done well because of the tough winters. Once they'd changed to Black Angus cattle, the ranch had thrived.

"I saw the horses out in the pasture," she said. "Are they yours?"

"Do you ride?"

She laughed and shook her head. "But I've always wanted to."

"Tomorrow I'll teach you," he said on impulse.

"Really?" She looked excited about the prospect. There was a peacefulness to her that he hadn't seen since they were on the dance floor last night.

"I think you'll like it, and when you're ready, I'll show you more of my part of Montana by horseback."

"I'd love that," she said and finished her sandwich.

"You liked the elk?" he asked amused at the way she ate. He had joked that she acted as if she wasn't sure where her next meal might be coming from, but now wondered if that wasn't the case. She'd said that the sports car she'd been driving didn't belong to her. For all he knew, she might not have anything more than the clothes on her back.

Maybe she *had* been a guest at the Grizzly Club, but he had a bad feeling he'd been right and she'd borrowed a car she shouldn't have.

He shook his head at the thought that he might be harboring a criminal. And such a beautiful, engaging one at that.

As they finished the elk steaks, Logan looked across the table at his guest and saw how exhausted she was. He felt a strange contentment being here with her like

this. It surprised him. He never brought any of his dates
back to his house. But then this woman wasn't exactly
a date, was she?

"There's a quilt up on the bed that my great grandmother made," he said. "You look like you're ready to
crawl under it."

She smiled, appearing almost as content as he felt.

He got up and cleared the dishes, putting them in
the sink, then he went to the closet and pulled down
the extra blankets he kept there. Winters in this old
farmhouse were downright cold, and there were many
nights when he'd fallen asleep in front of the fire—the
only really warm place in the house.

Dropping them on the couch, he turned to find her
standing in the kitchen doorway. "Don't you want me
to help you with the dishes?" She looked cute wearing
his robe. He watched her pull it around her, hugging
herself as if even the spring night felt cold to her. It
slid over her curves in a way that made him realize he
would never look at that robe the same way again.

"The dishes can wait. Why don't you get some sleep?
I'll saddle up the horses in the morning and we'll get
you ridin'."

She seemed to hesitate for a moment, then smiled
gratefully. "Thank you. For everything."

He nodded. "It's nice to have you here." It was true,
but still he hadn't meant to say it, let alone admit it.
He'd never been without female company if he'd wanted
it. But he often found women confusing. He preferred
his horse.

Not this woman, though.

Even after she went upstairs, he could smell lilac and felt a stirring in him at the mere thought of her. He'd felt drawn to her from that moment he'd seen her expression on the dance floor. He recalled the way she had moved to the music.

As he heard her close his bedroom door, he groaned to himself. He must be losing his grip. His brothers would think him a damned fool. Not just for bringing a woman he knew nothing about back to his house, but for letting such a beautiful woman go to bed alone— and in his bed.

Whatever her reason for being here, it wasn't because she couldn't resist him, he thought with a laugh. Logan Chisholm wasn't used to that, either.

As he lay down on the couch and pulled a blanket over him, he told himself she would be gone in the morning—and probably with his pickup and any cash she could find.

But as he heard her moving around upstairs, he found himself smiling. He could always get another truck.

Chapter Five

The motorcycle that the guard at the Grizzly Club said had gone after the woman in the silver sports car was registered to Logan Chisholm, the address Chisholm Cattle Company, Whitehorse, Montana.

Sheriff Buford Olson let out a low whistle. Hoyt Chisholm was one of the wealthiest ranchers in the state, so it was no surprise his son might be visiting the Grizzly Club. Or even that he might know the woman who'd been visiting Martin Sanderson, as the guard had suggested.

So what had he been doing on this side of the Rockies? Visiting his friend JJ? Did that mean that Logan Chisholm also knew Martin Sanderson?

Buford picked up the phone. His stomach growled again and he noticed how late it was. He'd call him tomorrow. Probably a waste of time anyway, since Logan Chisholm hadn't actually gone into the Grizzly Club.

But Chisholm had seen Jennifer James leaving and possibly followed her. He might know where she'd gone between the time she was seen leaving the club and going out in a blaze that evening beside Flathead Lake.

Sighing, Buford put the phone back. He was starved

and it was late. Also, he didn't relish telling Logan Chisholm about the dead woman—that was if Logan even knew this JJ. Chisholm was probably still in the Bigfork area, which meant he would read about it in the papers.

There was always the chance that if Chisholm knew something about either death, he would come forward with any information he had. Buford had never heard much about Hoyt Chisholm's sons except that they were adopted and there were a bunch of them. Which meant they hadn't been in too much trouble. With a father as well known as Hoyt Chisholm, it would be hard to stay out of the headlines if the sons had run-ins with the law. Even Chisholm's money could only do so much when it came to the press.

It certainly hadn't been able to keep Hoyt's name out of the headlines when he'd lost first one wife, then another. The first wife had drowned, the second had been killed in a horseback riding accident, the third had disappeared, recently turning up dead, murdered.

Buford had followed the case with interest. Hoyt had been arrested, but later cleared. An insurance investigator by the name of Agatha Wells had been arrested for the third wife's murder. Last Buford had heard, Agatha Wells had been sent to the state mental hospital for evaluation and had escaped.

It had been nasty business, since Hoyt Chisholm had recently taken a fourth wife, Emma. The insurance investigator had come after her as well, abducting her at one point. Later Agatha Wells was believed to have drowned in the Milk River after being shot by a sheriff's deputy on the Chisholm ranch. Her body, though, had never been found.

He hoped Logan Chisholm didn't have any connection to Martin Sanderson's death. The Chisholm family had been through enough.

Picking up his hat, Buford pushed himself up out of his chair. He'd spent too much time on his feet today and he ached all over. As he turned out his office light, all he could think about was his big leather recliner waiting for him in front of the television. He had a lot on his mind. And he couldn't quit thinking about that note that had been pinned to Martin Sanderson's body. He'd give anything to know what it said. He had a feeling it would solve this case.

So much about the case nagged at him. Why had Martin Sanderson invited all of the members of the former Tough as Nails band to Montana and left keys for them when he had to know that the one called Luca was dead?

And what, if anything, did this Jennifer James, JJ, have to do with it?

It wasn't until he got home to discover his granddaughter visiting that he found out just who JJ had been.

BETSY HARPER GLANCED AROUND the table in the motel restaurant dining room, marveling at how little they had all changed. Loretta was still brassy, loud and demanding. Karen had always been quiet, never letting anyone know what she was thinking.

And Jett was Jett, she thought with no small amount

of bitterness. He had barely acknowledged her, but what did she expect? He'd dumped her for JJ ten years ago and done her a favor in retrospect.

He would have made a lousy husband, an even worse father. Still, he'd been her first, and she somehow thought that might have made a difference to him. Apparently, it didn't.

"So what do you think of this whole mess?" Jett asked after he'd joined them in the motel restaurant dining room.

They'd decided to all stay at the same motel. Jett had joked about keeping enemies close. Betsy supposed that was how he felt. Just like JJ, he'd definitely betrayed them all, some of them more than others.

Conversation had been stilted. Loretta had gone on for a while complaining about how bad her life was. As if they couldn't just look at her and see that she was hard up for money. Loretta blamed Martin and was convinced Tough as Nails could have been great if he hadn't broken up the band.

"I'm not sorry Martin's dead," Loretta said now. "I just wish I'd shot him."

"Who says you didn't?" Jett said. "We all think it was JJ, but maybe she didn't do it."

"I think she did it," Betsy said. "Why else would she take off the way she did?" Jett had told them that JJ had been staying in a wing of the main house and that he'd seen her prints in Martin's blood—and so had the sheriff.

"Maybe she ran to avoid *us*," Karen said without looking up from her meal. "If like you said Martin was

threatening her with this reunion tour… She was probably afraid that we all hated her."

Jett laughed. "Like you don't. I would have loved to
have seen her face when she found out what Martin was
up to. I'm surprised she didn't kill him with her bare
hands."

"I can't believe she agreed to a reunion tour," Betsy
said.

Karen gave her a you-can't-be-that-naïve look. None
of them knew just how naïve she'd always been about
a lot of things.

"Jett just said JJ knew nothing about it," Karen said
impatiently to her. "There was never going to be a tour.
It was just Martin messing with us again."

"Well, he's dead now." Jett waved the waiter over.
"Anyone else want to drink to that? I'm in the mood to
celebrate. Champagne," he told the waiter.

"You're the only one who thinks this is a celebra-
tion," Karen said. "A man has been murdered and
you're all ready to string JJ up for it."

"Well, if one of *us* didn't kill him, then who else was
there?" Jett said. "We're the only ones who had motive,
opportunity and means, since there was a handgun on
the floor beside him. I heard the sheriff check. It belonged to Martin."

"But JJ is the only one missing, isn't she?" Loretta
pointed out.

The waiter brought the champagne and glasses. Jett
poured himself a glass and lifted it for a toast. "Here's
to JJ, wherever she might be. If she was here I would
thank her."

No one else reached for a glass, but that didn't keep Jett from emptying his.

As he set his down, his gaze settled on Betsy. She felt the heat of his look as he asked, "What do you girls have planned to amuse yourselves until we can get out of this godforsaken place?"

KAREN FELT DISGUSTED BEING around Jett again. She hated that they were all acting as if nothing had happened ten years ago.

Betsy was the worst. Jett had broken her heart. Karen remembered how despondent she'd been. She'd had to hold Betsy's hand through that horrible time while keeping her own pain and anger to herself.

Now as she watched Jett turning his charm on Betsy, she wanted to throw something at him. Throw something at Betsy, too. Hadn't the woman learned what a no-count Jett was? He used people, then discarded them. One look at Jett and Betsy should have known the man hadn't changed.

"I, for one, am going to turn in early," Karen said tossing down her napkin and rising. "I regret ever coming here."

"You came because you felt like you owed us," Loretta said snidely.

Karen turned on her. "It wasn't your guilt trip that made me change my mind and come after you pleaded with me," she snapped. "I did it because I got tired of listening to you whine."

"Now, ladies," Jett said.

"There are no ladies here," Loretta said with a laugh.

"I think I *will* have a drink, Jett. That is, if you're buying." She picked up one of the champagne glasses and held it out. He happily filled it.

"I didn't want to come, either," Betsy said. "But I also didn't want to be the one band member who ruined it for the others."

"How could we have had a reunion tour without Luca anyway?" Karen said.

"Bands do tours all the time without the original members," Jett said.

"There wasn't going to be a reunion tour," Karen snapped as she started to step away from the table.

"Then why get us here?" Betsy said, sounding surprised and disheartened.

Karen was tired of Betsy's apparent naïveté. No one could be that sweet and innocent, she thought as she walked away.

Behind her, she heard Jett say, "I think he was hoping one of you would kill JJ."

Loretta's laugh and words followed Karen out of the room. "What makes you think we didn't?"

EMMA CHISHOLM STOOD AT THE window looking out at the rolling prairie. Chisholm land as far as the eye could see. She'd fallen in love with this place, the same way she had with Hoyt Chisholm, only months ago.

Of course, she hadn't had any idea what was in store for her when she'd agreed down in Denver to run off with him to Vegas for a quickie marriage. They hadn't known each other. They hadn't cared. Love does that to you. He'd told her the ranch was large and isolated.

"Sounds wonderful," she'd said, and he'd laughed.

"Some women can't take that kind of emptiness."

"I'm not some women." But she'd heard the pain in his voice and known there had been others before her who he'd taken back to the ranch. All she'd known then was that they hadn't lasted. A man in his late fifties would have had at least a wife or maybe even two, she'd thought then.

It wasn't until she'd come to Whitehorse, Montana, and met Aggie Wells that she'd found out she'd underestimated Hoyt's history with wives—and pain. He'd been married three other times, all three ending tragically, as it turned out.

Former insurance investigator Aggie Wells had brought the news along with a warning that Emma was next. "He killed his other wives. I can't prove it," Aggie had said, "but I keep trying. Watch yourself."

Emma hadn't believed it. She knew Hoyt soul deep, as they say. He wasn't a killer. She'd just assumed like everyone else that Aggie was either obsessed with her husband—or just plain crazy.

That was months ago, she thought now as she looked out across the land and realized she'd been living with ghosts—the ghosts of her husband's exes and now Aggie's ghost.

So why did she still expect to see one of them coming across the prairie with only one goal in mind, killing her, the fourth and no doubt final wife of Hoyt Chisholm?

No one knew about the ghosts she'd been living with.

As much as she and her husband shared, she couldn't share these thoughts with Hoyt.

"Aggie Wells is dead," Hoyt had said. "She was shot. You saw her fall into the river. She didn't come up."

But when the sheriff had dragged the river, they hadn't found her body.

"She got hung up on something, a root, a limb, an old barbed-wire fence downriver," Hoyt said. "When the river goes down this summer, we'll find her body. But until then, she's gone, okay?"

But it hadn't been okay, because Emma had come to know Aggie, had actually liked her, maybe worse had believed in her heart that the woman might not be crazy. Nor dead. If anyone could survive being shot and even drowned, it would be Aggie.

The insurance investigator wasn't the only ghost Emma now lived with, though. Hoyt's first wife, Laura Chisholm, was the ghost that caused her sleepless night. Aggie had come to believe Laura hadn't drowned that day on Fort Peck Reservoir but was still alive and vengefully killing Hoyt's wives.

Aggie had even provided photographs of a woman who looked so much like what Laura Chisholm would look like now after all these years that it had made Hoyt pale. Seeing the effect the photographs had on her husband had made a believer out of Emma. And if you believed Laura Chisholm was alive, then you also had to believe that she had murdered not one but possibly all of Hoyt's other wives—and would eventually come for Emma herself, like the living ghost she was.

Hoyt didn't believe it. At least that's what he said.

But if that were true, then why would he continue to insist on someone hanging around near the ranch house so Emma was never left alone?

She laughed softly at a thought. Didn't Hoyt realize that she was never really alone? Either Aggie's ghost or Laura's was always with her—at least in her thoughts. She was merely waiting for one of the ghosts to appear. Either Aggie trying to save her again or Laura determined to kill her.

"What are you baking?" Hoyt asked as he came into the kitchen and pulled her from her thoughts.

"Gingersnaps," she said, stepping away from the window and back to her baking. Baking was the one thing that took her mind off the waiting. She was always baking or cooking or cleaning. Hiring help had proved to be difficult after all the trouble here on the ranch. Suspicion hung over the place like thick smoke.

"I hate seeing you work so much," Hoyt said now. "I've called an agency in Billings. We have that guest-room at the far wing. What would you think about live-in help? No one wants to drive all the way out here from Whitehorse. I think this will work better."

She didn't correct him. It wasn't the drive and he knew it. Maybe people in Billings didn't know about the Chisholm Curse, as it was called.

"I don't need any help. You know I like to keep busy," Emma said, but she could tell he was determined to hire someone. Normally she would have put up a fight, but the truth was, having someone living in the house and helping sounded like a blessing. That way

Hoyt and his sons could go back to running this ranch instead of babysitting her.

Hoyt came up behind her, put his arms around her and pulled her close. She closed her eyes and leaned back into him. Never had she felt such love.

"Dawson just left for home," her husband said, nuzzling her neck. Her stepson Dawson had been assigned to Emma duty that day, which meant he'd spent the day pretending he had things to do around the ranch's main house and yard. Did any of them really believe they were fooling her?

Certainly not Hoyt, she thought as she turned off the mixer and let him lead her upstairs to their bedroom. The cookies could wait. Being in her husband's strong arms could not.

She knew as he closed the bedroom door that he believed their love was like a shield that would protect them. She prayed he was right, but alive or dead, his first wife and Aggie Wells were anything but gone for good.

FORMER INSURANCE INVESTIGATOR Aggie Wells had come close to dying. She still wasn't her old self. For months, she'd felt her strength seep out of her and now wondered if she would ever be the same again.

She told herself she was lucky to be alive. If the bullet had been a quarter of an inch one way or the other it would have nicked a vital organ and she would have drowned in that creek.

It surprised her that she'd survived against all odds. How easy it would have been to give in to death. She still had nightmares remembering how long she'd had to stay underwater to avoid the sheriff's deputies catching her.

That memory always came with the bitter bite of betrayal. She'd trusted Emma Chisholm. That stupid, stupid woman. Aggie had been trying to save her life and what did she get for it? Shot and almost drowned.

In her more charitable moments, she reminded herself that she *had* abducted Emma just months before that day on the river. Still, she'd risked capture to bring Emma important information about Laura Chisholm.

Also, Emma had seemed as surprised as Aggie had that day when they'd heard the sheriff and her deputies coming through the trees. Maybe Emma hadn't informed them about the meeting by the river. At least that's what Aggie liked to believe. She liked Emma and now there was nothing she could do to save her. *The die is cast,* she thought. After surviving the cold water and the bullet wound, Aggie had gotten pneumonia and barely survived.

Her weight had dropped drastically and she didn't seem to have any strength to fight it. She told herself she was bouncing back, but a part of her knew it wasn't true. Worse, she feared she would never see this case through.

A small, bitter laugh escaped her lips. It wasn't her case, hadn't been for years. The insurance company she'd worked for had fired her because she hadn't been able to let the Chisholm case go.

She couldn't really blame them. She'd gotten it all wrong anyway. When Hoyt Chisholm's first wife,

Laura, had allegedly drowned in Fort Peck Reservoir, Aggie had been convinced Hoyt had killed her.

He'd remarried not long after. He had adopted six sons who needed homes, and if any man was desperate for a wife, it would have been him. Tasha Chisholm had been killed in a horseback-riding accident.

Aggie couldn't believe he'd kill another one. And then along came Krystal. Did he really think he could get away with a third murder?

Krystal Chisholm had disappeared not long into the marriage. By then Aggie had been pulled off the case, but that hadn't stopped her. She couldn't let him get away with killing another wife.

The first two deaths appeared to be accidents—at least to the unsuspecting. The third wife's disappearance could never be proved to be anything more than that.

"But I knew better," Aggie said to herself. Her faint voice echoed in the small room of what had once been a motel and was now a cheap studio apartment where she'd been hiding on the south side of Billings.

She'd hit a brick wall in her covert investigation back then. The insurance company had warned her off the case. But eventually they found out and fired her.

Fortunately, she'd saved every dime she'd ever made, so money wasn't a problem. She'd taken on private investigations when she felt like it. She was good at what she did, putting herself in someone else's shoes until she knew them inside and out.

Thankfully, she'd helped people who, when called

on, couldn't say no to helping her. Like the surgeon she'd had to call after she was shot.

She might have given up the Chisholm cases—if Hoyt Chisholm hadn't married a fourth time all these years later. Aggie had no choice but to warn Emma Chisholm. The woman was blind in love.

"Just as you had no choice but to abduct her once you figured out who the murderer really was," Aggie said to the empty room, then pulled herself up some in the threadbare recliner where she sat.

Only a little sun spilled in through the dirty window between the two frayed and faded curtains. The light bothered her now. Her illness had seemed to affect her eyes. She drew her attention away from the crack in the curtains, feeling too weak to get up and close them tighter.

But no one believed her. Instead, law enforcement was convinced that Aggie herself had killed Hoyt's second and third wives in an attempt to frame him for murder.

She scoffed at that. This was about obsession. Not Aggie's with this case, but Laura's with Hoyt. Aggie understood obsession, she knew how it could take over your life.

If only the sheriff had listened to her. Instead, she'd been arrested and sent to the state mental hospital for evaluation. They thought *she* was crazy?

Aggie smiled to herself as she remembered how she'd slipped through the cracks, sending another woman to the state mental hospital who actually needed the help.

Her smile faded quickly though as she reminded herself that she had failed. That day beside the river she had brought Emma the proof that Laura Chisholm was alive and living just hours away in Billings as a woman named Sharon Jones.

But when she'd come out of her fever, surfacing again at death's door, she'd asked the doctor if a woman named Sharon Jones had been arrested.

"I had hoped and yet I knew better," she said to herself. Laura was like a warm breeze in summer, drifting in and out unnoticed. She had to be to stay hidden all these years, appearing only to kill and then disappear again.

The doctor had given her the bad news. Sharon Jones hadn't been arrested and now she'd disappeared again. "I went by the house you asked me to check," the doctor told her. "It was empty. No sign of anyone."

Laura Chisholm was still on the loose. She would take another identity and when the time was right, she would strike again. Emma Chisholm was going to die and there wasn't anything Aggie could do about it.

Chapter Six

It was late by the time Logan headed for the barn to saddle his horse the next day. He must have been more tired than he'd thought. He couldn't remember sleeping this late in the day since college.

Once saddled, he rode down the half-mile lane to pick up his mail from the box on the county road. As much as he loved being on the back of his motorcycle, he loved being on the back of a horse just as much.

It was a beautiful Montana spring day, the sky a brilliant blue, no clouds on the horizon and the sun spreading warmth over the vibrant green land. He loved this time of year, loved the smells, the feel of new beginnings.

He wondered if that was what his houseguest was looking for. She'd apparently bailed—at least for a while—on her old life, whatever that was. He hadn't slept all that well last night knowing she was upstairs. And this morning he had no more idea what she was all about than he had when he'd met her the other night at the bar. He hadn't heard a sound out of her by the time he'd left. For all he knew she'd sneaked out last night and was long gone.

At least she hadn't taken his pickup.

He'd already decided to take a few days off work and, if she hadn't bailed on him as well, show her his part of Montana if she was still up for it. But then what, he wondered? Eventually, he had to get back to work. His father and brothers would be wondering what was going on. The last thing he needed was for one of them to show up at the house, he thought as he reached the county road.

Logan realized Blythe didn't really know who he was, either. He felt almost guilty about that—even though she had been anything but forthcoming about herself. He wanted her to like him for himself and not for his family money. Of course, it could be that she already knew who he was—knew that night at the bar when he'd asked her to dance. His family had certainly been in the news enough with that mess about Aggie Wells.

He pushed away the memory, just glad that it was over. With Aggie Wells dead, that should be the end of speculation about his father's other wives' deaths.

Logan thought instead of Blythe and his reservations about her. He recalled her new cowboy boots. She wouldn't be the first woman who'd come to Montana to meet herself a cowboy. Even better a rich one.

But with a self-deprecating grin, he reminded himself that she hadn't even made a play for him. Maybe that was the plan, since it seemed to be working. He couldn't get her off his mind.

Swinging down from the horse, he collected his mail and the newspapers that had stacked up since he'd been gone. He glanced at today's *Great Falls Tribune,* scanning the headlines before stuffing everything into one of his saddlebags, climbing back into the saddle and heading home.

As he rode up to the house, he saw her come out onto the porch.

"Good morning," he called to her as he dismounted, relieved she hadn't taken off. Even without his pickup.

"Out for a morning ride?"

"Just went down to get the mail and my newspapers," he said as he dug them out of the saddlebag. "You up for a ride?"

She eyed the horse for a moment. "Do you have a shorter horse?"

He chuckled as he turned toward her. "I have a nice gentle one just for you." He noticed that she was wearing one of his shirts. It looked darned good on her. "Want to ride or have something to eat first?"

"Ride."

Logan knew he would have granted her anything she wanted at that moment. She was beautiful in an understated way that he found completely alluring. Her face, free of makeup, shone. There was a freshness about her that reminded him of the spring morning. She seemed relaxed and happy, her good mood contagious.

"Let's get you saddled up, then," he said, and led her out to the barn.

"This isn't going to be like a rodeo, is it?"

He laughed. "No bucking broncos, I promise. Don't worry, you're in good hands."

He showed her how to saddle her horse, then led it outside and helped her climb on.

"I like the view from up here," Blythe said, smiling down from the saddle. "So what do I do now?"

He gave her some of the basics, then climbed on his own horse. At first he just rode her around the pasture, but she was such a natural, he decided to show her a little piece of the ranch.

"This is what you do every day?" she asked, sounding awed.

He laughed. "It's a little more than a ride around the yard."

"You said you chase cows." She glanced around. "So where are these cows?"

"They're still in winter pasture. We'll be taking them up into the mountains pretty soon."

"You and your brothers. You ranch together?"

Her horse began to trot back toward the barn, saving him from answering. He rode alongside her, giving her pointers. She had great balance. It surprised him how quickly she'd caught on, and he wondered if she really had never ridden before.

"You're a natural," he said when they reached the house. It was late afternoon. They'd ridden farther than he'd originally planned, but it had been so enjoyable he hadn't wanted to return to the house.

"I had so much fun," she said as she swung down out of the saddle. "I wish we could do it again tomorrow." She groaned, though, and he could tell she was feeling the long ride.

"We can do it again tomorrow, if you're up to it," he said, liking the idea of another day with her.

"You probably need to start chasing cows again and I should be taking off, though, huh?" She looked away when she said it.

He really needed to get back to work, but he said, "I can take a few days off." As she helped him unsaddle the horses and put the tack away, he wondered again how long she planned to stay and where, if anywhere, the two of them were headed.

He knew he wouldn't be able to keep his family from Blythe long. Since his father Hoyt had remarried after years of raising his six sons alone, all six sons were expected to be at supper each evening. His stepmother Emma wanted them to spend time together as a family, and she was a great cook. It was just a matter of time before the family heard he was back and started wondering why he hadn't been around.

LORETTA WAS WAITING FOR THE others late the next morning down in the coffee shop. She'd already had a cup of coffee, which had only managed to make her more jittery. How long was the sheriff going to keep them here? She was broke and wondering how she was going to pay her motel bill, let alone eat.

Not to mention the latest news she'd just heard before coming down to the coffee shop. JJ had been killed yesterday in a car accident.

As Betsy and Karen joined her, she said, "You heard?"

"It's on all the news stations," Karen said.

"You and JJ had been closer than the rest of us," Loretta said, noticing that Karen had been crying.

"They were best friends when they were kids, huh," Betsy said.

That was news to Loretta.

"We grew up next door to each other," Karen said. "People thought we were sisters." She smiled at the memory, her eyes filling with tears.

"Must have been hard when she left the band," Loretta said. "So did she keep in touch with you?"

"No." Karen looked away.

"I thought it was just us," Betsy said. "But then none of us kept in touch either after that first year. Not surprising, I guess."

"Yeah, after everything that happened," Loretta agreed. She'd called Betsy a couple of times but felt like she'd gotten the cold shoulder. Karen, who she thought always acted as if she thought she was better than everyone, she hadn't even bothered to call.

"So we know what Betsy's been doing the last ten years, cranking out kids," Loretta said. "What about you, Karen?"

"I work in New York as a magazine editor."

Beat the hell out of Loretta's bartending job and part-time drumming gigs.

"So you never married?" Betsy asked.

"Three times. None of them stuck," Loretta said. "What about you, Karen?"

Karen shook her head.

"You got married quick enough after the band split," Loretta said to Betsy. "But I get the feeling you're still carrying a torch for Jett." Loretta couldn't help herself, even though Karen shot her a warning look.

"Jett made the rounds among us," Karen said pointedly, "but I don't think any of us were ever serious about him."

"Is that right?" Jett said shoving Karen over as he joined them in the booth.

Loretta didn't miss the look Jett and Betsy exchanged. He was up to his old tricks, she thought, and wondered what Betsy's husband would have to say about it. That was, if anyone bothered to tell him.

She discarded the idea. What did she care? She hadn't come here to bond with her former band members. She'd come for the money and now there wasn't any.

"You all heard about JJ?" Jett said, glancing around the table. He looked solemn for a moment before he asked with a grin, "So which one of you killed her?"

"Why would any of us want to kill JJ?" Karen asked with obvious annoyance.

Jett shrugged. "Jealousy. I've already told the sheriff to check the brakes on her rental car."

"Jealous? Not over you," Loretta said.

"Maybe," he said still grinning. "But I definitely felt some professional jealousy. JJ became a star while the rest of you—"

"Did just fine," Karen said. "Let's not forget that JJ, according to the tabloids, had been trying to get out of her contract. I don't think her life was a bed of roses."

"So we're all supposed to feel sorry for her?" Loretta asked. "Excuse me, but she dumped us. Sold us right

down the river. I, for one, haven't forgotten or forgiven."
When she saw the way everyone was staring at her, she
added, "But I had nothing to do with her driving her
car off a cliff."

"I'm sure it was just an accident," Betsy said.

"Sure," Jett replied with a chuckle. "Just like Martin
getting shot through the heart."

BUFORD'S PHONE HAD BEEN ringing off the hook all day.
As hard as Kevin had tried to keep the news of Martin
Sanderson's death from the media, he'd failed.

"Mr. Sanderson's death is under investigation," the
sheriff said. "That's all I can tell you at this time."

When his phone rang yet again, he'd snatched it up,
expecting it would be another reporter.

"You knew about JJ's accident last night," Jett Atkins
said the moment Buford picked up.

He recognized his voice but said, "I'm sorry, who is
this?"

"Jett Atkins. You knew JJ was dead when you called
me last night."

"The accident was under investigation."

"It's splashed all over the papers, television and internet. You could have told me last night. Instead I have
to see it on TV."

"Well, you know now." Buford didn't have the time
for the rock star's tantrum.

"They killed her. JJ was too good a driver. You'd
better check the brakes on that car. I already warned
them that I was going to tell you."

Buford loved nothing better than being told what he

needed to do. But he was reminded of the lack of skid marks on the highway. It had appeared that the driver of the car hadn't braked.

"Who are *they?*" he asked, even though he suspected he knew.

"Her former band members. The more I've thought of it, the more I think one of them killed Martin and then sabotaged JJ's car and killed her, as well."

"I thought you were convinced JJ killed Martin," he reminded him.

"Well, she could have after what he did to her. But if anyone is murderous, it's the members of her former band. They hated her enough as it was. Once they found out that JJ wasn't doing any reunion tour—"

"They knew that for sure?"

"I don't know. But if Martin told them and they figured out that he'd used them—"

"Mr. Atkins—"

"Check the brakes on her car. I'm telling you one of them or all three of them killed her. You should have seen their faces this morning at breakfast when I asked them which one of them did JJ in."

Buford groaned. "Please let me do the investigating."

"Let me know what you find out about the brake line."

"You must be starved," Logan said after he and Blythe returned from their horseback ride. They'd eaten elk steak sandwiches late the night before, but that had been hours ago now. "I'll make us something to eat."

"Can I help?" She had picked up the newspapers he'd brought home earlier.

"No, you've had a strenuous enough day. Anyway, it's a one-man kitchen. I'm thinking bacon, scrambled eggs and toast." He liked breakfast any time of the day, especially at night.

"Yum." She sounded distracted.

He left her sorting through the newspapers on the couch and went into the kitchen. The sun had long set, the prairie silver in the twilight. Blythe must be exhausted. He hadn't meant to take her on such a long ride. But she'd been a trooper, really seeming to enjoy being on horseback.

It wasn't until the meal was almost ready that he realized he hadn't heard a peep out of her. She must have fallen asleep on the couch.

He put everything into the oven to keep it warm and was about to go check on her when he smelled smoke. Hurriedly, he stuck his head into the living room to find her feeding the fire she'd started in the fireplace.

"I hope you don't mind," she said quickly, no doubt seeing his surprise. "I felt a little cool."

"Sure," he said, but noticed she'd used one of the recent newspapers he hadn't had a chance to read instead of the old ones stacked up next to the kindling box by the fireplace. Also she'd made a pitiful fire. "Here, let me help you."

She'd wadded up the front pages of the most recent *Great Falls Tribune* and set the paper on fire, then thrown a large log on top. The paper was burning so quickly there was no way it would ignite the log.

He pulled the log off. The newspaper had burned to black ash.

"Oh, I'm sorry. You probably wanted to read that," she said behind him.

"Probably wasn't any good news anyway," he said not wanting to make her feel bad.

"Don't bother to make a fire," she said. "I'm fine now. What is that wonderful smell coming from the kitchen?"

He studied her a moment. "You're sure?"

She nodded.

He told himself it was his imagination that she looked pale. Earlier she'd gotten some sun from their long ride and her cheeks had been pink. Now all the color seemed to have been bleached out of her. She seemed upset.

"Maybe I'll teach you how to build a fire while you're here, too."

Her smile wasn't her usual one. "That's probably a good idea."

As they went into the kitchen, he couldn't shake the feeling that her purpose in burning the newspaper had nothing to do with a chill. It seemed more likely that it had been something she'd read in the paper.

Logan tried to remember the headlines he'd scanned before riding back to the house. Scientists were predicting a possible drought after low snowfall levels. A late-season avalanche had killed a snowmobiler up by Cooke City. Some singer named JJ had been killed in a car wreck in the Flathead Valley.

He couldn't imagine why any of those stories might

have upset her and told himself he was just imagining things. Who got upset about an article and burned the newspaper?

"Are you sure I can't help?"

He started at the sound of her voice directly behind him and checked his suspicious expression before he turned. "Nope, everything is ready." When he studied her face, he was relieved that her color had come back. She looked more like that laid-back, adventurous woman who'd climbed onto his motorcycle yesterday.

"I hope you're hungry," he said as he handed her a plateful of food.

But something had definitely ruined her appetite.

"Blythe," Logan said after they'd eaten and gotten up to put their dishes in the sink. He touched her arm, turning her to face him. She was inches from him. She met his gaze and held it. "Tell me what's going on with you." He saw her consider it.

But then her expression changed and even before she closed the distance between them, he knew what she was up to. Her lips brushed over his cheek, the look in her eyes challenging. She put her palm flat against his chest as she leaned in again, lips parted and started to kiss him on the mouth.

He grasped her shoulders and held her away from him. "What was *that?*" he demanded.

"I just thought…"

"If you don't want to tell me what's really going on with you, fine. If you want to make love with me, I'm all for it. But let's be clear. When you come to my bed, I want it to be because you want me. No other reason."

Disbelief flickered across her expression. He knew he was a damned fool not to take what she was offering—no matter her reasons. The woman was beautiful and just the thought of taking her to bed made his blood run hotter than a wildfire through his veins.

He wanted her. What man wouldn't? But he wouldn't let her use sex to keep him at a distance. Even as he thought it, he couldn't believe it himself. Why did he have to feel this way about this woman?

Her eyes burned with tears. "I appreciate everything you—"

"Don't," he said. "I'm glad you're here. Let's leave it at that. I'm going to check the horses."

BLYTHE COULDN'T ESCAPE upstairs fast enough. Just his touch set something off in her, while the kindness in his eyes made her want to confess everything. She had wanted to bare her soul to him.

Instead, she'd fallen back on what she'd always done when anyone got too close. She had tried to use the same weapon her mother had: sex. To her shock and surprise, Logan wasn't having any of it. He'd shoved her away and what she'd seen in his gaze was anything but desire. Anger burned in all that blue. Anger and disappointment. The disappointment was like an arrow through her heart.

He'd gone out to check the horses and she'd hurried upstairs to run a bath before she did something crazy like confess all. How would he feel about having a murderess under his roof? Worse, a coward? She'd gotten at least one person killed, maybe two, if she counted Martin.

Even the hot lilac-scented water of the clawfoot tub couldn't calm her. She was still shaken and upset about the almost kiss. Logan had seen right through her. Another man, she thought, would have taken what she was offering and not cared what was going on with her. But not Logan.

He saw through her. No doubt he'd also figured out why she'd burned the newspaper. She couldn't believe what she'd read in the paper. A young woman had apparently stolen her rental car, lost control and crashed, the poor woman, and now everyone thought it had been her and that she was dead?

Not her. *JJ.* The fantasy performer that Martin Sanderson had created. Now they were both dead.

She'd seen the way Logan had looked at her when she'd attempted to destroy the news articles in the fireplace. But she couldn't let him see either story—not the one about JJ's sports car convertible ending up down a rocky embankment, catching fire and killing its driver or about Martin Sanderson's murder.

When the bath water cooled to the point where she was shivering, she got out and, wearing Logan's robe, went to his bedroom. On the way, she listened for any sound of him on the couch below. Nothing. Maybe he was still out with the horses.

Still embarrassed, she was glad she didn't have to face him again tonight. Once in his bedroom, she moved to the window of the two-story farmhouse and looked out at the night. She still felt numb. What had she thought would happen when she left everything in the car beside the lake?

Nothing. She hadn't thought. If she had, she would have realized that someone could have come along, found the car, the keys, her purse and thought she'd killed herself in the lake. Instead, someone had taken the car and died in it.

How could she have ever suspected something like that was going to happen? Still she felt to blame. Someone else was dead because of her.

She remembered what it had said in the article. The police had speculated that the woman had been driving too fast and had missed the curve. Officers were investigating whether drugs and alcohol might have been involved.

Not her fault.

She sighed, close to tears, knowing better. Just like Martin Sanderson being dead wasn't her fault. Now she wished she'd been able to keep the newspaper article, to read it again more closely, but she'd panicked. If Logan saw it he might connect the car she'd been driving with this woman's death—and her. She wasn't ready to tell him everything. If she ever was.

Maybe the best thing she could do was clear out. He didn't need her problems, and eventually those problems were going to find her here. She didn't kid herself. All burning the articles had done was buy her a little time. Logan was too smart. He was going to figure it out. Eventually the police would figure it out, as well.

Isn't it possible Fate is giving you a second chance?

JJ was dead and she was alive.

She had wanted out of her life and she'd been given a chance to start over. A clean slate. With everyone thinking she was dead, she could start life fresh. Did it matter that she didn't deserve it?

As she turned away from the bedroom window, she recalled her conversation with Martin. "I would give anything to do it differently."

He'd laughed. "You're what? Barely thirty and you're talking as if your life is over? Save the drama for when you get paid for it. I'm not letting you out of your contract. Period. If you keep fighting me, I'll make you do a reunion tour with your former Tough as Nails band."

She'd been shocked he would even threaten such a thing. "You wouldn't do that."

"Wouldn't I?"

"You can't make me," she'd said, knowing that Martin Sanderson could destroy her and he knew it.

"I'll sue you, and take every penny I made for you."

"Take it. I'm done," she'd said and meant it.

He'd studied her for a moment. "Okay, you're not happy. I get it. So let's do this. Take some time tonight to unwind. Go into town. Have some fun. Then sleep on it. If you feel the same way in the morning, then… well, we'll work something out that we can both live with."

She remembered her relief. She'd actually thought things might be all right after all. Isn't that why she'd gone to that country-western bar that night? And luck had been with her. She'd met Logan Chisholm.

But by the next morning everything had changed. Martin was dead and she'd realized that she had worse problems than getting out of her contract and a tour with her former band members.

She didn't know what she would have done if Logan hadn't shown up when he did at the Grizzly Club. It had been desperation and something just as strong—survival—that had made her abandon her car and get on the back of his motorcycle. She had wanted to run away with him. Just ride off into the sunset with the cowboy from her girlhood dreams.

Now another swift change of luck. Everyone thought JJ was dead.

Especially her former band members.

Even if they suspected she was still alive, they wouldn't think to look for her in this remote part of Montana.

A bubble of laughter rose in her chest as hot tears burned her eyes. She was too exhausted to even think, let alone decide what to do tonight. She would decide what to do tomorrow. She moved to the bed. She was a survivor. Somehow she would survive this, as well. Or die trying.

As she climbed between the sheets, she didn't fight the exhaustion that pulled her under. The last thing she wanted to think about was what a mess she'd made of that old life. Or the look on Logan's face when she'd tried to kiss him.

SHERIFF BUFORD OLSON WAS IN his office when he got the call from the coroner's office.

"I've just spoken with the state crime investigators. Martin Sanderson's death has been ruled a suicide," the coroner said without preamble. "He was dying. Cancer. His personal physician confirmed my findings. He'd known he had only a few weeks to live."

Buford ran a hand over his thinning hair. All the evidence had been there indicating a suicide—except for the note. Because someone had taken it.

The moment he'd seen the safety pin with the tiny piece of yellow sticky note stuck to it, he'd thought suicide. But again, without the note…

Martin Sanderson had been shot in the heart—and not through the robe. For some unknown reason suicide victims rarely shot themselves through clothing.

The gun found at the scene was registered to Sanderson. Its close proximity to the body, the lack of evidence of a struggle, the powder burns around the wound, the gun powder residue on the victim's hands and the sleeves of his robe all pointed toward suicide.

Even the angle of the shot appeared to be slightly upward, like most suicides. Another sign of a possible suicide was the single shot to the heart. All the scene had needed was a reason for the suicide, and now the coroner had provided it. Sanderson was dying. If only they had that damned note, this case could have been tied up a lot sooner.

"Good work," the mayor said when Buford gave him the news. "Case closed. I'll alert the media."

Closed as far as the mayor was concerned, Buford thought after he hung up. But there was that missing note and the mystery of who—and why—the person had taken it. If it had been Sanderson's guest Jennifer "JJ" James, then they would never know what the note said.

Buford told himself it didn't matter. Martin Sanderson's death had been ruled a suicide. The infamous JJ had died in a car wreck. All the loose ends had been neatly tied up. What more did he want?

With a curse, he called the garage where Jennifer James's car had been taken and asked the head mechanic to check to see if someone might have tampered with the brake line.

Chapter Seven

The next day Logan was still angry with himself and Blythe. Why wouldn't she let him help her? Stubborn pride? He, of all people, understood that.

What bothered him was that the night he'd danced with her, he'd seen a strength in her that had drawn him. Now though she seemed scared. What had happened between their last dance and now? Something, and whatever it was had her on the run and hiding out here with him.

He couldn't help but feel protective of her. Whatever she needed, he would do his best to give it to her if she would just let him. He was worried about her. But he told himself the woman he'd danced with was too strong and determined to let whatever had happened beat her. Maybe she just needed time.

As for what had happened last night… He'd wanted to kiss her, wanted her in his arms, in his bed. He was still mentally kicking himself for pushing her away. He could imagine what his brothers would have said if they'd heard that he turned down a beautiful, desirable woman.

But Blythe wasn't just any woman.

And he'd meant what he'd said last night. He wanted more than just sex with her. Logan chuckled, thinking again about what his brothers would say to that.

Speaking of his brothers, he thought with a curse. One of the Chisholm Cattle Company pickups was coming down the lane in a cloud of dust. As the truck drew closer, he recognized his brother Zane behind the wheel.

He glanced toward the stairs. Blythe hadn't come down yet this morning. He'd hated the way he'd left things last night. But by the time he'd come in after mentally kicking himself all over the ranch yard, her door upstairs had been closed, the light off.

Late last night, unable to sleep, he'd decided that whatever Blythe was running from had something to do with an article in yesterday's newspaper. He'd ridden down this morning, but today's paper hadn't come yet. Maybe the best thing to do was go into town to the library so he could go through a few days papers on the internet. He couldn't imagine what she was hiding, just that she was here hiding because of it.

Now, though, he had a bigger problem, he thought as he stepped out onto the porch and walked down the steps to cut his brother off at the pass.

"Hey, what's going on?" Zane asked as he climbed out of the pickup. "Dad said you called and needed a few more days off."

"Is there a problem?"

"We're shorthanded, that's the problem," his brother said as he glanced toward the house. "Dad wants one of us staying around the main house to keep an eye on

Emma until some agency in Billings can find someone to come up here and live in the guest wing."

"He's still worried about Emma?" Their lives had been turned upside down the past six months, but should have calmed down after Aggie Wells had drowned in the creek. Once winter runoff was over, they'd find her remains and then that would be the end of it.

Logan knew his stepmother had been put through hell and all because of his father's past. But then again, she should have asked a few more questions before she'd run off with him for a quickie marriage in Vegas.

He thought about Blythe and realized he'd put himself in the same position Emma had. What did he know about the woman now sleeping in his bed? And had he let that stop him?

"You know Dad," Zane said.

"Can't today. Sorry."

"Oh?" His brother looked past him. "Emma was worried you were sick. She wanted to send some chicken soup along with me. I got out of there before she baked you a cake, too."

"I'm fine."

Zane looked at him suspiciously. "How was the Flathead?"

"Pretty this time of year."

His brother laughed. "I see you bought yourself some new clothes."

Logan looked to where Zane was pointing and swore under his breath. Blythe had left her jean jacket with the embroidered flowers on it lying over the porch railing.

His brother was grinning from ear to ear. "I knew you wanting time off had something to do with a woman."

Just then, as luck would have it, Blythe came out the front door onto the porch.

Zane let out a low whistle. "It's all becoming clear now," he said under his breath. "Aren't you going to introduce me?" When Logan said nothing, his brother stepped around him and called up to the porch, "Hello. I'm Logan's brother Zane, but I'm sure he's told you all about me."

Blythe smiled. "As a matter of fact, I think he said you were his favorite."

Zane laughed. "I like her," he said to Logan. "Why don't you bring her to supper tonight. I'll tell Emma to set another plate."

Logan could have throttled him. Zane knew damned well that if he'd been ready to tell her about the family, he would have already brought her by the house.

"Oh, and I'll cover for you today, but I'll expect you back to work tomorrow. You get babysitting duty." With that Zane climbed into his pickup, waved at Blythe and drove away.

SHERIFF BUFORD OLSON WAS about to leave his office for the day when he got another call from the coroner's office. What now, he thought as he picked up.

"The woman's body found in that car accident wasn't Jennifer James," the coroner said in his usual all-business tone. "This woman was in her early twenties. The crime lab took DNA from a hairbrush Jennifer

James left at the Grizzly Club. This Jane Doe is definitely not the woman the media calls JJ."

"We have no idea who she is?"

"She was wearing a silver bracelet with the name Susie on it. I would suggest sending her DNA to NDIS to see if they have a match. That's the best I can do." The National DNA Index System processed DNA records of persons convicted of crimes, analyzed samples recovered from crime scenes as well as from unidentified human remains and analyzed samples for missing person cases.

"Thanks," Buford said, still processing this turn of events. If JJ hadn't died in her rental car, then where was she? She'd have to be on the moon not to hear about the accident that had allegedly claimed her life at the edge of Flathead Lake. So why hadn't she come forward?

He'd barely hung up when he got a call from a gas station attendant in Moses Lake, Washington.

"Is this the sheriff in that town where JJ was killed?" a young female voice asked.

"Yes?" he said, curious since the dispatcher had motioned to him that he might actually *want* to take this call.

"Well, I wasn't sure if I should call or not, but I just had this guy in an old pickup buy gas? The thing is, he used one of JJ's credit cards. It has her on the front, you know one of those photos of her with her guitar, the kind you can get on certain credit cards? I have all her CDs, so I recognized her right off. The man tried to use the card at the pump but it didn't work so he brought it in and when it was denied again, he just took off."

Buford felt his heart racing, but he kept his voice calm. "Did you happen to get the plate number on the pickup?"

"Yeah. He didn't look like the kind of guy JJ would have dated, you know?"

"Yeah." He wrote down the license plate number she gave him and thanked her for being an upstanding citizen. She gave him a detailed description of the pickup driver. He told her to hold on to the credit card and that he'd have someone collect it from her shortly.

Even before he ran the plates on the pickup, he suspected it would be stolen—just like the credit card. It was.

Buford put an all points bulletin out on the pickup and driver, then sat back in his chair and scratched his head. JJ wasn't dead. At least her body hadn't been found, and right now Logan Chisholm might be the only person who could tell him where she went that day after leaving the Grizzly Club.

When he called directory assistance and no listing was found, he put in a call to the Chisholm Cattle Company.

LOGAN DIDN'T WANT HER meeting his family, Blythe thought with no small amount of surprise. She'd been so busy hiding her former life and who she'd been from him, she'd never considered that he might be hiding her from his family and friends.

"You can get out of it," she said as Zane drove away.

"Out of what?" Logan asked, clearly playing dumb.

She smiled. "Out of taking me to supper with your family."

"It isn't what you think." He dragged his hat off and raked his fingers through his thick blond hair. He wore his hair longer than most cowboys, she thought, but then again she didn't know many cowboys, did she? His eyes were the same blue as the sky. She'd met her share of handsome men, but none as appealing as this one.

"You don't have to explain. We just met. We don't even know each other. There is no reason I should meet your folks." Even as she said it, she was curious about his family. Curious about Logan. She felt as if she'd only skimmed the surface, but she liked him and wouldn't have minded getting to know him better—if things were different.

The thought surprised her. She hadn't had roots since she left home at fourteen and thought she didn't want or need them. But being here with Logan had spurred something in her she hadn't known was there.

"Is there any coffee?" she asked as she turned back toward the house.

"Blythe, it isn't that I don't want you to meet them."

In the kitchen, she opened a cupboard and took down a cup. She wasn't kidding about needing some coffee. She felt off balance, all her emotions out of kilter. She could feel him behind her, close.

She turned to him. "Look, you don't really know me. Or I you. I don't even know what I'm doing staying here. I should go." She started to step past him, but he closed his hand over her arm and pulled her close.

His alluring male scent filled her, making her ache with a need to touch him and be touched. She turned to find him inches from her. He took the coffee cup from her hand and set it on the counter. Then he pulled her to him.

He felt warm, his shirt scented with sunshine and horse leather. His hands were strong as they cupped her waist and drew her close. As his mouth dropped to hers, she caught her breath. She'd known, somewhere deep inside her, that when he kissed her it would be like rockets going off. She hadn't been wrong.

Logan deepened the kiss, his arms coming around her. He stole her breath, made her heart drum in her chest, sending shivers of desire ricocheting through her. She melted into his arms. He felt so solid she didn't want him to let her go.

As the kiss ended, he pulled back to look into her eyes. "I've wanted to do that since the first time I saw you."

Her pulse was still thundering just under her skin. She wanted him and she knew it wouldn't take much for him to swing her up into his arms and carry her upstairs to that double bed of his. Just the truth.

She took a step back, letting her arms slip from around his neck. She almost didn't trust what she might say. "I'm sorry about last night."

He shook his head. "I just want us to be clear. I want you. I have from the moment I laid eyes on you at the country-western bar."

"I want you, too. And I want to tell you everything. I just need some time to sort things out for myself."

He grinned and shoved back his Stetson. "And I want to take you home to meet my family, but I need to warn you about them."

"No, don't spoil it. Let me be surprised," she joked.

"I called my stepmother. We're on for tonight. But you might change your mind about everything once you meet them all."

She knew it was crazy, but she was relieved he wanted her to meet his family. It was dangerous. What if one of them recognized her? Blythe knew she had worse worries than that.

And yet, right now, all she wanted to think about was meeting Logan's family. "I need to go into town and get myself something to wear." She hadn't been this excited about a date in a long time.

Logan seemed to hesitate, as if he was thinking about kissing her again. Desire shone in his eyes. Her own heart was still hammering from the kiss. She *did* want him. More than he could know. But he wanted more from her than a roll in the hay. When was the last time she'd met a man like that?

"I better go start the truck," he said.

She was glad now that she'd stuffed a few hundred dollar bills into the pocket of her jeans before she'd left Martin Sanderson's house that awful morning. It seemed like weeks ago instead of days.

Blythe took a sip of the coffee, needing the caffeine to steady her after the kiss. She hadn't slept well last night, and the sound of the vehicle coming down the road this morning had made her heart race until she reminded herself that not a soul in the world knew she was here—other than Logan.

Now his brother Zanc knew, and soon so would his family. But they knew her as Blythe. She heard the pickup door slam, the engine turning over, and downed the rest of the coffee. She felt nervous about meeting Logan's family and unconsciously touched a finger to her lips.

She couldn't help smiling as she thought of his kiss. *You're falling for this cowboy.*

No, she told herself, as messed up as her life was, she couldn't let that happen. Once he knew the truth about her, that would be the end of it. Maybe she should go to the door and call him back in and tell him everything. Nip this in the bud before it went any further and they both got hurt. Tell him before she met his family.

Logan would be hurt enough once he knew everything. How long did she really think she could keep that old life a secret, anyway? What if someone in town recognized her?

Blythe put down her cup and pushed out through the screen door to the porch to pick up her jean jacket from where she'd left it. As she did, she looked out at this wide-open land. It was like her life now. Wide open. Now that she had this new life—at least for a while—she was surprised by what she wanted to do with it.

She had put away most of the money she'd made in an account where she could get to it. She could do anything she pleased, go anywhere in the world. To her surprise, though, she realized she didn't want to leave here, didn't want to leave Logan. She wanted to meet his family.

Couldn't she just enjoy this life for a little while?

As she headed out to the pickup, she saw him sitting behind the wheel. He smiled at her and her heart took off in a gallop as she climbed into the cab next to him. She knew this couldn't last, but was it so wrong for just another day?

LOGAN HAD SOME TIME TO KILL while he waited for Blythe to shop for clothes. He'd offered to buy her anything she needed, but she'd told him she had money.

"Nothing fancy," he'd warned her. "You're in the real Montana now."

After he'd left her, he'd headed to the library. He felt a little guilty, but he had to know what had been in the newspaper Blythe had burned. She was in trouble. He felt it at heart level. The only way he could help her was to know what had her running scared. Something in that newspaper had upset her. He was sure of it.

It didn't take him long at the library to find the section of the paper Blythe had burned. He scanned the articles. One caught his eye—the one about the woman who'd been killed in a car wreck at the edge of Flathead Lake. Was it possible Blythe had known the woman? He read the name. Jennifer James. Apparently she was best known as JJ, a rock star who shot to meteoric fame.

According to the story, she'd missed a curve and crashed down a rocky embankment, rolling multiple times before the car burst into flames and finally came to rest at the edge of the lake. The infamous JJ was believed to have been driving at a high rate of speed. It was not determined yet if she was under the influence of drugs or alcohol.

All it said about this JJ person was that she had led a glittering life in the glare of the media after her sky-rocketing career. She had died at the age of thirty.

It wasn't until he focused on the sports car convertible that he knew he'd been right about something in the newspaper upsetting her.

The sight of the car stopped him cold. That and a sentence in the cutline under the photograph. JJ had been discovered by legendary music producer Martin Sanderson. Sanderson was a resident of the Grizzly Club, an exclusive conclave south of Bigfork.

That's when Logan saw the second headline: Famous Music Producer Found Dead.

He quickly scanned the story until he found what he was looking for. Martin Sanderson had been found dead in his home Saturday.

Saturday? The day Logan had gone to the club looking for the mysterious woman from the bar. The day Blythe had come tearing out of the gate to race down the highway like a crazy woman, then climb on the back of his motorcycle and ask him to take her away with him.

He hurriedly read the article. Investigators from the Missoula Crime Lab had been called in on the case. They thought it was a homicide? He checked to see the estimated time of death. Saturday morning.

Logan groaned. No wonder she'd wanted to get as

far away from the Flathead as possible. She'd known the sheriff would be looking for her.

The article mentioned that Sanderson had discovered the recently deceased JJ who, according to sources, had been visiting Sanderson at the Grizzly Club.

His heart began to pound as he reread the first newspaper article. Who had died in the car? Someone named Jennifer James better known as JJ, according to the story. He double-checked the car photo. It was the same make and color as the one Blythe had left beside the highway two days ago. No way was that a coincidence. Add to that the connection to the Grizzly Club…

Logan shook his head. Blythe had to have known this woman. But then why not say something? Because she felt guilty for leaving the car for her friend? They both must have been staying at the Grizzly Club with Sanderson.

So who was this JJ? From the grainy black-and-white photo accompanying the short article, it was impossible to tell much about her, since she was duded out in heavy, wild makeup and holding a garish electric guitar.

Logan glanced at his watch. He'd told Blythe he would pick her up back on the main drag after running a few errands of his own. He still had thirty minutes, enough time to see what else he could learn about the woman who had been killed.

He typed in Pop Singer JJ. Pages of items began to come up on the computer screen. He clicked on one and a color photograph appeared.

His breath rushed out of him as he stared at the photograph in shock. Blythe. No wonder he hadn't recognized her. He wouldn't have ever connected the woman who'd climbed on the back of his motorcycle with this one even without the wild makeup and masks she wore when she performed.

He thought about her that first night at the Western bar in her new cowboy boots. There had been a look of contentment on her face as she'd danced to the music. No, she'd looked nothing like this woman in the publicity photo.

It didn't help that he wasn't into her kind of music. He'd never heard of JJ or a lot of other singers and bands she'd performed with, since he was a country-western man himself.

But who was this woman staying with him really? The infamous JJ? Or the woman he'd come to know as Blythe? He had a feeling that whoever she was, she was still wearing a mask.

At least now he knew why she'd run. It had to have something to do with music producer Martin Sanderson's death. Had she killed him?

He didn't want to believe he'd been harboring a murderer. But with a curse, he reminded himself that everyone thought she was dead and she had let them. She'd seen the article. She knew someone else had died in her car. If she was innocent, then why hadn't she said something? Why hadn't she come forward and told the world she was still alive?

AGGIE WELLS WOKE COUGHING. Sun slanted in the crack between the curtains. She'd fallen asleep in her chair again and lost another day. But what had brought her

out of her deathlike sleep was that same horrible nightmare she'd been having for weeks now.

She sat up, fighting to catch her breath.

The doctor had said that the pneumonia had weakened her lungs. The gunshot wound had weakened her
body. Add to that failure and she felt like an old woman,
one foot in the grave.

"You have to call Emma," she said when she finally
caught her breath.

Call and tell her what? That you had a horrible
dream—most of it unintelligible, but that you've seen
how it all ends?

Aggie realized how crazy that sounded. She had
nothing new to tell Emma or the sheriff. No one believed that Laura Chisholm was alive, let alone what
she was capable of doing.

The nightmare seemed to lurk in the dark shadows
of the room. Aggie pulled her blanket around her, but
couldn't shake the chill the dream had left in her bones.

She remembered glimpses of the nightmare, something moving soundlessly in a dark room, the glint of
a knife. Aggie shuddered. She hadn't seen Laura in the
shadows, but she'd sensed something almost inhuman.

Aggie reached for the phone, but stopped herself.
She was sure the sheriff would be tracing any calls
coming into the ranch. Hoyt might answer. She might
not even get a chance to talk to Emma at all.

And what would be the point? She didn't know
where Laura Chisholm had gone or who she had
become. She just knew the killer was headed for Chis-

holm ranch soon and Emma would never see her coming.

All calling would accomplish was to give the sheriff Aggie's own location. She couldn't bear the thought of spending what was left of her life in the state mental hospital or behind bars in prison.

In her weakened state, she didn't have the energy to escape again. Nor could she go out and find Laura Chisholm again for them. Just the thought of Laura Chisholm made the hair stand up on the back of her neck. She shifted in her chair. She realized sitting there that somehow she'd gone from being the hunter to the hunted.

It wasn't what Laura was capable of that terrified her. It was that the woman could somehow be invisible— until it was too late for her prey. It took a special talent to go unnoticed. To seem so safe that she didn't even stir the air, didn't appear to take up space, didn't seem to exist in any form other than a ghost.

Maybe the worst part was that Aggie *knew* Laura. She'd become Laura when she'd believed Hoyt Chisholm had killed his first wife. Aggie had worn the woman's same brand of perfume and clothing, had her hair cut in the same style, had learned everything she could about Laura. She'd tried on the woman's skin.

She *knew* Laura and, she thought with a shudder, Laura knew *her*.

A lot of people thought Aggie Wells was dead.

Laura Chisholm wasn't one of them.

In Aggie's nightmare, Laura found her.

Chapter Eight

Logan's cell phone rang, echoing through the small, quiet library. He quickly dug it out, saw that it was his stepmother calling and hurried outside to take it. "Hello."

"Where are you?" Emma said sounding excited about having company tonight.

"In town. Blythe——" She might be the pop rocker JJ, but he thought of her as Blythe and knew he always would. "Had to get something to wear for tonight."

"You didn't tell her she had to dress up, did you?" Emma scolded.

"Just the opposite. But she's a woman. You know how they are."

His stepmother laughed. "We're looking forward to meeting her."

Logan wanted to warn Emma not to get too attached to her—just as he'd been warning himself since she'd climbed on his motorcycle. Since finding out who she really was, he was even more aware that she would be leaving soon, possibly prison. If innocent, back to her old life. No woman gave up that life to stay in his old farmhouse—no matter what she said.

"So you're still in town," Emma said.

"I have to pick up Blythe at the clothing store in about fifteen minutes and then we were headed back to my place."

"Don't do that. Come on over to the main house so we can visit before supper," she said. "Anything you want to tell me about this woman before you get here?"

He chuckled. "Nothing that comes to mind."

"Oh, you," Emma said. "Zane says she's lovely."

"She is that." And mysterious and complex and let's not forget a star—and quite possibly a murderer. Right now a star who is being immortalized because she died so young.

"Is this serious? Your brother seems to think—"

"Zane really should stop thinking," he snapped, realizing that Blythe wouldn't just be lying to him tonight at supper at the main ranch. She would be lying to his family. Involving them in this mess.

"I didn't mean to pry," Emma said, sounding a little hurt.

"You did, but that's what I love about you," he said softening his words. Emma was the best thing that had happened to their family. She only wanted good things for all of them.

"I just remembered an errand I have to run," Logan said, and got off the phone.

He checked his watch and then hurried back in the library. He wanted to check today's paper and see if there was anything more about Martin Sanderson's and JJ's deaths.

Logan found the most recent edition of the *Great*

Falls Tribune. Both JJ and Martin Sanderson had made the front page.

Mayor Confirms Music Producer's Death a Suicide

A tidal wave of relief washed over him as he quickly read the short update. Blythe might be JJ, but at least JJ wasn't a murderer. He knew that should make him happier than it did. There was a long article about JJ, about her humble beginnings, her rise to stardom, her latest attempts to get out of her contract and how she had died too young.

Her fans had been gathering across the country, making memorials for her. Logan remembered the waitress at the Cut Bank café and swore. The woman had recognized her. That's why Blythe had made them hightail it out of there.

But if she hadn't killed Martin Sanderson, then what was she running from? Was her life that bad that she'd rather let even her fans believe she was dead rather than come forward? Better to let them think she had died in a fiery car crash?

He realized that the whole world believed that the infamous JJ was dead. Everyone but him, Logan thought with a groan.

The only thing to do was call the sheriff over in the Flathead and let him know that JJ was alive. He started to reach for his cell phone and stopped himself. He couldn't do anything until he confronted her.

As he left the library, he recalled what she'd said to him when they'd reached Whitehorse that first night.

"Have you ever just needed to step out of your life for a while and take a chance?"

Is that what she was doing? Just taking a break from that life? Good thing he hadn't gotten serious about her, he told himself as he drove down the main drag and saw her waiting for him on the sidewalk ahead.

As he pulled in, she turned in a circle so he could see her new clothes. She was wearing a new pair of jeans, a Western blouse and a huge smile.

It was easy to see why he would never have recognized her even if he had followed pop rock. She looked nothing like the JJ of music stardom. Her dark hair was pulled back in a ponytail, her face, free of makeup, slightly flushed, her faded-denim blue eyes sparkling with excitement.

He felt a heartstring give way at just the sight of her.

"What do you think?" she asked as she slid into the cab next to him. "I don't want to embarrass you at supper. Is it too much?"

"You look beautiful."

She beamed as if that was the first time anyone had ever told her that.

"Emma called." Logan was going to tell her that supper was canceled but she instantly looked so disappointed, he couldn't do it. He had let her pretend to be someone she wasn't this long, what were a few more hours? "She wants us to come on by."

"If it's okay with you, sure," she said brightening. "Can you believe it? I'm nervous about meeting your family."

She wasn't the only one who was apprehensive, Logan thought as he drove out of town. At least he wasn't taking an alleged murderer to meet his family.

But he didn't have the faintest idea who this woman really was or what she was doing in Whitehorse. Once supper was over and they were back at the house—

"I have great news," she announced as he started the motor. "I have a job. I saw a Help Wanted sign in the window just down the street, I walked in and I got the job."

He stared at her. The sign down the street was in the window of a local café. "You took a *waitress* job?" He'd expected that she would tire of being the dead star soon enough and come out of hiding. He'd never expected this.

"I've slung hash before," she said sounding defensive. "It's been a while, but I suspect it's a little like riding a bike."

He didn't know what to say. Did she really hate her old life that much? Or was she still hiding for another reason?

"Tomorrow, if you'll give me a ride to town, I'll find myself an apartment so I can walk to work. As much as I've loved staying with you…"

Logan had driven out of Whitehorse, the pickup now rolling along through open prairie and sunshine. He hit the brakes and pulled down a small dirt road that ended at the Milk River. Tall cottonwoods loomed over them, the sunlight fingering its way through the still bare branches.

As he brought the truck to a dust-boiling stop, he said, "You can drop the front. I know who you are, JJ. So what the hell is really going on?"

SHERIFF BUFORD OLSON couldn't believe he was still sitting in his office waiting for phone calls. His stomach grumbled. He'd missed lunch and he didn't dare go down the hall to the vending machine for fear of missing one of those calls he'd been waiting for.

When his phone finally rang, he was hoping it would be Logan Chisholm. It wasn't.

"We picked up Charlie Baker," the arresting officer told him. The man who'd tried to use JJ's credit card at the gas station in Moses Lake, Washington. "He has several warrants out on him from Arizona and he's driving a stolen pickup."

"I just need to know where he got the credit card he tried to use for gas in Moses Lake," Buford said.

"He says his girlfriend took it from a purse she found in a convertible parked next to Flathead Lake. He swears the car keys were on the floorboard and that his girlfriend took the car, wrecked it and died."

"Did he say what his girlfriend's name was?"

"Susie Adams."

Now at least Buford knew who was lying in the morgue. What he didn't know was where JJ was, why she left her car beside the lake or why she hadn't turned up yet.

He thought about what Jett had said about checking the brake line on her rental car. Jett thinking that someone had tampered with the car bothered him.

First Jett was so sure JJ had killed Martin. Now he was sure that JJ had been murdered. The man just kept changing his tune. Why was that?

After Buford hung up from talking to the officer who'd picked up Charlie Baker, he called the garage and asked for the head mechanic.

"Tom, anything on that convertible yet?"

"You had it pegged," the mechanic said. "Someone tampered with the brakes."

That explained why the woman driving the car hadn't appeared to brake.

As he hung up, Buford wondered how it was that Jett had suspected foul play. Was he also right that one of JJ's former band members was behind this? Apparently they all had it in for JJ, including Jett.

The big question now was: where was JJ? And how long before whoever tried to kill her tried again?

BLYTHE TURNED TO HIM, THOSE blue eyes wide with surprise, then regret.

"We both know your name isn't Blythe."

Her chin came up. "It's Jennifer *Blythe* James."

The afternoon sun shone into the truck cab, illuminating her beautiful face. "Why didn't you just tell me you were this JJ?" he said with a curse.

Her smile was sad. "I'm sorry I kept it from you."

"Why did you?"

She shook her head. "It's such a long story."

He shut off the engine. "I have nothing but time."

Looking away, she said, "You wouldn't believe me if I told you."

"Try me."

With a sigh, she turned to face him again. "I saw a chance to put that life behind me—for even a little while. I took it."

"Who was Martin Sanderson to you?"

"He was my music producer. Basically he owned me

and my music," she said with no small amount of bitterness.

"You knew he was dead before you got on the back of my bike, didn't you?"

She nodded. "I didn't kill him, if that's what you're thinking."

"That was exactly what I thought, but his death has been ruled a suicide."

The news took her by surprise. "*Suicide?* No, that can't be right. Martin wouldn't—"

"Apparently he had cancer and only weeks to live."

She shook her head, letting it all sink in, then she smiled. "The bastard. That explains a lot. He insisted I come to Montana so we could talk about him letting me out of my contract. He was threatening to destroy my career—such as it was—and take everything I've made. I didn't care. I just wanted him to let me go."

"Did he?"

"Just before I met you that night at the bar," she said with a nod. "He told me to go have some fun and that if I didn't change my mind, then he would try to work something out with me in the morning." She let out a humorless laugh. "He knew he wouldn't be around by then."

"So you don't know how he left it."

She shook her head. "It doesn't matter. I'm done. If he sold my contract to someone else, let them take me to court. If they want, they can take every penny I made. I don't care." She smiled. "I have a job as of today. I don't need more than that."

Logan liked her attitude. He just wasn't sure he believed she could go from being rich and famous to being poor and unknown.

"Anyway, it probably doesn't matter," she added with a shake of her head.

"What do you mean, it probably doesn't matter?"

Again she looked away. He reached over to turn her to face him again. "What aren't you telling me? What was the real reason you ran away with me?"

"I told you. It was my girlhood fantasy to run away with a cowboy," she said.

He shook his head. "The truth, Blythe."

She swallowed, her throat working for a moment, then she sat up a little straighter as if steeling herself. "Someone has been trying to kill me."

BUFORD FELT HIS BELLY RUMBLE again with hunger. Clara was still putting hot chile peppers in everything, but he was building up a tolerance apparently. He couldn't wait to get home for supper, but he didn't want to leave until he heard back from Logan Chisholm.

When his phone rang, he thought for sure it would be Chisholm calling him back. He'd left a message at the ranch and been assured by Emma Chisholm that she would have her stepson call as soon as she saw him.

Instead the call was from a waitress from a café in Cut Bank, Montana.

"I saw in the newspaper that JJ was dead?"

"Yes?" Apparently she hadn't seen the latest edition.

"Well, that's weird because I saw her that day, you know, the day it said she died?"

Buford thought of the missing hours between when

she'd left her car beside the lake and when she'd left Martin Sanderson's house.

"What time was that?"

"It was late afternoon."

Cut Bank was hours from Flathead Lake. "Where was this that you saw her?"

"Here in Cut Bank at the café where I work. I recognized her right off, even though she pretended it wasn't her. I guess I scared her away. I should have been cooler."

"Scared her away? You saw her leave?"

"Yeah, I watched her and her boyfriend leave on his motorcycle."

Bull's-eye, Buford said under his breath. "What did the boyfriend look like?" He listened as she described a blond cowboy on a Harley, the same description the guard at the Grizzly Club had given him. Logan Chisholm.

"Did you see what direction they were headed?" he asked.

"East."

East, toward Whitehorse, Montana. East, toward the Chisholm Cattle Company ranch.

Buford thanked her for calling. The moment he hung up, he called Sheriff McCall Crawford in Whitehorse.

BLYTHE HAD FEARED HOW LOGAN would take the news. She had to admit he'd taken it better than she'd suspected. He was angry with her, but it was the disappointment in his expression that hurt the most.

"Someone is trying to kill you?" He sounded skeptical. She couldn't blame him. She didn't want to get into this with him, but she could see he wasn't going to take no for an answer.

"I started getting death threats a few months ago. I didn't think too much about it. People in the glare of the media often get letters from crazies." She shrugged, and she could see that he was trying to imagine the life she'd been living.

"Something happened to convince you otherwise," he said.

"There were a series of accidents on the road tour. The last time I was almost killed when some lights fell. You have to understand. I had wanted to quit for months. I guess that was just the last straw."

"You went to the police, of course."

"I did, but then Martin leaked the story to the media and it turned out looking like a publicity stunt. For a while, I thought it was. I thought Martin had hired someone to scare me back in line."

"Martin Sanderson really would have done something like that?" Logan asked, clearly unable to comprehend it.

She let out a humorless laugh. "Martin was capable of anything, trust me."

Logan took off his Stetson and raked a hand through his hair. "The note you dropped at the café in Cut Bank, is that part of this?"

She couldn't help her surprise.

"Yeah, I picked it up. It didn't seem important until now. *You're next?*"

"It was pinned to Martin's robe the morning I found

him lying dead next to the fireplace. I thought whoever had killed him—"

"Was coming after you next." Logan nodded. "That explains the way you came flying out of the club and why you climbed on the back of my motorcycle."

"Not entirely. When I saw you… I wanted to run away with you and would have even if none of this had happened." She could tell he wanted to believe that, but was having a hard time.

"You thought whoever killed him left the note for you."

She nodded.

"Why do I get the feeling that you know who's after you?"

She looked into his handsome face. It had been so long since she'd opened up to anyone. When had she become so mistrustful? She'd told herself it was the dog-eat-dog music business that had turned her this way. It was hard to know who your friends were, since it felt as if everyone wanted a piece of you.

But she trusted Logan. He hadn't asked anything of her. Still wasn't.

"I made a lot of mistakes in my life, especially when I signed with Martin Sanderson. Ten years ago, I was in a small all-girl band called Tough as Nails with some friends. Then Martin 'discovered' me." She couldn't keep the regret from her voice. "I wanted to get away from my life so bad then that I signed on the dotted line without thinking, let alone reading the contract. I dumped the band and my friends, latched onto that brass ring and didn't look back."

He frowned. "So you think this is about your former band members? Why now? Why wait ten years? Unless something changed recently."

She loved how quickly he caught on. "Martin was waiting up for me the night after I met you at the bar. He had some news, he said. He was planning to get Tough as Nails back together for a reunion tour and he'd invited them to Montana to knock out the details. He said after that, then he would let me out of my contract."

"You refused."

"I didn't trust him, let alone believe him. I'd lost track of the other members of the old band. As far as I knew, they'd all moved on, and since I hadn't heard anything about them, I'd just assumed they weren't involved in the music industry anymore." She looked out the side window for a minute. "Also we hadn't parted on the best of terms. They felt like I deserted them. I did."

"Still that doesn't seem like enough to want you dead."

She laughed. "You really don't know the music business." She quickly sobered. "But you're right. There *was* more. There was this young musician who was part of a band that we used to open for. His name was Ray Barnes. He'd been dating my best friend in the band and the others, as well. When I left, he left, too. With me. Today he's best known as Jett Atkins."

JETT ATKINS. LOGAN REMEMBERED seeing JJ with Jett in one of the photographs he'd uncovered on the library internet. "So you and Jett are—"

"History. A long time ago. But another one of my regrets."

"Who was the girl he was dating?"

"Karen Chandler, or Caro as we called her. But I think he might have been seeing the others at the same time. He was like that." Logan heard her remorse, saw the pain. He could understand why she had wanted to start her life over. "I don't want to believe it is Karen, but I hurt her badly. She and I grew up together. I should have fought harder for the band. After I left, it fell apart. Any one of them probably wants me dead."

Logan shook his head. "Isn't it possible the band would have fallen apart even if you'd stayed?"

"We'll never know, will we? But if Martin was telling the truth, then he got their hopes up. He was threatening to tell them I refused to be part of the band anymore, that I was too good for them. It wasn't true, none of it. He admitted he had never planned a reunion tour of Tough as Nails. He was just using them to get back at me."

Martin Sanderson really had been a bastard. He played with people's lives with no regard for them. Logan could understand why Blythe had wanted out, why she had felt desperate. Especially after Martin had apparently killed himself. Had he tried to make it look as if she had murdered him? Then why the note, he asked, voicing his thoughts.

"When I found Martin dead and saw the note pinned to his body..." She shuddered. "I couldn't be sure his killer wasn't still in the house and that I *was* next."

"So you think he wrote the note? Or someone else?"

She shrugged. "Maybe it was his final hateful act."

"I'm glad I was there when you needed me, but you can't keep running from this, Blythe. You have to find out who's after you—if they still are—and put an end to it. The Flathead County sheriff is going to figure out that you weren't in that car, if he hasn't already."

She nodded. "I would have told you the truth, but I wanted you to like the girl who always wanted to ride off into the sunset with a cowboy."

"I *do* like her," he said as he reached across the seat for her. "I like her a lot." He cupped her cheek, his thumb stroking across her lips.

She leaned into the warmth of his large callused hand and closed her eyes. Desire thrummed through her veins.

"Blythe?" His voice was low. The sound of it quickened her pulse.

She opened her eyes. Heat. She felt the burn of his gaze, of his touch.

He dragged her to him and dropped his mouth to hers. She came to him, pressing against him with a soft moan. Her arms wrapped around his neck as he deepened the kiss and her blood turned molten.

"I want you," she whispered when he drew back. "Here. *Now.*"

Chapter Nine

"Come on," Logan said as he opened the pickup door and pulled Blythe out behind him. Warm sunlight filtered through the new leaves of the cottonwoods. A warm spring breeze whispered softly in the branches as he led her along the riverbank.

At a small grassy spot, he turned and drew her close. His face was lit by sunlight. She looked into Logan's handsome face and felt her pulse quicken.

She'd wanted this from that first night they'd danced together at the country-western bar. There was something about this man. Being in his strong arms, she'd never felt safer—and yet there was a dangerous side to him. This man could steal her heart and there was nothing she could do about it.

As he pulled her closer, she swore she could feel the beat of his heart beneath his Western shirt. Her nipples ached for his touch as they pressed against the lace of her bra. His kiss, at first tender, turned punishing as the fever rose in both of them.

She grabbed the front of his shirt and tore it open, the snaps giving way under her assault. She pressed her palms to his warm, hard chest, breathing in the very male scent of him along with the rich primal scents of the riverbottom.

Logan pulled back, his gaze locking with hers, as he tantalizingly released each of the snaps on her Western shirt. She felt her blood run hot as his gaze dropped to her breasts. He freed one breast from the bra, his mouth dropping to the aching nipple. She arched against him, moaning softly like the trees in the spring breeze.

As he slid her shirt off her shoulders, he unhooked her bra freeing her breasts, and pulled her against him. Blythe reveled in the heat, flesh against flesh, as they stripped off the rest of their clothing, then dropped down in the sweet, warm grass.

Later she would remember the wonderful scents, the soft sounds, the feel of the Montana spring afternoon on her bare skin. But those sensations had been lost for a while in the fury of their lovemaking. It was Logan's scent, his touch, his sounds that were branded in her mind forever.

LOGAN LET OUT A CURSE AS HE checked the time. They had been snuggled on the cool grass as the sun disappeared behind the Bear Paw Mountains in the distance.

They got up, brushing off their clothes and getting dressed by the edge of the river.

"This might have been a better idea after the family supper," Logan said, but he was grinning. He picked a leaf out of her hair, laughed and then leaned in to kiss her softly on the mouth.

"Keep that up and we won't make supper at all," she

said, teasing. She would have been happy to stay here by the river forever.

Once in the pickup, she snuggled against him again as he drove toward the family ranch. Logan seemed less nervous about taking her home to meet his family. That was until they turned and passed under the large Chisholm Cattle Company sign and started up the road to the house.

She felt him tense and realized that she hadn't been paying any attention as to where they were going. Looking up now, she saw a huge house come into view. She tried to hide her surprise. She couldn't help but glance over at Logan.

"Nice place," she said playing down the obvious grandeur. Was this why he didn't want her to meet the family? He didn't want her to know that they were obviously well off? The irony didn't escape her.

As the front door of the house opened, a short, plump redhead in her fifties stepped out onto the porch.

"My stepmother, Emma," Logan said as he parked and cut the engine. Opening his door, he reached for Blythe's hand and she slid out after him. He squeezed her hand as they walked toward the house as if he was nervous again. She squeezed back, hoping there wasn't any reason to be.

"This must be Blythe," Emma said, pulling her into a warm hug. "Welcome to our home."

She felt herself swept inside the warm, comfortable living room where she was introduced first to Logan's father, Hoyt. He was just as she'd pictured the rancher, a large man with blond hair that was turning gray at the temples, a sun-weathered face and a strong handshake.

The brothers came as a surprise. Blond and blue-eyed, Colton resembled Logan and Zane and their father, but the other three had dark hair and eyes and appeared to have some Native American ancestry.

"You really do have five brothers," she whispered to Logan as they were being lead into the dining room.

"We're all adopted," Logan said.

That came as a surprise too, and she realized how little they knew about each other. It was the way she'd wanted it, actually had needed it. But that was before. Now she found herself even more curious about him and his family.

With the fiancées of the brothers Tanner, Colton, Marshall and Dawson, the dining room was almost filled. She was thinking how they would have to get a larger table if this family kept growing and at the same time, she couldn't help thinking of her own family table—TV trays in front of the sagging couch.

What was it like growing up with such a large family? She felt envious of Logan and wondered if he knew how lucky he was. A thought struck her. How could he ever understand her and the life she'd led? He'd always had all this.

Dinner was a boisterous affair with lots of laughter and stories. She couldn't remember a more enjoyable evening and told Emma as much.

"I'm new to the family myself," Emma confided. "Hoyt and I were married a year ago May."

Blythe could see that the two were head-over-heels

in love with each other. On top of that, it was clear that everyone at the table adored Emma, and who wouldn't?

"This meal is amazing," Blythe said. "Thank you so much for inviting me."

Logan had been quiet during supper. She wondered if he was always that way or if he felt uncomfortable under the circumstances. He wouldn't want to lie to his family, so keeping her secret must be weighing on him.

But when their gazes met, she saw the spark she'd seen earlier by the river and felt her face heat with the memory of their lovemaking.

"So I understand that Logan has taught you to ride," Hoyt said drawing her attention.

"She was a natural," Logan said sounding proud.

"I had a wonderful instructor and I loved it," she gushed. "I love the freedom. All this wide-open country, it's exciting to see it from the back of a horse."

"Where are you from that you don't have wide-open country like this?" Emma asked.

Blythe had known someone was bound to ask where she was from. "Oh, we had wide-open country in southern California. Desert. It's not the same as rolling hills covered with tall green grass and huge cottonwoods and mountains in the distance dark with pine trees."

"What do you do for a living?" Hoyt asked. Emma shot him a look. "I don't mean to be rude," he added.

"I'll get dessert," Emma said, rising from her chair.

Blythe smiled and said, "I don't mind. I've done a lot of different things, but today I got a job in town at the Whitehorse Café. I'll be waitressing."

"Waitressing's a good profession," Emma said, and shot her husband a warning look.

Blythe excused herself and went into the kitchen to help Emma get the dessert. The rest of the meal passed quickly and quite pleasantly.

It wasn't long until she was saying how nice it was to meet everyone, how wonderful the meal was and promising to come back.

"Oh, Logan, it slipped my mind earlier," Emma said as she pressed a bag full of leftovers and some freshly baked gingersnaps into his arms as they were leaving. "You had a call earlier from a Sheriff Buford Olson from Flathead County. He needs you to call him. I put the number on a slip of paper in the bag with the food. He said it was important."

LOGAN HAD SEEN BLYTHE'S panicked expression when Emma mentioned the call from the sheriff in Flathead County. He drove out of the ranch and turned onto the county road wondering why the sheriff was calling him, and realized the guard at the Grizzly Club had probably taken down the plate number on his motorcycle.

He glanced over at her, saw she was looking out at the night and chewing at her lower lip. "The sheriff knows. Or at least suspects I know where you are."

Blythe nodded. "I'll call him."

What if she was right and someone really was trying to kill her? She was safe here.

"It's too late now. Let's call him in the morning," he said.

They made love again the moment they reached the

house, both of them racing up the stairs to fall into his double bed.

Lying staring up at the cracked ceiling, Logan smiled to himself. His body was damp with sweat and still tingling from her touch.

Blythe was lying beside him. She sighed, then let out a chuckle.

Logan glanced over at her and grinned. "What's so funny?"

"Us," she said. "We both lied about who we are. You were afraid I was after your money. I was afraid you would only be interested in JJ."

"Pretty funny, huh," he said.

She nodded.

He studied her for a moment, then pulled her over to spoon against her backside. His breath tickled her ear, but she giggled, then snuggled closer.

"I love the feel of you. I can't remember a time I've felt happier."

Logan felt the same way. He breathed in her warm scent, languishing in her warmth and the feel of her flesh against his, and tried not to worry.

But if she was right and someone wanted her dead, then as soon as everyone knew she was alive, Blythe wouldn't be safe. He couldn't bear the thought of any harm coming to her.

She would be safe here with him.

That was if she didn't go back to her old life.

The thought was like an arrow through his heart.

Of course she would go back.

He felt his heart break. He'd fallen for this woman from the moment he'd seen her on that dance floor only days ago.

"WE CAN'T KEEP LIVING LIKE THIS," Emma Chisholm said after everyone had left. She'd said this before, but this time she saw that Hoyt knew she meant it.

"The house is armed to the teeth with weapons," she continued. "You never leave my side or have one or two of my stepsons here watching me."

She wasn't telling him anything he didn't already know, but she couldn't seem to stop. "You have done everything but build a dungeon and lock me in it. I can't leave here without an armed guard. You're killing me, Hoyt, and worse, I see what it is doing to you."

He nodded as if he knew she not only meant it, but that he could see the strain this had put on their family.

"I know you're sick to death of me hanging around," he said.

"It's not you. It's knowing that you should be working this ranch and not babysitting me. Your sons are going crazy, as well. They need to be on the back of a horse in wild country, not cooped up here in this kitchen. And I need to do something besides bake!"

He smiled then as if he'd noticed the extra weight she was carrying. "I like your curves."

"Hoyt—"

"I have some news," he said quickly. "I was going to tell you tonight. I found a woman through that service in Great Falls. She sounds perfect, older, with experience cooking for a large family. The service explained how isolated we are out here and that it would be a live-in position and she was fine with that."

Emma didn't necessarily like the idea of someone living in the house with them. But the house was large. The woman would have her own wing and entrance and they would all have plenty of privacy. Anyway, what choice did Emma have?

She knew Hoyt flat out refused to leave her alone. It was nonnegotiable, as he'd said many times. If this was the only way she could have some freedom, she would take it. It was at least a step in the right direction.

"Wonderful. I could use the help," she said agreeably.

Hoyt eyed her suspiciously. "She comes highly recommended. She will be doing the housework and helping with the cooking, if you let her. She'll accompany you wherever you need to go."

Emma mugged a face, but was smart enough not to argue.

He smiled and moved to embrace her. "I'm so sorry about all of this."

"Stop that. None of this is your fault."

His expression said he would never believe that. "If Laura is alive, if she's what Aggie believed she was, then it has to be my fault. I failed her. Failed all of us, especially you."

Emma was surprised to hear him even entertain the idea that his first wife might be alive. He'd sworn he didn't believe it. Apparently she wasn't the only one living with ghosts.

She shook her head and took her husband's face in

her hands. "Listen to me. We can't know what's in another person's heart let alone their mind, even those
closest to us. You said yourself that Laura was like a
bottomless well when it came to her need. No human
can fill that kind of hole in another person."

He leaned down to kiss her.

"So when do I meet my new guard?" she asked.

"She's coming at the end of the week."

Emma hated the idea, but at least Hoyt and his sons
could get back to running the ranch. She would deal
with the housekeeper and find a way to get some time
away from the ranch—alone.

She couldn't live her life being afraid, thinking every
person she met wanted to kill her. Emma had lost some
of her old self and she intended to get it back.

Not that she was going to take the gun out of her
purse that was always within reach. She was no fool.

AGGIE WELLS HAD BEEN DOZING in her chair. She jumped
now at the sudden tap on her door. Holding her breath,
she waited. Another light tap.

Aggie realized it was probably her doctor friend
coming back to check on her. He'd wanted to put her
in the hospital but she'd refused, knowing that would
alert the authorities and be the end of her freedom.

With effort, she pushed herself up out of the chair
and moved to the window. Parting the curtain, she
peered out, surprised that it was dark outside.

Even in the dim light, she could see that it wasn't the
doctor. It was the elderly woman who lived in the unit
at the end of the building. The old woman was horribly

stooped, could barely get around even with the gnarled cane she used. She wore a shawl around her shoulders, a faded scarf covering most of her gray hair.

Aggie had seen her hobbling by, headed for the small store a few blocks away. She'd thought about helping the woman but everyone who lived in the old motel units kept to themselves, which was fine with her.

The old woman tapped again, so bent with age and arthritis that she probably saw more of her shoes than she did where she was going. For a moment she leaned into the door as if barely able to stand, then tapped again, swaying a little on her cane, and Aggie realized she must need help or she wouldn't be out there.

Aggie quickly opened the door. "Is something wrong?" she inquired, reaching for the elderly woman's arm, afraid the woman was about to drop onto the concrete step.

But the moment she grabbed the arm she realized it wasn't frail and thin but wiry and strong.

Aggie had always been a stickler for details. Too late she noticed that while everything else was like the old woman's who lived a few doors down, the shoes were all wrong.

Chapter Ten

The woman Aggie Wells had opened the door to brought the cane up, caught her in the stomach and drove her back into the room. She quickly followed her in, closing and locking the door behind them.

As the formerly stooped woman rose to her full height, she shrugged off the shawl and faded scarf. Aggie saw why she'd been fooled. The shawl and faded scarf were *exactly* like the old woman's who lived in the last unit.

She let out a cry of regret, knowing that the old woman wouldn't be in need of either again.

Aggie had stumbled when she'd been pushed and fallen, landing on the edge of the recliner. Weak and gasping for breath, she now let herself slide into the seat while she stared at the old woman's transformation into a woman nearer her own age. It was a marvel the way Laura Chisholm shed the old woman's character.

"We finally meet," she said to Laura, realizing the woman must have known where she was for some time. Laura had been watching and waiting for just such an opportunity.

Only the shoes would have given her away, had

Aggie noticed them before she opened the door. Laura Chisholm's feet were too large for the old woman's shoes. When she'd disposed of the poor old woman, taken the shawl and scarf and cane, she'd had to use her own shoes.

There was a time when Aggie wouldn't have been fooled. She would have noticed the small differences and would never have opened the door. But that time had passed, and a part of her was thankful that she had finally gotten to meet a woman she'd unknowingly been chasing for years.

"Aggie Wells," Laura said, as if just as delighted to meet her.

How strange this feeling of mutual respect, two professionals admiring the other's work.

"Just tell me this," Aggie said, not kidding herself how this would end. "Why?"

"Why?" Laura cocked her head almost in amusement. There was intelligence in her blue eyes but also a brightness that burned too hot.

"Do you hate Hoyt that much?"

Laura looked surprised. "I *love* Hoyt. I will *always* love him. Haven't you ever loved someone too much and realized they could never love you as much?"

Aggie hadn't. Other than her job. "Let me guess, everything was fine until he adopted the boys."

Laura's face darkened. "I wasn't enough. First it was just three boys, then three more. He said he had enough love for all of us." She scoffed at that.

"You could have just divorced him and made a life for yourself."

Laura smiled. "Who says I haven't?"

"But you couldn't let go. You've been killing his wives." There was no accusation in her voice. She was just stating what they both knew.

Laura looked down at the thick gnarled wood cane in her hand, then up at Aggie. "If I couldn't have him, no one else could either."

"Why didn't you just kill him?"

The woman looked shocked at the idea. "I *loved* him. I couldn't do that to him."

But killing his wives was another matter apparently. "I'm curious. How did you get away that day at the lake?"

Laura frowned and waved a hand through the air as if the question was beneath Aggie. "I told Hoyt I was afraid of water, that I couldn't swim. He believed anything I told him. I grew up in California on the beach and learned to scuba dive in college. I set everything up beforehand, the scuba gear, the vehicle on a road a few miles from the spot where I would go overboard. I simply started an argument with Hoyt and let the rest play out. When he realized that I'd filed for divorce, it made him look guilty. I thought he would never remarry. I was wrong."

She shrugged, and Aggie realized what Laura had been able to do since then was much more impressive. Laura had dedicated her life to making sure Hoyt found no happiness with another woman.

Just as Aggie had dedicated hers to chasing the truth. Other people had balance in their lives, they had their job, their family, their friends, but not her and Laura.

They'd both sacrificed their lives for something intangible: a cockeyed sense of being the only ones who could get justice.

Was this woman's quest any crazier than her own? Aggie had lost the job she loved because she couldn't let go of that thin thread of suspicion that something wasn't quite right about Laura Chisholm's death.

Had she been able to let go, where would she be now? Certainly she wouldn't be wanted for murder, nearly committed to a state mental hospital and about to die at the hands of the real killer.

And Laura? Had she felt loved, wouldn't she still be with Hoyt, raising six sons, getting old with him in that huge house on the ranch?

"We don't choose this, it chooses us," Aggie said seeing the truth of it.

Laura nodded as if she had been thinking the same thing.

Then again Laura might simply be crazy.

The difference now was that Laura would win.

"Has it been worth it?" That was the real question Aggie had wanted to ask. She watched Laura lift the thick wooden cane and step toward her.

"Worth it?" Laura asked as she closed the distance between them. A smile curled her lips, her eyes now bright as neon. "What do you think?"

Aggie's last thought was Emma. She said a quick prayer for her. The fourth wife of Hoyt Chisholm didn't stand a chance against a woman this obsessed.

LOGAN WOKE TO FIND HIS BED empty. For just an instant, he thought he'd dreamed last night. But Blythe's side of the bed was still warm, her scent still on his sheets. He heard the soft lap of water in the tub of the adjacent bathroom, then the sound of the water draining, and relaxed.

A few moments later Blythe came out, her wonderful body wrapped in one of his towels. He grinned at her and pulled back the covers to pat the bed beside him.

"Sorry, but I have to call the Flathead sheriff, then get to work, and so do you," she said, reaching for her clothes. "Zane said you have Emma duty today."

He couldn't believe she was really going to go to that waitress job, but he was smart enough not to say so. With a groan, he recalled that she was right. He had Emma duty today. He much preferred working on the ranch than hanging out at the house. Today though, he much preferred staying in bed with Blythe. He reached for her, thinking they had time for a quickie.

She giggled, pretending to put up a fight.

At the sound of a vehicle coming up the road, they both froze. "Are you expecting anyone this morning?" she whispered.

He shook his head and reluctantly rose from the warm bed to pull on his jeans. Going to the window, he looked out and felt a start. It was a sheriff's department patrol SUV coming up the road. He watched it grow closer until he could see the sheriff behind the wheel. She had someone with her.

He swore under his breath as he hurriedly finished dressing.

"Who is it?" Blythe asked sounding worried.

"The sheriff. She has someone with her. I'll go see what they want."

"You know what they want."

He gave her a smile he hoped was reassuring, kissed her quickly and went downstairs. He'd wanted to call the sheriff before anyone found out that JJ was staying with him. He figured it would look better for Blythe.

As the patrol car came to a stop in front of his house, he stepped out onto the porch. "Sheriff," he said as McCall Crawford climbed out. He felt as if he'd seen too much of her during the mess with his father's former wives.

"Logan."

His gaze went to the big older man working his way out of the passenger seat. He was big-bellied, pushing sixty, his face weathered from years in Montana's sun.

The man merely glanced in Logan's direction before reaching back into the patrol car for his Stetson. As he settled it on his thinning gray head, he slammed the patrol car door and stepped toward the house.

"This is Sheriff Buford Olson from the Flathead County," McCall said. "We're here about Jennifer James. JJ?"

Logan nodded as the door opened behind him and Blythe stepped out.

JETT ATKINS GROANED AT THE sound of someone knocking on his motel room door. It was that damned sheriff, he thought as he went to the door. Sheriff Buford Olson acted as if he wasn't all that sharp. But Jett wasn't fooled.

He hurriedly hid the suitcase he'd had by the door. The sheriff hadn't told him he could leave town yet— even after Martin Sanderson's death had been ruled a suicide. It was that damned JJ. The sheriff had said he was waiting for the coroner's report.

All Jett knew was that he'd had enough of this motel room, this town, this state. He wanted to put as much distance as he could from whatever Martin had been up to with JJ's former band members.

But when he opened the door, it wasn't the sheriff. Loretta stood in the doorway.

"What are you—"

She didn't give him a chance to finish as she pushed past him. He closed the door and turned to find her glaring at him. It reminded him of all those years ago when the two of them had dated. Well, he wouldn't really call it dating. More like what people now called hooking up.

"Where's JJ?" she demanded.

"What are you talking about? She's dead."

"You haven't seen the news today?"

He hadn't. He was sick of sitting in this room with nothing to do but watch television. Last night he'd packed, determined to leave town no matter what. Then he'd finished off a half quart of Scotch and awakened with a hangover this morning. He hadn't even turned on the TV.

"No, why?" he asked now. Loretta said she sang in a bar and nightclubs. He knew she was just getting by. He'd shuddered at the thought, since it was his greatest fear. At least she hadn't been famous and had the rug pulled out from under her. Most people hadn't even heard of her or Tough As Nails.

"That body that was found in JJ's rental car turned out to belong to some woman from Arizona. The cops think the woman stole JJ's car and crashed it. I heard just now that they are investigating the crash as a homicide."

He had to sit down. He lowered himself to the edge of the bed. "You're saying someone tried to kill JJ but killed some other woman instead? Then where is JJ?"

"That's what I just asked you."

"I haven't seen her. She was gone by the time I reached Martin and found him dead..." He stared at Loretta. "I wasn't joking about one of you wanting her dead."

Loretta rolled her eyes. "If I wanted to kill her, it would be more personal than a car wreck. I'd want to be the last person she saw before she died."

He shuddered. "Maybe you were."

She scoffed at that. "I vote for Betsy. That sweet act of hers? I've never bought it. It's women like that who kill, you know."

He didn't know. He figured any of the three were capable of it. Especially if they acted together.

"Or Karen," Loretta said, as if she'd been giving it some thought. "After all, JJ was her best friend—or so she thought. Also, I heard that Martin went to Karen first." She nodded at his surprise. "Karen had the talent. But I heard she turned him down flat, saying she could never desert JJ."

Jett let out a low whistle. "Then JJ deserted her without a thought."

Loretta shrugged. "There is another possibility," she said eyeing him intently. "You."

He laughed. "Why would I want to kill JJ?"

"According to the tabloids, she dumped you."

"Do you really believe *anything* you read in them?" he challenged. "Anyway, that was just the spin Martin put on it after *I* dumped JJ." He could see Loretta was skeptical. "You have no idea what it's like to date someone with her kind of star power. It was exhausting."

"She did outshine you, didn't she?" Loretta said with no small amount of satisfaction.

"Well, whoever tried to kill JJ...apparently they failed," Jett said. "And now she's disappeared."

"So it would appear," Loretta said mysteriously.

"If you know where she is, then why were you asking me?" he demanded.

She smiled. "I just wanted to see if you knew where she was. You don't. She'll turn up. She owes me for this mess and I intend to get my money out of her, one way or another." With that she left, slamming the door behind her.

"WE WERE GOING TO CALL YOU this morning," Logan said as Sheriff Buford Olson's gaze went to Blythe.

"Is that right?" he said, not sounding as if he believed it for an instant. "I think we'd better sit down and talk about this."

"Do you mind if we come in?" McCall asked.

Logan shook his head. "Come on in. I'll get some coffee going."

"So why don't we start with you telling me who you are," Buford said after they'd all taken chairs and cups of coffee at the kitchen table.

Blythe braced herself as she looked into the sheriff's keen eyes. "My name is Jennifer Blythe James, but I think you already know that."

"JJ," he said. "Okay, now tell me what you're doing here."

"Getting on with my life," she said.

"You do realize that you left the scene of a death without calling anyone, then left the scene of an accident that resulted in another death, not to mention let everyone believe you were dead."

"At first I panicked," she admitted. She had felt no need to clear her name. Not her name, JJ's. How strange. JJ had become a separate persona over the past ten years. Blythe had lost herself and only found that girl she'd been the other night at a country-western bar dancing with Logan Chisholm.

But she doubted the Flathead sheriff would understand that.

"I'd been getting death threats and having some close calls on my music tour," she continued. "I was convinced someone was trying to kill me. Martin had made it appear that the incidents were nothing more than a publicity stunt. I left the tour and came to Montana to try to talk him into letting me out of my contract. I'd had enough."

Sheriff McCall Crawford sipped her coffee and

didn't say a word. Clearly, she'd just come to bring the Flathead sheriff.

"Did you talk him out of it?" Buford asked.

Blythe shook her head. "I thought I had. But that night when I returned to the house, he told me he had contacted the members of my former band and was going to make me do a reunion tour with them if I didn't go back on my music tour. I told him to stuff it and left the room."

"Did you hear the shot that killed him?"

"No, that house is too large, I didn't hear a thing. I didn't know he was dead until I came back down to the living room the next morning and saw him."

"Saw him and the note pinned to him," Buford said. "What did the note say?"

She had to quell a shudder at the memory. *"You're next."*

The sheriff studied her. "Why did you take the note?"

"I don't know. I grabbed it before I thought about what I was doing, wadded it up and stuck it in my pocket. I guess it made everything a little less real. Then I realized that whoever had killed him could still be in the house. So I ran. I thought if I could get far enough away from there, go some place that no one knew about…"

"That was pretty shortsighted," Buford said.

She nodded and glanced at Logan. "I just wanted to escape my life for a while. By the way, Logan didn't know anything about what I was running from or even who I was."

"Did you recognize the handwriting on the note?" Buford asked.

A chill snaked up her spine. Hadn't she known how vindictive Martin was? How deceitful? The man had made his fortune using other people and their talents.

"No," she said. "I just assumed the person who'd killed him was the same one who'd been threatening me. Now I think he might have written the note himself."

"Why would he do that?" Buford asked.

"He wanted me to fear for my life. I think he killed himself hoping I would be under suspicion for his death." If it hadn't been for fate and a car thief, she might have been arrested.

"You're that sure he wrote the note," the sheriff said. "What about his other guests?"

"Other guests?" she echoed.

"You weren't aware your former band members were staying in the guesthouse just out back?"

She could feel the color drain from her face. Reaching for her coffee, she took a drink, burning her tongue.

"So you didn't know that Karen, Loretta and Betsy had already arrived?" he said.

She shook her head.

"Is it possible one of them found the body and wrote the note?" he asked.

Blythe couldn't speak. She looked from her coffee cup to him and knew he saw the answer in her eyes.

"You said there had been death threats before this? Do you have copies of those?" he asked.

"No, I threw them away. They didn't seem…serious at the time."

"A death threat that didn't seem serious?" Buford asked.

"I've had them before and nothing happened. Other musicians I've known have gotten them. They aren't like, 'I'm going to kill you.' They're more vague, like, 'You have no idea what you're doing to the kids listening to your horrible music. Someone should shut you up for good.' That sort of thing."

"I have a granddaughter who listens to your music," Buford said. "She listens to Jett Atkins, as well. I think whoever wrote that note might have a point."

"That's another reason I wanted out of my contract," she said. "Martin had total control of my career as well as the music. I hated what I was singing. I signed the contract with him when I was very young and stupid."

"Your former band members aren't the only ones in Montana. Your boyfriend Jett is here, as well," Buford said.

"He's not my boyfriend."

The sheriff nodded. "No love lost there either, huh?"

"If you're asking if I have enemies—"

"I know you do," Buford said, cutting her off. "The brakes on your rental car had been tampered with. The death of the woman driving it has been ruled a homicide."

Blythe felt all the air rush out of her. She shot to her feet and stumbled out of the room.

"If you know someone is trying to kill her," she heard Logan say as she pushed open the screen door and stepped out onto the porch. Blythe didn't catch the rest. Logan couldn't blame the sheriff. She was the one who'd run. If she'd called the sheriff the moment she'd found Martin's body—

She heard the screen door open behind her. The next moment, Logan's arms came around her.

"Don't worry," he said as he drew her close. "I'm not going to let anyone hurt you."

"YOU CAN'T ARREST HER GIVEN the circumstances," Logan said when he and Blythe returned to the kitchen and the two sheriffs sitting there.

Buford studied him for a moment, then turned his attention to Blythe. "You should know that at least one member of your old band is dead. Lisa Thomas."

"Luca?" Blythe said.

"Apparently she died recently," Buford said. "In a hit-and-run accident."

Logan saw Blythe's expression. She had to be thinking the same thing he was. It had been no accident.

"I'm going to talk to the former members of your band again," Buford was saying, "but in the meantime…"

Blythe glanced at her watch. "In the meantime, I have a job in town I need to get to."

The sheriff raised two bushy eyebrows, but it was McCall who spoke before Logan could.

"Are you sure that's a good idea?" the Whitehorse sheriff asked. "You seem to have a target on your back."

"It's a terrible idea," Logan interrupted, but he saw the stubborn set of Blythe's jaw.

"What am I supposed to do, sit around and wait for someone to come after me again?" she demanded.

Buford chuckled as he rose slowly from the kitchen chair. "What kind of job did you say this was?"

"Waitressing." She raised her chin defiantly.

"Making it easy for whoever wants you dead to find you, huh?" He nodded smiling.

Logan stared at her. "You're using yourself as *bait?* Have you lost your mind?"

"Could I speak with you outside?" she asked.

"You betcha," he said taking her arm and leading her back out to the porch. "What the hell, Blythe?"

"I don't expect you to understand this," she said. "But ten years ago I signed away all control of my life when I took Martin Sanderson's offer to make me a star. I have that control back and it feels really good."

"You're right, I don't understand. There is someone out there who wants you *dead.*"

She nodded. "And I might have kept running like I did when I left my car beside the lake and climbed on the back of your motorcycle. But you changed that. I don't want to run anymore."

"You don't have to run. You can stay here. I will—"

Blythe leaned into him and brushed a kiss across his lips silencing him. "I need a ride to town. I hate being late my first day of work. Is that offer to lend me a pickup still open?"

He didn't know what to say. It was clear that she'd made up her mind and there was no changing it. He swallowed the lump in his throat, trying to fight back his fear as the two sheriffs came out onto the porch. All he could do was reach into the pocket of his jeans and hand her his truck key.

"I'll get one of my brothers to come pick me up," he said his voice tight.

"You sort it out?" Buford asked as Blythe headed for his pickup.

"Find out who is after her," Logan said between gritted teeth. "Find them before they find her." Meanwhile he was going to do everything in his power to keep her safe.

The problem was that the woman was as stubborn as a damned mule. But he was glad that Blythe seemed her former strong, determined self again. Not that he wasn't worried about what she would do next.

Chapter Eleven

Betsy came out of the shower to find Loretta and Karen sitting on the ends of the bed, glued to the television screen. Her heart kicked up a beat. "What's happened now?" she asked with a sinking feeling.

Loretta grabbed the remote to turn up the volume. A publicity shot of JJ flashed on the screen, then a news commentator was saying that an inside source had confirmed that the body found in the rented sports car convertible was not pop rocker JJ.

"Authorities are asking anyone with information regarding JJ to call the sheriff's department." A number flashed on the screen.

"I don't understand," Betsy said. She knew now why she never watched the news. It depressed her.

"JJ," Loretta said. "She's not dead. She wasn't driving the car that crashed."

"Then who was?" Betsy asked.

Loretta shrugged.

"Then where is JJ?" Betsy asked.

Karen looked over at Loretta. "That's the million-dollar question, isn't it?"

Loretta was already heading for the door. "I need

a drink. Call me if you hear anything. I already asked Jett about JJ. He swears he doesn't know where she is. But I wouldn't be surprised if the two of them cooked this up. When I find JJ, she is going to pony up some money for this wasted trip. I swear, that bitch is going down."

As she went out the door, Karen sighed.

"Does she really believe that Jett and JJ cooked up letting some poor young girl die in JJ's car?" Betsy asked. "Is that really what she thinks?"

"Loretta has always had her own way of thinking," Karen said distractedly. "Just as she sees this as JJ owing her."

"What do *you* think about all this?"

Karen seemed surprised that Betsy would ask her. But Karen had always seemed the most sensible one in the band and Betsy said as much.

"Thanks for the vote of confidence, but I have no idea. The police will sort it out. In the meantime, I wish I knew where JJ was."

"You miss her, don't you?"

Karen smiled. "Hard to believe after what she did to all of us, huh."

"She was just offered an opportunity and took it," Betsy said. "I don't blame her. But you were just as good as she was, if not better. I've never understood why Martin chose her and not you."

"I guess he saw something in JJ that I lacked."

"Do you still play and sing?"

"I don't really have the time," Karen said, but Betsy knew it was more than that.

"It hurt us all when the band broke up. Don't you think we could have found another lead singer? I mean, we didn't have to break up the band when JJ left."

Karen smiled as she turned back to her. "We'll never know."

"Loretta says that JJ's leaving was like having the heart ripped out of us because we felt betrayed," Betsy persisted. "Is that how you felt?"

When the door opened and Loretta came in with Jett, Betsy noticed that Karen seemed glad for the interruption. Clearly, she hadn't wanted to talk about JJ anymore. Or how she felt about the girl she considered her sister walking out on her.

"It's all over Twitter," Jett announced. "JJ was seen east of here."

BLYTHE HAD SOME TIME TO think on the way into town. She needed an apartment so she could walk to work. She couldn't keep driving around town in a Chisholm Cattle Company pickup. But she knew that wasn't the real reason she couldn't stay with Logan any longer.

She couldn't put him in any more danger than she already had.

What she'd told Logan had been heartfelt. He had changed everything. She would have kept running, but he made her want to end this so she could get on with her life—and she hoped Logan would be in it.

But until she found out who was after her, she had to put some distance between them. Whoever had put the note on Martin Sanderson's body could have killed her that morning at the Grizzly Club. She figured the only reason they hadn't was that they wanted her running scared still.

She wouldn't let them use Logan Chisholm to do it.

As she drove into the small western town of Whitehorse, she spotted the local newspaper office. The idea had been brewing all the way into town, but as she pushed open the door to the *Milk River Courier,* she was aware that what she was about to do could be the signing of her death warrant.

"Can I help you?" The young woman who rose from behind the desk had a southern accent and a nice smile.

"Are you a reporter?" Blythe asked.

"Andi Jackson, at your service," she said, motioning to the chair across from her desk.

Blythe saw that the small newspaper office was deserted as she took a seat. "You're a weekly paper? Is it possible to get a story in this week's paper?"

"It would be pushing my deadline, but if it's a story that has to run, I can probably get it in tomorrow's paper," Andi said.

"It is. My name is Jennifer Blythe James, better known as JJ, and until recently everyone thought I was dead."

Andi picked up her notebook and pen and began to write as Blythe told her JJ's story, starting with the small trailer in the middle of the desert, then a band called Tough as Nails and ending with her waitressing at the local café in town.

"This is one heck of a story," Andi said when Blythe had finished. "I'm curious how it's going to end."

Blythe laughed. "So am I." After Andi took her

photo, she bought a paper so that she could look for an apartment after work, then she headed for the White-horse Café. The last thing she wanted was to be late for work her first day.

"YOU AREN'T GOING TO HAVE to babysit me much longer," Emma said when Logan came through the back door into the kitchen. "Your father has hired someone to keep an eye on me so you can all get back to ranching. The woman is supposed to be here by the weekend."

She glanced at him as he dropped into a chair at the table. "Logan?"

He blinked and looked over at her as if seeing her for the first time that morning. "Sorry, I was lost in thought."

"I can see that." She'd never seen him this distracted and would bet it had something to do with the young woman he'd brought to supper last night.

Having just taken a batch of cranberry muffins from the oven, she put one on a plate for each of them and poured them both a mug of coffee before joining him at the table.

"Okay, let's hear it," she said as she sliced one muffin in half and lathered it with butter.

"It's Blythe," he said with a curse.

She laughed. "Big surprise." Emma took a bite of the muffin. It was warm and wonderful, the rich butter dripping off onto the plate as she took another bite. She really had to quit baking—worse, eating what she baked. "So you've fallen for her."

"No, that is…" He started to swear again but checked himself. "I've never met anyone like her."

"So what's the problem?"

"Someone is trying to kill her."

Emma leaned back in surprise. "It must be something in the water around here," she said, and then turned serious. "Why would anyone want to hurt that beautiful young woman?"

"It's a long story," Logan said with a sigh.

Emma listened, seeing how much this woman had come to mean to him. Chisholm men were born protectors. What they didn't realize sometimes was that they were also attracted to strong women who liked to believe they could protect themselves. Hoyt was still learning that.

"It doesn't sound like there is much you can do if she's set on doing things her way," Emma said. "But you certainly don't have to hang around here babysitting me today. I'll be just fine."

Logan shook his head, grinning across the table at her. "Blythe reminds me a lot of you."

"That's a good thing, right?" she asked with a laugh.

"Stubborn and a woman hard to get a rope on," he joked.

"You Chisholm men. When are you going to learn that you have to let a woman run free if you ever hope to hold on to her?"

"It's a hard lesson," Logan said. "I'm not sure I can do that."

"But then again, you've never been in love before.

Love changes everything. Have you told her how you feel?"

"About her determination to stick her neck out and get herself killed?"

"No, Logan, how you feel about *her*."

"It's too soon."

"Or is it because you're afraid you'll scare her off?" she asked, eyeing him.

He chuckled. "You see through me like a windowpane. You have any more of those muffins? Also, I need to borrow your computer. I have to find out everything I can about who's after Blythe. So far, they don't know where she is. But once they find out..."

AFTER HER INTERVIEW WITH THE newspaper, Blythe hurried to the café to get to work. Within minutes after putting on her apron, she was waiting tables and joking with locals as she refilled coffee cups and slid huge platefuls of food in front of them.

It *was* like riding a bike, she thought.

As she worked, she tried not to glance out the front window at the street or the small city park across from the café. The newspaper article wouldn't come out until tomorrow. Reporter Andi Jackson had told her the Associated Press would pick up the story and it would quickly make every newspaper in the state.

"You realize your story is going to go viral after that," Andi had said. "With communications like they are, everyone in the world will know that JJ is waitressing in Whitehorse, Montana."

That was the plan, Blythe thought.

Still, she couldn't help but feel a little nervous about the repercussions that were to come when Logan found out—not to mention the fact that the story was bound to bring a killer to town.

Right before quitting time, she saw Logan pull up out front. Just the sight of him as he stepped from one of the Chisholm ranch pickups made her heart take off at a gallop. She ached for a future with him. They were just getting to know each other. If she let herself, she could imagine the two of them growing old together in that farmhouse of his, raising kids who Logan would teach to ride horses before they learned to walk, just as he had done.

She could see them all around that long table at the home ranch. She'd never had siblings, let alone lived close to any cousins. She'd always wished for a large family like Logan's and guessed it wouldn't be long before Hoyt and Emma had more grandchildren running around than they could count.

"Hi," she said as she stepped outside, so glad to see him it hurt.

Logan looked into her eyes and she saw the pain in all that blue as he dragged her to him and kissed her. As he drew back, he said, "How was your first day of work?" She could tell it was hard for him to even ask.

"My feet are killing me," she said with a laugh. "How was your day?"

He gave her a look that said he couldn't take any more chitchat. "We need to talk."

Blythe nodded and they walked across the street to the park and took a bench.

"You know how much I want to protect you," he began. "But I can't if you're working here in town."

"I see what your stepmother has been going through waiting for a possible murderer to come after her," she said. "Look what it is doing to your family. I don't want that. If someone wants to kill me badly enough, they will find a way no matter what."

"No, I won't—"

"Worse, if I was with you at the time, then they might kill you, as well." She shook her head. "That isn't happening. That's why I'm getting an apartment here in town, that's why I can't see you—"

"No," he said shooting to his feet and pulling her up with him. He grabbed her shoulders and looked into her eyes. "This is hard enough. If I can't see you... No."

"It's only temporary," she said touched. "I'm sorry. You had no idea what you were getting into when you met me."

"Oh, I had some idea." He let go of her but she could see this was killing him. "What now?"

"Now I find an apartment." She hesitated, knowing what Logan's reaction was going to be when she told him about the newspaper article coming out in tomorrow's paper. "Then when the article comes out tomorrow about JJ being alive and well and waitressing in Whitehorse—"

Logan swore, ripped his Stetson from his head and raked one large hand through his thick blond hair. "You know what bothers me?" He bit off each word, anger cording his neck. "You are filled with so much guilt over leaving behind your former band members that you think you *deserve* this."

She shook her head. "You're wrong. I do regret what I did, but I'm not ready to die. I want to live, really live, for the first time in a long time," she said with passion. "You know why that is? Because of you. I can't wait for the next time I get to make love with you. That's why I'm doing this. I want it over and I don't want you in the cross fire."

He dragged her to him and dropped his mouth to hers for a punishing kiss. "You aren't going to have to wait long for the next time we make love," he said when he pulled back. "Let's find you an apartment. That article doesn't come out until tomorrow, right?"

SHERIFF BUFORD OLSON HADN'T wanted to like JJ any more than he had Jett Atkins. But the young woman he'd met on her way to her waitress job had impressed him. He couldn't help but like her—and fear for her.

He'd seen the look in her eye. She was planning to use herself as bait. Not that he could blame her for wanting to flush out the killer. He wanted that as badly as she did.

"You'll keep an eye on her," he'd said to Sheriff McCall Crawford.

McCall had nodded. "You think it's one of her former band members?"

"Likely, given what we know. They had motive and opportunity. I'll see what I can find out as far as means and get back to you. The music business sounds more dangerous than law enforcement."

"The nice thing about Whitehorse is that the town is small enough that anyone new stands out like a sore thumb. I'll be waiting to hear from you."

Buford had a lot of time to think on his way back to Flathead. The moment he reached his office, he had a call waiting for him from Jett Akins.

"Is it true?" Jett asked. "Is JJ alive and living in Whitehorse?"

The sheriff shook his head at how fast news traveled. "Where did you get that information?"

"It's all over the internet."

Of course it was. "Under the circumstances, I'm not at liberty to say."

"The circumstances? You don't think I want her dead, do you?"

"It has crossed my mind," Buford said.

"It's these women JJ should be worried about. I just went down to the room where they were staying," Jett said. "They've cleared out."

"Only the Sanderson case is closed, but I can't keep all of you in town any longer."

"That's it?" Jett demanded. "If you knew these women the way I do—"

"I heard that you dated all of them at one time or another. I guess I'm just surprised you aren't the one they want dead," Buford said.

"I'll be leaving town now, *Sheriff.*" Jett slammed down the phone in his ear.

Buford hoped that was true. With the news out on the internet, Blythe was already bait—but she might not realize it.

He put in a call to the cell phone number she'd given him. It went straight to voice mail. When he called Logan Chisholm's cell, he answered on the first ring.

THE MOMENT EMMA SAW THE sheriff drive up, she knew it was bad news. She stood in the doorway, holding the screen open, afraid to step out on the porch.

Sheriff McCall Crawford climbed out of her patrol SUV. She stopped when she saw Emma watching her, slowing as if dreading what she'd come to tell her.

"Emma," the sheriff said as she mounted the stairs. Not Mrs. Chisholm at least.

"I just made iced tea," Emma said and turned back into the house for the kitchen. She heard McCall behind her. "As I recall, you like my gingersnaps," she said over her shoulder. She wanted to avoid whatever bad news the sheriff had brought as long as possible, since she had a feeling she already knew.

She set about putting a plate of cookies on the table and pouring the tea as the sheriff took a seat at the kitchen table.

"It's about Aggie, isn't it?" Emma said as she put the tea and cookies on the table and dropped into a chair across from McCall. Zane, she noticed, was out by the barn. He was her babysitter today. She told herself the news might turn out to have a silver lining. Maybe it would put an end to this house-arrest life she'd been living.

"We found Aggie," the sheriff said.

"She's dead."

Another nod. "I'm sorry."

"Did you find her in the river?" Emma asked around the lump in her throat. Aggie. She thought of the vibrant, interesting woman, obsessed, yes, but so alive, so filled with a sense of purpose.

"No, not in the river. In Billings." The words fell like stones in the quiet room.

Emma crossed herself, mumbling the Spanish she'd grown up with, the religion Maria and Alonzo had given her.

Neither of them had touched their tea or the cookies.

"I don't understand." That was all she could think to say because she feared she *did* understand.

"She'd apparently fallen ill after going in the river."

Emma raised her gaze from the table to stare at the sheriff with an accusing look she could no longer control. "Don't you mean, after being shot by one of your deputies?"

"She was a wanted criminal who was getting away, though I'm sure the bullet wound added to her deteriorated condition," McCall said without looking away. "She was living in an old motel on the south side of Billings."

Hiding, trying to get well, Emma thought. Her stomach roiled with both grief and anger. "Is that what killed her?"

Now the sheriff looked away. "She was murdered."

"Murdered? Then you know who killed her?"

As McCall finally looked at her again, there was regret in her dark eyes. "After Aggie gave you the photos of the woman she believed was Laura Chisholm, I called in the FBI. They are tracking the woman."

"Without any luck," Emma said.

"We don't know who killed Aggie. She lived in a place where some of the residents had records for violent behavior. One of them could have killed her for a few dollars in her purse. Another woman was also killed in the same building. I wish I had better news."

She scoffed. "How could the news be any worse?"

McCall shook her head as she rose to her feet. "I'm sorry."

Emma looked at the young woman. She wanted to blame her for Aggie's death, blame someone. But if anyone was to blame, it was herself. If she'd gone to McCall and told her she was meeting Aggie...

Water under the bridge now. She studied the sheriff. "When is your baby due?"

McCall's expression softened. "November."

Emma smiled. "Do you know—"

"We want to be surprised." Her smile was strained, guarded and Emma remembered thinking McCall was pregnant once before, months ago.

"Miscarriage?" Emma said. "I'm sorry. I will keep you and your baby in my prayers."

"Thank you," McCall said, her voice thick with emotion. "I'm sorry about Aggie."

Emma nodded. She couldn't blame the sheriff anymore than she could blame Hoyt. He had called the sheriff when he suspected his wife was up to something involving Aggie that day. Emma would never forgive herself. Aggie had been trying to save her, was no doubt still trying when she was killed. The woman would never give up—that was her downfall as well as her appeal.

Apparently the person who killed her was the same way.

Emma listened to the sheriff leave, then laid her head on her arms on the kitchen table and let the hot tears come. A woman who'd tried to save her was dead and now her murderer was coming for Emma.

If Laura Chisholm had gotten to Aggie, then Emma knew there was little hope for her. Aggie wouldn't have been easily fooled. Laura would find a way to get to her and Emma doubted she would see her coming.

THE NEWS GOT OUT FASTER THAN Blythe had anticipated. Logan had told her it was all over the internet after Sheriff Buford Olson had called to warn him.

"Don't go to work today," Logan had pleaded with her. "Come out to my place. We'll take a long horseback ride up into the mountains."

"Don't tempt me," she'd said.

"Blythe—"

"I have to go back. I'm working a split shift. Maybe I'll see you after work." There was nothing she would have liked better than staying in bed with him. Her heart ached at the thought of giving up a horseback ride with him. Yesterday they'd found her a furnished apartment and made love late into the night.

But Blythe knew the only way she could be free to be with Logan was to end this, one way or another.

Now, at work at the café, there'd been a steady stream of diners since the newspaper article had come out that morning. Most just wanted coffee and pie and to check out this pop rock star who was now waitressing in their town.

Things had finally slowed down when Blythe saw a car pull up out front of the cafe. The car caught her attention because there were so few in this Western town. Pretty much everyone drove trucks.

She'd just served a tableful of ranchers who'd joked with her and still had her smiling, when she saw the woman climb out of the car. A cold chill ran through her. Karen "Caro" Chandler.

Her former best friend from childhood was tall and slim. She wore a cap-sleeved top in a light green with a flowered print skirt and sandals. As she removed a pair of large dark sunglasses, Blythe saw that she was even more beautiful than she'd been when they were girls.

"I'm going to take my break now, if that's all right," she called over her shoulder to the other waitress. Removing her apron, she tossed it on a vacant booth seat and stepped outside.

Karen looked up as Blythe came out the door, her expression softening into a smile. "It's been a long time."

"Too long," Blythe said, and motioned to the park bench across the main street. The sun felt warm and reassuring as they crossed the street. Only a few clouds bobbed along in a clear, blue sky. The air smelling of spring and new things seemed at odds with the conversation Blythe knew they were about to have. The past lay heavy and dark between them.

"So how is waitressing again?" Karen asked. "Remember that greasy spoon where you and I worked in high school? You broke more dishes and glasses than I did. But Huck always forgave you."

"Huck," she said smiling at the memory. "I wonder whatever happened to him?"

"He died a few years ago after rolling his car on the edge of town." Karen nodded at her surprise. "I went back to the desert to take care of Dad. He had cancer."

"I'm sorry." She studied her friend, surprised not that Karen had gone back to take care of her father but that she was stronger than Blythe had ever imagined. When they were girls, Blythe had been the one who made all the decisions about what the two of them did and Karen had let her. She watched Karen brush back a lock of hair and look up toward the warm blue of the sky.

"I know why you're here," Blythe said.

"Do you?" Her former friend looked over at her, their gazes locking.

"I'm sorry. I should never have left the band, left you behind."

Karen laughed. "Is that why you think I'm here?" She shook her head, smiling. "Tough as Nails breaking up was the best thing that ever happened to me. I went to college, met a wonderful man. We live together back east. We have a good life. I'm happy, Blythe. I didn't come here to tell you that you ruined my life. Quite the opposite. After you left, I realized I could do anything I set my mind to, I didn't need you to tell me what to do anymore."

"I'm still sorry. I wish I had kept in touch," she said,

hearing bitterness in Karen's voice no matter how much she denied it. "If not to tell me how much you hate me, then why are you here?"

"Luca came to see me before she died," Karen said. "She told me something that I thought you should know. She wrote some songs when she was dating Jett. When they broke up, he took the songs."

That didn't surprise Blythe. "He must not have recorded them or—"

"He did. Right after the two of you signed with Martin. Luca went to Martin. They settled out of court. A couple of the songs were his biggest hits."

"I had no idea," Blythe said, shaking her head.

"Luca felt that she'd been swindled by Martin and Jett. She was going to go public if they didn't pony up more money. The next thing I heard, she'd stepped in front of a bus."

Blythe felt her blood run cold. "You think it wasn't an accident? That someone pushed her?"

Karen nodded. "You were with Jett during the time when he recorded the songs. Do you remember seeing Luca's small blue notebook?"

The chill that ran through her made her shudder. She hugged herself against it, the warm spring sun doing nothing to relieve the icy cold that had settled in her.

"I was afraid that might be the case," Karen said. "Luca had found out that Jett planned to release another of her songs. That is why she was so upset with Martin and Jett. Jett had told her he no longer had the notebook."

He'd lied. No big surprise there. "You think either he or Martin killed her to shut her up."

"If I'm right, then you might be the only one who saw him with that notebook of Luca's songs," Karen said. "Luca's song that he recorded is set to come out next month."

Could this explain the accidents on her road tour? Jett was always around since he'd been closing for her. And he was in Montana. But if anyone had rigged the brakes on the sports car she'd rented, it must have been Martin. Unless Jett had come to town earlier and Martin had let him into the Grizzly Club without anyone knowing it.

She would bet there was a back way out of the club, one only the residents used.

Blythe felt sick. "Thank you for telling me."

Karen shrugged. "You were once like my sister. Whatever happened after that…" She stood. "Good luck, JJ." Her tone said she thought Blythe would need it.

Karen was studying her. "You seem…different."

"I'm not JJ anymore. As far as I'm concerned, she's dead. I'm Blythe again." She'd started going by Blythe in high school because it had sounded more mature, more like the musical star she planned to be. "JJ" had been Martin's idea.

"You do know that there never was going to be a re-union tour of Tough as Nails," Blythe said.

Karen looked amused. "I knew that. I think Betsy

and Loretta did, too. Got to wonder why they came all the way to Montana, don't you."

Blythe could see that Karen was trying to warn her. Jett might not be the only who wanted her dead.

"You going to keep waitressing when this is all over?" Karen asked, sounding skeptical.

"I might. It's honest work and I think I need that right now." She didn't say it, but the next time she picked up a guitar, she hoped it would be to sing a lullaby to one of her children. With Logan Chisholm.

"If you're ever in Whitehorse again…" She realized that Karen didn't seem to be listening. She was staring across the street.

Blythe followed her gaze and saw Logan leaning against his pickup watching the two of them.

"A friend of yours?" Karen asked, turning her gaze back to Blythe. She broke into a grin. "You finally found that cowboy you always said you were going to run away with."

Blythe knew they would never be close again, not like they'd been as kids, but she hoped they stayed in touch. Maybe time would heal the friendship. She sure hoped so. Impulsively, she hugged her former friend.

Karen seemed surprised at first, then hugged her tightly. "Be careful. I hope I get to hear about this cowboy someday."

Blythe glanced at Logan. She'd asked him to stay clear of her. "He's one stubborn cowboy," she said as they started back across the street toward Karen's car.

The truck came out from behind the space between

two main drag buildings where there'd been a fire a year ago. Sun glinted off the windshield, the roar of the engine filling the spring air as the driver headed right for the two of them.

Chapter Twelve

Buford called the airport only to find that none of the four, Jett, Karen, Loretta or Betsy had taken a flight out of town. He was in the process of calling rental-car agencies when Betsy walked into his office.

"There is something I think you should know," she said. She was nervously twisting the end of a bright-colored scarf that hung loosely around her neck.

He motioned her into a chair across from his desk. "What do I need to know?"

"It probably doesn't mean anything, isn't even important," she said haltingly.

"But you're going to tell me so I can be the judge of that, right?"

She nodded solemnly. "Ten years ago I overheard a conversation. I didn't mean to. Everyone thought I'd already left. I was always slower than the rest of them at getting out after a performance."

Buford tried to curb his impatience. "What did you hear?"

"Martin Sanderson. He was making one of the band members an offer," she said.

"JJ." He quickly corrected himself. "I'm sorry, I guess she was Blythe then."

Betsy shook her head. "It was Karen. She was apparently Martin's first choice. I heard him tell her that she had more talent than Blythe and that he could make her a star."

"Karen didn't take the offer," Buford said afraid he saw how this had gone down.

"She said she couldn't do that to her friend. Martin laughed and said, 'Well, she won't feel the same way when I make her the same offer.' Karen said he was wrong. That he didn't know Blythe the way she did."

"I would imagine Karen was upset when she heard that her friend had taken the deal and not looked back," Buford said.

Betsy shook her head. "That's just it. Karen didn't react at all. We all knew she had to be devastated, but she is so good at hiding her true feelings. If anyone hates JJ, it has to be her. She was betrayed worse than any of the rest of us. So you can see why there was no way the band could survive after all that. It was clear that Karen's heart definitely wasn't into it."

Betsy had quit worrying at the end of her scarf. She got to her feet and seemed to hesitate. "Jett said JJ's car had been tampered with and that's what killed that girl who took it."

"Your point?" he asked even though he had a good idea where this was headed.

"Karen's father was a mechanic. She loved to work with him on weekends. She knew all about cars and didn't mind getting her hands dirty. One time, when they were dating, she even fixed Jett's car for him."

LOGAN HAD BEEN WATCHING Blythe and another woman he'd never seen before visiting across the street. Was the woman one of the former members of her old band? They had seemed deep in conversation, making him anxious.

When they'd finally stood, hugging before heading across the street, he'd relaxed a little. Whoever the woman was, she apparently didn't mean Blythe any harm.

Then he'd heard the roar of the pickup engine, saw it coming out of the corner of his eye and acted instinctively. Later he would recall rushing out into the street to throw both women out of the way of the speeding truck. Now as he knelt on the ground next to Blythe, his heart pounding, all he could do was pray.

"Blythe! Blythe!" When she opened her eyes and blinked at the bright sunshine, then closed them again, the wave of relief he felt made him weak.

"Blythe," he said, part oath, part thanks for his answered prayer.

"Logan," she said, opened her eyes and smiled up at him.

"Is she all right?" he heard a voice ask behind him.

"She'd better be." There'd been a few moments when she hadn't responded. They'd felt like hours. He'd never been so scared.

She looked around at the small crowd that had gathered. He saw her confusion.

"Do you remember what happened?" he asked.

"Karen?" she said and tried to sit up.

"I'm right here," the woman who'd been with Blythe answered. "I'm fine." She didn't sound fine though. She sounded scared. Her skirt was torn, her top soiled, and like Blythe she'd scraped her elbow and arm when Logan had thrown himself at them, knocking all three of them out of the way of the pickup.

Logan could still hear the roar of the engine, the sound of the tires on the pavement, and see the truck bearing down on the two women crossing the empty street.

"Okay, everybody stand back, please." Sheriff McCall Crawford worked her way through the small crowd as Logan was helping Blythe to her feet. "Someone tell me what happened here."

A shopkeeper told the sheriff what he'd seen. "It appeared the pickup purposely tried to run the two women down."

Blythe leaned into Logan, clearly still shaken. He put his arm around her and tried not to be angry with her, but it was hard not to be. She was determined to risk her life—and push him away. He wasn't having it after this. Whatever he had to do to keep her safe, he was doing it.

"Did anyone see the driver?" McCall asked.

Blythe looked to Karen who shook her head. "The sun was reflecting off the windshield."

"So you couldn't tell if it was a man or a woman?" the sheriff asked.

"No."

"What about you?" McCall asked Logan.

"I heard it coming but I was just trying to get to Blythe before the pickup hit her."

"None of you saw the pickup's license plate, either?" the sheriff asked.

More head shakes.

"It was covered with mud," Logan said. "The pickup was an older model Ford, brown, that's all I can tell you."

She nodded. "I'd suggest you see a doctor," she said to Blythe, who instantly started to argue.

"I agree," Logan spoke up. "She definitely needs her head examined. I'm taking her over to the emergency room now."

"Very funny, Logan," she said under her breath.

"Okay, if you remember anything…" McCall turned to Karen. "I'd like to speak with you if you don't mind."

"We'll be at the emergency room, if you need us," Logan said. "I'll see that Blythe is safe from now on whether she likes it or not."

He'd expected Blythe to argue and was surprised when she didn't. Had it finally sunk in that she was in serious danger?

Blythe glanced around. "Where is Karen?" she asked.

"She left with the sheriff," Logan said.

"I was hoping to at least say goodbye," Blythe said.

"Sorry, but I think she wants to put as much distance between the two of you as she can. Apparently she's having trouble with the idea of someone almost killing her—unlike you."

* * *

It wasn't until they reached the hospital that Blythe finally felt her scraped elbow and the ache in her hip where she'd hit the pavement. Logan had refused to leave her side, standing in the corner of the emergency room watching the doctor check her over.

The incident had scared him badly. She could see that he was still worried about her. There was a stubborn set to his jaw that told her he'd meant what he'd said about not leaving her side. The thought warmed her and frightened her. Whoever had tried to run her down today would be back. She was determined that Logan Chisholm not be in the line of fire when that happened.

"No concussion," the doctor said. "I'll have the nurse put something on the scrapes and you are good to go."

As the doctor left, Logan stepped over to her bed. She looked into his handsome face and saw both anger and relief. He'd hurled himself at her and Karen, throwing them out of the way, risking his own life to save hers. Could she love this man any more?

"You saved my life," she said.

He chuckled. "Doesn't that mean you owe me some debt for eternity?"

She knew what was coming. "I hate that you risked your life today because of me. I can't let you keep doing that." He could have been killed today. Karen, too.

"How do you plan to stop me?" he asked, leaning toward her.

She felt her breath catch, her heart a rising thunder in her chest as he leaned down, his lips hovering just a heartbeat away from her own before he kissed her. Her pulse leaped beneath her skin. But when she reached to cup the back of his neck and keep his mouth on hers, he pulled back.

"You are coming home with me or I'm moving into your apartment," he said. "Which is it going to be?"

She could see that there was no changing his mind. "I've missed the ranch and the horses. I've missed you, too." All true. "But Logan—"

"Then it's my place," Logan said, cutting her off.

AFTER THE SHERIFF'S VISIT ABOUT Aggie's murder, Hoyt had insisted on staying at Emma's side until the new housekeeper arrived. He took several weapons from his safe and dragged her out to the barn for more target practice.

"I want you to be able to shoot without hesitation," he told her, thrusting a pistol into her hand.

"I can shoot and you already gave me a gun," she said. "That's not what you want me to be able to do."

"No," he agreed meeting her gaze. "I want you to be able to kill if you have to and without a second thought."

Anyone could be taught to shoot a weapon. Killing, well, that was something else.

"What about you?" Emma asked after shooting several pistols and proving that she could hit anything she aimed at.

"I'm not worried about me," he said.

"I am." She looked into his handsome face, saw how much this had aged him. They'd been so happy when they'd first married—before Aggie Wells had come back into his life first with accusations of murder and then with her crazy story about Hoyt's first wife being alive and a killer.

"Can you kill her?" Emma asked him.

His gaze locked with hers. She saw that he wanted to argue that his first wife was already dead. But maybe even he wasn't so sure now.

"I would do anything to keep you from being hurt. *Anything*." He pulled her into his arms and held her so tight she couldn't breathe.

He believed he could kill his first wife, his first love, a woman who had broken his heart in so many ways.

But Emma prayed he would never have to look into Laura's eyes and pull the trigger. If anyone had to do it, Emma hoped it wasn't him.

She took the pistol he handed her and aimed at the target on the hay bale and fired. Bull's-eye. But could she put a bullet through another woman's heart?

"SO DID YOU SEE HER?"

Buford smiled as his fourteen-year-old granddaughter Amy met him at his front door. "I saw her."

Since the call from the Whitehorse sheriff about an attempt on JJ's life, he'd been distracted with the case. He'd forgotten that this granddaughter knew he'd been to Whitehorse to see her music idol.

"Is she more beautiful in person than even on television?"

"I couldn't say. She's quite attractive." He could tell his granddaughter had hoped for more. "She seems very nice."

Amy rolled her eyes. *"Nice?"*

He didn't know what else to say. "I *liked* her."

That too met with an eye roll. "You like everyone."

If only that were true.

"Can't you even tell me what she looked like? Pretend it's a description of one of your criminals," his granddaughter persisted.

He thought for a moment. "She's tall and slim and has really amazing eyes. The color of..."

"Worn blue jeans?"

He nodded smiling. "She was wearing jeans, a Western shirt, blue I think, and red cowboy boots. Her hair is dark and long and looks natural. And she just learned how to ride a horse."

Amy seemed pleased to hear that. "Did she say anything about when she would be singing again?"

"No. I think it could be a while." If ever. "She's taking a break. Waitressing at a café in Whitehorse."

"That is so cool," Amy exclaimed excitedly. "Can you imagine walking into a café in the middle of Montana and *JJ* was the one who took your order?"

He couldn't. "Are you still listening to Jett Atkins's music?" He was afraid if he told her how much he disliked Jett, it would only make her like the man's music simply out of rebellion.

"I don't like him as well as JJ."

Buford was glad to hear that.

"He really needs a new hit."

"What about that one you played for me?" He'd heard it several times on the alternative radio station since this whole thing started with JJ. He'd been listening to the station realizing it was high time he knew what his granddaughter listened to. "What was the name of that song again?"

"Poor Little Paper Doll." She said it as if she couldn't believe he had forgotten. "That song is really *old,*" she said. "It came out in 2002!" The way she said it, 2002 was centuries ago. He supposed it seemed that way to a fourteen-year-old.

"Hasn't he had other hits?" He realized how little he knew about the music business, just as he'd been told numerous times lately.

"Not really. Especially lately. His songs haven't been very good. I read online that his sales are lagging and his last concert didn't even sell out," she said.

Interesting, he thought. Jett hadn't had a hit for a while and his career was faltering. He said he didn't know why Martin Sanderson had invited him to Montana, but of course he could have been lying about that.

What if Martin was putting some kind of pressure on *him?*

But what could that have to do with JJ?

Buford shook his head. He was too tired to think about it anymore tonight.

"It's funny, the songs that did well for Jett were nothing like the ones he's been singing lately," Amy said thoughtfully as they went to find her grandmother and see what was for supper. "Maybe he's writing his own songs." Apparently seeing that her grandfather had lost interest, she added, "Maybe his songwriter died. Or was *murdered.*" She'd always known how to get Buford's attention.

* * *

"What's wrong?" Blythe asked, sitting up in bed to find Logan at the dark window looking out.

"One of the horses got out," he said. "I must not have closed the gate again. Nothing to worry about."

She watched him as he reached for his jeans, pulled them on, then leaned over the bed to give her a kiss.

"I'll be right back."

Blythe lay back down, content and snug under the soft, worn quilt. A cool breeze blew in one of the windows bringing the sweet new smells of the spring night. She smiled to herself, listening as she heard Logan go down the stairs and out the front door.

Rolling to her side, she placed a hand on his side of the bed. The sheets were still warm from where his naked body had been only minutes before. She breathed in his male scent and pulled his pillow under her head, unable to wipe the smile from her face.

This was a first for her, falling in love like this. She'd thought it would never happen. The men she'd met were more interested in JJ and being seen with her. She'd never met a man like Logan who loved Blythe, the girl she used to be.

A horse whinnied somewhere in the distance. She closed her eyes, wonderfully tired after their lovemaking, and let herself drift.

Logan would be back soon. She couldn't wait to feel his body next to her again, have him put his arms around her and hold her close as if he never wanted to let her go.

She just hoped he was right about them being safer

together. She couldn't bear it if something happened to Logan because of her. Just as she couldn't bear being out of his arms.

LOGAN WALKED ACROSS THE starlit yard. No moon tonight, but zillions of stars glittered in a canopy of black velvet. Dew sparkled in the grass, the starlight bathing the pasture in silver.

He had pulled on his jeans and boots, but hadn't bothered with a shirt. The air chilled his skin and he couldn't wait to get back to Blythe. He smiled to himself as he thought of her, but then sobered as he remembered that she was a star.

Maybe she thought she didn't want to go back to it now, but she would. She would miss being up on stage, singing for thousands of screaming fans. Living out here in the middle of Montana certainly paled next to that. Right now, all of this was something new and different—just like him.

She was living her childhood dream of riding off into the sunset on the back of a horse with a cowboy. But that dream would end as the realization of a cowboy's life sunk in. He didn't kid himself that even the fact that he'd fallen in love with her wouldn't change that.

The thought startled him—just as the horse did as it came out of the eerie pale darkness. It was the big bay, and as it thundered past him, he saw that its eyes were wide with fear.

The horse shied away. Something in the darkness

had startled the big bay. He'd never seen a rattlesnake near the corral at night, but he supposed it was possible.

Watching where he was walking, he moved closer to the open gate. The barn cast a long dark shadow over most of the corral and the horses inside it.

He heard restless movement. Something definitely had the horses spooked. As he neared the gate, he looked around for the shovel he'd left leaning against the post earlier. If there was a rattler in the corral tonight, the shovel would come in handy. But as he neared the corral, Logan saw with a frown that the shovel wasn't where he'd left it.

Something moved off to his left in the shadowed darkness of the barn and for a moment he thought it was another one of the horses loose.

The blow took him by surprise. He heard a clang rattle through his head, realization a split-second behind the shovel blade striking his skull.

The force of it knocked him forward. He stumbled, his legs crumbling under him as he fell face-first into the dirt.

BUFORD COULDN'T SLEEP. IT was this damned case. Slipping out of bed, careful not to wake his wife, he went to his computer. Something his granddaughter had said kept nagging at him.

First he checked to see when Jett's hit song, "Poor Little Paper Doll," came out. Six months after Tough as Nails broke up. Six months after Jett and JJ were "discovered" by Martin Sanderson.

Did that mean something?

He looked at the time line he'd made of the lives of the former members of the band. The only musician whose life changed at that time was Lisa "Luca" Thomas. She'd apparently come into money.

He checked his watch. It was late, but not that late, he told himself. He was afraid this couldn't wait. He called his friend who worked in the U.S. Treasury Department and explained that it was a matter of life and death and there wasn't time to go through "proper" channels.

"Lisa 'Luca' Thomas was employed as a songwriter. Ten years ago? She had a very good year with her songwriting."

"Who paid her the most?"

"Martin Sanderson."

He hung up and called the deputy he'd had working on the backgrounds of his suspects—the former members of the Tough as Nails band as well as Jett Akins. So far, the deputy hadn't come up with anything of real interest, but Buford had told him to keep digging until he did.

"I just put what I found on your desk at the office," the deputy said. "It's a birth certificate."

"Give it to me in a nutshell," Buford snapped.

"Betsy Harper Lee had a baby seven months after the band broke up," the deputy said.

"And I care about this why?"

"At the time the band broke up, according to Jett, who I called to confirm this, he and Betsy were hooking up. She hadn't even met her soon-to-be husband. Jett was the father of the baby Betsy was carrying. I suspected that might be the case when I saw the baby's middle name: Ray, Jett's real name.

"Did Jett know she was pregnant?" Buford asked.

"He did. He came up with all kinds of reasons he couldn't 'do the right thing' ten years ago, but the bottom line was that he left her high and dry because of his career—and he was with JJ by then."

Who would Betsy blame for the father of her baby leaving her? Not Jett—but the woman she believed had stolen him from her: JJ.

Now too wound-up to quit, Buford hung up and called the dispatcher to see if any of the rental agencies had gotten back to him.

"There is a message on your desk. Four different rental agencies called. All four of the names you gave them rented vehicles," the dispatcher said.

"Does it say what kind of cars they rented?" he asked. It did.

Only one had rented a pickup.

BLYTHE WOKE WITH A START. She hadn't intended to fall asleep, wanting to wait until Logan returned. The bed felt cold, the air coming in the window sending a chill over her bare flesh. She started to pull up the quilt to cover her shoulders and arms when she heard what had awakened her.

The phone was ringing downstairs.

She glanced at the clock on the nightstand next to the bed.

11:10 p.m.?

She blinked in confusion. Logan had gone to check

the horses a little after ten. He hadn't returned from putting the horse back in the corral?

The phone rang again.

Something was wrong. Hurriedly she sat up and swung her legs over the side of the bed to reach for Logan's robe. As she hurried out of the room and started down the stairs, the phone rang again.

"Logan?" She thought he might have come back in and decided to sleep on the couch for some reason. But he would have heard the phone, wouldn't he?

The whole house felt empty and cold. Starlight shone in through the windows, casting the living room in a pale otherworldly light as she came down the stairs.

As the phone rang again, it took her a moment to find it. She hadn't even realized that Logan had a landline. Another ring. She realized the sound was coming from the kitchen. From the moonlight spilling in the window, she saw the phone on the kitchen wall, an old-fashioned wall mount.

She snatched up the phone. "Hello?"

"JJ?" The voice was gruff and familiar and yet it took her a moment to place it. She hadn't been sure who might be calling this time of the night—and somehow she'd expected it would be Logan, though that made little sense. He'd only gone out to put the horses back in. Unless there was a phone out in the barn.

"I'm sorry to wake you. Is Logan there?" Sheriff Buford asked. There was an urgency to his tone that sent her heart pounding harder.

"No, I…he went out to check the horses and he

hasn't come back. I thought it might be him calling from the barn—"

"Listen to me," the sheriff snapped. "You have to get out of—"

Blythe heard the creak of the old kitchen floor behind her. As she turned, a hand snatched the phone from her and hung it up. She stumbled back as the kitchen light was snapped on, blinding her for an instant, as the last person she'd expected to see stepped from the shadows.

"What are you…" The rest of her words trailed off as she saw the gun.

Chapter Thirteen

"Thought I'd left? Or thought I'd forgiven you?" Karen asked as she leveled the gun at her.

Blythe remembered that bitter edge she'd heard in Karen's voice. She hadn't forgotten or forgiven. "But that truck. It almost hit us both."

Her old friend smiled. "Nice touch, huh. I thought you would appreciate the drama. I certainly lived through enough of yours when we were kids. Remember all the nights you used to crawl in my bedroom window to get away from one of your mother's drunk boyfriends?"

Until one night one of Blythe's mother's boyfriends followed her and threatened to go after Karen if she ever went to her house in the middle of the night again. That's when Blythe had started going to her own bed at night with a knife under the pillow.

"You had to know how much I appreciated that. I don't know what I would have done without you." She thought she heard a sound outside. Logan could be coming in that door at any moment.

"Until you got the chance to make something of yourself and left me behind," Karen snapped.

"I didn't want to. I told Martin I wouldn't go without you."

Karen seemed surprised by that. "What did he say?"

"He told me that he'd already offered you a music contract, but that you'd turned it down. Are you telling me he lied about that?"

"It's true I turned down his offer."

"Karen, why would you do that? Martin told me that you were his first choice because you were the one with all the talent."

Tears welled in her eyes. "Because of you. I couldn't leave you and the band."

Blythe studied her in the harsh glow of the overhead kitchen light. She could see the clock out of the corner of her eye. Logan should be coming back at any moment.

"He won't be coming," Karen said with a smile.

"What did you do to him?" Blythe cried, and took a step toward her.

Karen waved her back with the gun. "Don't worry. I didn't kill him. He's tied up out in the barn. I didn't want him interrupting our reunion. You did plan on the old band doing that reunion tour, didn't you, *JJ?*"

"That was Martin's doing. Not mine. He knew how much you all resented me. I'm sure the twisted bastard was hoping one of you would want to kill me."

"Or maybe he knew all along it would be me," Karen said. She hadn't let the gun in her hand waver for an instant. There was a determination in her eyes that Blythe remembered from when they were kids.

"I'm going to be someone someday," Karen used to

say. "Those people who look down their noses at me now will regret it one day. I want fame and fortune. I want people to recognize me when I walk down the street and say, 'Isn't that her? You know that famous singer.'"

Blythe's dream had been to get out of the desert trailer park and away from her drunk mother's boyfriends. She hadn't dreamed of fame and fortune and yet she'd gotten both.

"You could have had fame and fortune just like you used to say you wanted when we were kids. You turned it down, and not because of me."

Karen started to argue, but Blythe cut her off.

"Martin always said that what I lacked in talent I made up for in guts. He said it was too bad you were just the opposite."

"Don't I look like I have guts?" Karen demanded and took a threatening step toward her. Karen aimed the gun at Blythe's heart. "If you think I won't kill you, you're wrong. I can't bear the thought of you living the life that should have been mine any longer."

"I'm a waitress now, Karen," Blythe snapped. "You want that life, go for it."

The gun blast was deafening in the small kitchen.

LOGAN WOKE TO THE FEEL OF THE cold hard ground beneath him and a killer headache. For a moment, he couldn't remember what had happened. If not for the ropes binding him, he might have thought one of the horses had clipped him and he'd hit his head when he went down.

He tried to sit up, straining against the ropes around his wrists and ankles. His head swam at the effort, but as his thoughts cleared, he let out a curse. Blythe.

Whoever had hit him and tied him up was after Blythe.

Rolling to his side, he looked around for something to free himself. In the corner, he spotted an old scythe that he sometimes used to cut weeds behind the barn. He began to work his way over to it, scooting on the cold earth, his mind racing.

He remembered that he'd come out to put the horses back in the pasture. He'd thought he'd left the gate open. It wouldn't have been the first time one of the horses had gotten out. Even when he realized that something was spooking the horses, he thought it must be a rattler.

Never had he thought anyone would come after Blythe out here. His mistake. One he prayed wouldn't cost her her life.

He reached the scythe, knocked it over and positioned it between his wrists as he began to saw. He couldn't believe anyone would want to harm Blythe, certainly not one of her former band members, and yet someone had taken a shovel to the back of his head and left him hog-tied in the barn.

What were they going to do to Blythe?

Not kill her. No, just scare her. Logan desperately wanted to believe that in the end, they wouldn't be able to hurt her. But then he had no concept of the kind of hatred that could bring another person to kill.

Logan sawed through the ropes on his wrist and was

reaching for the scythe to cut the bindings around his ankles when he heard the gunshot. His heart dropped.

KAREN SMILED AS A CERAMIC container on the kitchen counter exploded, sending shards flying and startling Blythe. "I planned all of this. Hired someone to make it look like someone else from the band had tried to run us down on the street. I know Martin thought I was a coward, that I blamed you because I didn't go for what I wanted ten years ago and instead let you take it from me. Martin told me to my face just before I killed him."

Blythe stared at Karen in shock. "I thought his death was ruled a suicide."

"He said he was going to kill himself when I found him that morning about to write his suicide note," Karen said with a smile. "But we both knew he wouldn't have called me to meet him over at the house unless he lacked the courage to do it. He had the gun pointed at his chest, but I was the one who had to press the trigger. He goaded me into it because he didn't have the guts to do it himself. I was the last person he saw."

"Oh, Karen." She felt sick as she stumbled back against the kitchen table. Her fingers felt the smooth brim of Logan's Stetson and her heart lurched at the thought of him. She prayed Karen was telling the truth and hadn't hurt him.

"You're the one who left the note for me," she said, seeing it all now. "Martin must have told you I was there in another part of the house. All these years. You could have had a career. It didn't have to be either me or you."

"Do you know what makes me the angriest?" Karen said as if Blythe hadn't spoken. "You had it all and you were going to throw it away. Martin told me how you didn't appreciate it. You had everything I'd dreamed of and yet it meant nothing to you."

"Karen, that's not—"

"Don't bother to lie. You took what was mine." Her face twisted in a mask of fury. "Martin was right. You don't deserve to live."

Blythe had only a split second to react as Karen brought the gun up and squeezed the trigger. The Stetson brim was already in the fingers of her right hand. She drew it from behind her and hurled the hat at Karen as she dived for the floor.

LOGAN HURRIEDLY CUT THROUGH the ropes. As he stumbled to his feet, he felt the effects of the blow to his head. He could barely breathe, his fear was so great, but it was the dizziness that made him grab hold of the barn wall for a moment. His vision clearing, he raced toward his pickup and the shotgun that hung in the rack in the back window.

Two gunshots. His heart was in his throat as he saw that the kitchen light was on. But he saw no one as he quietly opened his pickup door and took down his shotgun. From behind the seat, he found the box of shells and popped one in each side of the double barrels. Snapping it shut, he headed for the front door.

He knew he couldn't go in blasting. If Blythe wasn't already dead—

The thought clutched at his heart. He'd brought

her out here so he could protect her. If he'd gotten her killed—

He eased open the front door and instantly heard what sounded like a scuffle just inside.

BLYTHE WASN'T SURE IF SHE'D been hit or not. She felt the hard floor as she hit her already scraped elbow. But even that pain didn't register at first as she knocked Karen's feet out from under her.

Karen came down hard next to her. A loud "oof!" came out of her as she hit the floor. Blythe saw that there was a red welt on Karen's cheek where the Stetson brim must have hit her.

Blythe grabbed for the gun, but Karen reacted faster than she'd expected. She kicked out at Blythe, driving her back as she brought up the gun and aimed it at her head.

As Karen scrambled to her feet, Blythe slowly got to hers.

"I'm sorry this is how it has to end," Blythe said as she saw the front door slowly swing open behind Karen. "I never wanted to hurt you. You were like a sister to me. I missed you so much. I can't tell you how many times I wanted to pick up the phone and call you."

"Why didn't you?" Karen demanded, sounding close to tears. Her arm was bleeding from where she'd gotten skinned-up earlier on the main drag in Whitehorse. She must have hit it when she fell, Blythe thought as she tried to think about anything but Logan.

He had slipped in through the front door, a shotgun

in his hands, and was now moving up behind Karen. He motioned for her to keep talking.

"I didn't think you would want to hear from me after the band broke up," she said. "I blamed myself for leaving it and leaving you. I guess I also didn't believe Martin that you'd turned down an offer to do what I was doing. I thought he'd lied. It wouldn't have been the first time."

Logan was now right behind Karen, practically breathing down her neck. She was crying, big fat tears running down her face.

"He was right, you know?" Karen said and made a swipe at her tears with her free hand. "I was afraid that I wouldn't be good enough to make it. I hoped you would fail but when you didn't…" She seemed to get hold of herself, inhaling and letting out a long sigh. "It's too late now. I've burned too many bridges. This has to end here. You and me. Just as it always should have been."

Something in Karen's gaze suddenly changed. Blythe saw Logan raise the shotgun and cried out to warn him as Karen suddenly spun around.

Blythe felt her legs give under her. She dropped to her knees as she watched Logan bring the butt of the shotgun down on the side of Karen's head. As she crumbled like a ragdoll, she managed to get off another shot. It whizzed past Logan, missing him only by inches, before shattering something in the living room.

In the distance, she heard the sound of sirens and remembered the call from Sheriff Buford Olson earlier. He must have called the local sheriff, McCall Crawford, for moments later the ranch yard filled with flashing lights and the sound of doors slamming and running feet on the porch steps.

Blythe buried her face in Logan's shoulder as he dropped to his knees beside her. His breath was ragged, his heart a drum in his chest as he dragged her to him. She heard his voice break with emotion as he thanked God that she was alive.

Then he lifted her face to his and told her he loved her.

Epilogue

"If I could have your attention please." Logan rose from his chair at the long table in the dining room of the main house at Chisholm ranch. He touched his knife to his wineglass again. A hush fell over the room as all eyes turned in his direction.

Blythe felt her heart kick up a beat as Logan smiled down at her. She wanted to pinch herself. So much had happened since that night in the kitchen. Everything about JJ and the past had come out. Logan's family had been so supportive, just the memory brought tears to her eyes.

They'd spent the rest of that night giving their statements to the sheriff, having the doctor check Logan over to make sure he didn't have a concussion and filling his family in on JJ and everything else that had happened.

Sheriff Buford Olson had picked up Loretta and charged her with attempted murder after discovering that she'd rented the pickup and had been the driver in the near hit-and-run. Karen had paid Loretta to do it, but Loretta told Buford that she'd been happy to. In fact, she'd done her best to hit both of them.

Karen had hired herself a good lawyer. When Blythe had tried to visit her in jail, Karen had refused to see her. As she'd left the sheriff's department, she didn't look back. She was through blaming herself for the events of the past.

Before he died, Martin Sanderson had also released Jett from his contract, but Jett was quickly finding out that no other recording studio was interested. On top of that, Betsy had produced a sworn affidavit from their deceased band member Lisa "Luca" Thomas, stating that Jett had stolen songs from her and what she'd been paid for them—after he'd recorded the songs as his own. Her estate was suing Jett for full disclosure.

That had pretty much driven a stake through the last of his singing career.

Blythe had been glad to see that Betsy had more backbone than any of them had seen before. She'd known that Betsy was pregnant all those years ago before the band broke up. But if her oldest son was Jett's, then it was a secret Betsy intended to take to her grave.

A few days ago, Blythe had been sitting on the porch in the shade after a long horseback ride with Logan when he joined her.

"I love you," he said. Blythe started to speak, but he stopped her.

"You don't have to say anything. I know that staying here, on this ranch, in the middle of nowhere is the last thing in the world you want to do."

"Logan—"

He touched a finger to her lips. "Let me finish. I

didn't tell you I love you to try to get you to stay. I just wanted you to know that if you ever need to get away from your life again, I'll be here."

She smiled and shook her head. "I'm not going to want to escape my life again. All of this has helped me know what I want to do with the rest of it." She touched his handsome face, cupping his strong jaw with her palm. "I love you, Logan Chisholm, and there is no place I want to be other than right here with you."

He'd stared at her in surprise. "What about your career—"

"Martin freed me from my contract, so I do still have my singing career if I wanted it. But since climbing on the back of your motorcycle that day over in the Flathead, I've known that the only singing I want to do is to my babies. You do want children, don't you?"

"There's something I need to ask this woman," Logan said now as he reached down and took Blythe's hand. "Jennifer Blythe James, would you be my wife?"

Blythe felt tears blur her eyes as she looked around the table and saw all the smiling welcoming faces. Then she turned her face up to Logan. "There is nothing I would love more," she said.

He dragged her to her feet and into his arms. She leaned into him, felt his strength and that of his family around them, all the things a good marriage needed.

The room burst with applause and cheers around them as Logan kissed her. Blythe could see their children running through this big house, all the holidays and birthdays, all the cousins, aunts and uncles.

She'd dreamed of a big family, but the Chisholms were bigger and more loving than any she had ever dreamed possible.

When Logan finally released her, she found herself hugged by everyone in the room. Emma was last. She'd cupped Blythe's shoulders in her hands and just looked at her for a long moment.

"You are going to make the most beautiful bride and such a good wife to our Logan," she said, her voice breaking with emotion. "Welcome to the family." Emma pulled her into a hug.

Through her tears, Blythe saw her future husband standing nearby looking at her as if he would always see her as she was now. She smiled back, picturing getting old with this man. Yes, after all the fame and fortune, this was exactly where she wanted to be.

HER NAME WAS NOW CYNTHIA CROWLEY. She'd picked the name out of thin air—just as she did most of her names.

She thought of it as reinventing herself. She cut her hair, dyed it, got different colored contact lenses, changed her makeup, her address, became the woman she imagined Cynthia Crowley was. A widow with no family and no real means of support.

Laura had first discovered in high school drama class that she could don a disguise like an outer shell. She'd loved acting and she was good at it. Everyone said she seemed to transform into her character. The truth was, her characters had felt more real to her than whoever she'd been before she pulled on their skin.

She liked to think of herself as a chameleon. Or a snake that was forever shedding its skin. She had changed character so many times that some days she could hardly remember that young woman who'd married Hoyt Chisholm. Laura suspected though that Mrs. Laura Chisholm had been as big a fake as Cynthia Crowley was now.

Women did that when they married for life. They became who their husbands *thought* they had married. That's what she had done with Hoyt. She'd played the role of his wife. At least for a while.

It was no wonder that her life had led her to the special effects department of several movie studios in California. It was amazing how the new products could transform an actor. She especially loved a type of substance that reminded her of the glue she'd used in grade school. As a special effects makeup artist, she had worked with actors to make them look old and wrinkled or badly scarred.

The work was rewarding. She loved what she did and often experimented with her own disguises. But ultimately, there was only one constant in her life. Hoyt Chisholm.

Laura remembered the first time she'd seen Hoyt. She'd known then that she would love him until the day she died. She'd also known that he would never love her as much as she loved him. It had broken her heart every moment she'd been with him. That was why she hadn't been able to stay. It had been too painful knowing that one day he would see the real her and hate her.

She was tortured by the way other women had

looked at him. It had been impossible not to imagine him with one of them instead of her. Hoyt would become angry when she'd voice her fears and she'd feel another piece of her heart gouged away by his lack of understanding.

Once he'd decided to adopt the boys, she'd lost more of him. He'd actually thought the boys would bring the two of them closer, but when she'd seen his love for babies that weren't even his own blood, she'd felt herself losing more and more of him. He tried to make it up to her, trying so hard it made her hurt even worse. She'd seen him start to pull away from her and knew she had to escape before it got any worse.

Divorce was out of the question. She would always be his only wife till death parted them. She could have warned him not to ever remarry before she faked her death that day on Fort Peck Reservoir. But Hoyt wouldn't have understood. You had to love someone so much it hurt to understand.

She'd known he would remarry. She'd thought he would have to wait seven years to have her declared dead. But he'd found a way around it, marrying that bitch Tasha. Unlike her, Tasha had shared Hoyt's love of horses. Oh, the horrible pain of watching the two of them together, until one day she couldn't take it any longer and had rigged Tasha's saddle.

After that, she'd hoped Hoyt wouldn't marry again. But Hoyt hadn't been able to resist the young woman who'd been helping take care of his boys. Krystal appealed to Hoyt's need to protect a woman in trouble.

He would have continued to try to save Krystal if Laura hadn't helped him by getting rid of her for good.

From a safe distance, she had watched him raise the boys alone, all six of them, and build an empire. She'd been proud of him, had actually loved him more.

Then Emma had come along.

Laura shook her head. Just the thought made her hands ball into fists, her jaw tightening, her heart on fire.

Hoyt was in love. Or so he thought. She knew the power of love, but it was a weak emotion compared to hate. Hate, now there was something with substance, something you could feel deep in your bone marrow, something to live for.

Laura lived now for only one thing. To see Emma Chisholm dead and gone. But this time she thought Hoyt might have to go, as well. Maybe his sons and their fiancées too. Maybe it was time to finally end this pain once and for all. If only Hoyt had loved her and only her.

As she parked her car and got out, it looked as if they were having a party, but she knew Emma made a big deal out of suppers at the ranch. Everyone was here. Perfect.

She stood for a moment, looking at the huge house all ablaze with lights, remembering when it had been hers and Hoyt's.

Then she made her way up to the front door and rang the doorbell. It would be her house again in a few moments, she thought with a crooked smile.

* * *

When the doorbell rang, everyone turned in surprise toward the front door.

"Are you expecting someone?" Emma asked her husband.

Hoyt shook his head. "Unless it's the live-in housekeeper. She wasn't supposed to be here until tomorrow though. I'll go see."

Emma asked her future daughters-in-law to serve dessert and went into the living room. Hoyt was already at the door, opening it as the bell rang again.

Standing back, Emma waited. She wondered what this woman Hoyt had hired to babysit her would be like. Dreaded, was more like it. Older, he'd said. Experienced, he'd said.

Emma feared she would be dull as dirt, when what she needed was to kick up her heels after everything she'd been through since marrying Hoyt.

But she wasn't going to complain. If the woman wasn't any fun, then Emma would find a way to sneak away from her.

Bracing herself, Emma watched Hoyt open the door. He hadn't turned on the porch light so she couldn't see the woman standing on their doorstep clearly.

"Come on in, Cynthia," Hoyt said. "We expected you tomorrow, but tonight is fine. You're just in time for dessert."

"Call me Mrs. Crowley," the woman said in a low hoarse voice. She spoke strangely as if out of one side of her mouth. Had the woman had a stroke?

And as she stepped into the light, Emma saw that

her face was badly scarred on one side as if she'd been burned in a fire.

"Whatever you prefer," Hoyt said and turned to see Emma standing at some distance behind him. "Mrs. Crowley, I'd like you to meet my wife, Emma."

The woman looked up then and Emma felt a chill race through her. One of the woman's eyes was a dark brown. The other one on the side that had been burned was completely white and sightless.

"I know I don't look like much," the woman said in her hoarse voice. "But I'm a hard worker."

"I'm sure you are," Emma said stepping to her to take her hand. "Welcome to Chisholm ranch."

The woman's grip was strong. "Thank you, Mrs. Chisholm."

She hated that the woman was hard to look at because of her injury, but she knew over time, they would all adapt to it, just as Cynthia Crowley had herself.

"Please call me Emma," she said warmly.

"Don't you worry, Emma. I am much stronger than I look. Before long, I promise you'll be surprised at what I'm capable of doing."

* * * * *

Zane squeezed her hand, and leaning toward her, drew her into his arms.

He hadn't planned to kiss her. But at that moment, it seemed the most natural thing in the world.

Her lips parted, her breath warm and sweet. He felt a quiver run through her, his pulse kicking up as his mouth dropped to hers.

Dakota gently pushed him away. "Sorry, but your reputation precedes you."

He heard the slight tremble in her voice. She pulled free of his arms and he leaned back, telling himself he shouldn't have kissed her. Especially given why they were together. Didn't he have enough women problems right now?

"You're going to believe rumors about me?" he joked as he tried to cover up how even that quick kiss had affected him.

She smiled but there was hurt in her gaze.

His gaze caressed her face for a moment before meeting her eyes. "But that kiss? I was just fulfilling a promise I made you before you moved to New Mexico. Remember?"

WRANGLED

BY

USA TODAY BESTSELLING AUTHOR
BJ DANIELS

First published in Great Britain 2012
by Mills & Boon, an imprint of Harlequin (UK) Limited,
Eton House, 18-24 Paradise Road, Richmond, Surrey TW9 1SR

© Barbara Heinlein 2012

ISBN: 978 0 263 89542 1
ebook ISBN: 978 1 408 97241 0

46-0712

Harlequin (UK) policy is to use papers that are natural, renewable and
recyclable products and made from wood grown in sustainable forests. The
logging and manufacturing processes conform to the legal environmental
regulations of the country of origin.

Printed and bound in Spain
by Blackprint CPI, Barcelona

USA TODAY bestselling author **BJ Daniels** wrote her first book after a career as an award-winning newspaper journalist and author of thirty-seven published short stories. That first book, *Odd Man Out,* received a four-and-a-half-star review from *RT Book Reviews* and went on to be nominated for Best Intrigue that year. Since then she has won numerous awards, including a career achievement award for romantic suspense and many nominations and awards for best book.

Daniels lives in Montana with her husband, Parker, and two springer spaniels, Spot and Jem. When she isn't writing, she snowboards, camps, boats and plays tennis. Daniels is a member of Mystery Writers of America, Sisters in Crime, International Thriller Writers, Kiss of Death and Romance Writers of America.

To contact her, write to BJ Daniels, PO Box 1173, Malta, MT 59538, USA or e-mail her at bjdaniels@mtintouch.net. Check out her website at www.bjdaniels.com.

This book is dedicated to Julie Miller and Delores Fossen, two fellow Intrigue writers I greatly admire. I was with them in Los Angeles at the *Romantic Times* convention relaxing when I came up with the ending of this book. Thank you both for your friendship. I'm looking forward to our *January Ice Lake* anthology together.

SAVE UP TO 25%

Subscribe to Intrigue today and get 5 stories a month delivered to your door for 3, 6 or 12 months and gain up to 25% OFF! That's a fantastic saving of over £40!

MONTHS	FULL PRICE	YOUR PRICE	SAVING
3	£43.41	£36.90	15%
6	£86.82	£69.48	20%
12	£173.64	£130.20	25%

As a welcome gift we will also send you a FREE L'Occitane gift set worth £10

PLUS, by becoming a member you will also receive these additional benefits:

- FREE Home Delivery
- Receive new titles TWO MONTHS AHEAD of the shops
- Exclusive Special Offers & Monthly Newsletter
- Special Rewards Programme

No Obligation - You can cancel your subscription at any time by writing to us at Mills & Boon Book Club, PO Box 676, Richmond. TW9 1WU.

To subscribe, visit
millsandboon.co.uk/subscriptions

MILL
BOO

Chapter One

The knock at the door surprised Zane Chisholm. He'd just spent the warm summer day in the saddle rounding up cattle. All he wanted to do was kick off his boots and hit the hay early. The last thing he wanted was company.

But whoever was knocking didn't sound as if they were planning to go away anytime soon. Living at the end of a dirt road, he didn't get uninvited company—other than one of his five brothers. *So that narrows it down,* he thought as he went to the window and peered out through the curtains.

The car parked outside was a compact, lime-green with Montana State University plates. Definitely not one of his brothers, he thought with a grin. Chisholm men wouldn't be caught dead driving such a "girlie" car. Especially a lime-green one.

Even more odd was the young, willowy blonde pounding on his door. She must be lost and needing directions. Or she was selling something.

His curiosity piqued, he went to answer her persistent knock. As the door swung open, he saw that her eyes were blue and set wide in a classically gorgeous face. She wore a slinky red dress that fell over her body like water. The woman was a stunner.

She smiled warmly. "Hi."

"Hi." He waited, wondering what she wanted, and enjoying the view in the meantime.

Her smile slipped a little as she took in his worn jeans, his even more worn cowboy boots and the dirty Western shirt with a torn sleeve and a missing button.

"I wasn't expecting company," he said when he saw her apparent disappointment in his attire.

"Oh?" She looked confused now. "Did I get the night wrong? You're Zane Chisholm and this is Friday, right?"

"Right." He frowned. "Did we have a date or something?" He knew he'd never seen this woman before. No red-blooded American male would forget a woman like this.

She reached into her sparkly shoulder bag and pulled out a folded sheet of paper. "Your last email," she said, handing it to him.

He took the paper, unfolded it and saw his email address. It appeared he had been corresponding with this woman for the past two days.

"If you forgot—"

"No," he said quickly. "Please, come in and let's see if we can sort this out."

She stepped in but looked tentative, as if not so sure about him.

"Why don't you start with how we met," he said as he offered her a seat.

She sat on the edge of the couch. "The Evans rural internet dating service."

"Arlene's matchmaking business?" he asked in surprise. Arlene Evans, who was now Arlene Monroe, had started the business a few years ago to bring rural couples together.

"We've been visiting by email until you…"

"Asked you out," he finished for her.

"Are you saying someone else has been using your email?"

"It sure looks that way, since I never signed up with Arlene's matchmaking service. But," he added quickly when he saw how upset she was, "I wouldn't be surprised if Arlene is behind this. It wouldn't be the first time she took it upon herself to play matchmaker." Either that or his brothers were behind it as a joke, though that seemed unlikely. This beautiful woman was no joke.

She looked down at her hands in her lap. "I'm so embarrassed." She quickly rose to her feet. "I should go."

"No, wait," he said, unable to shake the feeling that maybe this had been fate and that he would be making the biggest mistake of his life if he let this woman walk out now.

"You know, it wouldn't take me long to jump in the shower and change if you're still up for a date," he said with a grin.

She hesitated. "Really? I mean, you don't have to—"

"I *want* to. But you have the advantage over me. I don't know your name."

She smiled shyly. "Courtney Baxter." She held out her hand. As he shook it, Zane thought, *This night could change my life.*

He had no idea how true that was going to be.

Chapter Two

Dakota Lansing got the call at 3:20 a.m. She jerked awake, surprised by the sound of the ringing phone. She hadn't had a landline in years. Glancing around in confusion, for a moment she forgot where she was.

Home at the ranch. It all came back in a rush, including her father's death. She turned on the light as the phone rang yet again and grabbed the receiver.

As she did, she glanced at the clock, her mind spinning with fear. Calls in the wee hours of the morning were always bad news.

"Hello?" Her voice broke as she remembered the last call that had come too early in the morning.

This is Dr. Sheridan at Memorial Hospital in Great Falls. I'm sorry to inform you that your father has had a heart attack. I'm afraid there was nothing we could do. Your sister is here if you would like to speak with her.

My sister? You must have the wrong number, I don't have a sister.

"Hello?" she said again now.

At first all she heard was crying. *"Hello?"*

"Dakota, I need your help."

Her sister, half sister, the one she hadn't known existed until two weeks ago, let out a choked sob.

"Courtney? What's wrong?"

More sobbing. "I'm in trouble."

This, at least, didn't come as a surprise. Dakota had expected her half sister was in trouble when she'd asked after their father's funeral if she could stay at the ranch for a while.

"I want to get to know you," Courtney had said. But it had become obvious fairly quickly that her half sister wanted a lot more than that.

"Speak up. I can barely hear you," Dakota said now.

"I can't. He's in the next room."

Dakota rolled her eyes. A man. Not surprising, since Courtney had been out every night in the two weeks since their father's funeral.

"I think he might be dead."

Dakota came wide awake. *Dead?* "Where are you?" There was a loud crash in the background as something fell and broke. "Tell me where you are," Dakota cried as she stumbled out of bed. *"Courtney?"*

Her father's secret love child, a woman only two years younger than herself, whispered two words before the line went dead.

"Zane Chisholm's."

ZANE WOKE TO POUNDING. He tried to sit up. His head swam. He hadn't really drunk champagne last night, had he?

Numbly he realized the pounding wasn't just in his head. Someone was at the door and it was still dark outside. He turned on a light, blinded for a moment. As he glanced over at the other side of his queen-size bed, he was a little surprised to find it empty. Courtney had come home with him last night, hadn't she?

As he got up he saw that he was stark naked. Who-ever was at the door was pounding harder now. He quickly pulled on a pair of obviously hastily discarded jeans and padded barefoot into the living room to answer the door.

"What the hell happened to *you?*" his brother Marshall asked in surprise when Zane opened the door.

"I'm a little hungover." A major understatement. He couldn't remember feeling this badly—even during his college days when he'd done his share of partying.

"Your face," Marshall said. "It's all scratched up."

Zane frowned and went into the bathroom. He turned on the light and stared in shock into the mirror. His pulse jumped. He had what looked like claw marks down the side of his left cheek. As he looked down at his arm, he saw another scratch on his forearm.

What the hell had happened last night?

"Are you okay?" Marshall asked from the bathroom doorway. He sounded worried, but nothing like Zane felt.

"I don't know. I'm having trouble remembering last night."

"Well, it must have been a wild one," Marshall said. "I hope it was consensual with whatever mountain lion you hooked up with."

"Not funny." His head throbbed and his memory was a black hole that he was a little afraid to look into too deeply.

"You do remember that you and I are picking up horses in Wolf Point today, right?" Marshall said. "I'll give you a few minutes to get cleaned up, but don't even think about trying to get out of this. I need your help and we're already running late. I told you to be ready at four forty-five."

Zane nodded, although it hurt his head. What time was it, anyway? The clock on the wall read 5:10 a.m. "Could you make me some coffee while I get ready?"

His brother sighed. "Aren't you getting a little too old for partying like this?" he grumbled on his way to the kitchen.

Zane stepped into the bathroom, closed the door and stared into the mirror again. He looked like hell. Worse, he couldn't remember drinking more than a glass or two of champagne, certainly not enough to cause this kind of damage.

He thought about Courtney. She had to have done this to him. He touched his cheek. What scared him was, what had *he* done to get that kind of reaction from her?

EMMA CHISHOLM HAD been an early riser all her life. She liked getting up before the rest of the world when everything was still and dark. Since marrying Hoyt Chisholm a year ago, she especially liked seeing the sun come up here on the ranch.

As she stepped into the big ranch kitchen, she heard a sound and froze.

"I hope I didn't scare you."

Emma shuddered as a chill raced down the length of her spine. She tried to hide it but knew she'd failed when she turned to see amusement in their new live-in housekeeper's one good eye. Up before sunrise and often the last one to bed, the woman moved around the house with ghostlike stealth.

"There really is no need for you to work such long

hours," she said as Mrs. Crowley stepped out of the dark shadows of the kitchen. The fifty-eight-year-old woman moved with a strange gait—no doubt caused by her disfiguring injury. It was hard to look into Mrs. Crowley's face. The right side appeared to have been horribly burned, that eye white and sightless. Behind her thick glasses, her other eye shone darkly.

"I'm not interested in sleeping anymore," Mrs. Crowley said. Her first name was Cynthia, but she'd asked them to refer to her by her married name.

The moment she'd come to the house, she had taken over. But Emma couldn't complain. Mrs. Crowley, a woman about her own age, was a hard worker and asked for little in return. She lived in a separate wing of the house and was Emma's new babysitter.

Not that Emma's husband, Hoyt, would ever admit that was the case. But last year his past had come back to haunt them. It had to do with the deaths of Hoyt's last three wives. An insurance investigator by the name of Aggie Wells had been convinced that he'd killed them.

When Aggie had heard about Hoyt's fourth marriage—this one a Vegas elopement to Emma—she'd come to Montana to warn Emma that she was next.

Aggie was dead now. While the police hadn't found her killer, Emma was fairly certain that the perpetrator was the same one who'd murdered at least one of Hoyt's wives.

Aggie Wells had originally been convinced that the killer was Hoyt, but as time went on she'd thought Hoyt's first wife might still be alive. Laura had allegedly drowned in Fort Peck Reservoir more than thirty years before. Aggie had even found a woman named Sharon Jones, whom she believed was Laura. Unfortunately, Sharon Jones had disappeared before the police could question her.

For months now Hoyt had been afraid to leave Emma alone. Either he or one of his six sons hung around the house to make sure no harm came to her.

She'd been going crazy, feeling as if she was under house arrest. Hoyt and his sons had to be going crazy as well. They were ranchers and much more at home on the back of a horse than hanging around the kitchen with her.

Finally Hoyt had come up with the idea of a live-in housekeeper. Emma was sure that Mrs. Crowley wasn't what he'd had in mind. But after all the rumors and suspicions that were flying around, it was next to impossible to get anyone to work at the ranch.

Fortunately, Mrs. Crowley had been glad to come. She said she liked that Chisholm Cattle Company was so isolated.

"People stare," she'd said simply when Emma had asked her if she thought she could be happy living this far away from civilization.

She was an abrupt woman who had little to say. Emma knew she should be thankful, but sometimes it would be nice to have someone who would just sit and visit with her. That definitely wasn't Mrs. Crowley, but Emma kept trying.

"I see you've made coffee," Emma said now. "May I pour you a cup? We could sit at the table for a few minutes before Hoyt comes down."

"No, thank you. I'm cleaning the guest rooms today."

Emma could have argued that the guest rooms could wait. Actually, they probably didn't need cleaning. It had been a while since they'd had a guest. But Mrs.

Crowley didn't give her a chance. The woman was already off down the hallway to that wing of the house.

As Emma watched her go, she noticed how the woman dragged her right leg. That's what gave her that peculiar gait, she thought distractedly. Then she heard Hoyt coming downstairs and poured them both a cup of coffee.

It wasn't until she took the mugs over to the table that she realized Mrs. Crowley always made herself scarce when Hoyt was around. Maybe she just wanted to give them privacy, Emma told herself. "Strange woman," she said under her breath.

A moment later Hoyt came into the kitchen, checked to make sure they were alone and put his arms around her. "Good morning. Want to sneak out to the barn with me, Mrs. Chisholm? Zane and Marshall have gone to Wolf Point. Dawson, Tanner and Logan are all mending fences and Colton has gone into town for feed."

She laughed, leaning into his hug. It had been a while since they'd made love in the hayloft.

CYNTHIA CROWLEY WATCHED Emma and Hoyt from one of the guest room windows. They had their arms around each other's waists. Emma had her face turned up to Hoyt, idolization in her eyes. She was laughing at something he'd said.

Cynthia could only imagine.

She let the curtain fall back into place as Hoyt pushed open the barn door and they disappeared inside. As she turned to look around the guest room, she mumbled a curse under her breath. The decor was Western, from the oak bed frame to the cowboy-print comforter. *Emma's doing,* the housekeeper thought as she moved to look at an old photograph on the wall.

It was of the original house before Hoyt had added onto it. The first Chisholm main house was a two-story shotgun. It was barely recognizable as the house in which Cynthia now stood. Hoyt had done well for himself, buying up more land as his cattle business had improved.

On another wall was a photograph of his six adopted sons, three towheaded with bright blue eyes, three dark-eyed with straight black hair and Native American features. In the photo, all six sat along the top rail of the corral. The triplets must have been about eight when the picture was taken, which made the other three from seven to ten or so.

They looked all boy. There was a shadow on the ground in the bottom part of the photograph. Hoyt must have been the photographer, since she was sure the shadow was his.

Now the boys were all raised—not that Emma didn't get them back here every evening she could. All but Zane were engaged or getting married so the house was also full of their fiancées. Emma apparently loved it and always insisted on helping with the cooking.

Not that Cynthia Crowley minded the help—or the time spent with the new Mrs. Hoyt Chisholm. Emma fascinated her in the most macabre of ways.

The new Mrs. Chisholm had definitely been a surprise. A man as powerful and wealthy as Hoyt Chisholm could have had a trophy wife. Instead he'd chosen a plump fifty-something redhead.

"There is no accounting for tastes," the housekeeper said to the empty room as she went to work dusting. Before she'd been hired on, she'd been told about Hoyt's other three wives—and their fates.

"Do you think he killed them?" she'd asked the director of the employment agency where she'd gone to get the job.

"Oh, good heavens, no," the woman had cried, then dropped her voice. "I certainly wouldn't send a house-keeper up there if I thought for a moment…"

Cynthia had smiled. "I'm not afraid of Hoyt Chis-holm. Or his wife. I'm sorry, what did you say her name was?"

"Emma. And I've heard she is delightful."

"Yes, delightful," Cynthia grumbled to herself now. At the sound of laughter, she went to the window. Through the sheer curtains she saw Emma and Hoyt coming out of the barn. They were both smiling—and holding hands.

Cynthia Crowley made a rude noise under her breath. "The two of them act like teenagers."

A loud snap filled the air, startling her. It wasn't until she felt the pain that she looked down. She hadn't been aware that she'd been holding anything in her hands until she saw the broken bud vase, and the blood ooz-ing from her hand from where she'd broken the vase's fragile, slim neck.

ONCE THEY HAD THE HORSES loaded at a ranch north of Wolf Point, Marshall suggested they grab lunch. Zane wasn't hungry, wasn't sure he ever would be again. He was anxious to call Courtney and find out what had happened last night.

Stepping outside the café to call her, he realized that he didn't have her number. Nor was she listed under

Courtney Baxter. He tried the couple of Baxters in the Whitehorse area, but neither knew a Courtney.

With no choice left, he called Arlene Evans Monroe at the woman's rural internet dating service that had allegedly put them together in the first place.

"Did you set me up with a woman named Courtney Baxter?" he asked Arlene, trying not to sound accusing. Arlene used to be known as the county gossip. In the old days he wouldn't have put anything past her. But he'd heard she'd changed since meeting her husband Hank Monroe.

"Yes," she said, sounding wary. "Is there a problem?"

"Only that Courtney showed up at my door last night saying I had a date with her through your agency and I didn't have a clue who she was."

"Are you telling me you didn't make a date with this woman?"

"I never even signed up for your dating service. I thought maybe someone had done it as a joke."

"Zane, I have your check right here."

How was that possible? He knew he was still feeling the effects of the hangover; his aching head was finding it hard to understand any of this. But all morning he'd been worried about what had happened last night. He had a very bad feeling and needed to talk to Courtney.

"When does it show that I signed up?" he asked Arlene.

"Two weeks ago."

Two weeks ago? A thought struck him. About two weeks ago he'd come home to find someone had been in his house. Like most people who lived in and around Whitehorse he never locked his doors, so the intruder

hadn't had to break in. Nor had the person taken anything that he could see—not even his laptop computer.
But enough things had been moved that he'd known
someone had been there.

He swore now, realizing that must have been when
the person had gone online and signed him up for the
dating service—and taken at least one of his checks.
He hadn't even noticed any were missing.

"What is the number on that check?" he asked Arlene. She read it off and he wrote it down, seeing that
it was a much higher number than the checks now in
his checkbook. He wouldn't have missed it for months.

Who went around signing someone up for a dating
service? This made no sense. It had to have been one of
his brothers. Or his stepmother, Emma? She had made
it clear she thought it was time her six rowdy stepsons
settled down. Maybe she was behind this.

But neither Emma nor his brothers would have come
to his house when he wasn't home, gotten on his computer and then taken one of his checks to pay for the
rural dating service. Who then? And why? This was
getting stranger by the moment.

"I need Courtney Baxter's telephone number," he
told Arlene.

"According to the service policy you agreed to—"

"I didn't agree because I never signed up," he said,
trying not to lose his temper. He caught his reflection
in the café window and saw the four scratches down
his cheek where someone had definitely clawed him.

"Zane, what if I call her and make sure it's all right
first? Do you want to hold?"

He groaned, but agreed to wait.

She came back on the line moments later. "She's not

answering her cell phone. I left her a message to call me immediately. I'm sorry, Zane, but that's the best I can do. It's policy."

He swore under his breath. The old Arlene would have handed it over. She would also have asked why he was so anxious to talk to his "date" and the news would have gone on the Whitehorse grapevine two seconds later.

"The moment you hear from her…"

"I'll let you know," she said.

Zane didn't hear anything from Arlene on the long drive back to Whitehorse. He hoped that once he got home there might be a note or something from Courtney.

Not wanting to drag the loaded horse trailer down the narrow lane to the house, Marshall dropped him off by the mailbox on the county road.

"You sure you're going to be all right?" Marshall asked.

He'd been sick all day and still had a killer headache.

"You really did tie one on last night," his brother said, looking concerned. "What were you drinking anyway?"

"I remember having some champagne."

Marshall shook his head. "That all?"

Zane couldn't recall if it had been his idea, but he doubted it. Courtney must have suggested it. "And I only had a couple of glasses, I'm sure."

His brother lifted a brow. "You sure about that?"

He wasn't sure of anything. "Don't worry about me. I'm fine," he lied as he climbed out of the Chisholm Cattle Company truck and headed down the narrow dirt road to his house.

The early summer sun was still up on the western horizon. It warmed his back as he walked. Grass grew bright green around him, the air rich with the sweet scents of new growth. Grasshoppers buzzed and butterflies flitted past. In the distance he could see that there was still snow on the tops of the Little Rocky Mountains.

As he came over a rise, he slowed. A pickup he didn't recognize was parked in front of his house. Courtney? Or maybe one of her older brothers here to kick his butt. He quickened his step, anxious to find out exactly what had happened last night—one way or the other.

Zane was still a good distance from the truck when he saw the woman and realized that it wasn't Courtney. This woman was dressed in jeans, boots and a yellow-checked Western shirt. Her chestnut hair was pulled back into a ponytail. She stood leaning against the truck as if she'd been waiting awhile and wasn't happy about it.

When she spotted him, she pushed off the side of the pickup and headed toward him. As she came closer, his gaze settled on her face. He felt the air rush out of him. She was beautiful, but that was only part of what had taken his breath away.

He'd seen Dakota Lansing only once since she was a kid hanging around the rodeo grounds. She'd been cute as a bug's ear back then and it had been no secret that she'd had a crush on him. But, five years his junior, she'd been too young and innocent so he'd kept her at arm's length, treating her like the kid she was.

The last time he'd seen her he'd happened to run into her at the spring rodeo in Whitehorse. He'd been so surprised to see her—let alone that she'd turned into this beautiful woman—he'd been tongue-tied. She must have thought him a complete fool.

The whole meeting had been embarrassing, but since she'd moved to New Mexico, he'd thought he would never see her again. And yet here she was standing in his yard.

"Dakota?" he said, surprised at how pleased he was to see her.

Smiling, he started toward her, but slowed as he caught her body language. Hands on hips, big brown eyes narrowed, an angry tilt to her head. His brain had been working at a snail's pace all day. It finally kicked into gear to question what Dakota Lansing was doing here—let alone why she appeared to be upset.

She closed the distance between them. "Where is my sister?" Those big brown eyes widened, and he knew she'd seen the scratches on his face just seconds before she balled up her fist and slugged him.

The punch had some power behind it, but it still had less effect on him than her words.

"Your sister?" he asked, taking a step back as he rubbed his jaw and frowned at her. He'd known Dakota Lansing all his life. She didn't have a sister.

Chapter Three

"Courtney Baxter," Dakota said. "The woman I know you were out with last night." She looked as if she wanted to hit him again. Her eyes narrowed. "What did you do to her?"

He rubbed his jaw, feeling as if he was mentally two steps behind and had been since Courtney Baxter had knocked on his door not twenty-four hours before. "Courtney Baxter is your sister?"

"My *half* sister. Where is she?"

His head ached and now so did his jaw. Dakota had a pretty good right hook. "How do you know I was with her?"

"She called me sounding terrified. What did you do to her?"

Taking a step back, he raised both hands. "Hold on a minute. We can figure this out."

"What is there to figure out?" she demanded.

He noticed something he hadn't earlier. Dakota's left hand. No wedding ring. No ring at all. The last time he'd seen her, she'd had a nice-size rock on her ring finger. He'd heard she was engaged to some investment manager down in New Mexico.

She saw him staring at her left hand and stuck her

hands into the back pockets of her jeans, her look daring him to say anything about it.

No chance of that.

"We should put something on those knuckles," he said, having noticed before that her right hand was swelling. Hitting him had hurt her more than it had him. Well, physically at least.

Dakota Lansing. He still couldn't believe that the freckle-faced tomboy who used to stick her tongue out at him had grown into this amazing-looking woman.

"Why don't you come into the house for a minute," he said, and started for the front porch.

"Zane, I'm only interested in finding my sister."

"So am I." He left the door open, went into the kitchen and opened the freezer door. By the time he heard her come in he had a tray of ice cubes dumped into a clean dishcloth.

"What did you do to her?" Dakota demanded again from the kitchen doorway.

He motioned to a chair at the kitchen table. "Dakota, you know me. You know I wouldn't hurt anyone."

She didn't look convinced, but she did sit down. He reached for her injured hand, but she quickly took the ice from him, pushing his hand away.

"Courtney said on the phone last night that she was in trouble. I heard something crash in the background. Just before the connection went dead she said your name."

The whole time she'd been talking she was glaring at him, challenging him to come up with an explanation. He wished he could.

"Dakota, I have to be honest with you. I can't remember anything about last night. I woke up this morning alone with these scratches on my face and—" he pushed up his sleeve "—my arm."

Her eyes widened a little when she saw the scratches on his arm. He saw fear flicker in her expression, fear and anger. "How long have you been dating my sister?"

She sounded almost jealous. Which he thought just showed how hungover he was. "I had never laid eyes on her until she showed up at my door last night claiming we had a date," he said. He saw she was having trouble believing it. "I swear it. And I certainly didn't know she was your sister. So how is it I never knew you had a sister?"

"She's my father's love child." Dakota sighed and shifted the ice pack on her swollen knuckles. "I only found out two weeks ago after my father died."

He remembered seeing in the newspaper that her father had passed away. He'd thought about sending a card, but it had been so many years, he doubted Dakota would remember him.

"Are you sure she's even—"

"I saw her birth certificate. It had my father's signature and his name on it. Apparently Courtney's mother and my father got together either when my mother was dying or right after."

He could see how painful this was for her. Dakota had idolized her father, and to find out on his death that he'd been keeping a lover and a sister from her for years...

"So you're claiming that Courtney just showed up at your door?" Dakota asked, clearly not wanting to talk about her father.

Zane told her about his call to Arlene at the dating service, the check someone had used to enroll him and that he was waiting to hear from Courtney, since he, too, was worried about what might have happened last night.

She studied him for a long moment. "So a woman you have never seen before shows up at your door claiming you have a date, and you just go out with her anyway?"

He guessed Dakota had probably heard about his reputation with women. "I didn't want to hurt her feelings."

Her chuckle had a distinct edge to it, and he remembered why he'd always liked her. Dakota had always been smart and sassy. She'd been a daredevil as a kid, always up for just about anything, from climbing the three-story structure that held the rodeo announcer's booth at the fairgrounds, to trying to ride any animal that would hold still long enough for her to hop on. Since her father had raised rodeo stock, she'd had a lot of animals to choose from. He'd liked her a lot. Still did, he thought.

"How well do you know her?" Zane asked.

"Not as well as you know her, apparently," Dakota said, and shoved the ice pack away as she reached for her phone.

"Who are you calling?" He hated to think.

"I'm trying Courtney's cell." She punched in the number and hit Send. "I've been trying to call her all day and—"

At the distant sound of a phone ringing they both froze for an instant. Then, getting to their feet, they followed the muffled ringing.

Zane hadn't gone far when he realized the sound was

coming from his bedroom. He pushed open the door and stepped in, Dakota on his heels.

The ringing seemed to be coming from the bed, but when he drew back the crumpled covers, it was empty. As the phone stopped ringing, no doubt going to voice mail, he knelt down and looked under the bed.

He could just make out the phone in the shadowy darkness under the bed—and what was left of the lamp that had been on the nightstand on the other side of the bed. The lamp lay shattered between the bed and the closet.

Refusing to think about that right now, he reached for Courtney's phone.

It wasn't until he pulled it out and heard Dakota gasp that he noticed the cell phone was smeared with something dark red. Blood.

He dropped the phone on the bed, realizing belatedly that he should never have touched it. He had a bad feeling it would be evidence—against him.

As he turned, Dakota took a step back from him. The frightened look in her eyes hit him like a blow. There were tears in her eyes; the look on her face was breaking his heart.

"I didn't harm your sister. Dakota, you *know* me."

"I *knew* you, Zane, but that was a long time ago."

"Not so long. I haven't changed. Drunk or sober, I would never hurt a woman. You have to believe me." But how could he keep telling himself that nothing bad had happened last night when the evidence just kept stacking up?

They both turned toward the front of the house as they heard a vehicle pull up. Zane moved quickly to look out, hoping it would be Courtney and he could get this cleared up and relieve his mind.

But it wasn't Courtney's lime-green compact with the MSU plates.

It was a Whitehorse County Sheriff's Department patrol SUV.

"Mrs. Crowley," Emma cried when she saw the woman's bandaged hand.

"It's nothing."

"Oh, here, let me see it." She reached for the woman's hand.

"I said it was nothing," Mrs. Crowley said, taking a step back and drawing her hand behind her. Her face had closed up, her one good eye glinting as hard as the tone of her voice.

Emma fell silent. She'd held out hope that she would like the woman Hoyt had hired as her housekeeper-babysitter. Being close in age, she'd thought they might have things in common.

But every time she had reached out to Mrs. Crowley, offering her friendship, it had been quickly rebuffed.

"Just let me do my work," the woman said now. Her wrecked face caught the light; the burn scars looked angrier today than usual.

Unlike Hoyt, Emma made a point of looking Mrs. Crowley in the eye. She refused to be put off by her injuries—or her manner.

Hoyt just steered clear of the woman and often apologized for hiring her.

"She's fine," Emma always said in Mrs. Crowley's defense. She suspected that the woman had trouble getting other positions and couldn't afford to lose this job.

Hoyt paid her well and the living accommodations were probably nicer than any she'd had before. Not that Emma's kindness or the house or the pay had softened Mrs. Crowley in the least.

"Whatever happened to her has made her push people away," Emma told her husband. "We just need to keep trying to make her feel at home here."

Hoyt had been skeptical. "You probably pick up stray dogs, too, don't you? Honey, this time I don't think even you can make that woman civil—let alone happy."

Emma couldn't help but wonder what had happened to Mrs. Crowley that made her like this. She suspected it was more than whatever accident she'd had that had left her disfigured. But Emma doubted she would ever know. It wasn't like Mrs. Crowley was going to tell her anytime soon.

"DID YOU CALL THE SHERIFF?" Zane asked without looking at her as Dakota joined him at the window.

"No." With a sinking feeling, Dakota watched Sheriff McCall Crawford climb awkwardly out of the patrol vehicle. Dakota saw that the sheriff was pregnant, a good seven or eight months along.

"Maybe Courtney called her, or—"

Or Courtney had been found. Dakota didn't let him finish that thought. "Courtney wouldn't have called the sheriff." If her sister had had any intention of calling the sheriff, wouldn't Courtney have done so last night instead of calling her?

Whatever Courtney was up to, Dakota suspected the sheriff was the last person she wanted involved.

"Well, if you didn't call her, and Courtney didn't…" Zane let the thought hang between them.

Dakota glanced over at him, saw his freshly scratched face in the glow of the afternoon sun coming through the window and could guess what was about to happen.

Once the sheriff saw the scratches, she wouldn't need to hear about the phone conversation Dakota'd had with Courtney in the wee hours this morning. Nor would the sheriff need to see the bloody phone from under Zane's bed before hauling him off to jail.

Common sense told Dakota, given the evidence, jail was probably the best place for him. But not if she had any hope of him helping her find her sister.

"Here's what I want you to do," she said as the sheriff's footfalls echoed on the old wooden porch. "Go in the bathroom and stay there. Let me handle this."

Zane shook his head as the sheriff knocked at the front door. "If you think I'm going to hide behind your skirts—"

"What you're *going* to do is help me find Courtney, and you can't very well do that behind bars," Dakota said through gritted teeth as the sheriff knocked again. "Turn on the shower. There's something I haven't told you about Courtney. Now trust me."

She shot him an impatient look and waited until he disappeared into the bathroom and shut the door before she went to answer the sheriff's third knock.

As the door swung open, Sheriff McCall Crawford couldn't help her surprise.

"Dakota Lansing?" McCall said. "Haven't seen you in a while." She'd been several years ahead of Dakota and they'd gone to different schools—McCall in Whitehorse, while Dakota had gone to Chinook—but they'd crossed paths because of sports.

"I've been living in New Mexico. I only recently returned. For my father's funeral," she added.

"Yes, I heard. I'm sorry." The sheriff looked past her. "Is Zane around, by any chance?"

"He's in the shower, but you're welcome to come in." She stepped back and McCall entered the house. "He's getting ready so we can go out for dinner."

McCall glanced around the small house. There wasn't much to see. Zane Chisholm obviously wasn't into decorating. She doubted he spent much time here.

"I came out to talk to Zane, but since you're here…" McCall said. "Is there a problem I should know about?"

Dakota looked confused by the question. "A problem?"

"I got a call that there was a domestic disturbance out here."

"When was that?"

"Twenty minutes ago," McCall said.

Dakota let out a laugh. "You didn't really take that call seriously, did you? The closest neighbor is a half mile away. Hard to really see or hear a domestic disturbance, unless of course they said there was gunfire involved."

"True," McCall said. "Unless, of course, *you* made the call."

"I can assure you, I didn't call. But I suspect caller ID would have confirmed that," Dakota said.

The sheriff smiled. She remembered Dakota Lansing as being smart and capable. "Just had to check. Actually the call came from a woman who said she was your sister."

"Courtney?"

McCall saw that she now had Dakota's attention. "Is Courtney Baxter your sister?"

"My half sister. Long story. Why would she make a call like that? I haven't seen her for several days."

"Good question." McCall glanced toward the bathroom door. She could hear the shower still running. Zane Chisholm took an awfully long shower.

As she felt the baby kick, McCall rested her hand on her swollen belly. For a moment she was lost in that amazing feeling. The whole pregnancy had been like this, stolen moments from her job when she felt as if she wanted to pinch herself. She just couldn't believe she and Luke were having a baby.

"Is it possible your sister is jealous?" McCall asked as she turned to leave. "I heard Zane was out with a pretty blonde last night. Apparently they were celebrating rather hard."

Compliments of the Whitehorse grapevine first thing this morning. McCall even knew that Courtney Baxter had been wearing a very sexy red dress. Who needed Twitter? *No one in this county,* she thought.

That Courtney was Dakota Lansing's half sister had come as a surprise. The scuttlebutt now around town was that the girl was the product of an affair Clay Lansing had years ago.

"I actually set up the date," Dakota said. "I knew the two of them would hit it off. Zane and I are just friends. But I can understand why Courtney might be jealous after a date with Zane. He is a catch."

McCall nodded as she glanced into the kitchen and bedroom, saw the unmade bed and figured this was merely a case of sibling rivalry. "Well, you two have a nice supper. Have Zane give me a call when he gets a chance."

As she started for the front door, she heard a cell phone ring from somewhere in the bedroom. "If that's your sister calling, please tell her I'd like to talk to her, too," McCall said, and let herself out.

DAKOTA LET OUT THE BREATH she'd been holding since the moment she'd realized it was Courtney's cell phone ringing. Zane had left it lying on the crumpled covers of the bed. Fortunately it had been out of the sheriff's sight.

She hurried into the bedroom and gingerly picked up the phone. Private caller. "Hello?"

No answer, but she could hear breathing on the line. "Who is this? Courtney? If that's you—"

Whoever it was hung up.

Dakota stood holding the phone for a moment, then quickly dropped it back on the bed. She felt a rush of anger. Courtney was fine. She'd called the sheriff twenty minutes ago. She must have seen Dakota's pickup parked in front of Zane's house from the county road.

Or she'd called so the sheriff would see Zane's scratched face.

"What are you up to, Courtney?" Dakota said to the empty bedroom. No good, that much she was sure of. "And what really happened here last night?"

The room provided few answers. Unless you read something into the crumpled sheets on the bed. She felt a surge of anger mixed with something she didn't want to admit. Jealousy. Zane had gone out with her sister.

I didn't want to hurt her feelings. She swore under her breath.

Too bad he hadn't felt that way when they were kids, Dakota thought, remembering how he'd pushed her away.

"You're just a kid," he'd said when she tried to hang around him at the rodeo grounds. "Go on. Find someone your own age to bug."

She ground her teeth at the memory. She'd had the worst crush on him. And, stupidly, she'd written it all down in her diary, every horrible tearful account, including her conviction: *Zane doesn't know it, but some day I'm going to marry him.*

Two days ago, when she'd realized that someone had been in her things, she'd discovered that her diary and some old photographs were missing. Courtney. She was the only one who could have taken the diary.

Now Dakota wondered when Courtney had taken it. Two weeks ago—about the same time that someone had mysteriously signed Zane Chisholm up for a dating service?

It was no coincidence that Courtney had tricked Zane into a date. Dakota was sure of that. Courtney had the diary. She knew how her sister had felt about Zane. So Courtney had done this out of meanness?

What had she hoped to accomplish by this? More than sibling rivalry, Dakota thought, remembering the scratches on Zane's face and the frantic phone call in the wee hours this morning.

Whatever Courtney was up to, Dakota was going to find her and put a stop to it. And Zane was going to help her.

Unlike him, Dakota had a bad feeling she knew exactly why Courtney had targeted him. She couldn't wait to get her hands on her diary—and her sister.

MRS. CROWLEY STEPPED into her room and closed the door firmly behind her. She had always been so good at playing her roles—she now thought of herself as Mrs. Crowley. Smiling at the thought, she locked the door to listen. She had to make sure she wouldn't be disturbed.

It hadn't taken long to learn the sounds of the house. The older section had more to say than the newer one, but she knew all of its many voices—which floorboards creaked, which doors opened silently, which spot in the house carried the most sound for eavesdropping.

She'd explored every square inch of the house until she knew she could move through it blind if she had to. That was a possibility if the house were ever to catch fire.

Satisfied that everyone was down for the night, she stretched, relieving her back from the strain of walking hunched over. She had taught herself to move silently and now chuckled to herself at how many times she'd been able to come up behind Emma without her knowing it and startle her.

Moving just as silently now, she stepped into the bathroom and studied herself in the mirror over the sink a moment before she reached up and took out the white contact lens. She blinked, waiting for the eye to focus. Then she removed the dark brown contact lens.

She slowly began to remove the burn scar, peeling it off as she peeled away Mrs. Crowley. At last she stood at the mirror, her face scrubbed clean, her eyes blue again.

As she stared at herself, though, she felt she was

looking at a stranger. It had been so long since she'd been herself, her image came as a shock.

But it was nothing compared to the shock it would give others in the house when the time came to end this charade, she thought with a wry smile.

Chapter Four

The moment Zane had gone into the bathroom and turned on the shower, he'd changed his mind about staying hidden while Dakota handled the sheriff.

He'd never run from trouble in his life, and he wasn't going to now. But as he'd reached for the bathroom door handle, he'd glimpsed his face again in the mirror over the sink. The scratches were an angry red and, maybe worse, he had no explanation for them.

Dakota was right. He needed to find Courtney and he couldn't do that behind bars. He feared anything he said to the sheriff would come out sounding like a lie. If Sheriff McCall Crawford saw Courtney's cell phone…

He'd stayed put even though it was hard. He couldn't hear what was being said. For all he knew, Courtney had been found and that was why the sheriff was here.

Zane jumped at the tap on the bathroom door. He quickly turned off the shower and opened the door.

"The coast is clear," Dakota said as he came out.

"What did McCall want?" He hated the fear he heard in his voice. From Dakota's reaction, she'd heard it too. She had to be wondering if she was wrong about him.

"Apparently Courtney called about a disturbance out here between you and me."

"*Courtney* called? Then she's all right?"

"Apparently."

He shook his head. "But why would she..." The thought struck him like a brick. "She wanted the sheriff to see the scratches on my face and arm. What the hell is going on with her?"

"She seems to have it in for the two of us," Dakota said. "That's why we have to find her and find out what she's up to."

"The *two* of us?"

Dakota looked away for a moment as if she hadn't meant to say that. "The last time I saw her was a few days ago. Right after that I realized she'd been in my house and taken something of mine." She waved a hand through the air. "The point is, I want it back. She had no business in my house, let alone taking anything of mine."

He nodded, seeing that whatever Courtney had taken, Dakota didn't want to talk about it. He changed the subject. "What did McCall make of all this?"

"She seemed to think it was my sister being jealous."

"We know better." The date last night, what he could remember of it, hadn't been anything special. In fact, he recalled before he'd lost his memory that he hadn't planned to see Courtney again. She was beautiful, but not that interesting.

His head still hurt, but a thought wormed its way through. "You said Courtney showed up two weeks ago. That's the same time someone broke into my house and used my computer to set up the rural dating account. Could she have been planning this that long ago, trying to set me up for more than a date?"

"Why go to the trouble?" Dakota asked, frowning as if she was trying to work it out herself.

"Why me at all?" It didn't make any sense to him either. "The requirements I put down for the perfect date apparently made Courtney the perfect match."

Dakota raised an eyebrow.

"I didn't put down *any* requirements, but whoever signed me up must have rigged it so that my requirements matched Courtney's. It had to be Courtney."

"A lot of trouble and to what end?"

"I guess that depends on what happened last night," he said as he glanced around the living room. Nothing seemed to be missing, but then he'd made that mistake before.

"You really don't remember what happened after your date?" she asked.

"I've never had a hangover like this before."

Dakota was looking at the scratches on his face again. "Maybe you should get a drug test at the hospital."

Dakota was willing to consider that he'd been drugged? Zane was surprised and relieved. But why hadn't he thought of it? Because he'd been running scared from the moment he'd opened his eyes this morning.

He had to know what he was dealing with. Courtney Baxter seemed to be setting him up. But why? He was just grateful that Dakota seemed to be on his side. If he'd just gotten drunk and didn't remember, that was one thing. But if Dakota was right and Courtney had drugged him...

"I think a drug test is a good idea," he said, but Dakota didn't seem to hear him.

She was looking at Courtney's cell phone. She had picked it up by two fingers. He could see the smeared blood from here.

"Any idea how it got blood on it?" she asked. "Or how it ended up under your bed? I noticed there was also a broken lamp on the other side of the bed. You probably don't know anything about that either."

He shook his head. "You said you heard something crash in the background when you were on the phone with her."

"Could have been the lamp." She looked down at the phone again. "Maybe we should see about getting DNA off this phone to find out if it is even Courtney's blood. We can have a doctor run a blood test on you at the same time for possible drugs. Do you have a small plastic sandwich bag we can put this in?"

"Top drawer on the right." He watched her head for the kitchen, trying to figure out what about Dakota was bothering him. She certainly was taking all this better than he would have thought.

"I doubt there will be fingerprints other than ours, but…" She stopped on her way back from the kitchen, the cell phone in a plastic bag she'd found in the drawer. "What's wrong?"

He wasn't sure. "You just kept me out of jail—at least temporarily—and now you're going to help clear me? What's going on, Dakota?"

"I told you. I need your help to find Courtney."

"Because she took something of yours that you want back. If you just wanted to find Courtney, you could have told the sheriff everything you know and thrown me to the wolves," he said. "The sheriff, with all her resources, would be looking for your sister right now.

So why didn't you? It wasn't just to keep me out of jail so I could help you find her. I hate to sound suspicious, but I have to wonder why you're so anxious to find her that you would throw in with *me*."

"She's my sister."

"Uh-huh."

Dakota sighed. "Okay, maybe I've suspected she was up to something from the first time I laid eyes on her."

"You said your father's name and signature are on her birth certificate. Are you saying you're questioning that?"

She shrugged. "All I know is that something's wrong with her story. After what you've told me, I'm even more convinced."

"But not enough to go to the sheriff."

"I want to do some investigating of my own before I get the sheriff involved," Dakota said.

He suspected there was more, something she was hiding, but right now he was just glad he wasn't in jail.

"Then you believe me?"

"I'm willing to consider you were set up." She stepped to the door and opened it. "On the way into town, I think we should see who Courtney's been calling—and who's been calling her."

DAKOTA HADN'T BEEN completely truthful. Not that she didn't have her reasons for wanting to believe Zane and, if she was being honest with herself, some of them had to do with the crush she'd had on him when she was a girl.

He was even more handsome now. Not that she was the kind of woman who was overcome by good looks. Zane hadn't made fun of her like the other boys when she'd been the skinny, freckle-faced, buck-toothed, mouth-full-of-braces girl who'd hung around him like a lovesick puppy.

Nor was she that smitten girl anymore. But she also believed that Zane, while no longer the lanky boy she'd known as a girl, was still honorable and decent. She had to trust her instincts. Her instincts told her that Zane was telling the truth.

"I'll drive," she said, and Zane didn't argue. He looked like death warmed over, making her also believe she might be right about him having been drugged.

She could tell that his greatest fear was that something really awful had happened to Courtney last night. Dakota told herself it was more likely, after what the sheriff had said, that Courtney was up to her pretty little neck in this and not as the victim. Another reason Dakota wanted to find her as quickly as possible.

As she drove, she watched Zane out of the corner of her eye as he began to check the numbers on the cell phone through the plastic bag.

"There are no contact numbers," Zane said. "I get the feeling this is a fairly new phone, since there are so few calls and messages. The last outgoing call was…" He read off the number.

"That's the number at my ranch from when Courtney called last night. Do you recognize any of the other numbers?"

"As for incoming, there are calls and messages from you and Arlene Evans Monroe. I had asked her to call Courtney and get back to me when she heard from her." He studied the numbers for a moment. "Otherwise there are two incoming calls from numbers that I don't recognize. Courtney returned one of those calls, but not the most recent one."

Dakota realized she hadn't told Zane about the phone call earlier. "Someone was looking for her. Before the sheriff left your house, Courtney's cell phone rang. I answered it. I could hear breathing on the other end of the line, but the person didn't say anything before hanging up."

"Courtney? If she was the one who called the sheriff about a disturbance at my house," he said, his brows furrowing.

"Or someone else looking for Courtney."

"Do you recognize either of these numbers?" He read the numbers off to her.

"Sorry, they don't sound familiar. There's a notebook and pen in the glove box," she told him as they neared town.

Zane jotted down the numbers as Dakota pulled into the back of the hospital.

Whitehorse County Hospital was small. As they walked in the back door, Zane spotted Dr. Buck Carrey. He looked more like a rancher than a doctor. A big man, he had a weathered face wrinkled from the sun and from smiling. His gray hair was uncharacteristically long for Whitehorse and pulled back in a ponytail. Today he was wearing jeans, boots and a Western shirt, with his white Stetson cocked back on his head.

He greeted Zane warmly, then shook hands with Dakota, whom he hadn't had the pleasure of meeting before, and invited them into his office. "You said this was a confidential matter?" he asked, closing the door.

Dakota listened while Zane gave an abbreviated version of what they needed. Doc raised a brow when Zane showed him the phone. "Let's start with the blood test. As for the DNA, I need something to compare it to."

"I'm her sister. Well, half sister. Will that work?"

"Close enough." Doc left and came back with the items he needed to do both tests. He took blood from Zane, then a swab of Dakota's mouth and another swab of blood from the phone.

"I'll have to get back to you on your blood test," he told Zane. "Same with the blood on the phone." Doc seemed to study Zane's scratches for a moment. "You sure you don't want the sheriff in on this?"

"If we can't find Courtney, we'll go to the sheriff," Dakota promised. Her sister was in trouble, she'd bet on that. But she feared it was Courtney's own making.

"I'M SORRY ABOUT ALL THIS," Zane said as they left the hospital. "First your father's death, then a sister you never knew you had and now this."

Dakota shrugged as she opened her pickup door and slid behind the wheel. "I think what hurt the most was that I'd always wanted a sister and apparently I've had one since I was two—I just didn't know it."

"Why do you think your father kept it from you?"

She shook her head. "Guilt maybe. Everyone says he adored my mother, but when she got sick, I don't think he could handle it."

"I can't imagine your father living a double life, not the way he felt about your mother." He also couldn't imagine Clay Lansing keeping all of this from his daughter. There had to be more to the story. "So what do you know about Courtney's mother?"

"Nothing, really," Dakota said. "Courtney said she died and that she doesn't like to talk about it."

"Did she mention where she was raised, at least?"

"Great Falls. She wasn't even that far away, just a few hours. My father must have seen her when he went there, since she was at the hospital when he died."

"He died in Great Falls?" Zane asked in surprise.

Dakota nodded and seemed to concentrate on her driving. "All of it has come as such a shock—his death, Courtney, the lie he lived all these years." He could hear the hurt in her voice. "She had more time with him at the end than I did," Dakota said, voicing her pain.

"If she's telling the truth," Zane said as he looked over at her. "You suspected something about her story was a lie, didn't you?"

She glanced at him in surprise.

He smiled. "I know you, Dakota. You wouldn't have believed me so quickly if you didn't suspect your sister was up to something." True, they hadn't seen each other in years, but in so many ways she was that kid he knew from the rodeo grounds. She'd always seemed too smart for her own good.

"If you're right and you were set up, then Courtney is in on it," Dakota said. "I can't imagine any other reason she would sign up for Arlene's rural dating service. One look at her tells me she's never had trouble finding a date."

Zane had been one of those men. He cursed himself for it. "I need to see her room where she was staying."

"She's not there," Dakota said. "I checked and her car wasn't there before I came looking for you."

"She might have dumped her car somewhere."

"Why would she do that?"

He shook his head. "Why would she pretend we had a date and possibly drug me?"

"You don't know she was the one who signed you up for Arlene's rural dating service," Dakota pointed out.

"No, but she had to be in on it. That's the only thing that makes any sense. You didn't check to make sure she wasn't at home, a friend maybe had given her a ride home?"

Dakota shook her head. "She doesn't have any friends here."

"That you know of," Zane said. "Let's try her room first. If she set me up…"

"You think she's cleared out."

"Yeah, that's exactly what I'm thinking. I'm sure there's more, but I have a feeling this next part is her being scarce until the other shoe drops," he said.

THEY REACHED CHINOOK, a small, old town along the railroad, down the Highline from Whitehorse. She turned north on a dirt road toward the Lansing ranch, traveling through the rolling prairie.

It had been a clear blue day, the kind that are almost blinding. Now the sun had dipped behind the Bear Paw Mountains, the sky a silken blue-gray and still cloudless. A meadowlark sang a song that traveled along with them as she drove.

"You say she doesn't have any friends," Zane said as he watched the countryside roll by and tried to get a clear picture of what Courtney Baxter was really like. He couldn't shake the feeling that he hadn't been out with the "real" Courtney last night. "No one you've seen her with, no phone calls?"

Dakota shook her head.

"When I woke up and Courtney was gone, I just assumed she'd left on her own," he said. "But what if there'd been someone else with her at my house last night after I passed out?"

He felt her studying him again, stealing glances at him as she drove. "Dakota, you know me. I wouldn't have hurt her."

She let out a breath. "I know."

"Thank you for believing in me. I suspect whatever this is, Courtney isn't in it alone and I have a bad feeling your sister doesn't realize how dangerous the person she got involved with really is."

"Oh, I don't know about that. I get the feeling Courtney can take care of herself."

Dakota drove past the large old, white, single-story ranch house to the small matching guesthouse out back. Zane remembered when they were kids and Dakota had told him that her father had built a house on the ranch for her to stay in when she reached sixteen. He recalled her excitement because she was like him. She never wanted to leave the ranch; she just didn't want to live at home.

But something had changed for her to end up in New Mexico, engaged to a guy involved in investment managing.

Zane saw as they climbed out of the pickup that Courtney's compact car was nowhere in sight.

Dakota knocked at the front door. "Courtney?"

He held his breath, praying she would open the door. Dakota knocked again, then pulled out a key and opened the door.

As the door swung in, Zane caught the scent of perfume, the familiarity of it making him a little sick to his stomach and increasing his dread. What had happened last night? The harder he tried to remember, the worse he felt.

The guesthouse was small, one bedroom, one bath with a kitchenette and living area. The bedroom door was ajar. Dakota stepped over to it, carefully pushing the door all the way open to expose an empty, unmade bed.

"It doesn't look like she's been back," Dakota said as he headed over to the closet and eased the door open.

Only a handful of clothes hung there. He frowned and moved to the chest of drawers. The top drawer held a few undergarments. The next drawer had even less, only a couple of tank tops and pajama bottoms. The third drawer had two pairs of jeans, and the bottom drawer was empty.

He closed the last drawer and turned to look at Dakota. "What woman has so few clothes?"

She shrugged. "Maybe this is all she owns."

"Or maybe she left most of her belongings somewhere else. Does she have a job?"

"She said she's been looking locally."

He smiled at that. "Not looking very hard, right?"

Dakota sighed. "I got the feeling she was waiting for me to offer her half the ranch."

If Courtney Baxter really was Clay Lansing's love child, then she could probably legally force Dakota to split the ranch and the rough stock business with her. He swore under his breath. How could Clay have done this to Dakota? Worse, he'd kept her sister from her—and let Dakota learn about her after he was gone. Didn't he realize the repercussions of his actions?

Zane moved to the bed. A clock radio sat on one of the bedside tables, nothing else. He bent down to look under the bed and was hit again with the smell of Courtney's perfume. For a moment he thought he would be sick. He stilled his stomach and squinted into the darkness under the bed.

Something glinted. Reaching in, he felt the cool, weathered vinyl surface, found the handle and pulled the old suitcase from under the bed.

He glanced at Dakota.

"Maybe you'd better make sure it isn't ticking before you open it," she said.

He popped the latches on each side. The suitcase fell open.

EMMA CHISHOLM GLANCED OUT the window, surprised to see Mrs. Crowley silhouetted against the fading twilight.

Instinctively, Emma stepped back, afraid the woman might have seen her. She was relieved when she stole another glance and saw that Mrs. Crowley had her back to the house.

What was she doing out there? The woman never went outside. At least not that Emma had ever noticed.

Peering around the edge of the curtain, it took her a moment to realize the housekeeper was on a cell phone. Emma had never seen her make or take a call. No cell phone had ever rung while Mrs. Crowley was working. Emma was actually surprised that the housekeeper even owned one.

She couldn't help but wonder who the woman was talking to. Mrs. Crowley made it clear she had no one who would interfere with her ability to stay at the ranch and work every day except one each week.

When pinned down, the housekeeper had said she

was widowed, no children. She'd quickly made it clear she thought Emma had stepped over some invisible line by even asking.

"It could be a friend," Emma muttered to herself. But even as she said it, she had her doubts. "Maybe a friend from before the accident."

That was something else that Mrs. Crowley made clear she wasn't going to talk about.

"People don't just stare at me," she said, her voice sharp with bitterness and anger. "They want to know what happened. Like vultures, they would love to hear every horrible detail." Mrs. Crowley's one good eye glinted like granite. "Well, they won't be hearing it from me and neither will you."

With that, she'd turned and limped off.

Emma watched now from the edge of the curtain as Mrs. Crowley finished her phone call and stood for a long moment as if admiring what little remained of the sunset.

As she turned to come back to the house, her gaze rose to the second floor as though she sensed Emma watching her.

Emma jerked back, heart hammering. The last thing she wanted Mrs. Crowley to think was that she was spying on her, true or not.

After a moment, Emma dared to take another peek. Mrs. Crowley was still standing in the same spot. The harsh glow of the sunset fell across the woman's disfigured face. She was smiling her crooked half smile, her gaze mocking as she looked up at the second-floor window, making sure that Emma knew she'd been caught spying on her.

Chapter Five

Empty. The suitcase was empty? Dakota laughed, letting out the breath she'd been holding. She'd been so afraid of what they were going to find. "It's just an old suitcase. Looks like it belonged to another generation."

"Like her mother?" Zane said with the lift of an eyebrow.

"More like her grandmother." Dakota leaned over it and caught a whiff of stale air that reminded her of her own grandmother. "My nana had a similar suitcase. It even smelled a little like this one."

The suitcase had been expensive because it had been made to withstand even a fall from a plane, supposedly. She realized what Zane was getting at. These particular suitcases, because of their expense, often had the name and address of the owner engraved on a plate inside.

She peered into the silky lining. Her fingers brushed over something cold and slick at the edge. She looked up at Zane and smiled as her fingers found the engraving. Turning the suitcase to the light, she read, "Frances Dean, 212 W. River St., Great Falls, Montana."

"Don't get too excited. Your sister could have picked this suitcase up at a garage sale," Zane said.

"Or this could be a relative." As she started to pull her hand back from the metal tag, her fingers caught on the lining. It tore. When she looked down she saw why her fingers had caught. The lining appeared to have been cut.

"Well, would you look at that," Zane said as he peered into the space between the lining and the hard cover of the suitcase.

He reached in and drew out a thin stack of hundred-dollar bills.

Dakota felt her eyes widen. "Do you think Courtney knew the money was in there?"

Zane sent her an are-you-serious look. "Who do you think put this money in there? The bills are new."

"How much is it?" Dakota asked as he began to dig out the stacks.

"I'd say at least ten thousand."

Ten thousand dollars? "I don't understand this. Courtney let me think she was broke. She'd been borrowing money from me until she could find a job, she said."

Zane shook his head sympathetically. "Apparently your sister took us both in. Any idea where she might have gotten it?" He tossed the money into the suitcase, snapped it shut and grabbed the handle.

"Probably from whoever put her up to whatever no good she's involved in," she said, still in shock. Courtney had played them both. "You're taking the suitcase?"

He smiled. "Looks like we're going to Great Falls to find out if Frances Dean knows where we can find Courtney. In the meantime, we have the money. Which means it's only a matter of time before Courtney comes looking for *us*."

DAKOTA GLANCED AT HER WATCH. It was several hours to Great Falls. There was no way they would get there in time to talk to anyone—at least not tonight.

"Don't you think we should wait and go in the morning?" she asked.

He shook his head. "I'm afraid of what Courtney will do next if we wait. This way we can try to track down whoever lives at the address on the suitcase first thing in the morning. You don't have to come if you don't want to."

No chance of that. "Just let me go over to the house and throw a few things into a bag."

"Dakota," he said as she started to turn away. "Thank you. I'm glad you're in this with me."

She felt a stab of guilt. *Tell him about the diary. He needs to know that you're the one who involved him in this.*

"Give me ten minutes," she said, and hurried across the yard, telling herself that Courtney had to have more of a motive for involving Zane than sibling rivalry. Dakota hadn't even seen Zane in years.

But she realized as she packed a few items of clothing in an overnight bag that Courtney might be using Zane because she felt cheated. Maybe she thought she should have had everything Dakota had since she didn't get to live on the ranch with their father.

Who knows what made Courtney do what she has, let alone what she is planning to do next, Dakota thought. Zane wasn't the only one worried about that.

On impulse, Dakota went into her father's den. Once she'd realized that Courtney had been in the house and taken her old diary, she'd been so upset that she'd only given a cursory look for what else her sister might have taken.

Now she had a bad feeling as she went behind her father's desk and saw that the bottom drawer was partially open. There were gouges in the wood where someone had used something sharp to break the lock.

With trembling fingers, Dakota pulled the drawer out, knowing what had been inside was gone—and who had taken it.

ZANE FOUND DAKOTA standing in her father's study. He tried to read her expression, but the afternoon light cast her face in shadow.

"Is everything all right?" he asked.

She looked up and seemed surprised to see him, as if she'd forgotten about him. He figured she was thinking about her father, missing him. He regretted interrupting her but they had to get going.

"I hate to rush you—"

"You're not," she said quickly. "I'm ready."

He saw her overnight bag by the door and picked it up. "Anything else?"

She shook her head. She seemed distracted, but he didn't press her as they walked out to her pickup.

"I thought we'd go to my place if you don't mind. I can pack a few things and we can take my truck. I'm feeling much better."

"Whatever you think," she said. He could tell wherever her mind had been, it was still there.

They were both quiet on the drive back to his house. It wasn't until they were on the road to Great Falls that Dakota broke the silence.

"You think Courtney was paid to set you up?" she asked.

That's exactly what he thought. But ten thousand dollars? That was a lot of money. Way more money than he was worth setting up.

"I just can't understand why anyone might have paid your sister to do this," he said. "Especially that *much* money. And other than me looking like I got into a catfight and feeling hungover, what was the point? Unless she was supposed to kill me...."

"Don't say that. Even if Courtney drugged you, I'm sure she didn't mean to take it that far."

Zane looked over at Dakota. "I thought her phone call to you was part of the setup, but what if she really was in trouble? What if she *was* supposed to kill me and couldn't go through with it? That could explain why she's disappeared. She's hiding from whoever paid her to do the job."

"Why would she want you dead? And why didn't she come back for the money? Unless the money wasn't her real reason for what she did."

"That's why I don't think she acted alone. But it has to be someone with a grudge against me." He glanced over at Dakota and gave her a crooked grin. "As I recall, you had quite a temper when I riled you up. You out to get me, Dakota?"

"That's not funny." She turned away.

Zane stared out at the Montana evening as they drove through the rolling green prairie. This was such a beautiful time in this part of Montana. The mountain ranges were capped with pristine white snow from the last snowfall in the high country. The snow and deep blue mountains were in stark contrast to the lush green of the prairie. Creeks ran wild with the beginning of summer runoff and there was a feeling of new beginnings in the air.

It was the kind of evening he loved and yet he was too aware of the woman sitting just inches away from him.

Dakota didn't seem to be aware of him. Something was bothering her. But apparently it wasn't anything she wanted to share with him. He'd been joking earlier about her being a part of this. What if she was?

DAKOTA WAS FURIOUS with her half sister and couldn't wait to find her. If Courtney even really was her sister.

She'd been so shocked when she'd first learned about Courtney that she now realized she should have demanded more proof. All she'd had was a glance at Courtney's birth certificate. Once she'd seen her father's name and his signature...

Why hadn't she questioned that the birth certificate might have been a fake? She'd invited Courtney to come live at the ranch—a stranger. Now she regretted that terribly. What else had Courtney taken from the house? Dakota didn't know. Just as she didn't know why Courtney was doing this or what she had to gain other than possibly ten thousand dollars.

Dakota had put off telling Zane what she'd discovered missing in her father's den. She needed time to let all of this sink in so she could sort it out. At least that's what she told herself. But she hadn't sorted it out and Zane needed to know. He already suspected that Courtney was supposed to kill him last night. What if he was right? What if Courtney tried again?

"There's something I need to tell you," she said as

they left the meandering Milk River behind and headed south toward the Missouri—and the city of Great Falls. "I told you Courtney took something of mine."

"But you don't want to tell me what she took."

She knew it was silly not to confess about the diary. But she was embarrassed by all the things she'd written. With luck, she would get it back and Zane would never have to know.

Letting out a breath, she said, "Courtney took some old photos along with a pistol my father kept in the bottom drawer of his desk. It's a .45."

Zane let out a curse. "You're just now telling me about this?"

"I didn't check until I went in to pack for this trip. But after everything that has happened…"

"Wait," he said, holding up a hand. "You came looking for her because of something she took, right? Something that had you upset enough that you actually believed I had been set up."

"Courtney had also taken some personal things of mine, including some old photographs."

"Old photographs?"

"Some of my father at several rodeos and one of you and me."

He blinked at her. "She took a gun and a photo of your father and one of the two of *us?*"

"I'm sorry. I should have told you."

"You think she *targeted* me because of a photograph of the two of us? That's why you believed me! That's why you're so anxious to find her and why you didn't want the sheriff involved." He shot her a look, then laughed. "Dakota, you aren't responsible for this. Seriously. You can't believe that's all that's behind this."

She shook her head, feeling close to tears.

He grinned. "You had a photo of the two of us?"

She brushed at the tears. "It was a good one of *me*. You just happened to be in the picture," she said, and looked away, but she knew he was still grinning. Just as she knew he was wrong. She *was* responsible somehow for what was happening.

EMMA CHISHOLM HEARD the steady throb of an engine and slipped out of bed. At the window, she saw one of the ranch pickups pull around to the side of the house. She glanced back at the clock beside the bed. 2:11 a.m.

As the driver cut the engine, she thought it must be one of her six stepsons. But since they each had their own homes it would be unusual for one of them to come by this late—unless there was trouble.

Emma was surprised when Mrs. Crowley stepped from the pickup.

"I will need a vehicle at my disposal," Mrs. Crowley had announced the day she'd appeared at their door. "I'd prefer not to drive my own car given the condition of your…rural roads."

Emma had to shoot Hoyt a warning look to keep him from saying what she knew he was thinking.

"There is always a ranch pickup around. Will that do?" Emma had asked the woman. She was determined to make this work, one way or the other.

Mrs. Crowley had turned her nose up, but said that would have to do.

"Who the hell does she think she is?" Hoyt had demanded later when the two of them had gone out to the barn. That was where they escaped to, knowing that Mrs. Crowley wouldn't set foot out there. "If you

knew what I was paying her…" He'd broken off, looking chagrined.

"It's all right. I know she didn't come cheap." Emma
appreciated that he'd gone to so much trouble to make
sure she was safe. She knew that Hoyt would pay any
price for her safety.

"Yeah, well, the problem is that no one wants to work
for a murderer. Even an acquitted one."

"Stop that," Emma had snapped. "The problem is
that no one wants to be more than a mile from a mall."
She'd laughed. "They just don't realize that there isn't
a mall anywhere that can beat being out here."

Hoyt had smiled as he'd cupped his hand behind
her neck and pulled her close. "How did I get so lucky
with you?"

Emma could have told him, since he was the sexi-
est man she'd ever known and the biggest-hearted. Any
woman would have been a fool not to love this man and
appreciate the land that he loved. But she'd bit back her
words. His first wife, Laura, hadn't appreciated either.

Now Emma wondered what Mrs. Crowley was doing
out at this time of night. She didn't seem like the type
of person to close down the bars in Whitehorse, but as
secretive as she was, who knew her type?

The woman reached back into the pickup cab for the
large purse she carried. It was more like a carpetbag,
and tonight it seemed fuller than ever. What did Mrs.
Crowley carry in there, anyway?

With a start, Emma realized that the woman could
have a secret life at night. It wasn't the first time she'd
taken off after supper without a word. She could have
come in late all those nights as well and Emma just
hadn't heard her before.

Still, as she watched Mrs. Crowley carefully close the pickup door so as not to disturb anyone and then disappear into the lower floor of the house, Emma was amazed at the woman's stamina. As hard as she worked, refusing even a break, how could she stay out this late and still be up before the sun in the morning?

On her day off, Mrs. Crowley stayed in her room, not even interested in food. Everything about the woman was a mystery to Emma. The weather was beautiful this time of year and yet she showed no interest in the land right outside her window. In fact, the drapes on her windows were always closed.

Maybe the sunlight bothered her burned skin and eye, Emma thought, chastising herself for finding fault with the woman. Mrs. Crowley had made it possible for Hoyt to return to work with his sons. No more babysitting Emma day after day.

Emma stepped back from the window, telling herself it was none of her business. Climbing back into bed beside Hoyt, she snuggled closer. It didn't matter what the woman did late at night or on her day off in her room.

But Emma had a terrible time getting back to sleep. What did they really know about the woman who lived in their house with them?

ZANE FROWNED AS HE TOOK IN the house. The house at 212 W. River Street was a narrow, two-story wood structure that had once been white before all the paint had peeled off. Like the neighborhood, it had an abandoned look.

He glanced over at Dakota. They hadn't said much since he'd knocked on her motel door to see if she was ready for breakfast. Last night when they had stopped at a motel, it had felt awkward.

He'd stopped thinking of her as a kid and that was part of the problem. She seemed embarrassed and clearly hated admitting that she'd kept a picture of the two of them from when she'd had a crush on him. He couldn't help being flattered that she'd kept it. He'd always pretended to his friends that Dakota hanging around bugged him. But he'd been sorry when her father had moved his rough stock part of the ranch to New Mexico and Dakota had gone with it.

Right now, he was glad that they had that history together. True, she had her reasons for wanting to find her sister, but he doubted she would have believed him about Courtney otherwise. Just as he was sure she wouldn't have wanted his help if she didn't somehow feel responsible.

But Zane didn't believe that Courtney Baxter had come after him because of some photo she'd seen of the two of them from years ago. If Courtney wanted to hurt Dakota, the best way was to try to take Lansing Ranch. Not only would it kill Dakota to lose it, the ranch was worth a lot of money, not to mention the rough stock business. Worth a lot more than ten thousand dollars.

The question still remained though: Why come after *him?* What was to be gained other than the money?

The money alone meant Courtney hadn't come up with this by herself. He suspected Dakota was right about the phone call from her sister. Maybe Courtney really had been scared and crying out for help. Or maybe that had been part of the setup. Maybe Courtney wanted to throw the two of them together. He felt foolish this morning for ever suspecting Dakota.

Now, as they climbed out of his pickup, he feared the address they'd found in the suitcase was a dead end.

He'd hoped the name plaque might lead them somewhere, but it appeared the house was empty and had been for some time.

Everything around the house was overgrown to the point that the vegetation was slowly taking over the structure. No one had lived here in a very long time.

"Hello?" The voice was small, just like the woman whose head barely topped the fence between the properties. "Can I help you?" the neighbor asked.

She had a shock of white hair that seemed to float like a halo around her head. Dressed in worn blue overalls, a red long-sleeved shirt and tennis shoes, the woman stepped out from behind the fence. She surveyed them with keen blue eyes. In her hands was a hedge trimmer.

"You live next door?" Zane asked, unable to hide his surprise. He'd thought for sure that the entire neighborhood was abandoned.

"Have for almost ninety years," she said proudly. "I was born here. But you're not looking for me, are you?"

"We were looking for Frances Dean," Dakota said, stepping forward.

"Dead, I'm afraid," the woman said. "Entire neighborhood's been dying off for years now. I'm about the only one left. A developer is just waiting for me to die so he can tear down what houses haven't fallen down and build a bunch of condos."

From her tone it was clear she was holding out until her last breath. "You aren't with that low-life vulture, are you?"

"No," Dakota assured her. "Did you know Frances Dean well?"

"All my life."

"Did she happen to have a daughter?" Zane asked.

"Camilla," the woman said with a nod. "Married one of the Hugheses. Widowed, I'd heard. Nice girl."

"Do you know if she has a daughter by the name of Courtney?" Dakota asked.

"Can't say. Last I heard of Frances she was worried because Camilla was having trouble getting pregnant." The old woman shrugged. She eyed Zane's scratches. "You look like you tangled with a rosebush. Did that once. Nasty thorns on those little devils."

"Well, thank you for your time, Mrs...."

"Miss. Abigail Warden." They introduced themselves. "Pleased to meet you. I suppose I should ask why you're looking for Frances's kin."

"A woman named Courtney Baxter has gone missing. We're trying to find her mother and we have reason to believe she might be related to Frances Dean," Dakota said.

"Might be. Might not. Good luck to you." Miss Warden turned back to the hedge with her clippers. As they left, they heard the *snap, snap, snap* of her blades.

"You know they're going to find that poor old woman under that hedge someday," Dakota said.

"There are worse ways to go," Zane said as they got back into the pickup. When his cell phone rang he pulled it out of his jacket pocket, hoping it was Courtney.

"It's Doc," he said to Dakota, then snapped open the phone. "Hello?"

"I got back your blood test," Doc said. "There were a variety of drugs in your system."

"One that would cause memory loss?"

"Several that would. You're lucky that mix of drugs didn't kill you."

Maybe it was supposed to. "What about the DNA on the phone?"

"I put a rush on it. We can get a basic preliminary test within twenty-four hours, so we should be hearing soon."

Zane thanked him and hung up, more upset than he wanted Dakota to know. Her sister had targeted him. To what end, he couldn't imagine. In fact, knowing what he did now, he was surprised he hadn't heard from Courtney. He wouldn't have put some sort of blackmail past her.

Of course, there was another option. That the reason Courtney hadn't turned up was because of whoever had put her up to this. Someone she hadn't trusted entirely and that's why she'd taken the gun from Clay Lansing's desk drawer. It made sense—if Courtney had feared she was going to need it.

Chapter Six

At a convenience store, Dakota borrowed a phone book. There were a half dozen Hugheses in the book, but only one C. Hughes. She jotted down the address, opting not to call first.

Fortunately, when they arrived at the address, there was a car in the driveway.

The first thing Dakota noticed about Camilla Hughes when she answered the door was how little she looked like Courtney. Camilla was a petite woman in her late fifties with dark brown hair and eyes. There was a cultured softness to both her manner and her speech. Again nothing like Courtney.

"May I help you?" Camilla asked, looking from Dakota to Zane and back.

"Hi, we're friends of Courtney's, just passing through town and we were hoping she might be around," Dakota said.

"Oh, I'm so sorry," Camilla said. "Courtney isn't here. Did she tell you she was going to be here?"

Dakota stole a look at Zane, pleased that she'd been right about the suitcase. Still, Courtney's lack of resemblance to this woman worried her. That and the fact that their last names were different.

"No," Dakota said. "Since we were in town we thought we'd just take the chance that she might be."

"Have you tried calling her?" Camilla asked.

"I'm not sure I have her number with me," Dakota said.

"Come in." Camilla waved them into her spotless, well-furnished home. "I'll get it for you." She went to a small desk just off the living room. As she was writing a number down for them on a notepad, Dakota moved to the fireplace.

There was a line of framed family photographs along the mantel. Dakota picked one up and turned it so Zane could see the woman in the studio shot. It was the same woman who'd showed up at Dakota's father's funeral, the same one Zane had taken to dinner last night. Courtney Baxter.

The other photographs were all of Camilla, a tall slim man with red, thinning hair and beautiful Courtney at various ages over the years. Dakota put the photo back on the mantel as Camilla Hughes came over to hand her the piece of notepaper.

The cell phone number Camilla had written down was different from the phone they'd found under Zane's bed. *Was that phone even Courtney's?* she wondered with surprise.

"Your name is Hughes but your daughter goes by Baxter?" Zane asked, expressing what Dakota had been wondering.

All the color washed from Camilla Hughes's face in an instant. She took a couple of steps to the side and lowered herself into a chair. "That's the name she's going by?"

He nodded, and Dakota could see that like her, he

was surprised that the woman had become so upset. As Camilla waved Zane into a seat across from her, Dakota joined him on the couch. "I'm sorry. I didn't know she was doing that. Baxter was her biological mother's name."

"She's *adopted?*" Dakota asked, unable to contain her surprise even with the obvious difference in appearance between mother and daughter. It explained why Courtney didn't resemble either her mother or father, though. But then Courtney didn't resemble their father or Dakota either. That meant she must have taken after her mother. Her *biological* mother?

"Yes, Marcus and I adopted her when she was only a few days old," Camilla said, still looking shaken.

"Her mother couldn't keep her?" Dakota had to ask, wondering about the mystery woman who'd had an affair with her father.

Camilla looked even more upset. "A nurse told me in private that the mother didn't want her, wanted nothing to do with her." Camilla instantly bit her tongue. "I've never told Courtney that, of course. I shouldn't have told you either. I'm just upset that Courtney has chosen to go by a woman's name who didn't want her."

"It's all right," Zane said. "I'm sorry this news has upset you so."

"Courtney has always known she was adopted, but she never seemed to have any interest in finding her birth parents," Camilla said. "I didn't even know that she knew her birth mother's last name." She seemed to shake herself out of her thoughts. "I'm sorry, but how is it that you know my daughter?"

Dakota felt telling Camilla about her relationship to Courtney would upset the woman further. Not to mention finding the ten thousand dollars tucked in the suitcase and the fact that her daughter seemed to be missing.

"We only recently met her," Dakota said. "Your daughter has been staying with me up north of Chinook."

"Staying with *you?*" Camilla asked, frowning.

"In my guesthouse. When we met, she said she needed somewhere to stay until she could find a job and get a place of her own," Dakota said.

Camilla shook her head in obvious bewilderment. "A few weeks ago she told me she was going on a short trip. She came over and borrowed her grandmother's suitcase. I haven't heard from her since and she hasn't been answering her phone...." She frowned. "If she's been staying up north, then why were you looking for her here?"

"She didn't come home the last two nights," Dakota said. "We were coming to Great Falls and thought she might be here. I wanted to let her know that a man at one of the jobs she'd applied for wanted to do a second interview."

She hated lying but the explanation seemed to relieve Camilla a little—that is, until she took a good look at Zane's scratched face.

"Rosebushes," Dakota said.

"Are there any high school friends or college friends she might be staying with?" Zane asked.

"She really hasn't been in touch with any of them that I know of." Camilla looked close to tears. "They all have jobs. Courtney was still trying to figure out what she wanted to do." She pursed her lips. Dakota could tell that she hated telling complete strangers such personal information. She only did so because of her obvious concern for her adopted daughter.

"Is it possible one of her birth parents contacted *her?*" Dakota asked.

Camilla seemed surprised by the question. "I hadn't thought of that. Maybe that's where she is now." She brightened at the thought. "Now that you mention it, Courtney hasn't been herself lately. She's been distant, secretive. I thought it was just growing pains, a sign that she wanted to be more independent from me."

"You said 'lately,'" Zane asked. "The past few weeks?"

Camilla nodded. "She even purchased a second cell phone a couple weeks ago. I thought that was odd. Clearly she didn't want me to know who she was calling—or who was calling her. I thought it might be a young man she wasn't ready to tell me about."

"Do you have that number?"

She shook her head. "She said she needed space. We've always been so close. Marcus and I spoiled her, no doubt about that. But maybe we should have pushed her out of the nest sooner. Then after Marcus died...I know I leaned on Courtney more than I should have."

"What about Courtney's birth father?" Dakota asked, trying to keep the emotion out of her voice.

Camilla shook her head. "The nurse I talked to didn't know anything about him."

"Isn't his name on the birth certificate?" Zane asked.

"No. Courtney's birth certificate shows my name and Marcus's."

"I'm confused," Dakota said. "Where was Courtney born?"

"It was a home birth somewhere in Montana. We got

a call. We didn't even realize that anyone knew how much we wanted a child and hadn't been able to have one of our own." She looked worried now. "It wasn't through an adoption agency exactly."

The Whitehorse Sewing Circle, Dakota thought. That group of old women had been secretly orchestrating adoptions for years. "Did your daughter get a quilt shortly after she was born?"

"Why, yes," Camilla said.

"So you don't know the names of her birth parents?" Zane asked.

"Just the mother's name. Lorraine Baxter."

Dakota recalled now that she had only glanced at the mother's name on the birth certificate that Courtney had shown her. It could have been Lorraine Baxter.

"You never tried to find her then?" she asked.

"Good heavens, no! That's why I was shocked when you told me that Courtney was going by the woman's name. You must be right about the woman contacting her. But why now? She didn't want her when she was born, why would she contact her now?"

Dakota knew there could be all kinds of reasons. She feared, though, given what they now knew, the reason wasn't a good one.

"When she picked up the suitcase, she didn't say where she was going?" Zane asked.

"No. That was something else that worried me. She said she had something she needed to do." Camilla's voice broke and tears welled in her dark eyes. "When she left, she hugged me and told me how much she loved me. But I had the most horrible feeling that she wasn't ever coming back, that she was telling me goodbye."

ZANE COULD SEE THAT DAKOTA was upset as they left. She'd promised to let Camilla know if they heard anything from Courtney.

"That poor woman," Dakota said as they climbed back into the pickup. "What if something bad has happened to my sister?"

"If she *is* your sister," Zane said.

Dakota frowned. "Courtney offered to take a DNA test anytime I wanted, but I didn't see any reason since she'd already showed me the birth certificate with my father's name and signature."

"I suspect that birth certificate could be a fake."

"I'm not sure how the Whitehorse Sewing Circle operates. But wouldn't there be an original birth certificate with the birth parents' names on it?"

He shrugged. "Maybe. If the mother thought she was going to keep the baby, then changed her mind, and the women of the Whitehorse Sewing Circle found the Hugheses, who were ready to adopt the baby, and saw that another birth certificate replaced the first. You heard what she said about the quilt. The Circle makes every baby it handles a quilt."

"If the mother didn't want the baby, then why would she keep the original birth certificate?" Dakota asked.

"Maybe she thought it would come in handy someday."

"Those women in the Circle have placed a lot of babies illegally and gotten away with it. If Courtney was my father's daughter then she was probably born somewhere near Whitehorse. Anyone with relatives or friends in Great Falls could have known about the Hugheses and their desire for a baby."

Zane nodded. "Your father would have known about

the Whitehorse Sewing Circle, which means that Courtney's mother would have probably known as well."

"Or maybe he sent her to the women so she could get rid of the baby," Dakota said.

"You know your father would never have done that."

"Do I? What if it was a woman he never should have gotten involved with?"

"A married woman?"

"Possibly."

Zane shook his head. "We won't know until we find Lorraine Baxter." He started the truck engine and drove, wondering where to go next. "This birth certificate Courtney showed you, did you ask Courtney for a copy?"

"I was so shocked I didn't ask for anything. But why put his name on the birth certificate if he isn't involved in this?"

Zane shot her a look. Was she serious? "He had money, a ranch, a good business."

"Still, Lorraine Baxter would have had to know him. She had to get a copy of his signature if she was going to forge his name. She didn't just pick his name out of thin air."

"Okay, let's say she knew him. Maybe had been intimate with him. Maybe Courtney *is* your half sister. The only way we're ever going to know everything is if we can find this woman. Don't look so skeptical," he said, glancing over at her. "If we're right, she's been in contact with Courtney and recently."

Dakota smiled at him. "You amaze me."

"Really?" he asked, grinning at her.

"You're a lot smarter than you look."

He had to laugh because he knew how he looked

with his face scratched up. He really wanted to find Courtney and get some answers, Dakota's sister or not.

"We need to try the numbers we found on her phone," he said.

"It might not even be Courtney's phone."

"Or it could be the extra phone she bought."

"So Courtney could talk to her birth mother without Camilla knowing about it," Dakota said.

"You're pretty sharp yourself," he joked as he pulled over. No reason to keep driving when they didn't have a clue where to go next.

He shut off the engine and turned to look at Dakota. He still wasn't used to the woman she'd grown into—or his reaction to her. He felt so close to her and yet they hadn't been around each other in years.

"Courtney must have gotten the birth certificate from her biological mother," Dakota said, frowning. "How else could Courtney have known about her birth father? Her adoptive mother didn't know his name and, apparently, neither did the nurse who delivered Courtney."

"If the birth mother was telling the truth and your father is really Courtney's father, then I doubt he ever knew he had a second daughter," Zane said. "I spent a lot of time around your father when I was rodeoing. Your father adored you. I can't believe he didn't have plenty of room for another daughter in his heart. He wouldn't have kept her a secret, and he wouldn't have given her up for adoption."

Her eyes filled with tears. "I want to believe that. I know he had wanted more children. If my mother hadn't gotten sick…"

Zane saw the pain behind the tears. She had hated

the thought that Clay had kept Courtney from her. Dakota had idolized her father. He'd been everything to her even before her mother died. To have a sister sprung on her like this must have been more painful for her than he could imagine.

But if Courtney really was the daughter of Clay Lansing, then her mother had had an affair with him either while his wife was dying of cancer or right after.

Zane just hoped the whole thing was a scam and that Courtney Baxter shared no blood ties with Dakota.

Dakota reached over and took his hand. "Thank you," she said, her voice breaking. "I've been struggling with this for weeks. I hated that I was suspicious of Courtney and I've been so angry with my father for keeping it from me."

Zane squeezed her hand. Leaning toward her, he drew her into his arms. He hadn't planned to kiss her. But at that moment, it seemed the most natural thing in the world.

Her lips parted, her breath warm and sweet. He felt a quiver run through her; his pulse kicked up as his mouth dropped to hers.

Dakota gently pushed him away. "Sorry, but your reputation precedes you."

He heard the slight tremble in her voice. She pulled free of his arms and he leaned back, telling himself he shouldn't have kissed her. Especially given why they were together. Didn't he have enough woman problems right now?

"You're going to believe rumors about me?" he joked as he tried to cover up how even that quick kiss had affected him.

She smiled, but there was hurt in her gaze. "Let's

not forget that you went out with a woman who simply showed up at your door."

"Yeah," he said, sobered by the memory. And not just any woman. Possibly Dakota's half sister. "You make a good argument." His gaze caressed her face for a moment before meeting her eyes. "But that kiss? I was just fulfilling a promise I made you before you moved to New Mexico. Remember?"

DAKOTA FELT HER FACE HEAT with embarrassment. Oh, she remembered all right.

"Don't you want to be the first boy I ever kiss?"

Zane looked down at her, sympathy in his gaze. "Your first kiss should be with someone special."

"That's why I want it to be with you." Her voice cracked, her eyes filling with tears. *"I'm moving away and if you don't kiss me…"*

"Dakota." He touched her shoulder, crouching down so that they were at eye level. His voice was soft. *"That's real sweet, but there are going to be so many boys who want to kiss you. Boys you're going to want to kiss, too."*

"Then will you at least save a kiss for me?"

Zane nodded and smiled, the caring look in his eyes making her love him all the more.

"Promise me that you'll kiss me one day. Promise?"

"I promise."

"I was just a silly kid," she said now.

"Yeah, you were. But you aren't anymore, are you? And I'm not sorry about the kiss."

Courtney's cell phone rang—the one they'd found under Zane's bed and at least believed was hers.

The sound startled Dakota and yet she'd never been

so glad for the interruption. She had wanted Zane Chisholm to kiss her since she was that silly kid who hung around him at the rodeo grounds.

But the phone was a good reminder that Zane had been with her sister two nights ago. She knew his reputation, and while she'd thrown herself at him when she was a girl and he was a teenager, she was no longer that starry-eyed tomboy. And Zane was definitely not that still-innocent teenager.

As for the kiss… Dakota told herself that as nice as it had been, it was just a kiss. But the purring of her pulse beneath her skin, the erratic beat of her heart, the quick breaths, all of those spoke of the true effect that Zane Chisholm's kiss had on her.

Dakota only hoped Zane hadn't noticed. Or if he had, that he thought it was the phone ringing that made her hand tremble as she pulled the bagged phone out of her purse.

She looked down at the phone as it rang again. "It's the same number calling from before, the one that hung up when I answered. What should I do?"

The phone rang a fourth time. "Don't answer it. Maybe they'll leave a message."

The phone rang once more, then fell silent.

SHERIFF MCCALL CRAWFORD stood in front of the mirror, studying her changed figure.

"It's beautiful. *You're* beautiful," her husband, Luke, said as he came up behind her and placed his palms over her bare, round abdomen. He kissed her on the back of the neck, then peeked at her in the mirror.

"Why are you frowning?" he asked.

"Was I?" she asked, quickly checking her expression. "I'm just so…big. I'm going to have to get a new uniform."

"Or you could go ahead and take maternity leave," Luke suggested.

She met his gaze in the mirror. "I have another month before the baby's due." She wasn't telling him anything he didn't already know. McCall turned in his arms to face him. "You want me to quit."

"No, I…" He sighed. "I just don't want anything to happen to you and the baby. I know that is horribly selfish. Sorry. It's just how I feel."

She started to tell him that she was the sheriff and had a job to do and that he knew that when he married her, but she stopped herself. She had to admit that lately she'd been feeling the same way.

She would be out on a call and feel their baby move inside her and all she could think about was that little life. The thought of putting their baby in jeopardy scared her. She didn't want to be afraid to do her job. If that happened, she told herself she would quit.

"Nick will be back in a few days." Her undersheriff would be filling in while she was on maternity leave. "I'll see about taking my leave then."

What she couldn't tell Luke was about her fears. Ruby hadn't been a bad mother, just not a great one. McCall wanted to be a great one.

But that was only one of her fears. She was afraid that she wouldn't want to go back to being sheriff after their daughter was born, that she had worked this hard to be the best law enforcement officer she could only to give it up. She felt torn and hated that feeling. Why couldn't she have it all?

Her cell phone rang.

Luke groaned. "Duty calls."

She kissed him and reached for her phone, listened, then said, "I'll be right there."

As she snapped the phone shut and reached to put on her clothing she saw her husband's expression. "A lime-green compact was found south of town in a ravine," she told him. "I'm sure there is nothing for you to look so worried about."

But as she climbed into her patrol SUV and headed south toward the isolated wilderness of the Missouri Breaks, McCall had a bad feeling about the car and driver.

The deputy had told her the car was registered to a Courtney Hughes. But in the purse found inside, he'd discovered a credit card under the name Courtney Baxter—the woman who'd been seen out with Zane Chisholm two nights ago.

McCall hated to jump to conclusions. But neither Zane Chisholm nor Courtney Baxter had called her back, she reminded herself as she drove the narrow dirt road south into the rugged breaks country.

Chapter Seven

"The caller didn't leave a message," Dakota said after checking. She couldn't help being disappointed, though not surprised.

"If Courtney left that phone under my bed on purpose—"

"Then that was probably her calling before to see if you'd found it," Dakota said.

"If she didn't, then someone else is looking for her. Might as well try the numbers she called and received calls from."

Dakota punched in the last number that had called.

The phone rang four times and went to voice mail. An electronic voice instructed her to leave a message.

She didn't.

She tried the only other different number. A male voice answered on the second ring.

"Where the hell are you?" the man demanded. "You leave in the middle of the night without a word? And what the hell am I supposed to do with your bar tab? If you think I'm picking it up, you're crazy."

Dakota looked over at Zane wide-eyed and mimed, "What do I do?"

"Talk?" he mouthed back.

She opened her mouth, but feared the man would hang up the moment she spoke. She let out a sigh, an impatient one like she'd heard Courtney do numerous times.

Silence.

"You're in trouble, aren't you?" he said, then swore angrily. "I told you not to get involved with these people." *These people?* Silence. "Courtney?"

"You were right," Dakota said, dropping her voice in the hopes she would sound enough like her sister.

Silence. Then he let out a curse. She heard the telltale sound of the phone disconnecting.

"Well," she said after repeating what the man had said, "Courtney's involved in something."

"Yeah, we kind of figured that. Bar tab, huh? Would you recognize the man's voice if you heard it again?"

"I think so."

"Sounds like she hooked up with a bartender at one of the local bars and ran up a tab," Zane said. "We might have to hit the bars."

Dakota nodded as she looked down at the list of phone numbers. "No other numbers we don't know."

THE LIME-GREEN COMPACT CAR was almost hidden in a stand of old junipers at the bottom of the ravine.

McCall found her deputy waiting for her beside a patrol car parked at the side of the road. As she walked over to the edge of the ravine, she noted the tire tracks where the car had gone off the road.

"No skid marks, no sign of the driver trying to brake," the deputy said as he joined her.

"Could have been going too fast and missed the curve, didn't have time to brake," McCall said.

"Yep, could have," he agreed.

That was, if Courtney Baxter had been driving the car.

"Got to wonder what she was doing way out here," the deputy said.

"No sign of the driver?" McCall asked.

The deputy shook his head. "I couldn't find any tracks, but then we had that big storm down this way the other night. Could have covered 'em."

"Let's go see," McCall said, and saw the deputy shoot her a look.

"It's pretty steep," he warned.

She ignored him and started down the slope. It *was* steep, the ground unstable. The dirt moved under her, an avalanche of soil. She began to slide and realized too late how she'd let her pride overrun her good sense.

Fortunately, the embankment ended at the edge of the junipers. She slid to a stop near the bottom of the ravine, grabbed a branch on one of the juniper trees and used it to keep from sliding any farther.

She felt the baby kick and smiled. That had actually been fun, she thought as she moved around the junipers to the side of the lime-green vehicle.

One glance told her what she already knew. The car was empty.

McCall glanced around, checking the ground for footprints. The only ones in the dirt were the deputy's. Either he was right about the storm erasing them, or no one had been in the car when it had gone off the road.

McCall pulled on the latex gloves from her pocket and opened the driver's side door. She caught the smell of something sour and felt her stomach roil. She'd been this way since the beginning of her pregnancy. No three months of morning sickness for her. Every smell affected her.

As she drew back from the odor, she noticed that the keys were in the ignition and the car was in Neutral. She checked the seat. It was pushed all the way back.

Whoever had last driven this car was long-legged, possibly longer-legged than Courtney Hughes aka Courtney Baxter.

McCall suspected that someone had pushed the car off the road into the deep ravine. Hoping it wouldn't be found?

Hard to hide a lime-green anything, though.

Holding her breath, she leaned into the car to check under the seats. She found the bloody rag stuffed under the passenger seat. It was wrapped around something heavy. Carefully, she turned back the dark-stained edges of the rag to reveal a gun.

The grip was stained with what appeared to be blood. The smell of the dried blood turned her stomach. She quickly wrapped the gun back up, leaving it on the floor of the passenger side, and stepped away from the car.

Taking large gulps of fresh air, McCall fought to keep her breakfast down. The last thing she wanted to do was contaminate the scene. She took a few more deep breaths, steadied herself, then called to the deputy to contact the state crime lab.

After a few moments, she made the climb back up to her patrol SUV. The baby kicked again. She placed her hand on her stomach, felt the movement and made a promise to her infant and her husband that she would stop this—as soon as the undersheriff got back. Just a few more days.

"Everything is going to be fine," she whispered as much to herself as her baby.

But she feared that wasn't the case for Courtney Baxter.

DAKOTA DROVE PART OF THE WAY back to the Lansing ranch while Zane slept.

She'd had a lot of time to think. Too much time apparently, since she'd found herself reliving Zane's kiss. A part of her wished she hadn't cut it off when she had. Another part of her, the logical, smart part, thought she should have stopped him sooner.

She was more than aware of Zane's reputation with women. She had no intention of becoming one of them. Last night, lying in her motel room bed, knowing he was only feet away in the next room, she'd had a terrible time getting to sleep.

Dakota hated that he still had that effect on her. She felt like that silly girl who'd trailed after him hoping for even just a smile from him.

As she turned down the road to the ranch, she knew she couldn't keep spending day after day with him.

Zane jerked awake as she pulled into the yard and cut the engine. Without a word, he was out of the pickup and striding toward the front door of the guesthouse.

She went after him. "Courtney's car isn't— Just a minute. I have the key…." Her words died off as she saw Zane try the knob. It turned in his hand and the door swung open.

He glanced back at her, all his fears culminating in his expression. He seemed to brace himself as he waited for her to join him before he stepped inside.

Dakota wasn't sure what she expected. She had a

pretty good idea that Zane might have anticipated finding Courtney sprawled dead on one of the Navajo rugs gracing the hardwood floors.

The small living area was empty. So were the kitchen and bedroom and bath, as well as the closet.

"She's cleared out," Zane said, turning to look at her.

Dakota stared at the empty closet in surprise. When Courtney had shown up at their father's funeral with evidence that she was her half sister, Dakota had been afraid Courtney was after half the ranch.

After the shock of having a sister had worn off, Dakota had decided that Courtney deserved half interest in the ranch and their father's business. She was Clay Lansing's daughter, after all, and she'd missed out on a lot. Why shouldn't she have a chance to live on the ranch if she wanted to?

"I always wanted a sister," she said.

Zane gave her an odd look.

"I was just getting used to the idea." She sighed. "She would have noticed that her suitcase and money were missing, don't you think?"

"Unless she wasn't the one who cleaned everything out. Whoever gave her the money might not know what she did with it."

"Why would someone else remove all her things?"

"To make us think she is still alive."

Still alive. Dakota felt a chill at his words.

"If Courtney came back and realized her suitcase was missing, I'm sure she'll be in contact with you soon." He didn't sound as if he believed that was going to happen any more than she did.

She watched him search the small guesthouse. "What are you looking for?"

"Anything she might have left behind. You didn't happen to write down her license plate number, did you?"

"No, I had no reason to." But now that she thought of it, it would have been a good idea. She had just assumed that her biggest worry was that her sister would try to force her to sell the ranch so Courtney could get her share.

So what had changed?

Zane, she thought as she watched him move the bureau away from the wall. Zane and ten thousand dollars, is that what had changed? If they were right and her birth mother had contacted her, was it possible she'd put Courtney up to this? But why? It made no sense.

No, Dakota thought. This had to have something to do with her and Zane and Courtney being spiteful. But how far was her sister planning to take this? That's what scared her.

She stepped closer to see what Zane was reaching for. "You found something?"

"A credit card receipt. Looks like it was for food and drinks at the bar in Zortman." He held it up. "Is it yours?"

"I can't imagine how it could be. What is the date on it?"

"A week ago."

She shook her head. "I hardly ever get down to Zortman." It was a small old mining town an hour to the south.

"Has anyone else been in this room since then?"

"No. Just Courtney."

He met her gaze. "This could be the bartender who called. He apparently knows more than we do about what Courtney's been up to. How do you feel about hitting that bar down in Zortman? I need to check in at home first. I'm surprised that my brothers don't have the National Guard out looking for me."

"Give me a call when you're ready and I'll drive over to Whitehorse later," Dakota said. "I need to take care of a few things around here first." The lie seemed to hang between them.

"Sure. You know you don't have to go. I can go down and talk to the bartender on my own."

Dakota hesitated, caught between wanting to find Courtney and wanting to put distance between her and Zane and the old feelings he evoked in her.

"No," she said, finding Courtney and her diary winning out. "Just give me a call."

WHEN ZANE'S CELL PHONE RANG, he thought it was Dakota calling to say she'd changed her mind. He'd seen that she hadn't wanted to go with him to Zortman. He didn't blame her. They'd been together now for almost forty-eight hours. Clearly, she'd had enough of him.

He mentally kicked himself for kissing her as he took the call. Had he thought she was still that starry-eyed girl who'd had a crush on him? What had he been thinking?

"Just received those DNA results from the cell phone," Doc said by way of introduction, then paused.

"Yes?"

"Whoever's blood is on the phone, I can tell you that the person is female and related to Dakota Lansing."

"Could it be a sister with the same father, different mothers?" Zane asked.

"Definitely could be from what I see in the DNA report," Doc said.

So Courtney really was her sister. He'd been so sure she wasn't and that she'd been pretending to be Clay Lansing's love child as part of some elaborate scam—a scam that somehow involved him.

And the blood *was* Courtney's. That thought was slow coming, but hit him like a brick. There hadn't been a lot of blood, but enough to scare him.

He had hoped it had been staged and would end up being animal blood.

"You still there?" Doc asked.

"Yeah, sorry, I'm just surprised. Thanks." As he hung up, he turned down his lane and saw the sheriff's SUV sitting in front of his house. He swore under his breath.

He glanced in the rearview mirror and saw his face. It wasn't that much better than it had been yesterday. The scratches were starting to heal, but still shocking.

Worse, he couldn't explain any of it, including the blood on Courtney's phone. Glancing over, he saw the bagged phone sitting on the seat where Dakota had left it. He pocketed the plastic bag with the phone inside and parked next to the SUV, hoping the sheriff wasn't here with bad news.

As he climbed out, he caught a glimpse of McCall's expression and knew whatever she was here for wasn't good.

"Zane," the sheriff said as she climbed awkwardly out of her rig.

He saw the exact moment she got a good look at his face and the scratches. Her expression darkened even more.

"Want to tell me how you got those scratches?" She sounded angry and disappointed.

He was pretty sure she now knew that he'd been hiding in the bathroom the other day so she wouldn't see his face. He swore silently. He looked even more guilty. Worse, the sheriff would know Dakota had been in on it.

"I don't know how I got the scratches," he said honestly. "But I'll tell you what I do know."

She nodded slowly. "Maybe we better step inside your house. You have a problem with that?"

He shook his head. He knew he should probably call the ranch lawyer. At the very least make her get a warrant. But he feared that would only make matters worse. He knew McCall, knew the kind of sheriff she was. All he could do was put his cards on the table.

Once inside the house, he offered the sheriff a seat as well as something to drink. Not surprisingly, she wasn't in the mood for either.

He told her everything, leaving out nothing but making sure he covered for Dakota.

When he finished, McCall said, "Where is this suitcase with the money in it?"

"It's in my truck behind the seat."

"Let's go get it," the sheriff said.

While he dug out the suitcase, she stood behind him.

"If you don't mind, you can put it in my car," she said, opening the passenger side door of the SUV for him to load the suitcase. "Then I'd like to have a look around your house. With your permission."

"Fine with me," he said as he led her back to the house. As they entered, he told her, "There's a broken lamp on the other side of the bed. I have no idea how it got broken."

"And the cell phone you found under the bed?" she asked.

Reluctantly, he produced it from his pocket.

She raised a brow when she saw that he'd placed it in a sandwich bag—and that it had what she must recognize as blood on it.

"The blood belongs to Courtney Baxter, although that's not her legal name, according to her mother. It's Courtney Hughes."

The sheriff didn't seem surprised at that news. "You should have come to me right away."

"I knew even less then than I do now. I wanted to find Courtney first."

McCall looked around the small house, going into the bedroom last. The covers on the bed were still rumpled; everything looked as it had when he'd awakened from what he now thought of as his mystery date from hell.

He watched McCall awkwardly bend down to look under the bed, saw her freeze and felt his heart drop. What of interest could possibly be under the bed? There'd been nothing under there when he'd found the phone.

She rose long enough to pull on latex gloves, then bent down again to pull out a red dress—the dress Courtney Baxter had been wearing when she'd appeared at his door two nights before.

Even from the bedroom doorway, he saw the dark stains on the silken fabric. More blood.

"That wasn't under the bed when I left here yesterday," he said, his denial sounding hollow, his voice tight with dread. "I'm being set up. I swear to you...."

McCall pushed herself to her feet and turned to face him. The rest of his words died off as he saw her expression.

"Zane Chisholm. You have the right to remain silent," she began as she bagged the dress, then reached for her handcuffs.

Chapter Eight

Emma looked forward to trips into Whitehorse even though Mrs. Crowley was far from a fun companion. She spoke little and became irritated quickly if Emma tried to force conversation.

But being a recluse, Mrs. Crowley made it easy for Emma to have some free time away from everyone. It was their secret that Mrs. Crowley dropped her off to do her errands and picked her up hours later. For that Emma was eternally grateful.

Hoyt would have a fit if he knew. But Emma felt safe in Whitehorse. She still carried a pistol in her purse and kept on the lookout for anyone who didn't seem familiar.

It hadn't taken long to tell the locals from the occasional tourist passing through town. Whitehorse didn't get a lot of tourists. Most people came to Montana to see the mountains, towering pine trees and clear, fast streams. They had little interest in the rolling prairie, which was short on mountains, pines and streams.

Today though, Emma found herself wondering where Mrs. Crowley spent those free hours. The housekeeper never complained. In fact, she seemed to enjoy the time alone. Or maybe she just enjoyed being shed of Emma after the twenty-mile trip into town.

Emma knew she talked too much. But after being around so many men at the ranch, she was thankful to find herself in a woman's company—even Mrs. Crowley. She was excited at the idea of spending some hours on her own. The past year had been difficult. She had always been extremely independent. Being tied down and required to always have someone with her had been hell for her.

Not that she ever regretted marrying Hoyt. That was why she tried hard not to complain. This wasn't his fault, and she didn't want him blaming himself.

Today she had thoroughly enjoyed herself in town and was almost sorry when Mrs. Crowley pulled up in the truck for the ride home.

As she climbed into the passenger side, she noticed that Mrs. Crowley looked disheveled, which was completely out of character. Also the cab of the pickup smelled odd. She glanced more closely at the woman behind the wheel.

"Is something wrong?" she asked, taking in the death grip the housekeeper had on the steering wheel.

"I'm fine," Mrs. Crowley snapped.

Emma bit her tongue; however, she couldn't help noticing that there was dirt under the woman's fingernails. How odd.

It wasn't until she got out of the truck at the ranch that she saw the shovel in the pickup bed. It was covered with dark soil.

ZANE THOUGHT ABOUT USING his one phone call to contact the ranch lawyer. Instead, he called Dakota.

"I've been arrested," he said the moment she answered her cell. "When I got back to the house, the sheriff was waiting for me. She found something under the bed that wasn't there yesterday."

"What was it?" Dakota asked, sounding scared.

"It was the dress Courtney was wearing the night she showed up at my door. Dakota, it looks like there is blood on it."

"Oh, Zane. You're sure the dress wasn't under the bed when you found the phone?"

"Positive." He never locked his house. Hardly anyone around Whitehorse did. But he mentally kicked himself for not thinking to do it yesterday when they'd left. He had made it too easy for whoever was trying to frame him. He'd thought the damage was already done. He'd been wrong about that.

"Someone is definitely setting me up. I'm just scared that something has happened to Courtney. Could you call my dad? I used my one call to phone you."

"Of course. And I'll follow up on that receipt we found behind the bureau."

"No, don't. Please. It's too dangerous. Whoever is behind this…I'm afraid they're playing for keeps."

"You think Courtney is dead." Her voice broke and he could hear how scared she was that it was true.

"I hate to be the one to tell you this, but I heard as I was being led into the sheriff's department that Courtney's car was found in a ravine south of town. That was apparently why the sheriff was waiting at my house. I think McCall found more evidence against me in the car." He hesitated. "There's something else, Dakota. Doc called me. The DNA test results? Courtney *is* your sister."

DAKOTA HUNG UP, SHAKEN by the news. Zane in jail on possible murder charges. Courtney *was* her half sister—just as she'd claimed. And now she might be dead, her car in a ravine and more evidence against Zane in it?

She felt a sense of panic mixed with worry and heart-felt pain. She hadn't trusted Courtney. Still didn't. All she could hope was that her sister was alive and behind some scheme to make it appear Zane had done her harm.

It still made no sense. Courtney wouldn't take sibling rivalry this far. There had to be more to this.

Dakota reminded herself that her sister wasn't working alone. Who was this other person? Her birth mother?

She shuddered at the thought of Courtney's bloody dress being found under Zane's bed. Whoever was setting him up was building a strong case against him.

Dakota hurriedly called the Chisholm ranch, anxious to let Emma and Hoyt know what was going on so they could get Zane a good lawyer.

A woman answered the phone, her voice a little gravelly. "Chisholm Ranch, Mrs. Crowley speaking."

Mrs. Crowley? Zane hadn't mentioned anyone by that name. "I'm calling for Hoyt Chisholm."

"I'm sorry, he isn't in. May I take a message?"

Dakota heard someone ask, "Who is it?" then "I'll take it, Mrs. Crowley."

"Hello? This is Emma Chisholm, can I help you?"

Dakota introduced herself and quickly told her what had happened. "I'm sorry to have to tell you this over the phone."

"No, I appreciate you calling for Zane. It's just that… I'm shocked," Emma said.

"I'm sure Zane will fill you in on everything that's happened. You'll make sure his lawyer is called?"

"Of course. Thank you for letting me know."

Dakota hung up, unable to shake her fear for Zane—and Courtney. The way this was escalating, she couldn't believe Courtney had known what she was getting into.

As she glanced around the empty ranch house, she realized that she was spooked. She'd never been scared living out here so far from any other houses. The ranch had always been a safe place.

Until Courtney showed up, she thought with a shiver.

Zane had told her not to drive to Zortman and talk to the bartender, but when she considered all the evidence stacking up against him, she knew she couldn't just sit back and do nothing.

She didn't believe for an instant that Zane would hurt Courtney. It scared her though. If Courtney's car had been found and there was even more incriminating evidence in it... Was Courtney still alive? She shuddered at the thought that it might be too late for the sister she hadn't even gotten to know. Ultimately, blood was thicker than water. Whoever was behind this was going to pay.

Dakota reached for her purse. Maybe she couldn't save her sister; maybe no one could. But she would move heaven and hell to prove that Zane was innocent of this. She'd never been to the Miner's Bar in Zortman, but she'd heard stories about how rough it was when the gold mine had been up and running.

Still, she knew it would be at least a while before the ranch attorney could get Zane before a judge, and there was always the chance he wouldn't be able to make bail.

Dakota feared that whoever was behind this would

be tying up any loose ends. If Courtney was still alive, then Dakota had to move quickly. She felt as if the clock was ticking, the noose around Zane's neck tightening as well.

As she headed for her pickup, Dakota tried to imagine why Courtney would agree to be part of this. Ten thousand dollars? There had to be more to it. Courtney had grown up in a nice house with two parents who loved her and provided well for her. Also, Courtney hadn't thought enough about the money to put it somewhere safer than under the bed—or take it with her.

It had to be something more alluring than cash.

Courtney's birth mother. With a start, Dakota realized what a pull that could have had on her sister. Courtney was an only child who had never known her father or mother.

Dakota knew what it was like not having a mother. What had it been like for Courtney not knowing either of her birth parents? Maybe she had yearned for that connection, someone who she resembled, more than her adopted mother had known.

Family. Was that the hook that had gotten Courtney involved in what she might have thought at first was innocent?

Clearly she hadn't realized how dangerous it was. Now, if Courtney was still alive, she would definitely be a loose end.

DAKOTA CALLED MINER'S BAR on her way to Zortman. She figured that even if the bartender wasn't working, he wouldn't be that hard to find.

Zortman was a small, old mining town, even smaller

than Whitehorse. It squatted at the edge of the Little Rockies, surrounded by pine trees and rock cliffs.

"He ain't here," said a male voice as if this was his standard, humorous response when answering the phone. Dakota could hear chuckling in the background. It was an old bar joke, the typical line when a woman called.

She recognized the man's voice at once. It was the same man who'd answered the number on Courtney's cell phone earlier.

He laughed a little too long at his own joke. "Sorry, Miner's Bar. What can I do you for?" More chuckles.

Apparently the crowd was eating it up or was drunk enough to laugh at anything. Dakota figured it was probably the latter since it was late afternoon.

"Hello?" he said, his voice becoming muffled as if he'd turned away from the crowd at the bar. "Anyone there?" His tone changed. "Court?" he asked in a whisper.

Dakota snapped the cell phone shut and looked down the long straight road toward the Little Rockies. She didn't mind the drive south. This time of year the rolling prairie was lush and green, the sky a crystal clear, blinding blue. Only a few large white cumulus clouds hung on the horizon ahead.

A hawk called to her from a fence post as she passed. She'd just seen a bald eagle near a group of antelope. The antelope had spooked. She'd watched them race to the nearest barbed wire fence, scurry under it and take off again, disappearing over a rise. The eagle still hadn't moved, she saw in her rearview mirror.

As she drove through the ponderosas into Zortman, she spotted Miner's Bar among the other log buildings.

It appeared old, the logs weathered. She parked, got out, breathed in the scent of pines and went over again how she was going to play this.

She was Courtney's sister. That much wasn't a lie. Dakota was betting that if the bartender knew about the people her sister had gotten involved with, then the sister wouldn't come as a surprise.

Pushing open the door, Dakota was hit with the smell of stale beer. The bar was like so many in this part of Montana. Small and dark, a bunch of regulars on stools along the bar, a sad Western song playing on the jukebox.

And like bars in out-of-the-way places in Montana, everyone turned as she came in. She felt their gazes as the door shut behind her. Only a few were still staring at her as she made her way to an empty stool at the far end of the bar.

Once people didn't recognize you, they usually went back to their drinking. Only a couple of the younger cowboys at the bar leered at her longer.

"Go get her, Wyatt," one of them said, loud enough for her to hear, as the bartender stopped what he was doing to head in her direction. The others at the bar laughed. Clearly they'd had a few drinks and were looking for some fun.

Dakota studied the bartender as he made his way down the bar. Wyatt was tall, broad-shouldered and not bad looking. There was stubble on his jaw. His blond hair was rumpled and he had a look in his blue eyes that she recognized. She would bet he was exactly Courtney's type.

"What'll you have?" he asked, giving her a grin. She'd also bet someone had told him his grin was irresistible to women. It wouldn't be the first time the man had been lied to, or the last.

She could feel the group down the bar watching now. They'd probably been watching him in action for as long as he'd worked here.

"Whatever you have on tap," she told him.

Wyatt raised a brow. "Gotta love a woman who drinks beer," he said, flirting with her as he poured her one from the tap nearby.

"Does my sister drink beer?" Dakota asked quietly as he set down a bar napkin and her glass of beer.

He leaned toward her as if he wasn't sure he'd heard her. "Your sister?"

"Courtney," she said, still keeping her voice down.

He froze, then picked up a rag and killed some time wiping down the scarred surface of the bar. She could tell he was sizing her up, figuring out what to say, afraid he'd mess up.

"I know she spent some time here. With you." She met his gaze. She figured those nights Courtney had come in late she'd been down here. From Wyatt's expression, she'd figured right.

Wyatt put down the rag, wiped a hand over his mouth and asked, "She told you about me?"

"I'm her sister."

He seemed to relax, even let out a small laugh. "The uptight daddy's cowgirl."

The uptight daddy's cowgirl? So that was how Courtney had described her. Maybe her theory about the sibling rivalry wasn't that far off. Courtney *had* resented the fact that Dakota had had their father all those years and she hadn't. She bristled at the "uptight" part, though.

"And you're her latest sucker," Dakota said to Wyatt, and took a long drink of her beer.

He frowned, angry now. "Hey, watch it. I'm no sucker," he said in a tight whisper.

Dakota lifted a brow as she put down her beer. It was cold and tasted good. She wiped the foam from her upper lip. "So you're saying she didn't stick you with her bar bill?"

He leaned against the bar. "Are you trying to tell me she won't be back? Is that what this is about? She sent you with a message for me? Or didn't she get the money?"

"She got the money, but she seems to have disappeared. Actually, I'm looking for her myself."

He laughed. "She owes you money, too, huh?"

"She's part con artist, no doubt about that. But I'm afraid we're both going to be out of luck if I don't find her. I don't like the people she's…involved with."

"Yeah, me either."

Dakota took another drink of her beer. She had to go slow. If she rushed this, he might spook. But if she gave him too much time to think…

"Of course, she could be lying to both of us."

Wyatt shook his head. "Not if she already got the money. It must just be taking her longer than she thought it would."

So Courtney *had* been paid to do something. Dakota was dying to ask him if he knew what she had to do for the ten thousand dollars. "You think the money is why she's doing this?" Dakota let out a disbelieving sound and took another drink.

"Why else?"

She shrugged. "I think her birth mother has her hooks in her." She took a chance, winging it.

He looked surprised. "She told you about her?"

Dakota didn't bother to answer. "Courtney was worried she couldn't trust the woman. What do you think?"

She could see that he liked being asked what he thought. He even gave it a few seconds of thought before he spoke.

"I think family's what it's all about. Court got choked up even talking about her. It's her *blood,* you know what I mean?"

"Yeah. I get that." She held his gaze.

"Sure, you're her sister. So you're going to do right by her." The last came out almost sounding like a question. Courtney must have told him about the ranch and the business. She'd been eyeing it along with whatever else she was up to, just as Dakota had suspected.

"Still, I'd like to meet her mother, make sure she's on the up-and-up."

"Yeah, me too, but Court wasn't havin' it. I said, 'bring her down to the bar,' but she said her mother doesn't get out much." He shrugged.

"But if the mother's staying in Whitehorse…"

"Up north near the border, I think. Court never really said. I just got the feeling she wasn't in town."

"She mention what her mother wanted her to do for this money?"

He looked wary. "Nope." He didn't ask if Courtney had told her. Clearly, he knew Courtney had no intention of telling *her.* Did that mean he knew her old connection to Zane Chisholm?

Dakota tried a different tactic, seeing that she was losing him. "I would have thought she'd have told you how she had to earn this money her mother was giving her."

He smiled, proving he wasn't as stupid as he appeared. "I should get back down the bar."

"I know Courtney was worried. She took one of our father's pistols."

Wyatt tried to hide his surprise but failed. He held up both hands. "I don't know anything about it." One of the regulars called to him for another drink. He took a step in that direction.

Dakota put a twenty on the bar along with one of her father's business cards with the house's landline number on it. "My name's Dakota Lansing. If you hear from Courtney..." He started to argue. "She's already called me once saying she was in trouble and needed help. Unfortunately, the line went dead right after that."

He looked scared now. Another regular hollered at him, told him to quit flirting and bring them something to drink, but he didn't move. "I had a bad feeling about this. But I swear, she didn't tell me what she had to do for her mother. Just that she had to do it. She swore it was no big deal. Kind of a prank, really."

A prank? Dakota watched him hightail it down the bar. His hands were shaking as he reached for a couple of bottles of beer in the cooler. He'd suspected it was more than that. Who got paid ten thousand dollars by their mother to be part of a prank?

Wyatt had to know at least a little of what Courtney had been up to, Dakota thought as she left the twenty and her father's business card and walked out of the bar.

"Guess you didn't get far with that one," one of the regulars said, and they all laughed as the door closed behind her.

THE STATE CRIME TECHS FOUND the body buried under about six inches of dirt, fifty yards away from where Courtney Baxter's lime-green car was discovered.

McCall got the call late in the afternoon and drove south to the ravine. Coroner George Murphy was already on the scene.

"What have we got?" she asked after trudging through the cactus and sagebrush to the shallow grave. All the crime tech had told her on the phone was that they'd found a body in a shallow grave near where the car had gone off the road.

"The body was dumped here and hastily covered with dirt." George looked a little green around the gills. McCall knew the feeling. She never got used to violent death. It had gotten worse with pregnancy.

"Time of death?"

"I would estimate sometime in the past twenty-four hours. It appears the body was either thrown or rolled off that bluff," George said, pointing to a spot up by the road.

"It wasn't carried?"

He shook his head.

"So the killer might not have been very strong," McCall noted. "Could be why the body wasn't buried more deeply."

"Could be," he agreed. "I suppose you want to see the body." He didn't wait for an answer. He simply unzipped the black bag and stepped back.

McCall let out a surprised, "Who's that?" She'd expected to see Courtney Baxter.

"Your guess is as good as mine," George said. "He didn't have any identification on him. The crime techs took his fingerprints. He has what looks like prison tattoos, so they're pretty sure they'll get an ID on him as soon as they run his prints."

The man, short and slightly built, had been hit in the face with a flat, blunt object; his features were no longer recognizable. Blood was matted in his thinning, dark hair, his fingernails were dirty and broken, his clothing soiled from spending at least twenty-four hours under a pile of dirt.

McCall leaned away from the body, motioning for George to zip the bag up again. Her stomach lurched and she had to turn away from the smell not to be sick.

George handed her a mint. She mumbled her thanks and gazed up at the road, then over to the junipers where Courtney Baxter's car had been found.

"The crime team is broadening its search," George said. "They seem to think there might be another grave out here."

"Courtney Baxter's," McCall said, glad her stomach was finally settling down. "Unless Courtney's the killer."

"McCall, you are the most suspicious person I know," George said as he came over to stand by her. In the distance, crime scene techs were using cadaver dogs to search for more bodies. "I hope I never get like you."

"You will. If you stay at this long enough," she said.

ZANE DIALED DAKOTA'S CELL phone number the moment he made bail. One of the benefits of being a Chisholm was that his father was a powerful rancher and had pull when it came to the local judge. Thanks to his father, he wasn't going to have to spend even one night in jail. At least not yet.

Hoyt Chisholm and the ranch lawyer had convinced

the judge that Zane wasn't a flight risk. So far, all the sheriff had was incriminating evidence, but no body.

Zane knew that if Courtney was found dead it could change everything. He didn't even want to think about that. Whoever was behind this was bound to hear he'd made bail. He didn't doubt they would step up their plan to frame him.

As he listened to Dakota's phone go to voice mail, he knew he was waiting for the other shoe to drop.

He had to find out who was behind this before any more "evidence" appeared. His brother Marshall had dropped off his pickup when he'd come in with their father for the bail hearing. He started the engine as he listened to Dakota's voice mail message. Where was she?

He left a message saying he was out on bail and had to see her. He couldn't help being worried about her and didn't like the idea of her staying at the Lansing ranch by herself.

After a moment, he tried the number again. This time when it went to voice mail, he left a message saying he was headed for her ranch and for her to sit tight. He had to see her.

He knew his father and brothers, along with Emma, were anxious to see him. They wanted an explanation. He wished he had one to give them.

But he was too worried about Dakota to do that right now. Worse, he feared she might have decided to do some investigating on her own. She'd mentioned going down to Zortman to talk to the bartender. He'd told her not to go. Unfortunately, he feared that might have been like waving a red flag in front of a bull.

He quickly placed a call home. "I have to make a

stop before I come there," Zane told his father when he answered.

"Zane—"

"I'll be there as soon as I can. This is important. Would you ask Emma to make sure one of the guest rooms is ready? I'll be bringing a friend with me." He hung up before his father could question him further.

The hard part would be convincing Dakota to come back to the Chisholm ranch with him. The woman was independent, which he liked. But the more he'd thought about everything while in jail, the more he feared she was in danger.

Chapter Nine

It was late by the time Dakota left Zortman. Clouds scudded across a black velvet sky, giving her only fleeting glimpses of a sliver of silver moon.

Exhausted after a long, emotionally draining day, she drove back to the ranch. She was anxious to talk to Zane so she could tell him what she'd found out. She hadn't been able to get any service while on her way to Miner's Bar or on the way back until she reached Chinook.

She checked her messages. Both from Zane. He was out on bail and was headed for her ranch? She half expected to see his pickup when she pulled into the yard. *He must be on his way,* she thought as she climbed out and went inside.

It had been a long day. She wondered if she had time for a hot bath before Zane arrived. She was anxious to talk to him, even more anxious to see him.

Dakota sensed something was wrong the moment she walked into her father's ranch house. She hit the light switch and nothing happened. For just an instant, she thought the bulb in the overhead light had simply burned out.

Then she smelled him.

The hair shot up on the back of her neck. Goose bumps skittered over her flesh as she started to turn, her mouth opening as she tried to find her voice.

Her throat contracted and before she could squeeze out a sound, he was on her. His large hand clamped over her mouth, his arm wrapping around her, snatching her back against him in a viselike grip.

She kicked, tried to free her arms to fight him, but he was so much larger, so much stronger, that she was pinned. He dragged her toward the back of the house, knocking over a chair, then a lamp. The lamp broke, sounding like a shot, as he carried her away in the darkness.

Dakota heard a vehicle coming up the road. She tried to scream, but he had his hand over her mouth and his arm around her, pinning her own arms at her sides.

He shoved her through the open side door of a dark-colored van. She tried to scramble away from him. He caught her leg, dragged her to him and then hit her with his fist.

Stars glittered before her eyes just before the darkness closed in.

"DAKOTA?" ZANE KNOCKED, then tried her door. It swung open. He glanced back at her pickup parked outside. After he'd parked, he'd walked by her truck, felt heat still coming off the engine. She couldn't have been home long.

His fear was that she'd gone down to Miner's Bar in Zortman and put herself in even more danger. "Dakota?"

It was pitch-black inside the house. He tried the light switch. Nothing. Only a faint sliver of moon lit the sky outside, but was quickly extinguished by the cover of clouds. It did little to illuminate the interior of the house even though the curtains were all open. Out here in the middle of nowhere, curtains were seldom closed. No point.

"Dakota?" he called louder as his pulse took off.

The modest ranch house was single-level, the layout allowing him to move swiftly through it. "Dakota?" He heard the growing fear in his voice. Then, in a sudden shaft of moonlight he saw the upended chair and shattered lamp scattered across the floor, and felt the cool breeze coming through the open back door.

He raced to the door, his heart in his throat. In the distance, he heard a vehicle engine turn over. Swearing, he rushed outside into the darkness. He cleared the edge of the yard in time to see a van roar down the road.

Zane tore around the side of the house to his truck, leaped behind the wheel and cranked the engine over. He hadn't gone far when he felt the pickup lean to the right and heard the *whap whap* of the back rear tire.

Even before he stopped and got out he knew what he was going to find. Someone had cut his tire.

He stared after the taillights of the van as they dimmed on the horizon, his heart pounding with fear. Someone had Dakota. One sister was already missing. Now Dakota.

Call the sheriff.

As he reached for his phone, it rang.

"We have Dakota," a deep male voice said.

Zane had to tamp down his relief. He'd been expecting a call about Courtney and that one had never come. He'd feared the same might be true of Dakota.

"Who's *we?*" he asked, not expecting an answer but needing to fill the silence.

"If you ever want to see her again, you will do exactly as I say. Call the sheriff and I kill her."

"I won't. But don't you hurt her."

A hoarse chuckle. "Then you do what I say." He proceeded to give directions to an old mission cemetery outside of Whitehorse. "You know the place?"

"Yes." The mission building had been boarded up for years and the cemetery was surrounded by an iron fence. Both sat on a hill in the middle of nowhere. The perfect place for an ambush, especially on such a dark night.

"Twenty minutes? Bring the money."

"I'll be there."

"Come alone."

"Of course."

"And unarmed. You'd better get that tire fixed and get movin'. Time is running out for this cowgirl."

"I'm not movin' until I know that Dakota is all right."

The man started to argue, then swore. Zane could hear the scrape of his boot soles on the ground, then the groan of the rusty van door as he opened it.

A moment later, he heard what sounded like duct tape being ripped from her mouth. Dakota gave out a small cry.

"Tell him you're fine," the man ordered.

"Zane, don't—"

Another cry from Dakota, what sounded like a struggle, then the man's deep voice again. "Happy? She's fine as long as you do what I say."

Zane's free hand balled up in a fist. He couldn't wait to get his hands on the bastard. He hung up and dug out the .38 pistol he kept under his pickup seat, making sure it was loaded.

Then he stuffed the weapon into the pocket of his jean jacket and slipped his hunting knife in its scabbard into the top of his boot.

Twelve minutes later, he'd changed his pickup tire and was headed in the direction of the old mission. He didn't have the money. The sheriff had confiscated it. Apparently whoever had taken Dakota didn't know that.

So that would change how things went down, he thought, as ahead he saw the old mission etched against the dark sky.

MRS. CROWLEY HEARD the commotion shortly after the ranch phone rang. She glanced at her clock. Something was going on, since it was late in the evening. She'd been in bed, but not asleep, her drapes closed, making her room dark as the inside of a coffin.

Easing out of bed, she made her way to the door. Her room was in an empty wing away from the rest of the house. That was a blessing—and a disadvantage. She had to leave her room and sneak down the hallway to the stairs to hear anything that was going on.

Getting caught was not an option. But she was more than a little curious. She crept down the hallway to the top of the stairs, then settled herself into the deep shadows to listen.

"That's all he said?" Emma's insistent voice was followed by Hoyt's low rumble.

"I just know he was arrested because some woman he went out with is missing. He promised to come out here and tell me what's going on. But as you can see, he isn't here."

"Why would he want a guest room ready unless he was bringing someone with him?" Emma had dropped her voice. They were both on the lower wing where the guest rooms were located.

"I have no idea. Believe me, I'd like to know what the hell is going on as much as you do. I'm worried that something else has happened."

"Should we call the sheriff?" Emma asked.

"No. We'll wait and hope for the best."

Mrs. Crowley heard them go toward the kitchen. She knew Emma would make a pot of coffee, then probably bake something. The woman couldn't quit baking.

Sighing, she sneaked back to her room. Normally she never looked out her window, and kept the drapes shut tightly. But now she opened them a crack and peered out.

A breeze stirred the tall, old cottonwoods next to the house. Through the leafy limbs, she caught glimpses of moon and starlight. A dark night. Her favorite. She opened the window a crack and breathed in the air even though it tasted bitter to her, the scent too familiar, too painful.

She closed the window quietly and climbed back into bed. She knew she wasn't going to be able to sleep. As she lay staring up at the ceiling, she smiled to herself. Apparently there was trouble in Chisholm ranch paradise. There would be no lovemaking tonight in that king-size bed on the second floor of the other wing, or out in the barn.

Mrs. Crowley rubbed a hand over her smooth face. She would be glad when she no longer had to pretend to be someone she wasn't. And that time was coming. Soon.

ZANE SLOWED AT THE TURNOFF into the old mission. His headlights caught on a dark-colored van parked in the shadow of the church. It sat at an odd angle, the side door open. As the headlights hit it, Zane saw that the van was empty.

As he drove in, his headlights slashed over the terra-cotta-colored stucco of the church structure, then picked up the bone-white of some of the gravestones higher up the hill.

He parked next to the van, killed his lights and engine and sat for a moment, listening with his side window down.

Clouds played peekaboo with the crescent moon and sky full of stars, keeping the night dark with floating shadows across the landscape. An owl hooted from its perch on the ridge of the church roof. Back on the highway, a semi roared past. Silence followed.

Zane eased his door open and, grabbing an old duffel bag from behind the seat of his pickup, stepped out. The bag had a couple pairs of his old leather branding gloves in it. Ten thousand dollars in hundred dollar bills didn't take up a lot of space. He figured it would be enough weight to fool the kidnapper since Zane had no intention of ever letting the man look inside the bag.

The kidnapper couldn't be inside the church, since it had been boarded up for years. That didn't leave many hiding places.

Moving slowly, Zane climbed the slope toward the graveyard. At the edge of the building he stopped to make sure the kidnapper wasn't hiding in the shadow of the church.

The moon came out from behind a cloud, painting the side of the church in silver. No sign of anyone next to the church, but they could have moved around to the highway side.

He had his doubts about that. A man holding a woman at gunpoint could be seen in the glare of lights from the highway. Zane doubted the man would take that chance.

Turning his gaze back to the graveyard, he continued up the hillside. There could be only one other place the kidnapper was hiding with Dakota.

Most of the gravestones were too small and narrow to hide behind. But as he climbed higher, he saw several larger tombstones, these closer together and deeper in shadow.

"I'm here," he called as he moved toward the larger moss-covered gravestones.

Something moved in the dark twenty yards in front of him. He could make out the man's huge shape against the black sky and see the man's arm locked around Dakota's neck. As he moved closer, he caught the faint glint of a gun; the barrel was next to her head.

"Keep your hands where I can see them," the man called out. "Did you bring the money?"

Zane held the bag out away from his body as he moved toward the man, keeping his gaze on Dakota. She had a strip of duct tape over her mouth and her hands were bound behind her.

As Zane approached slowly, the moon and a few stars broke free of the clouds, casting an eerie, ghost-like glow over the graveyard. He locked eyes on Dakota and saw the determined gleam burning there. The man hadn't hurt her, but he had made her furious.

He smiled to himself in relief. Even after the years apart, he knew this woman. From the look on her face, she was ready for whatever he had in mind. With the relief came a surge of love. Dakota had always been strong. He needed her to be strong now as he prayed that he didn't get her killed.

When he passed one of the taller headstones, he pretended to stumble on the uneven ground and surreptitiously dropped his gun behind the gravestone before taking a few more steps toward the kidnapper.

"That's close enough," the man said.

Stopping ten feet away from the man, Zane set down the duffel bag and took a step back from it. "Now let her go."

The man shook his head. "Not until you hand over the money. Throw it to me."

Zane took another step back, now within feet of the tombstone where he'd dropped his weapon. "We had a deal. I brought your money. Let her go."

He could see the man's indecision even in the dark. He wanted the money badly. He was nervous and afraid; clearly this wasn't something he did every day.

Zane watched as the man took a step toward the bag, dragging Dakota with him. She was making it as difficult as possible for him to keep the gun on her and move her forward.

The man swore and released her, giving her a push that sent her sprawling between two old, bleached-white gravestones.

The moment she hit the ground, she disappeared into the darkness. Zane heard her scramble away from the man.

The kidnapper swore and hurried to the bag as Zane backed up to the gravestone where he'd dropped his pistol.

As the man reached for the bag, Zane reached for his gun. Slipping behind the tombstone, he raised it to aim at the kidnapper's chest.

The man, intent on the money, didn't seem to notice at first that Zane had suddenly dropped down behind a gravestone ten feet away.

But when he did, he brought his gun up and got off a shot. The bullet ricocheted off the crumbling stone inches from Zane's head. The man started to dodge toward one of the headstones for cover. But even moving, he made a large target. The first bullet didn't seem to faze him.

Zane fired again, dropping the man to his knees. He'd dropped the bag a few feet from him. He made a move for it. Zane fired into the dirt next to the duffel bag and the man jerked his hand back.

"Where is Courtney Baxter?" he called to the kidnapper. "What have you done with her?"

The kidnapper looked up, surprised by the question. "You're asking the wrong person," he called back as he made another lunge for the bag.

Zane's next bullet caught the big man in the leg.

He let out a howl, stumbled awkwardly to his feet again and charged, getting off two shots that pelted the gravestone around Zane and sent rock chips into the air.

Zane fired once more, the man just feet from him. The final shot stopped the kidnapper cold. He stood like a lumbering pine swaying in the wind before toppling, coming down with a crash that stirred the dust around him.

Zane kicked the man's gun away from him and then knelt down to check for a pulse. He found none. The air smelled of gunpowder, the night suddenly deathly quiet again.

"Dakota," Zane called as he got to his feet.

She stumbled out of the deep shadows of the gravestones. She had managed to cut the tape around her wrists on something she'd found in the cemetery and was freeing her hands as she came out of the dark.

He took her in his arms. "Did he hurt you?"

She shook her head, removed the tape from her mouth and pressed her face into his chest.

"Did you recognize him?" he asked.

"I'd never seen him before."

With one arm holding Dakota, Zane pulled out his cell and was surprised to get service this far from a town. He punched in 911.

EMMA TALKED HOYT INTO GOING to bed after Zane called to say something had come up. "He said he would see us in the morning. Whatever is going on, apparently it is going to have to wait until morning."

Hoyt tried Zane's number. It went straight to voice mail. He finally went to bed and instantly fell to sleep.

Emma felt as if she'd just closed her eyes when she heard a vehicle. She checked the clock and was surprised to see that she'd slept for hours. It was almost three in the morning.

She went to the window, expecting to see Zane and whoever he'd wanted the guest room for.

"Mrs. Crowley?" What could the woman possibly be doing out this late on these nights?

Even as she told herself it was none of her business, she watched Mrs. Crowley slip into the house. For a long moment Emma eyed the pickup the woman used.

Finally, knowing she wasn't going to get any sleep if she didn't, she pulled on Hoyt's dark robe and sneaked downstairs.

At the bottom, she stopped to listen. Not a sound came from Mrs. Crowley's wing of the house. Still, she waited. She would have a hard time pretending she'd merely come downstairs for a glass of water if Mrs. Crowley caught her.

Of course, there was always sleepwalking. Emma shoved that thought away with a snort. Mrs. Crowley would see right through that. The woman had an uncanny ability when it came to reading people.

Still not a sound.

In the kitchen, she slid open the utility drawer and felt around until her fingers closed on the small flashlight Hoyt kept there.

She ran the beam over the extra keys on the peg by the door until she found the spare key for the pickup Mrs. Crowley had been given to use.

Then she quickly turned off the flashlight and stood, gripping the key and listening.

She hated sneaking around her own house. But she knew that thought had more to do with her own guilty conscience, given what she was planning to do.

Snugging Hoyt's robe around her small frame, she tiptoed through the living room to the front door. The house was never locked—until Aggie Wells had come into their lives with stories about Hoyt's first wife coming back from the dead.

Emma eased the door open slowly. It creaked and her heart stopped. She listened, then slipped out onto the porch. The night air felt good. She breathed it in, studying the horizon.

She never got tired of the view of rolling grasslands, the Little Rockies in the distance, a dark purple smudge in the starlight. Emma loved the smell of fresh earth and new, green grasses. She loved Montana and Hoyt, she thought as her heart gave a small kick.

What was she doing spying on their housekeeper?

She almost changed her mind and went back inside. But then she noticed the muddy tires of the pickup they'd given Mrs. Crowley to drive.

There hadn't been any rain this far north, but she'd heard a storm had blown through down in the Missouri Breaks.

Maybe Mrs. Crowley had gone sightseeing.

Until three in the morning?

The air suddenly felt cold. She pulled the robe tighter and made her way quietly to the pickup, keeping to the shadows of the house.

Mrs. Crowley's room was on the far side of the wing, but she had access to every room in the house.

Emma glanced up. All the curtains on this side were open, the glass dark behind them. Fortunately Mrs. Crowley always parked the truck at the end of the wing in the darkest part of the yard.

Emma quickly slipped around the side of the pickup farthest from the house and eased open the passenger side door.

The dome light came on. She quickly turned it off. Then, leaving the door open, she slid across the seat and behind the wheel.

She didn't want to turn on the flashlight, so she felt around until she found the ignition. She slipped the key in after a few awkward attempts and turned it.

When she heard it click, she pulled the tiny flashlight

from the robe pocket and, shielding it with her hand, shone the light on the dashboard.

After quickly memorizing the mileage, she turned off the light, removed the key and slipped back out of the pickup.

As she started to ease the passenger side door shut, she caught a smell that made her stomach roil. It smelled like something had died in the cab of the truck. She thought about the shovel caked with fresh soil and the dirt under Mrs. Crowley's fingernails after the last trip to town and shuddered.

The pickup door clicked shut. She pushed to make sure it had latched and then sneaked back along the house. When she reached the porch, she took one of the chairs and sat for a moment, her heart pounding.

I'm too old for this.

The thought made her chuckle to herself. She would never be too old for this. A sense of satisfaction filled her. She was going to find out what Mrs. Crowley was up to at night, if for no other reason than her own curiosity.

The woman had way too many secrets.

Chapter Ten

"Oh dear, what happened to the two of you?" Emma cried as she ushered Zane and Dakota into the house.

Dakota knew they both looked a mess after what they'd been through last night. They were both dirty and exhausted, Zane's scratches still prominent.

They'd spent the rest of the night at the sheriff's department answering questions and being grilled about the dead man. Zane had been anxious to get to the ranch, so they hadn't even eaten since yesterday at noon.

Hoyt stepped up to his son, reached for his hand and then pulled him into a quick hug. Dakota saw the fear in the older man's face and knew how relieved he must be. Her own father would have felt the same way. She thought of him and felt her eyes blur with tears.

"What you must have been through," Emma said to Dakota. Dakota shuddered as she remembered being taken captive last night. "Oh, sweetheart, it's all right."

Zane put an arm around her and pulled her close.

"The sheriff called and told us some of it," Hoyt said. "But I'd like to hear it from you."

Zane nodded. "This is Dakota Lansing."

Hoyt Chisholm's eyes widened in surprise. "Clay's girl. I was sorry to hear about your father."

She nodded numbly, and Emma ushered them into the kitchen where she served them hot coffee and cranberry coffee cake. Dakota ate two pieces; the cake was the best she'd ever eaten.

"Can I fix you breakfast?" Emma asked, no doubt seeing how Dakota had scarfed down the coffee cake.

"Not now," Hoyt said, and waved a hand at her. Then he quickly smiled over at her. "I'm sorry. This is all so upsetting. First Zane is arrested and now this?"

Dakota listened as Zane filled them in on everything, from the woman he'd never seen before showing up at his door for the bogus date, to the shooting last night at the old mission graveyard.

"This woman is your *sister?*" Hoyt asked, frowning. "I guess I never knew Clay had another daughter."

"Neither did I," Dakota said. She explained how she hadn't found out until her father's funeral.

"How old is this sister?" Emma asked, sounding as shocked as Dakota had felt.

"Not quite two years younger than me."

Hoyt got up and went to the cupboard over the sink. He pulled down a fresh bottle of bourbon and poured himself a drink, took a swig, then turned to ask if anyone else would like some.

"Hoyt, it's eight in the morning," Emma said, glad she'd dismissed Mrs. Crowley for the rest of the day. She'd hoped the housekeeper would go into town but as far as she knew, the woman had only gone as far as her room.

"How is it you never knew about this sister?" Hoyt

asked. His voice sounded strained as he ignored his wife's scolding.

Dakota explained about her father's affair. "It had to be about the time my mother was dying or right after."

"Thirty years ago," Hoyt said more to himself than to anyone in the kitchen. He finished his drink and poured himself another.

Emma got up and went to him, touching his arm. Dakota heard her whisper, "Are you okay, honey?"

He nodded and turned back to Dakota. "Did your sister say anything about her mother?"

"No, and I didn't ask. Then when she disappeared…"

Zane took up the story, explaining about the trip to Great Falls, meeting Camilla Hughes and finding out about Courtney's trip north.

"We think her birth mother contacted her because she was going by the last name of Baxter," Dakota said. "The mother's name was Lorraine Baxter."

All the color drained from Hoyt Chisholm's face. The glass in his hands slipped from his fingers. It hit the tile floor and shattered, glass shards skittering across the floor.

Emma let out a small startled cry as the glass broke at her husband's feet.

"What's wrong?" Emma cried as she grabbed his arm. He was visibly shaking, pale with beads of sweat breaking out on his forehead.

Dakota feared he was having a heart attack.

"Did you know her?" Zane asked as he stared at his father.

Hoyt swallowed. "I was married to her."

McCall had put off calling Courtney Hughes's parents until she got the DNA test results from the blood found on the red dress she'd discovered under Zane Chisholm's bed.

She was anxious after everything that had happened. Zane Chisholm was adamant that he was being framed and Courtney and her birth mother were in on it. McCall didn't know what to believe. But she had a missing woman, an apparently abandoned car, evidence of possible foul play and two dead men.

The men had both been identified as escapees from a California prison. She had put a call in to the warden to see what she could find out about the men. Hopefully he might have some idea how they'd ended up in Montana, involved with Courtney Hughes aka Courtney Baxter.

When her phone rang, she jumped. The baby kicked as she reached for it. Just a few more days. In the meantime, she hoped to get some answers. She hated to leave this case for her undersheriff, who would be coming in cold on it.

She was relieved when she saw the call was from the state crime lab.

"The DNA found in the blond hair from the car matches the DNA found in the blood of the dress," the tech told her. "Same woman."

Time to call the young woman's parents.

"What was unusual," the tech continued, "was that the DNA search brought up a flagged comparison test from about thirty years ago."

"Flagged comparison test?"

"Another missing woman. This one was believed to have been drowned, but her DNA was sent to us and flagged in case any DNA test should produce a match."

Drowned, missing victim? McCall swallowed, her

heart pounding so hard she could barely hear herself think. "Are you telling me that a relative of Courtney Hughes is in the system?"

"Courtney Hughes's DNA results were a close enough match that the other one came up. Definitely related. I'd say mother and daughter. Interesting, huh?"

McCall thought about what Zane had told her. Courtney had been contacted by her birth mother. They suspected the Whitehorse Sewing Circle had been involved.

"You're saying that this other missing woman was Courtney's birth mother?"

"From the results, that is exactly what I'm saying. I pulled up the file. It's from a missing person's case from your area. A woman by the name of Laura Chisholm."

EMMA STARED AT HER HUSBAND. "There is another wife I don't know about?"

Hoyt shook his head and took her hands in his, his gaze filling with pain. "Lorraine Baxter was Laura Chisholm's maiden name. She thought 'Lorraine' sounded too old so she went by Laura. She had it changed legally, I think, at some point."

Everyone in the room fell silent as they let that sink in. Emma finally found her voice again.

"Courtney Hughes is Laura's daughter?" She looked over at Dakota. "You said she is about thirty-one or thirty-two? That means Courtney had to be born after Laura allegedly drowned," Emma said, even though she could see from everyone's faces that they'd all figured that out themselves.

Zane nodded. "So Laura Chisholm didn't drown, just as Aggie Wells said."

Emma felt sick to her stomach as she shooed her husband out of the way and cleaned up the broken glass. She needed the diversion. Her mind was spinning. Aggie had tried to warn her and now she was dead, all because no one had believed her. She reached behind her husband for the bourbon and poured herself a glass.

"I don't understand this," Hoyt said as he moved to the table and sat down heavily in one of the chairs. Some of his color had returned.

"It's pretty clear." Emma took a sip of the bourbon. It burned all the way down. "This is a message from Laura. All of this, setting up Zane, using Courtney— she wants you to know she's alive."

"Not just alive," Zane pointed out. "Capable of destroying our lives."

Hoyt rubbed a hand over his face. "Laura was so insecure, so needy. I was trying to build a ranch so I wasn't around enough. We were in the process of adopting the boys...."

"We have no proof that Laura is Courtney's mother," Emma said, knowing she was clutching at straws.

"I saw a birth certificate. It had both their names on it, but I suppose it could have been forged," Dakota said.

Hoyt shook his head. "Laura told me Clay was the father of her child."

Emma thought her husband couldn't surprise her further. She'd been wrong. She stared at him as if seeing a stranger. "When—"

"That day on the lake." He met her gaze. "I'm sorry I didn't tell you, but I couldn't bear to relive any more of the past than I've been forced to. Laura knew how badly I wanted a houseful of children. Her final blow was to tell me she was pregnant with Clay Lansing's baby."

"Did he know?" Dakota asked in a small voice.

"No. She told me she wasn't going to have it. I saw then that she had so little respect for human life and that was really the last straw. I told her I didn't love her and that I wanted a divorce. She went crazy."

"That's when she fell overboard," Emma said.

He nodded. "I wanted her out of my life but I didn't want her dead. I tried to save her...."

The room had fallen silent again.

Emma moved to her husband and wrapped her arms around him. "She's sick, obsessed and mentally unbalanced." None of those words came even close to describing Laura's kind of sickness.

"You realize we have no way of proving any of this," Zane said. "All we have is Camilla's word that the birth mother's name was Lorraine Baxter. Courtney has the birth certificate with both Lorraine's name and Clay Lansing's, and if Clay didn't know about the baby, then it is a forgery."

"She had the baby and gave it up for adoption?" Emma asked.

Dakota nodded. "We suspect through the Whitehorse Sewing Circle, so there will be no proof to find there."

"But surely one of the members..." Emma said. She'd heard about the group of women and what they'd done for years. It hadn't seemed like such a sinister thing to do, providing babies to good loving homes.

Now she feared that they might never know the truth. Unless Laura was found. She almost laughed at the thought. Laura would find them. She was probably close by, enjoying the pain she was causing them all.

"I'm worried about what she did to my sister," Dakota said.

"If we're right and Courtney is her daughter, then Laura wouldn't hurt her," Emma said with more conviction than she felt. Her words were met with silence.

Hoyt took her hand and squeezed it gently. "If Laura is alive, she's a murderer."

"How can you say *if?*" Emma demanded.

"Because I don't want to believe it," Hoyt said.

She softened her expression as she looked at him. Of course he didn't want to believe it. "Whatever she's done, it has nothing to do with you."

His laugh held no humor. "Emma, it has everything to do with me. I'm at fault. She didn't believe that I loved her enough. She turned to another man. Everything she's done is because I failed her."

"The woman is insane," Zane snapped. "You just happened to be the man she became obsessed with."

Dakota hadn't spoken for a while. When she did, everyone turned to look at her because of the anguish they heard in her voice.

"I think Laura might be responsible for my father's death," Dakota said. "I was so hurt that Courtney was with him when he died and not me…." Her gaze came up. Her eyes welled with tears. "If Courtney was with our father when he died, then it was her mother's doing. I wouldn't be surprised if Laura was there when he had his heart attack. I can only imagine my father's reaction to finding out what Laura had done and meeting a daughter he hadn't known existed."

Zane put his arm around her as a vehicle pulled up outside.

Emma glanced out the window and felt her stomach roil with dread. "It's the sheriff."

ZANE OPENED THE DOOR at the sheriff's knock, worried that she was here to take him back to jail.

"Sheriff Crawford," he said, hoping he was wrong because he couldn't leave Dakota, wouldn't leave her without a fight.

"Zane. I need to have a word with your father. Is he—" McCall looked past him.

"Please come in," Hoyt said. Zane moved aside to let her enter the house.

The sheriff glanced at Dakota, then Emma, and said, "I'm glad you're all here. I have some news on the DNA test the crime lab ran on Courtney Hughes's blood sample."

"Please sit down," Emma said. "Can I get you—"

"Nothing, thank you." She sat down and waited for everyone else to sit as well.

"Apparently when your first wife drowned, you gave the crime lab a sample of her DNA?" McCall asked Hoyt.

He nodded. Zane noticed how he stole a glance at Emma. They all seemed to know what was coming.

"The crime lab in Missoula ran Courtney's DNA. It brought up another close match. Laura Chisholm's," the sheriff said. "It appears that Courtney Hughes is Laura Chisholm's daughter."

She looked to Hoyt. He said nothing. They'd wanted confirmation. Now they had it.

"You already knew this?" the sheriff asked, looking around the room at them.

"We just learned that Laura Chisholm was Lorraine Baxter before she married my father," Zane said. "We hadn't known that she was definitely Courtney's birth mother."

"I don't think I have to tell you what this means," McCall said. "If Zane is right, then Laura Chisholm is behind her daughter's disappearance."

"She orchestrated all of this," Emma said.

The sheriff shook her head. "The only thing we're lacking is proof of that."

"She's not finished with this family," Hoyt said, his voice breaking with emotion.

"You have to find her," Emma said. "If she's using her own daughter to hurt my family…"

"I'm circulating copies of that age-progression photo Aggie Wells gave you not only locally, but also throughout the state," McCall said. "I'm doing everything possible to find her *and* Courtney." She didn't need to add, "If she is still alive." Everyone in the room had to be thinking the same thing.

"I'll make sure Emma is never alone," Hoyt said. "I'll have one of the boys stay with her as well as Mrs. Crowley."

The sheriff's cell phone rang. She glanced at it. "I need to take this." She got to her feet and stepped out of the room.

A few moments later, she came back into the room. Zane saw the expression on her face and felt his heart drop.

"Is it Courtney?" Dakota asked before anyone else could speak.

McCall shook her head. "That was the warden at the prison in California where the two dead men did time. Both are escaped criminals." She seemed to hesitate. "Three prisoners walked away from a work area last week."

"Three?" Zane said.

"The warden said they'd all three had a visitor a few weeks before. He described her as a woman in her late fifties to early sixties, blonde, blue-eyed. She was going by the name of Sharon Jones and used a Billings, Montana, address."

"Sharon Jones? The woman Aggie found and swore was Laura Chisholm," Emma cried.

"What more proof do you want that this whole thing is some sort of vengeance against our family?" Zane demanded.

"Until she is caught, all of you need to be very careful," McCall said. "There's a third man out there, not to mention Laura herself. I think everything going on with Zane is merely a diversion to bring the focus off the real target, Emma."

The sheriff turned to look at Emma. "If we're right and Laura is responsible for Hoyt's other wives' deaths, then Laura will be coming after you."

Chapter Eleven

Dakota was still stunned by everything that had happened in the past forty-eight hours.

"I'm not letting you out of my sight until this is over," Zane said as they left the Chisholm ranch.

She smiled over at him. His words were music to her ears. He'd saved her at the cemetery, risked his life. She couldn't help but think about the kiss as they went back to her ranch where she packed up what she would need.

From there, they drove back toward Whitehorse. "We can stay out at the home ranch with my folks, but I need to go by my place first."

She didn't say anything as they pulled into the yard of his house. There were no other vehicles around—just like at her house. She reminded herself that Courtney's car had been found.

But the third escaped prisoner from California was still at large. She wanted to believe that by now he had crossed the border into Canada and was long gone. Believing that Courtney and her mother had also skipped the country was a little harder to swallow.

"Doesn't look like anyone has been here," Zane said as he unlocked the door and stepped inside. "If you just give me a minute…"

"Zane." He stopped and turned to look at her, concern in his expression.

She stepped up to him and pushed a lock of his blond hair back from his handsome face. "Thank you."

He shook his head. "I got you into this."

"No, this started long before us. I just want to thank you. You saved my life last night."

His gaze locked with hers. "Dakota." The word came out like a prayer. She felt warmth rush through her. "Don't you know by now how I feel about you? I was half in love with that kid you used to be. Now…" He shook his head as if he couldn't put what he felt into words.

She leaned toward him and brushed her lips over his.

He drew back. "You sure about this?"

Had she ever been more sure of anything in her life? And yet, she knew that this would change everything between them—and possibly not for the better.

She'd taken chances in her life, plenty of them, but that was on the back of a horse in an arena or with the rough stock business. This was a whole different matter and she knew she was way out of her league.

He brushed her cheek with the rough pads of his fingertips, turning her face up to his so she couldn't avoid his blue gaze. She saw the cool blue and the heat behind it. With Zane Chisholm it would be all or nothing.

She nodded slowly and his hand slid behind her head, his fingers burying themselves in her long hair. He pulled her toward him until his mouth hovered over hers. Her breasts pressed against his hard chest, and his hold was strong and sure.

Her heart pounded like a war drum as he drew back

to meet her gaze again, as if searching for something to stop this before it got out of hand.

She met that steely gaze with one of her own. The one thing she had never lacked was courage. Those long-ago embers now fanned to a flame so hot she felt her blood catch fire.

Funny how nothing had changed and yet everything had. She was no longer that girl. He'd said men were going to want to kiss her. And they had. Just none of them had been Zane Chisholm. Until now.

His mouth dropped to hers in a stunning kiss that left her breathless. "That has been a long time coming," Zane said, sounding just as breathless.

She realized why he hadn't kissed her all those years ago. Nothing about Zane Chisholm was safe. She was just smart enough to know it now.

Zane swung her up in his arms, kicked open his bedroom door and carried her inside. As he laid her on the covers, she wrapped her arms around his neck and pulled him down, unable to go another moment without kissing him.

When she touched his lower lip with the tip of her tongue, she felt a shudder rock through him. With a curse he let her pull him down to the bed.

For a moment he stared down at her as if seeing her for the woman she'd become instead of that cowgirl she'd been.

Then he dropped his mouth on hers, taking possession of it, stealing her senses and proving that his earlier kiss was only a prelude of what was to come.

He grabbed her Western shirt and pulled the two sides apart with a jerk that made the snaps sing. A moan escaped his lips as he gazed down at her breasts straining against the lace fabric.

He undid the front hook with two fingers and she felt her breasts freed. His gaze took them in, then those blue eyes shifted to her face.

"You are so beautiful," he said, his voice sounding hoarse. He lowered himself to the bed beside her, his fingers brushing one hard nipple and making her shiver with a desire she knew only he could quench.

His mouth dropped to the other breast and she arched against him, silently pleading with him not to stop.

He trailed kisses, damp and sweet, over her body, making her wriggle in pleasurable agony until at last he shed his jeans and she felt the heat of his body against hers.

He took her in his arms and slowly made love to her with ever-deepening kisses. The release came like a train gathering speed. She clung to him, crying out as she felt wave after wave of ecstasy.

Zane collapsed next to her, his hand spread on her damp stomach. They lay like that, breathing hard, both of them knowing they wouldn't be going to the Chisholm home ranch tonight.

EMMA HAD A TERRIBLE TIME getting to sleep. Zane had called to say that he and Dakota were staying at his place. Emma hadn't argued. She'd smiled as she'd hung up the phone. It was clear Zane was crazy about the girl.

And to think that a year ago, Emma had thought she was going to have to help her stepsons find the perfect women for them. Somehow they'd all done it on their own. She guessed that was the way it was meant to be.

Of course, each of them had fallen in love with a

woman in trouble. So typical of Chisholm men, she'd thought as she'd climbed into bed next to Hoyt.

It was a little after two when she woke. She slipped out of bed and went to the window. The pickup Mrs. Crowley used was gone. Earlier, the housekeeper had complained of a headache and gone to her room. Which had relieved both Emma and Hoyt. They didn't really want her to know what was going on.

But apparently Mrs. Crowley had felt well enough later to go out after Emma and Hoyt had gone to bed.

"What are you doing?" Hoyt asked from the bed, making Emma jump.

"I couldn't sleep," she said when she found her voice. She didn't want him to know she was spying on their housekeeper. He'd think she had enough problems without that.

He blinked. "So you are just sitting in the dark?"

"Go back to sleep. I like sitting here. If it bothers you, maybe I'll go downstairs and read for a while."

"You sure you're all right?" he asked, sounding worried.

"I'm fine." She got up and went to the bed, leaning in to kiss him. "Go to sleep. I'll be back before you know it."

He smiled and closed his eyes. "You can read up here—I don't mind the light."

"I left my book downstairs." She waited for him to put up more of an argument but a moment later she heard him snoring softly.

As she crept downstairs, she admitted that spying on her housekeeper helped keep her mind off Laura Chisholm. But she knew that was only partly the truth.

Mrs. Crowley was too smug in her secrets. Emma was determined to solve this one.

Moving to the living room window, she didn't dare turn on a light. Mrs. Crowley might see it. Instead, she sat patiently in the dark, hoping Hoyt didn't awaken again and come looking for her.

Twenty minutes later, she saw headlights in the distance.

Emma waited another five minutes after Mrs. Crowley had parked the pickup and gone inside her wing before tiptoeing into the kitchen for the flashlight and spare truck key.

She knew she wasn't being as careful, but she had to put an end to this nightly spying. With the key and flashlight, she padded out of the kitchen, across the living room and out the front door.

It was colder out tonight. The sky was dark and the wind smelled of rain. She hurried along the side of the house in the shadows, feeling the bite of the wind. Rain was imminent.

It would serve her right to get wet, she thought as she slipped around the back of the pickup and through the passenger side door. If Hoyt caught her drenched in rain, how was she going to explain that?

This time, she didn't take the time to wait and see if anyone might have seen her. She turned the key and snapped on the flashlight.

The beam shone on the odometer reading.

Emma blinked and did quick subtraction. Eleven miles? Eleven miles round-trip, she realized. That meant the woman hadn't even left the ranch.

It was more puzzling than when she hadn't known

how far away the woman went in the middle of the night.

And more troubling somehow.

Rain pinged off the truck roof, making her jump. She hurriedly climbed out, slamming the door harder than she meant to.

Thunder rumbled in the distance. She hoped anyone who might have heard the slammed door would think that was what it had been.

As she started around the truck, a bolt of lightning splintered across the sky, lighting up the yard like daylight.

For a moment, Emma was blinded. She blinked and when her eyes focused again, she found herself face-to-face with Mrs. Crowley.

DAKOTA WOKE TO THUNDER that was so close it seemed to reverberate inside her chest. In the darkness she shivered and rolled over to face Zane. His features were lit by the light of the storm. He couldn't have looked more handsome than he did right now, she thought with a growing ache inside her.

Earlier she'd gotten up to get a drink and had pulled on his T-shirt. It smelled of him, filling her senses. As she'd slipped it over her head, her skin had tingled. Now she remembered the way the T-shirt had fit him, accenting the hard muscles, the washboard stomach, the tanned skin. She couldn't help but remember the way his jeans had hung on his hips, the fine blond line of hair that ran from his chest to disappear at the large rodeo belt buckle.

She had looked away, but not before he'd seen her

looking. A fire had burned in those blue eyes, hot as a welder's torch.

At just the thought of their lovemaking, she felt a fire burning in her. She'd never known this kind of passion, this kind of desire. Zane had been her childhood fantasy, the rodeo cowboy she'd planned to marry.

At the thought of her diary, she cringed inwardly. It embarrassed her that her sister, and who knew who else, had read about her longing. No doubt the reason it still embarrassed her was because that longing had never gone away.

Zane was the reason she hadn't gone through with her engagement. She'd felt as if there was something missing with her fiancé. Dakota had hated breaking it off, telling herself she was making a huge mistake still being in love with a fantasy cowboy.

But the truth was, Zane had corralled her heart and held it captive all these years.

In a flash of lightning that lit the bedroom, Zane opened his eyes. He smiled at her. "Nice shirt," he said.

Raindrops struck the partially open window next to them. Dakota felt the cool breeze rush over her bare skin as she brushed her lips over his, then pulled back a little to look at him. He seemed to be waiting to see how far she would go.

She shifted against Zane, feeling her aching nipples grow even harder beneath his T-shirt as she reached for the hem. Pulling his T-shirt up and over her head, she tossed it away.

He grinned. "You are insatiable."

She nodded as she wrapped her arms around his neck and pressed her naked breasts to his hard chest.

His hands came around her waist and drew her into

him until not even the cool breeze of the rainstorm could come between them. As his mouth dropped to hers, thunder boomed again as loud as the pounding of their hearts in the old ranch house.

"MRS. CROWLEY!" THE words flew from Emma's mouth with obvious surprise.

"Whatever are you doing standing out in the rain?" the woman demanded from beneath the umbrella she held.

Emma had been so careful the other time. Now she'd been caught red-handed. "The thunder and lightning. It woke me up."

Mrs. Crowley was giving her a sideways look that said, "And that explains your behavior how?"

"I woke up, couldn't sleep and wandered out on the porch. I thought I saw the dome light on in the pickup," Emma said. It was the only thing she could think of since she was pretty sure Mrs. Crowley had seen her in the truck.

"Really? Do you have trouble sleeping often?"

"Must have been the thunder," Emma said.

Mrs. Crowley glanced toward the pickup. "The dome light must have a short in it. I noticed it wasn't working the other night."

So she *had* noticed. Of course she had, Emma thought. The woman never missed anything.

"I'll have Hoyt take a look at it," Emma said.

"Don't bother. It's off now. Let's just leave it that way." Mrs. Crowley gave her one of her twisted half smiles. "You really should get in out of the rain."

With that the woman turned and went back inside. Emma stood for a moment, staring after her before she turned her face up to the rain. It felt good as she walked back to the front porch before entering the house.

Inside, she locked the door. Even as she did so she wondered what she was locking inside her house.

She shuddered at the memory of looking up to find Mrs. Crowley standing in front of her. Why did that poor woman scare her so?

Well, she'd never admit it. Especially to Hoyt.

Eleven miles, she thought as she went to the guest bathroom and dried herself off with a towel. Hoyt's robe was soaked. She hung it up.

Her nightgown was damp. She would change it upstairs.

As she headed upstairs, she mulled it over in her mind. Eleven miles round-trip. Where would that take you on the ranch?

Upset with herself, she knew she really *wouldn't* be able to sleep now. Retracing her steps, she went into the living room, turned on a lamp and picked up the murder mystery she'd been reading.

She was through spying on the poor woman, she told herself as she wrote down the mileage in the back of the book and wondered again where an eleven-mile round-trip would take a person on the Chisholm ranch.

THE NEXT MORNING THE STORM had passed. A brilliant glowing sun shone in the window from a sky of cloudless blue. Zane stirred to find the bed beside him empty. For one heart-stopping moment, he thought Dakota was gone.

Then he smelled bacon and heard the faint sound of music coming from his radio in the kitchen. He smiled and tried to still his pounding heart. Last night had been incredible. What surprised him was that it hadn't been like this with other women he'd known. He knew it sounded clichéd, but with Dakota it hadn't been just sex.

As he lay in the bed, it hit him like a boulder off a cliff. He loved her.

He'd never said the *L* word to any woman because he'd never loved any of them. For a few moments, he was shocked. But he realized this wasn't a spur-of-the-moment emotion. This had been coming for a long time.

Pulling on his jeans, he looked around for his T-shirt. Not seeing it, he grinned. He had a pretty good idea where he could find it.

Sure enough, as he stepped through the kitchen doorway, there was Dakota making breakfast in nothing but his T-shirt.

He moved behind her, put his arms around her, breathed in the scent of bacon and the woman he loved.

"I hope you're hungry," she said with a sexy chuckle.

"Hmm," he said into the side of her neck. She felt warm and soft, rounded in all the right places. He loved her strength as much as he loved her soft places.

Turning off the stove, he turned her in his arms. "What would it take to get you to come back to bed with me?"

EMMA HAD SLEPT. She woke sprawled on the couch with a crick in her neck and a page of her murder mystery pressed against her right cheek.

At first she didn't know what had roused her. Then she heard the phone and realized it wasn't the first time it had rung.

Still in her nightgown, she hurried to it, aware that it must be very early. Not even Mrs. Crowley was up yet.

"I just got a call from the Butte Police Department," Sheriff McCall Crawford said when Emma answered. "They've picked up a woman who matches Laura's description from the age-progression photo we sent around the region."

Emma couldn't help being afraid to get her hopes up. She'd prayed for this for so long. "But they aren't sure?"

"No, but they did find some evidence in her possession that makes them believe it's her," the sheriff said. "She had Courtney's number and Great Falls address on her and some gas receipts from a Westside convenience store in Whitehorse."

"Are they going to bring her to Whitehorse?"

"No," McCall said. "They need Hoyt to come to Butte to make a positive identification. They can only hold her for forty-eight hours so he needs to come as soon as possible."

Hoyt would have to face his first wife? Emma couldn't bear him having to do that. But if this was Laura and they couldn't hold her any longer because of lack of evidence...

"I'll tell Hoyt." She hung up and hurried upstairs only to find their bed empty. Hurrying back downstairs, she checked the kitchen and then headed for the barn.

She found him with his horses—the place he always headed when he was worried or upset. So he hadn't been able to sleep after all, she thought, wondering how long he'd been out there.

Emma watched him brushing one of his favorite horses. She could hear him talking softly to the mare and felt such a rush of love for him it almost floored her.

She took a step toward him, hating to interrupt. He looked so peaceful and she knew that this news would kill that instantly.

"Emma?" Hoyt seemed surprised to see her. "I thought you'd be asleep for hours." He smiled, making it clear he'd seen her sacked out on the couch. She probably still had the crease on her cheek where the page of her book had been pressed.

"I just got a call from the sheriff," she said. Hoyt put down the brush and stepped toward her. She quickly repeated what McCall had told her and watched an array of emotions cross his face.

"Then it's her," Hoyt said, sounding so relieved she stepped to him and put her arms around him. He pulled her close and she could hear the ragged emotion in his voice as he breathed words of love into her hair.

"I have been so worried about you, Emma," he said when she pulled back. "I have to go to Butte today? Why can't they just check her DNA since it is still on file?"

"I don't know. Apparently it would take too long. Or maybe she refused to take a DNA test. I hate for you to have to go, but if this woman is Laura..."

"Yes," he said. "It definitely sounds like she is. I'll do whatever I have to. I just want this to be over."

"Me, too," Emma said. She thought they would all be able to breathe again once Laura was locked up for good.

"I'll call one of the boys to stay with you until I get back," he said. Hoyt still referred to his sons as boys, even though they were all almost thirty or older.

She started to argue that it wasn't necessary. She had Mrs. Crowley. But her husband didn't give her a chance.

"I'd feel better if one of our sons is here with you until I'm positive they have Laura behind bars. Let's not forget that there is a third prison escapee still on the loose."

She hadn't forgotten. But with Laura locked up, she doubted they had to worry about the other escapee. By now he could already be across the border into Canada.

Chapter Twelve

Zane swore at the sound of the phone. He thought about not answering it. Right now the last thing he wanted was an intrusion from the outside world.

He glanced over at Dakota on the bed next to him. Her body felt so warm next to his, he never wanted to leave this bed.

The phone rang again. He reached for it and checked to see who was calling. When he saw that it was the ranch he quickly slipped out of bed.

He answered on the third ring. "Hello?"

"Zane, it's Dad." Zane listened as he filled him in about the trip to Butte and the woman the police there had behind bars. "Marshall is going to be staying with Emma, but I wanted the rest of you to know what's going on."

"They really think it's her?"

"Apparently she had Courtney's number and address on her and some gas receipts from the Westside here in Whitehorse."

"Then she'll be able to tell the police where Courtney is," Zane said, and heard Dakota come up beside him. She was wearing his shirt again and nothing else.

At this rate, they were never going to eat the breakfast she'd cooked.

"Let me know what happens." He hung up to take Dakota in his arms and tell her the possible good news.

"Has this woman they arrested said anything about Courtney yet?"

"Apparently not. But she did have Courtney's address and phone number and some gas receipts from Whitehorse."

Dakota snuggled against him, wrapping her arms around his waist and burying her face into his bare chest.

"Dad promised to call when he knew something definite."

She pulled back to look up at him. "I'm just so afraid that the more time that goes by…"

"I know." He thought about Courtney's car being found in that ravine—and one of the escaped prisoners' bodies found nearby. He regretted that he'd had to kill the other escaped convict last night before finding out anything about Courtney.

Zane swung Dakota up into his arms and carried her back to the bedroom. Putting her down gently, he lay beside her on the bed.

She was so beautiful. He touched her face, running his thumb pad over her smooth cheek. Her eyes widened and he saw desire stir in them.

"If we don't eat that wonderful breakfast you cooked pretty soon…"

HOYT REFUSED TO LEAVE until Marshall arrived. Emma was relieved when she saw Marshall drive up and Hoyt go out to talk to him. She and Hoyt had already said their goodbyes. She could tell Hoyt was just anxious to get to Butte.

A pilot friend had offered to fly him and was now waiting for him at the small airport outside of White-horse. It was no more than a wind sock, a strip of tarmac and an old metal hangar. But by flying, Hoyt could get there sooner—and get back just as quickly.

"Where's Mrs. Crowley?" Marshall whispered as he came through the back door and looked around the kitchen. Emma waved out the window to Hoyt as he climbed into his pickup. His gaze locked with hers for a moment before he started the motor and drove away.

"She wasn't feeling well and went to her room to rest," Emma said, turning from the window. "I'm worried about her. This isn't like her. But I don't dare go down to her room. She called me to say she had one of her headaches and asked if I would mind if she stayed in bed a little longer."

"She must have known I was coming over," he said. "She doesn't like me."

"That's not true," Emma said. He raised a brow and she laughed. "She doesn't like anyone," Emma whispered conspiratorially. "Sit down. I baked your second-most favorite cookies."

"I thought I smelled lemon." He smiled and slid into a chair at the table. "Dad eat all the gingersnaps?"

Emma closed the kitchen door so they would have privacy and turned on the radio to the country music station.

"Mrs. Crowley hates this kind of music," she said as she gave him a mug of hot coffee and a plate of lemon cookies and took a chair across from him.

He grinned at her. "How can you stand her?"

"Well…" She studied her stepson for a moment. "Can I tell you something? You just can't tell your father what I've been doing."

He made a cross with his finger over his heart and laughed. "If you've been slipping Mrs. Crowley happy pills, I've got some bad news for you. They aren't workin'."

Emma shook her head and leaned toward him. "I've been spying on her. And guess what? She sneaks off at night after we're asleep and she doesn't come back until the wee hours of the morning."

He frowned, clearly not expecting this. "Where does she go?"

"Well, that's what's so interesting. She only drives eleven miles, round-trip."

"That wouldn't even get her off the ranch."

"Exactly. But I think I've figured out where she goes. I just can't imagine why…unless she's meeting some man—" Emma realized "—at the old water mill house."

Emma realized Marshall wasn't listening to her anymore. He was looking past her out the kitchen window one moment, the next he was shooting to his feet, a curse escaping his lips.

She spun around to look out the window behind her, half expecting to see Mrs. Crowley's face pressed to the glass.

"Fire," Marshall said reaching for his cell phone. "Grass fire."

Emma saw it then. Smoke on the horizon. She'd learned about grass fires since moving to the ranch and knew how dangerous they could be, especially if pushed by wind. Outside the window she could see a brisk wind stirring the branches of the cottonwood trees.

She listened to Marshall barking information into the phone. He placed five more calls to his brothers.

"Go," she said when he snapped his phone shut. "I'm fine. Mrs. Crowley is here."

Marshall shook his head. "Zane is bringing Dakota to stay with you."

Emma liked Dakota and would be glad to spend some time with her. "Well, you don't have to wait for them to get here. Mrs. Crowley is in her room and I have your number if I have to reach you. You'll only be down the road."

The kitchen door suddenly opened. "What's going on?" Mrs. Crowley asked as she filled the doorway.

"Are you feeling better?" Emma asked.

"What's going on? I heard all the racket," the housekeeper said in answer.

"There's a grass fire. The boys have gone to fight it."

Mrs. Crowley went to the window and looked out as if she'd known where it was, had already seen it. "So what are you waiting for?" she demanded as she turned to face Marshall. "Shouldn't you be out there fighting it?"

He didn't get a chance to reply.

"I'm here with your stepmother now," Mrs. Crowley said in her no-nonsense tone. "Go."

"She's right," Emma said. "We'll be fine."

Marshall didn't have to be told twice. "Dakota is going to drop off Zane, then come here. She should be here soon," he said. "Call if you need me."

"I will," Emma said as she pushed him out the door. He took off running toward the ranch truck with the water tank on the back. A few minutes later, he was roaring down the road toward the dark smudge of smoke along the horizon.

"Marshall didn't even eat one of the cookies I made for him," Emma said. She turned to find Mrs. Crowley making tea.

"You must be feeling better," Emma said, looking out the window at the fire.

Mrs. Crowley could hear the woman's fear about the fire, but it was so like Emma to ask how *she* was feeling.

"I am better, thank you." Her employer turned in surprise at her words. "I appreciate how nice you've been to me. I know I haven't made it easy."

Emma's eyes widened a little as if she wasn't sure the words had really come out of her housekeeper's mouth.

Mrs. Crowley nodded, not having to pretend a look of chagrin. "You have been nothing but kind and I have rebuffed that kindness at every turn. I'm sorry."

Emma appeared not to know what to say for a moment. "I just wanted you to feel at home here. I have a tendency to come on too strong."

"I do feel at home here." Emma had no idea how much. "Please, let me make us a cup of tea and visit until your friend gets here."

"Are you sure you feel up to making the tea?"

"Yes. I only had a headache earlier. I'm fine now." She turned her back on Emma and began to fill the teapot, hoping the woman would take a seat and not insist on helping.

To her relief, Emma was more interested in the grass fire.

Mrs. Crowley tried not to hurry with the tea but

time was of the essence. Dakota Lansing would be arriving soon. She had to get at least one cup of tea into Emma before that. This opportunity might not present itself again.

"I suppose you won't be needing me soon," Mrs. Crowley said.

"Why would you say that?" Emma asked.

"Your husband's trip to Butte. I couldn't help overhearing. Is it really possible his first wife is alive?"

"I'm afraid so."

Mrs. Crowley shook her head as the teapot whistled. "I admit I did read a few things in the newspaper before I came here. I felt as if you and I had a lot in common actually. We are both haunted in a way by the past."

"That's true," Emma agreed as she poured a small pitcher of milk and prepared the cups.

"What I can't understand is why this woman would do what she's been accused of." She carefully filled Emma's cup and slipped in a fresh tea bag. "She must enjoy making other people miserable," she said as she watched the tea steep.

"I feel sorry for her," Emma said and Mrs. Crowley had to bite back a laugh. Of course Emma would.

"How can you possibly say that?" she demanded as she slipped a tea bag into her own cup, then took both cups over to the table, making sure she didn't accidentally mix them up as she saw the dust of a vehicle coming up the road in the distance.

"She must be a very unhappy person," Emma said.

"Maybe she just couldn't let go of her husband," Mrs. Crowley said as she pulled out a chair and sat down across from her. "Isn't it possible she loved him too much? That he was her life and she didn't need anything or anyone else?"

Emma took a sip of her tea and looked up in surprise. "You think she resented the children he adopted?"

Mrs. Crowley shrugged and sipped at her tea, watching Emma over the rim of her cup.

"I think she didn't want him but she doesn't want anyone else to have him," Emma said, then took one of the lemon cookies off the plate on the table and dipped it into the tea. She took a bite, then said, "That is the most selfish of all love."

EMMA DIDN'T LIKE THE TASTE of the tea and wondered how Mrs. Crowley could mess up even a simple cup of tea.

The woman was no cook. If Emma'd had her way, she wouldn't have let her in the kitchen. Every time Mrs. Crowley insisted on helping, nothing had turned out like it should have.

Emma prided herself on her cooking, especially her baking. Fortunately, Mrs. Crowley hadn't insisted on helping with the baking.

She took another sip of the tea. It tasted bitter. She tried not to grimace with the woman watching her.

"I think I need a little of that sweetener my future daughters-in-law insist on," Emma said.

Mrs. Crowley was being so nice, she rose quickly to get it.

Emma used the diversion to dump some of the tea out in the plant on the windowsill. She would have poured out more but Mrs. Crowley was too quick for her.

"Thank you," she said as she took one of the packets, tore it open and poured it into her cup under Mrs. Crowley's watchful eye.

Emma hated sweetener, but she had no choice now but to drink the tea. Mrs. Crowley knew she didn't take her tea with milk, but she added a little anyway, hoping it would make the brew go down easier.

Mrs. Crowley was making an effort to be friends. Too late if the woman in Butte turned out to be Laura. Emma would feel badly about having to let Mrs. Crowley go. Well, not that badly. She would never know, though, where the housekeeper went in the middle of the night.

Emma promised herself that she would give Mrs. Crowley a decent recommendation for her next job and make Hoyt give her a large severance package.

Even as she thought it, Emma knew she probably wouldn't have done that if the woman wasn't disfigured. She wondered if Mrs. Crowley was often overly compensated by her employers not for her work but because of her injury. Emma supposed that, too, could have made the woman the way she was.

Or at least had been. She'd been so pleasant today it was almost…spooky. Emma could feel Mrs. Crowley studying her. Now that she thought about it, many times since the housekeeper had arrived here she'd felt her studying her like a bug under a magnifying glass.

Another benefit of her injury, Emma thought vaguely. No one dared stare at Mrs. Crowley, which made it easier for her to stare at everyone else.

Emma put down her cup. She'd been forced to drink all but a little of it. She suddenly felt light-headed. She could barely keep her eyes open.

MRS. CROWLEY CONCENTRATED on her tea, letting Emma drink almost all of hers. A breeze stirred at the open kitchen window, bringing with it the smell of smoke. Hoyt was in Butte and by now all the Chisholm boys would be fighting the fire.

But the wind also carried the scent of dust. As she listened, Mrs. Crowley heard the vehicle she'd seen down the road approaching. It was only a matter of minutes before it reached the ranch house.

Mrs. Crowley glanced toward the window and the pickup that pulled into the yard. It was just a neighbor coming to refill the water tank in the back of his truck.

She looked over at Emma again. There was still time.

Emma was staring into her teacup as if reading her future in the small sprinkling of leaves at the bottom.

All things considered, not much of a future, Mrs. Crowley thought.

"I think Laura was scarred in ways none of us will ever understand," she said. "Did you know that her father deserted her when she was six? He was her life. Her mother remarried, of course, after transforming herself into whatever that man wanted her to be. The marriages never lasted so she kept having to become someone new for someone else."

Emma looked up and blinked as if having a hard time focusing.

"Laura's mother cared more about the men who traipsed through the house in a steady flow than she ever did about her daughter," Mrs. Crowley continued as she rose to take Emma's cup.

"You wouldn't know what it's like growing up feeling that you're not enough, that your love isn't valuable enough, that you're not even enough for your own mother. But I think you can imagine what something like that can do to a person," Mrs. Crowley said.

SOMETHING WAS WRONG. Emma had been trying to follow the conversation but Mrs. Crowley's words weren't making any sense.

She stared across the table at the woman. Mrs. Crowley looked different this morning, but Emma couldn't put her finger on what it was. She reached for a cookie, but hit the small pitcher of milk. Milk splashed onto the table.

"Here, let me help you with that," the housekeeper said, moving the pitcher out of her reach.

"I'm not feeling well." Her head was spinning and she could barely keep her eyes open.

"You must have what I did earlier. Headache? Lightheadedness? I was so tired I could barely stay awake."

Emma looked into the woman's face and had a moment of clarity. "Did you put something in my tea?"

Mrs. Crowley smiled. "It's all right. I only gave you a very strong sedative. It will knock you out, but it won't kill you. That comes later."

Emma tried to stand, but the housekeeper was on her before she could get out of the chair. She struggled to throw her off, but Mrs. Crowley was much stronger than she looked.

Nor was she limping, Emma thought as the housekeeper half dragged her toward the pantry. She gave up fighting to free herself from the woman's grip, realizing it was useless.

She was too weak. But she still fought to stay awake. Dakota was on her way. If she called out—

Emma opened her mouth, but only a low groan came out as the housekeeper dragged her into the pantry.

Emma's eyelids drooped and the last thing she heard as she lay on the floor was the hurried slamming of the pantry door. Then darkness.

MRS. CROWLEY LOOKED DOWN the road. No Dakota yet. She sat down, poured a little milk into her tea and idly stirred it with her spoon. It was dangerous, this game she was playing. She had let it go on too long. She'd been in this house since March. It was now June and she hadn't accomplished what she'd come here to do.

With a curse, she knew why it had taken her so long. Emma. The woman had intrigued her. Each day she'd relished watching her employer. Emma had an insatiable curiosity and a need to comfort. Mrs. Crowley smiled at the woman's pitiful attempts to befriend her.

The curiosity could have turned out to be a problem, though. While she was watching Emma, Emma had been spying on her. She chuckled to herself at Emma's attempts to find out where she'd gone at night. Taking a sip of tea, she almost spilled it as she recalled Emma's face when she'd caught her coming out of the cab of the pickup last night.

Feeling good for the first time in a long time, Mrs. Crowley considered having one of Emma's cookies. Normally she didn't allow herself the pleasure of sweets. She had just taken a bite when she heard the sound of a vehicle. Looking out the kitchen window, she saw the driver of the pickup park in front of the house and climb from behind the wheel.

Dakota Lansing. Before the other night, she hadn't

seen her since she was a cute little two-year-old, Clay Lansing's pride and joy.

She watched the now beautiful young woman head for the front door and felt a stab of remorse. Clay Lansing never knew it, but she could have fallen for him all those years ago. There was something so broken about him after his wife died. She'd been drawn to his pain and thrown caution to the wind.

She would have left Hoyt for Clay if it hadn't been for Dakota. It was ironic. She hadn't wanted a child, and in her reckless abandon had become pregnant with one.

She listened, but no sound came from inside the pantry. Smiling, she went to answer the knock at the door.

THE FIRE HAD RACED ACROSS the prairie, fueled by the wind and the tall grasses, and left charred, black ground. Smoke still billowed up along the horizon and could be seen for miles, but the flames had been knocked down.

This was the wrong time of the year for grass fires. Unfortunately an early spring, hot temperatures and abundant grass had kept the blaze going.

When Zane arrived he found his brothers, along with neighbors who had seen the smoke and come to help. They'd managed to get the fire contained and were now busy dousing any grass and brush still smoking.

Another truck pulled in equipped with a water tank in the bed. Zane saw that his brothers had almost emptied their tanks and would need to make a run back to the ranch to refill soon unless they got the fire completely out with this last tank of water.

Zane backed up his pickup and jumped out to grab the hose from the back and turn on the faucet of the water tank. The spray felt cold and blew back in his face as he began to douse the grass along the edge of where the fire had burned. Down the way, more neighbors were working along with several small community volunteer fire department crews.

Zane was thankful that his brothers were already winning the battle against the blaze. What he wanted to know now was how it could have started out here in the middle of nowhere—especially after a rain last night. Unless it had been started by a lightning strike and taken this long to get going.

After emptying the tank in the back of the truck, Zane moved across the blackened ground to the spot where the blaze appeared to have started. He hadn't gone far when he saw the containers of accelerant and the boot prints in the soft earth.

Hunkering down, he studied the track and then, on an impulse, looked to the horizon where the foothills rose in small clusters of pines. Zane caught a flash of light in the pines along the foothills not a half mile away.

Binoculars, he thought. The arsonist is watching to see how much damage he's caused.

A moment later Zane realized the arsonist had seen him and knew he'd been spotted. A pickup roared out of the trees in the distance. The driver was making a run for it.

Swearing, Zane sprinted for one of the ranch trucks. The bastard wasn't getting away.

As he neared the truck, Zane called to his brothers. "The man who started the fire. I saw him watching us from the trees. He's taking off."

Zane jumped behind the wheel. His brother Marshall

climbed into the passenger side as the truck engine roared to life, and Zane swung it around and headed for the county road to cut the man off.

Dust billowed up behind them as they raced across the pasture. Zane could see the blue pickup's driver careening down the road, hoping to escape before Zane could catch him.

"Can't this pickup go any faster?" Marshall joked, hanging on as the truck bounced over the ruts, fishtailing onto the road.

For a moment it looked as if the blue pickup would beat them to the spot where the two roads joined.

Zane feared that if the driver of the blue truck got there first, he might be able to outrun them. After all, his truck didn't have a water tank in the back.

He pushed the pickup harder, keeping his eye on the road as he and the other driver raced toward the point where the two roads intersected—and the trucks were about to meet, neither driver letting up off the gas.

Marshall was on the phone to the sheriff when he wasn't hanging on to keep from being bounced all over the cab.

"I suppose you have a plan," Marshall said, sounding a little anxious. "He doesn't look like he's going to give an inch."

Zane didn't answer. His mind was racing. Why start a grass fire? What had been the point?

Suddenly he knew. "Call our brothers," he cried. "Tell them to hightail it to the house. The fire was a diversion!"

The truck was almost to the intersection and so was Zane.

Marshall made the call and then braced himself for

the collision. He must have seen that his brother wasn't slowing down—and neither was the driver of the other pickup.

MRS. CROWLEY ANSWERED the front door on the second knock. She loved to see the expressions of people when they first saw her. Shock, then horror, then a nervous twitch of the eyes as their gazes slid away.

The young woman was even more striking close-up. She couldn't help but think of Clay's last words before his heart attack.

"Don't hurt my daughters." He'd grabbed her arm. "Laura, swear to me you won't hurt my daughters."

Fortunately he'd died before she had to answer.

"Is Emma here?" Dakota asked.

"She's lying down right now, but please come in. She told me to take care of you until she wakes up."

"I don't want to be a bother," Dakota said.

"Don't be silly," Mrs. Crowley said as she stepped aside to let Dakota into the house. "You're no bother. Come on back to the kitchen." She closed the door behind them, surreptitiously locking it. "Emma baked lemon cookies. She insisted you try one with a cup of my tea while you're waiting."

Chapter Thirteen

Hoyt Chisholm stood in the Butte Police Department, shaking inside with both anger and fear. An officer had brought him into a small room and told him to wait, and that he would bring the prisoner in.

Glancing at the chair on the other side of the table, Hoyt was too anxious to sit. He kept reliving that day on Fort Peck Reservoir. Huge waves had rocked the boat as the wind gathered speed and churned up the water from miles down the lake. He'd never seen waves like that and wanted to turn back but Laura had insisted they keep going.

Nor would she wear a life jacket even though she'd told him she couldn't swim. He hadn't wanted the day to turn into one of their horrible fights, so he hadn't made her put the life jacket on. For all these years, he'd regretted that maybe the most.

If she'd been wearing a life jacket, she wouldn't have drowned. Or been able to escape and perpetrate the cruel and inhuman hoax she'd pulled on him.

If she was really alive.

He knew she had to be. Everyone else believed it now, even Sheriff McCall Crawford. Aggie Wells had believed it. Emma, too.

Was the reason he didn't want to believe it because it would mean he'd not only fallen in love with a monster, but he'd married her?

He thought of how he'd nearly drowned diving into the water looking for Laura. Shuddering, he remembered the cold darkness of the water and felt the horror that Laura was down there fighting for her life and he had let her die.

In a body of water as large as Fort Peck, no one had been surprised that her body was never found.

He closed his eyes, hating that he'd married so quickly after her death. By then the adoption had gone through and he had six sons to care for. Tasha had loved them all so and he'd wanted so badly for the boys not to have to grow up without a mother.

Tasha's horseback-riding accident had been ruled just that, an accident. But he knew that if Laura was alive, she'd killed her. Just as she'd killed the next woman who'd come into his life, Krystal.

Laura had tried to frame him for Krystal's murder—just as she was now trying to frame his son. That thought sent a tidal wave of rage roaring through him.

He opened his eyes, fury trumping his terror at coming face-to-face with his dead wife. Whatever Laura's problem, it was with him. She'd taken it out on his wives and now one of his sons. He would stop her. If he had to do it with his bare hands.

He heard footfalls outside the room. The echo grew louder and he braced himself. Was a man ever ready for something like this? The footfalls stopped outside the door. The knob turned, the door swung open and two police officers escorted a dark-haired woman into the room.

She had her head down, but he recognized something familiar in the way she moved. She was the right height, the right body type and even appeared to be close to the age Laura would be now.

One of the police officers motioned for Hoyt to move behind the table.

He stumbled into the chair, gripping the sides as the other officer brought the woman all the way into the room and instructed her to sit down.

She did as she was told.

He watched her slowly lift her head. Her gaze met his.

Hoyt flinched as he looked into the familiar bright blue of her eyes. A sound came out of him, half cry, half curse. *"Laura."*

"I'M SORRY EMMA WASN'T feeling well," Dakota said as she took a seat at the kitchen table. She could see the smoke from the grass fire and silently prayed that Zane and the rest of the firefighters would be safe.

"You don't mind staying with my stepmother?" Zane had said on the way to the ranch.

"Of course not. Emma is delightful."

"She is, isn't she?" he'd said with a laugh. "I have to warn you, though. She'll ply you with cookies or cakes and try to find out everything about the two of us. She'll have us married by the time we get the fire out."

Dakota laughed.

Zane had taken her hand. "Do I need to tell you how crazy I am about you?"

She'd met his gaze and shaken her head. Looking into those blues, she had seen how he felt about her. She was just as crazy about him.

"Well, just in case you don't know, I…I…I'm crazy about you."

She'd laughed, shaking her head. "I love you, too, Zane," she'd said as he pulled up to where the others were battling the fire.

Marshall had come up to Zane's side window then. The next thing she knew she was driving one of the ranch pickups with an empty water tank on the way back down to the house and leaving Zane without another word.

He hadn't said he loved her. She tried not to think about that as she watched the billowing smoke on the horizon, her heart in her throat.

"Do you take milk in your tea?" Mrs. Crowley asked, drawing her attention back to the kitchen.

"No, thank you." Actually, she didn't drink tea, but she wanted to be polite so she said nothing more. One cup of tea wouldn't kill her. She just hoped Zane and the rest of the men were able to get the fire out, and soon.

Something about Mrs. Crowley made her uncomfortable, she thought as she looked over at the housekeeper. The woman had come as a shock. When she'd opened the door, Dakota had been taken aback not so much by the disfigurement, though she hadn't been expecting it, than the look in her one dark eye.

The woman seemed to look through a person.

Dakota shivered at the thought.

"Would you like a sweater?" Mrs. Crowley asked. She had her back to Dakota but she'd seen her shiver?

Dakota realized she'd seen her in the reflection in the microwave door next to her. The woman had been watching her. If Dakota hadn't been creeped out enough by the housekeeper before, she was now.

MRS. CROWLEY HURRIEDLY made a cup of tea for Dakota Lansing. She could feel time running out and knew she was cutting this one way too close. Anything could go wrong. She was usually much more organized. Maybe she was losing her touch.

She had planned on ending this quickly—her first day on the Chisholm ranch. Being back in this house had been excruciating. At the time, she hadn't been able to stand even the thought of spending another day here with Emma and Hoyt.

She'd waited until she'd heard Emma coming downstairs that first day. She'd been ready, the coffee made, a cup prepared for Hoyt's fourth wife.

The moment Emma walked in, she'd turned and said, "I have your coffee ready." She'd turned, cup in hand, knowing that Emma took hers black and strong.

"I thought *I* was an early riser," Emma said, clearly unhappy that she didn't have the kitchen to herself.

"I like to get an early start." She was still holding the cup of coffee out, a small tasteless dose of poison carefully stirred into the black brew. Fast and simple sometimes was the best.

"I really don't want you waiting on me," Emma had said as she took the cup. "I appreciate your thoughtfulness, but coffee's been bothering my stomach."

Mrs. Crowley had watched in horror as Emma poured the contents of the cup into the sink. She proceeded to wash out the cup, then pulled down a mug to make herself a cup of tea.

"I can do that," Mrs. Crowley said, trying to keep the frustration from her voice.

"Like I said, I won't have you waiting on me or Hoyt. We like doing for ourselves. I'm sure we explained that you are merely here to help with the housework and some of the cooking, when I need help."

All Mrs. Crowley had been able to do was nod, but she'd been fuming inside.

"I don't want you working too hard," Emma had said.

"I'm capable—"

"I know," her boss said, cutting her off. "But I hope you will be more of a friend than a…"

"Servant?" She could have told the impossible woman that there was more of a chance of that than ever becoming Emma's friend.

"No, more like family," Emma had said, and gave her a smile. "We really want you to feel at home here, Cynthia."

That's when she'd corrected her. "I prefer you call me Mrs. Crowley."

Not that it had stopped Emma from trying to get close to her. Her plan a failure, Mrs. Crowley had become intrigued by the woman and found herself amused enough that she'd felt no need to rush this. She began studying Emma Chisholm, curious about Hoyt's fourth wife.

And all that time, Emma had been curious about her, studying her, spying on her. When she thought about it, the whole thing was actually funny.

But now as she fixed Dakota's tea, she reminded herself that she was finally taking actions that would culminate in the end she had needed for so long.

She would have to hurry, though, and that made her a little sad. But all good things had to come to an end, she told herself as she turned with two cups of tea in her hands. "Emma says I make the best tea she has ever tasted. I hope you like it."

Hoyt Chisholm was glad he was sitting down. He stared at Laura, unable to believe his eyes. She'd aged, of course, in the past thirty years. They both had.

But she still looked enough like the woman he'd fallen in love with and married that he would have known her anywhere.

"How did you survive that day in the lake?" he asked. "I dove and dove for you and..."

She stared back at him. "I don't know what you're talking about. My name is Sharon Jones. I've never seen you before in my life."

He looked into her blue eyes. He was still so shocked to see her again that he knew he wasn't thinking clearly. Everyone kept telling him she was alive, but he hadn't believed it until this moment.

"If you don't know who I am, then..." Then she couldn't have been the one who had terrorized him and his family. She couldn't have killed his other wives. She couldn't have framed Zane.

"You're...lying," he said, telling himself this woman was Laura. He felt the weight of what that meant. It brought with it all the ramifications of what this woman had done to him and his family.

What scared him was whether or not the police would be able to prove it. What if they couldn't lock this woman up and throw away the key? He and Emma and his sons would have to live the rest of their lives in fear of what Laura would do next.

"You're a liar and a murderer," he said.

She shook her head slowly and gave him a small half smile. "You're…mistaken."

She even *sounded* like Laura. No one could look this much like his first wife or sound so much like her, unless…

He'd been so shocked to see her that for a moment he'd forgotten what the woman was capable of doing to him. She'd always messed with his mind. Her faked death, her affair with Clay Lansing—she'd put him through hell and had no intentions of stopping.

"She's Laura," he told the cops as he got to his feet. "Get a DNA sample from her and you'll be able to prove this woman is lying. She's wanted for murder in Whitehorse. I'll testify that she is my first wife, Lorraine Baxter Chisholm."

The woman looked up at him as one of the cops helped her to her feet. "You're wrong. Dead wrong."

He shook his head. If she wasn't Laura, then she was her twin sister. "It's her."

As the officer started to take her out of the room, she leaned toward Hoyt and whispered. "Are you really willing to stake your life on it? Or Emma's?"

Her words didn't surprise him. But when she gave him that half smile again, he realized where he'd seen it before—and where the real Laura Chisholm was right now.

DAKOTA TOOK ONE of the lemon cookies as Mrs. Crowley placed a cup of tea in front of her.

"Emma tells me that you recently lost your father," Mrs. Crowley said.

"Yes."

"I'm sorry. I understand he raised stock for rodeos."

Dakota didn't really want to talk about her father. "Yes." She wished Emma would wake up from her nap soon. The housekeeper continued to stare at her with that one dark eye, making her nervous.

She looked toward the kitchen door, hoping to see Emma's friendly face. Instead, she saw something odd.

Part of an apron was sticking out from the under the door of the pantry.

Mrs. Crowley followed her gaze. Dakota couldn't miss the change in the woman's expression.

"Why don't you finish your tea and I'll check on Mrs. Chisholm," the housekeeper said.

Dakota nodded mutely. Emma kept her kitchen spotless. Dakota had noticed when she'd helped her with the desserts the other night. She'd commented then about what a wonderful kitchen it was.

"It's my domain. Everything I wanted in a kitchen. Everything in its place," Emma had said. "I have my sons and husband trained not to touch anything in here. I try my best to keep Mrs. Crowley out as well." She'd made a face. "The woman never puts anything back where it goes. I swear, she'd rearrange everything if I let her."

Mrs. Crowley rose from her chair. Dakota picked up her teacup. She hadn't taken more than a sip. The tea tasted bitter and she didn't want any more of it. She pretended to drink, hoping she could get rid of it when Mrs. Crowley went to check on Emma.

Dakota waited until the woman left the room, then quickly got up and dumped the tea down the drain before hurrying back to the table.

She'd barely sat down again when Mrs. Crowley appeared in the kitchen doorway. Dakota jumped, even more nervous now. She'd come too close to being caught. Why hadn't she just told the woman she didn't like tea?

She hurriedly picked up one of the cookies and took a bite, hoping Mrs. Crowley didn't notice that her hand was shaking as she did.

Mrs. Crowley stood at the end of the kitchen table watching her. "You like her cookies?"

Dakota nodded. "They're delicious. She told me she loves to bake."

"Can't keep her out of the kitchen," Mrs. Crowley said.

Dakota noticed the housekeeper had her hand in the pocket of the apron she wore and she seemed to be standing more upright than she had before.

"You remind me of your father."

Dakota's gaze shot to the woman's face, settling on the one dark eye. "What?"

"Your father. I knew him."

Dakota stared at the woman. "You knew my father?"

"You didn't drink your tea," Mrs. Crowley said.

The swift change of topic threw her for a moment. "I'm sorry, I thought you just said you knew my father."

"As a matter of fact, we had a very short, intense affair when you were two."

Dakota felt her eyes widen in alarm at the woman's words—and the gun she pulled from her apron pocket. It was a short, snub-nosed revolver and it was pointed right at Dakota's heart.

"You could have made it so much easier if you had only drank your tea like a good girl," Mrs. Crowley said. "I cared about your father. I could have been happy with him had it not been for you. I've never liked children."

"Courtney." The word had slipped out.

"Yes, your sister."

"She's your daughter?" Dakota was still trying to make sense of what she was hearing—and seeing.

"I gave birth to her, if that's what you mean."

"You're…"

Mrs. Crowley smiled. "I used to be Laura Chisholm. Get up. We're going for a ride."

"Where's Emma?"

"Don't worry, she's coming with us."

The gravity of the situation was just starting to sink in. Hoyt was in Butte, his sons were fighting a grass fire and Dakota was looking down the barrel of a gun held by a crazy woman and known killer. She hated to think what this woman had done to Emma, let alone Courtney.

"What are you going to do with us?"

"If it makes you feel any better, before your father died he pleaded with me to promise that I wouldn't hurt you," Laura Chisholm said, then laughed. "Unfortunately he died before I promised him anything."

"You were there when he died." Hadn't she known that was the case? "You and Courtney. You must have taken him to the hospital. Or Courtney—"

"Don't be naive. I gave him something that caused the heart attack, why would I try to save him? Courtney took him, but not until I was sure he wouldn't survive."

Dakota took a step toward the woman, her anger overpowering her common sense. She wanted to take the gun away from this woman and—

"I wouldn't do that," Laura said. "I don't care where

you die but if you ever want to see your sister again, you will do what I tell you."

Dakota watched as Laura popped out the white contact from her eye without ever letting the gun trained on Dakota waver. She popped the other contact out and stared at Dakota with two familiar blue eyes. Courtney had inherited her mother's blue eyes.

EMMA STIRRED, EYELIDS flickering. Her body felt like it was made of lead weights. She didn't think she could move and didn't try for a few moments.

As her eyes finally managed to stay open, she looked around and saw that she was lying on the floor of the pantry.

Had she fallen? Fainted? She tried to sit up and found her muscles so lethargic it took all of her effort.

She was partway up into a sitting position when memory flooded her and she froze, listening.

Voices. She listened, recognizing Mrs. Crowley's monotone. It took her a moment to place the other voice. Dakota Lansing.

Emma sat up the rest of the way, thinking only that she had to save Dakota. She felt her head spin from the sudden movement and thought she might pass out.

She took a moment, trying to clear her head, her thoughts. How did she think she was going to save Dakota when she wasn't even sure she could get to her feet?

As she listened, she felt her blood turn to ice. Mrs. Crowley was Laura Chisholm. The woman had been living in their house all this time? Her heart pounded at the thought of the murderer this close to them.

But hadn't she known something was wrong? Hadn't

she been spying on the woman? She would never have guessed, though, that Mrs. Crowley was Laura Chisholm. Her disguise was too good. Now Emma understood why the woman had kept them all at arm's length. Finally, Emma knew the woman's biggest secret of all.

She heard Mrs. Crowley say, "I guess I don't need to check on Mrs. Chisholm. I hear her getting up now."

She'd heard her moving in the pantry.

From the conversation, Emma knew she didn't have much time. Mrs. Crowley had drugged her, and now the woman had Dakota and was planning on taking them to Courtney.

Emma, even through the haze of whatever she'd been drugged with, was betting the drive would be eleven miles round-trip.

She struggled to her feet. She knew she couldn't fight off the woman she'd known as Mrs. Crowley. All she could do was try to leave a message for Hoyt or the boys when they returned.

She looked around for something to write with and spotted her chalkboard on the back of the pantry door where she made her grocery lists.

Hurriedly, she grabbed a piece of chalk and as quietly as possible, began to write.

Chapter Fourteen

Hoyt called the house immediately, his heart dropping when the phone rang and rang. He left a message for Emma to call him at once.

Then he started to call Sheriff McCall Crawford as he watched the police take the woman he'd thought was Laura back to her cell.

She turned once to look back at him and mouthed, "Too late."

And then she was gone through a door.

Hoyt thought if he had to look at her another minute, he would have gone for her throat.

He'd call the sheriff and his sons on the way to the plane. He needed to get home as quickly as possible. Fortunately, he'd be flying back, but still it would take him too long. That had been the plan, though, hadn't it?

Hoyt couldn't take that thought any further because he knew the rest of her plan. Emma. The thought of losing her was almost his undoing. Ahead he saw the plane and pilot waiting for him.

As he hurried to the plane, he knew this was all his fault. He'd invited the woman into his house. Once as his wife. Now as his housekeeper.

Laura must be ecstatic that she'd fooled him so eas-

ily. She'd played him, getting him out of town, far from
the ranch and Emma. He prayed he was wrong, but the
more the thought about it, he knew Mrs. Crowley was
Laura. He racked his brain. Had Laura ever mentioned
a twin sister?

He couldn't remember, but the woman he'd just seen
at the police station was a close relative, there was no
doubt about that. And right now, the woman wasn't
going anywhere. The police would be able to hold her
until they could get to the bottom of this.

If Laura hurt Emma...

His heart ached from trying to hold in his terror. He
had married a monster. Or had he made her that way?

Hoyt didn't know. He just hoped he'd get a chance
to ask her—before he killed her.

McCALL HADN'T GOTTEN MUCH sleep last night. The baby
had kicked the entire night, it seemed. She'd called in
and told the dispatcher she'd be running a little late.

"Can you stay within cell phone range today?" she
asked Luke.

"The baby?" His eyes lit when he asked. He smiled
as he placed a large hand on her abdomen and felt the
baby kick.

She smiled and covered his hand with hers. Her undersheriff Nick Giovanni would be back tomorrow to
take over. She was more than ready.

She was hoping for a slow day at the office when
her cell phone rang.

Luke shot her a look. "Whatever it is—"

"Sheriff Crawford," she said, taking the call. She
listened, avoiding Luke's gaze and trying not to let

her true feelings show in her expression. "Don't worry, Hoyt, I'm on my way."

"Hoyt Chisholm? I thought he'd gone to Butte to identify his first wife."

"She wasn't Laura. But he thinks he knows where Laura is." She reached for her shoulder holster.

"I'm going with you."

She started to argue but felt the baby kick. Her stomach cramped and for a moment she held her breath, knowing Luke was watching her intently.

"All right." Even though Luke was a game warden, he'd had the same law enforcement training and was often called in when there was a need.

"Where does he think Laura is?" Luke asked as they headed for her patrol SUV.

"Chisholm ranch. He thinks Laura has been masquerading as his housekeeper, Mrs. Crowley."

Luke let out a low curse. "And Emma?"

"Hoyt tried the house and couldn't raise anyone, but they could all be at that grass fire I heard called in earlier. It's under control, but apparently Emma is missing and so is Mrs. Crowley."

ZANE COULD SEE THE DRIVER of the pickup and knew the man wasn't going to slow down. He was betting that the man driving the truck was the escaped prisoner from California and had nothing to lose and everything to gain if he got away.

"Zane." Marshall sounded worried. "Zane, I quit playing chicken when I was fourteen."

At the speed that they were traveling, the two pickups were going to meet at the same time where the two roads intersected.

"I'm not letting him get away," Zane said, and kept the pedal floored.

He watched the pickup out of the corner of his eye growing closer and closer. He saw Marshall reach for the dash to brace himself for the crash they both knew was coming.

At the last moment, the driver of the other truck veered to the left. Zane hit his brakes and cranked his wheel to the right, but he was still going too fast to keep from hitting the other truck.

The driver's side of Zane's pickup smashed into the passenger side of the other truck, driving it farther up the road and out into the open pasture. As Zane fought to keep control of his pickup, the other driver hit a dry irrigation ditch.

Zane swerved away, tires digging into the dirt, the truck rocking wildly.

"He's losing it," Marshall said as the other truck rolled. It churned up a cloud of dust as it rolled a second time and came to rest on its top out in the middle of the pasture.

When Zane got his pickup stopped at the edge of the road, he and Marshall jumped out and ran toward the truck. The driver had kicked out the windshield and was trying to climb out. The man matched the mug shot the sheriff had provided them of the third escaped prisoner so they could keep an eye out for him.

The escaped felon crawled out, bloody and bruised. He was hurt badly enough that he didn't put up a fight, just lay on his back in the grass.

"I need a doctor," the man cried. "You almost killed me."

"Where is Courtney Baxter?" Zane demanded.

"I'm not saying anything without a lawyer," the man said.

"I'll take care of him," Marshall said, no doubt seeing that his brother wanted to beat the truth out of the man. He grabbed some rope from the back of the pickup and began tying up the escaped prisoner for the ride to the sheriff's department.

Zane's cell rang. "Is everything all right at the house?" he asked when he saw that it was his brother Dawson calling.

"No one's here."

"What?" He looked at Marshall. "He says there's no one there."

"Wait a minute," Dawson said on the other end of the line. "I just found a note from Mrs. Crowley saying that they have gone into town."

Zane was shaking his head. "I'm going to the house," he called to Marshall, who signaled him to go.

Running to his pickup, he leaped in and tore down the road toward the ranch house. Emma wouldn't go into town, not with her stepsons fighting a grass fire burning down the road. She'd be baking something for when they finished with the fire.

He prayed he was wrong about the fire being a diversion. But the timing of the fire was too much of a coincidence. And now Emma, Dakota and Mrs. Crowley were gone?

He could see the house in the distance. Zane raced toward it, his heart in his throat. He kept seeing Dakota's face, remembering their lovemaking.

Why in the hell hadn't he told her that he loved her?

As the house loomed ahead, he prayed Dakota was all right.

"DID SHE HURT YOU?" Dakota asked Emma as they bounced along the road in the ranch pickup. Dakota was driving; Emma sat in the middle with Laura Chisholm holding a gun on her.

"No." Emma had been pretending to doze off and on from the time Dakota had helped Laura put her in the pickup.

"Just keep your eye on the road," Laura snapped. She'd peeled the scar off her face and no longer looked anything like Mrs. Crowley.

"Why are you doing this?" Dakota asked, trying to keep the fear out of her voice. She'd heard all about Laura Chisholm, knew at least some of the horrible things she'd done and suspected there was even worse they didn't know about. Dakota couldn't bear to think of this woman with her father.

"You wouldn't understand," Laura said, and leaned down a little to look into Emma's face. Emma had her eyes closed and her head on Dakota's shoulder.

As they'd been leaving the house, Emma had leaned heavily on her and seemed completely out of it. Until she'd whispered, "Be ready once we reach the well house." Then she had touched her fingers to her lips.

Dakota had nodded and squeezed her hand.

Now she wondered how Emma had known where they were going even before Laura had begun barking out orders.

"Can you drive any slower?" Laura snapped.

Dakota gave the pickup a little more speed. The road was narrow and bumpy as it cut through pasture. As they dropped over a hill, the house disappeared behind them.

"No one is coming to save you," Laura assured her

as she caught Dakota looking in the rearview mirror. "That's a nasty fire that could destroy most of their pasture on that side of the ranch. They aren't going to stop fighting the fire to save you."

Clearly, this woman was behind the fire. She'd managed to get everyone away from the house. Dakota wondered how the housekeeper had started the fire and realized it must have been the third escaped prisoner from California.

"Emma, I'm surprised you don't want to ask about me and Hoyt," Laura taunted.

Emma seemed to stir. "Hoyt?"

Laura laughed. "You do realize that you're not even legally married, since I am alive and well?"

Alive, yes. Well? Dakota thought not. She was just grateful she hadn't drunk the tea the woman had made her. She feared neither she nor Emma would still be alive for this little trip.

As Dakota drove over another hill, she saw the creek through a stand of pines and beyond that, what appeared to be a small stone building with an old waterwheel on one side and a cistern on the other.

At the house, Zane threw the pickup into Park and jumped out. As he was running toward the door, he noticed that the truck Mrs. Crowley drove was gone. Someone had left, maybe all three of them, but they hadn't gone to town. Of that he was sure.

He hit the front door, burst through it and into the house, already calling Dakota's name as he ran.

"Dakota!" The house felt empty long before he reached the large kitchen.

He glanced upstairs. "Dakota?" Taking the stairs

two at a time, he charged up to the next floor, all the time telling himself there was no one here. But he had to be sure.

He hadn't passed anyone on the main road but that didn't mean anything. There were numerous back roads on the ranch.

At the bottom of the stairs, he glanced toward the kitchen and noticed two teacups sitting on the table along with a plate of cookies.

Emma would never leave her kitchen without cleaning everything up.

He stepped in and noticed another teacup in the sink. The pantry door was ajar as well.

His phone rang, making him jump. For a moment he thought it was going to be Dakota. He imagined her telling him that she and Emma had gone for a drive with Mrs. Crowley to see the fire.

"Zane?"

It was his brother Marshall. "Is everything all right there?"

"No one's here, just like Dawson said. The pickup Mrs. Crowley has been using is gone."

"Zane, earlier Emma was telling me that she'd been spying on Mrs. Crowley. Apparently the old gal's been going out late at night and not coming back until the wee hours of the morning. She was telling me about it when I saw the fire. She thought Mrs. Crowley might have been meeting a man somewhere on the ranch."

Zane didn't even want to ask why Emma had been spying on the housekeeper. Racing to the far wing, Zane knocked at the housekeeper's door. No answer. He tried the knob. Locked. If he was wrong, his father would not be happy.

He stepped back, lifted his leg and kicked at the door. One more kick and the frame shattered, the lock broke and the door swung in.

The room was immaculate. In fact, it didn't even look as if anyone was staying here.

"Mrs. Crowley?" He stepped in. "Mrs. Crowley?" The bathroom door was ajar. He pushed it all the way open. Empty.

As he turned to leave, he spotted the framed photograph and froze in midstep.

It was a photograph of his father and a woman he'd never seen before. Why would Mrs. Crowley have a photograph of his father and some woman?

He stepped over to the picture and picked up the silver frame. His father looked incredibly young. Behind him was the original ranch house before the later additions, so that meant the woman in the photograph had to have been his father's first wife, Laura.

His gaze went to the woman in the photo. He felt his heart drop to his stomach. The frame slipped from his fingers and hit the floor, the glass shattering.

Laura Chisholm was Mrs. Crowley? She'd been living here all these months, right under their roof?

His cell phone rang. His father. He quickly answered it.

EMMA CONTINUED TO ACT as if she was still suffering from the drug Laura had given her. Through her half-closed eyes, she watched the landscape she had come to love blur past the window of the pickup.

Laura had a small, snub-nosed pistol pressed against her side. Emma felt the cold, hard metal with each bump that the pickup hit as Dakota drove them away from the prairie and up into the foothills.

Out of the corner of her eye, she saw the blackened, scorched earth from the grass fire off to the east. By now her sons would have the flames out and possibly be heading back to the house. She could only hope that they would find the note she'd left in the pantry.

"Don't you want to talk about it?" Laura asked.

Emma raised her head just a little to glance sideways at the woman. She looked so different now without the scarred face, the sightless eye. What gleamed in her two blue eyes was a brittle hatred that made her inwardly flinch.

"I would think you'd have questions for me. Don't you want to know how I survived, how I killed Tasha and Krystal, how I framed your stepson with the help of my daughter?"

Did any of that matter now? Emma didn't think so. "You're sick."

Laura laughed. "I'm no sicker than your friend Aggie."

That reminder stirred something in Emma. She had to tamp it down to keep from showing Laura that she wasn't as drugged as she was pretending.

"I know you killed her," Emma said, slurring her words.

"I hated doing it, though. I admired Aggie. We had a lot in common."

Aggie would have looked beyond Mrs. Crowley's disguise and not been fooled, Emma thought, then remembered that Aggie was dead because Laura had ultimately fooled her somehow as well.

"Why don't you just kill me?" Emma said. "Let Dakota go."

Laura smiled. "I'm afraid I've had to change my plans. You know, if you had drank that first cup of coffee I fixed you the morning after I started my job, it would have been all over right then. No one else would have gotten hurt."

Emma remembered the anger and frustration she'd seen in Mrs. Crowley's expression that morning. She'd misinterpreted it as the woman simply trying to establish herself in the house, the kitchen in particular.

"You could have poisoned me at any time after that," Emma said.

Laura chuckled. "You amused and intrigued me. I liked watching you, knowing that I could kill you at any time—and you had no idea who I was."

"That must have made you very happy." They were close to the old well house now. Emma cut her gaze to Dakota. The young woman was strong and determined, her hands on the wheel sure. Emma knew she could trust Dakota to put up a fight when the time came. She just hoped that she didn't get her killed.

"Park here," Laura ordered. She couldn't help being disappointed. She'd expected more out of Emma. She regretted giving her a drug that, while it had allowed Emma to regain consciousness, made her pathetically docile. She'd hoped for more fight out of her.

"Give me the keys," she told Dakota, who turned off the ignition and handed over the keys.

Laura saw them both looking expectantly toward the old stone well house and stone water tank.

"Let's go see Courtney," Laura said. "I know how

badly you want to see your sister. But remember. If you try anything, I will shoot Emma, then shoot you *and* Courtney."

"You would kill your own daughter?" Dakota demanded.

"I told you. I don't like children. Especially my own."

"What did my father ever see in you?"

Laura laughed. "I was beautiful and sexy and he was broken after your mother's death. I was touched by that kind of anguished love and wished Hoyt loved me half as much."

That got a small rise out of Emma. "Maybe he would have loved you more if you hadn't cheated on him."

Laura opened the pickup door and, keeping the barrel of the gun buried in Emma's side, pulled her out.

"You know nothing about it," she snapped, hating that she'd let Emma get to her. She couldn't have been more jealous of Emma than she was at that moment. Hoyt adored Emma. The two couldn't keep their hands off each other. He'd never been like that with her.

At the door to the well house, she tossed the key to the padlock to Dakota. The stone building had been perfect for her needs. It had no windows, only one door and was almost six miles from the ranch. Nor did anyone ever come up this way.

Laura remembered it because Hoyt had brought her out here the only time she'd ridden a horse with him.

"Open it."

DAKOTA CAUGHT THE KEY. Laura still had the gun pressed into Emma's side, a hand gripping her arm. Emma gave a slight shake of her head. Apparently she didn't want to try to do anything until they got inside.

She inserted the key into the padlock, fearing what they would find inside this odd building. The door was made of metal and had rusted over the years. She had to push hard to get it to open.

As it swung in, Dakota blinked. The only light in the stone structure came from the now open doorway and from four small openings high above in the circular stone walls.

The walls were smooth and there were several old watermarks on them. Dakota realized that this was part of the cistern used for water storage.

She spotted her sister in the shadows and felt a surge of relief. Courtney was alive. For a moment, that was all that mattered. Then she heard the rattle of chains and noticed the handcuff around Courtney's right wrist. The other end of the chain was attached to a pipe that ran along the wall.

Courtney began to cry at the sight of her. "Dakota, how did you—" The rest of her sister's words died on her lips as she saw Laura and Emma come into the room.

"A little family reunion," Laura said.

Courtney seemed to cower, a look of despair on her face. Dakota noticed that she was dressed in a pair of old jeans, a soiled T-shirt and sneakers. There were several containers that looked as if they had contained food stacked in the corner.

"You've kept my sister here chained to a pipe like an animal?" Dakota said, turning on Laura.

"Let's not forget that *your sister* was in on framing your boyfriend," the woman said.

"I haven't forgotten," Dakota said.

"I thought it was just a joke," Courtney cried. "I didn't know…." Her eyes filled with tears again as she bit off the rest of the lie. "Oh, Dakota, I'm so sorry."

As Laura started to shove Emma into the room, Dakota caught her signal. Emma whirled around, taking Laura by surprise, and knocked the gun from her hand. It skittered across the concrete floor. Dakota dove for it.

She heard Emma let out a cry and heard Courtney yell a warning. As her hand closed over the gun she was kicked hard in the side, knocking the air out of her.

Then Laura was on her, slamming her head against the concrete floor. Dakota felt blood run down into her left eye as she tried to fight the woman off. For her age, Laura was surprisingly strong and she fought dirty. She grabbed a handful of Dakota's hair, jerking her head back as she wrenched the gun from her hands.

In an instant, Laura was on her feet and holding the gun on them.

Dakota rolled over, wiping blood from her eye. Emma had gotten to her feet, but Laura had been too fast for her to intervene. She backed up as Laura swung the barrel of the gun toward her.

"Stupid. Stupid. Stupid," Laura said, sounding breathless and yet excited. "I should just shoot you right now. If Dakota moves a muscle, I will."

Dakota froze where she was on the floor as the woman backed her way to the open doorway.

"You aren't going to leave again," Courtney cried. "Please, Mother."

"Don't call me that. You were just a mistake of nature," Laura snapped. "My use for you is over. You wanted to get to know your sister? Well, now's your chance."

"Who is the woman the Butte police have in custody?" Emma asked.

"My cousin. People always thought we were sisters, we're so much alike. She owed me a favor," Laura said with a shrug.

Emma was just thankful that Hoyt was in Butte. By now he would realize he'd been sent on a wild goose chase, but he'd be safe from this woman.

"You know Hoyt will never remarry," Laura said.

"Yes, I know. Is that really all you want, for him to never find happiness with another woman?" Emma asked.

"You make it sound so simple." Laura shook her head. "I *loved* him. I should have been enough, but then suddenly he tells me he's adopting three infant sons and talking about getting another three who needed homes."

"Hoyt loves children," Emma said.

"Yes, but I don't."

"Clearly," Dakota said. "Anyone who could chain up her own daughter and keep her prisoner out here…"

"Don't judge me," Laura snapped, and waved the gun at her.

"You have what you want," Emma said quickly. "Let Courtney and Dakota go. By the time they walk back to the house, I'll be dead and you will be long gone."

Laura smiled. "I thought killing you would be enough, but I was wrong. By the time Hoyt gets back to the ranch, you'll be gone and so will his sons. He will have nothing left. Only then will he finally know how he made me feel."

With that, Laura stepped out through the door, slamming and locking the airtight metal door behind her as she plunged them into semidarkness.

"She's leaving us to die here," Courtney cried.

"No," Emma said as she quickly moved to Dakota and helped her up. "She's not. Are you badly hurt?"

Dakota shook her head as she heard what sounded like the crank of an old metal wheel. "She's not through with us, is she?"

Emma shook her head.

"What?" Courtney cried. "What are you whispering about?"

Before either could answer they heard the water. It cranked and creaked through the ancient pipes for a few moments before it began to fill the chamber where the three of them were now trapped.

Chapter Fifteen

Courtney let out a scream as water began rushing in around her feet. She tried to pull away but she was still hooked to the old pipe that ran along the wall.

"Stay calm," Emma ordered as she and Dakota hurried over to Courtney.

"I think if we both pull on this pipe we might be able to dislodge it," Dakota said. She met Emma's gaze as they both grabbed hold of the rusty pipe. They could feel the water surging through it. Once it broke, the chamber might fill even faster.

But the water was rising quickly and Courtney was manacled close to the floor. She would drown if they couldn't get her free.

"On the count of three," Emma said. "One, two, three!"

Dakota pulled as hard as she could. She heard Emma straining next to her. The pipe gave only a little.

Courtney began to scream. Water was lapping around their ankles now. A leak had sprung in the pipe. A spray of rust-red water showered over the three of them, drenching them to the skin.

"Courtney," Dakota snapped. "You can help. Grab

hold of the chain and pull on the count of three. One, two, three!"

The pipe came lose and the three of them were sent sprawling in the rising water.

"Okay, we can't panic," Emma said as even more water began to flow into the tanklike room. "I left a message. Someone will find it."

But they both knew there was little chance of Hoyt making it back in time. The rest of the Chisholms were fighting the fire. She and Dakota shared a look.

"Zane will come for me," Dakota said, praying it was true. Courtney was crying, pushing at the water with her hands as it rose to their thighs.

"All we have to do is swim when it gets too deep to stand," Emma said. "Once we reach those small windows up there, the water will rush out. We'll be able to breathe."

Dakota looked up at the four slits in the rock, then at Emma. Neither said anything, but Dakota knew the water wouldn't be able to rush out fast enough to save them, because the slits were too close to the top of the tank.

Their only hope was being found before they drowned.

LUKE HAD INSISTED on driving. "You'll be more comfortable in the passenger seat," he'd said, and McCall knew he'd been watching her. Nor was she feeling well enough to argue the point. She tried to get comfortable, but it was impossible with the baby being so active.

Time was of the essence if Hoyt was right and his housekeeper was Laura Chisholm. As far as Hoyt had known, the two were alone in the house, she told Luke.

"Hasn't this woman been working for them for several months?" Luke asked as he drove toward Whitehorse. She and Luke lived south of town on Luke's folks' old place. He'd built them a beautiful home, which he'd made her wedding present.

"So why would Emma have something to fear now, is that what you're asking?" McCall said. She'd been thinking the same thing. "I wonder if it doesn't have something to do with Zane." She had told him about Courtney Hughes aka Courtney Baxter. "Laura's her mother."

Luke shook his head. "If this Mrs. Crowley is Laura Chisholm, then where is Courtney?"

That was the question, and had been since she'd disappeared the night after her "date" with Zane. He was out on bail and if Courtney didn't turn up, or worse, turned up dead...

"Have you thought any more about what you want to do after the baby is born?" Luke asked.

McCall had her hand on her abdomen. She loved the feel of their child inside her. Safe. But once the baby was born... She flinched as she felt not a cramp, but what could only be a contraction.

"Honey?" Luke said, glancing over at her. "McCall?" He sounded alarmed.

"It's nothing. Just a twinge." That was all it had been, right? The baby moving so much must have caused it.

Suddenly she was scared. She would have gladly faced killers every day than to think about being the mother to this baby.

"Talk to me, McCall. I know something's going on with you."

"It was just a twinge," she said, hoping it was true.

She needed to carry this baby to term. It was a month too early.

"I'm talking about right now. I'm talking about the last eight months," Luke said. "I know you're worried about the baby because we lost the first one, but—"

"I'm scared." The words were out before she could call them back. She hated to admit to Luke how she was feeling. "I'm not sure what kind of mother I'll be. Look at my mother. Ruby was...well, Ruby."

"That's ridiculous," Luke said. "Is that all that's been bothering you? You're nothing like Ruby, thank heaven." He looked over at her and said, "McCall?"

She had another contraction, this one much stronger than the first one. "I think I'm in labor. It just came on so suddenly." She remembered losing the other baby. It had started much like this.

"I'm taking you to the hospital."

She nodded as she heard Luke on the patrol SUV radio calling the sheriff's office. "Halley Robinson is the closest to the Chisholm place. Have them send her," McCall said.

Luke passed on the message as he raced toward the hospital.

McCall prayed her baby would be all right. She was almost to term. But what would she do once the baby was born? She was terrified she might become like her mother.

AFTER THE CALL FROM HIS father, Zane raced back downstairs to the kitchen. Hoyt had already figured out somehow that Mrs. Crowley was Laura.

"You have to stop her," his father had pleaded. "Whatever you have to do."

Zane knew what he was saying. But first he had to find them. If Emma was right and Mrs. Crowley had been going somewhere on the ranch at night...

In the kitchen he noticed the partially opened pantry door—and the hem of Emma's apron sticking out. He quickly moved to it, heart in his throat as he prayed he wouldn't find her—

The pantry was empty. He breathed a sigh of relief, then saw the note on the chalkboard.

Well house. Laura/Crowley. Hurry.

The well house was an old cistern system that hadn't been used in years. Water had been diverted from the creek for storage for low precipitation years back when the ranch was started.

Zane placed a call to his brothers as he ran to his pickup. He told them everything, including what his father had said as he drove toward the well house. "Marshall has taken the third prisoner escapee into jail."

"We have a section of fire we're fighting near the house," Dawson said.

"I can handle this. I just needed you to know. Dad is flying in. He's going to be heading straight for the ranch the minute his plane touches down."

"Find them," Dawson said.

"I will." Zane snapped the phone shut and drove as fast as he could up the road toward the foothills.

LAURA COULD SEE DUST in the distance. She'd told Rex to pick off one after another of the Chisholm brothers.

Now she had a bad feeling he hadn't done as he was told. She should have killed him instead of his mouthy cellmate Lloyd. Lloyd would have gotten the job done.

As she started to climb into the ranch pickup, she

saw the flat tire. For a moment she just stood looking at it.

A flat? It seemed inconceivable that something so ordinary could foil her plans. For years she'd gotten away with murder, literally, because she'd planned every detail meticulously.

Laura glanced toward the road down in the valley again. Dust boiled up behind a rig headed this way fast.

She looked around for a place to hide, telling herself fate was playing right into her hand. She needed a vehicle and someone was bringing her one.

All she had to do was pull the trigger when the time came and then get out of here.

She could hear the water filling the tank and imagined the three women inside panicking. Especially Courtney.

For just an instant, Laura felt badly that Clay Lansing's daughters were part of the collateral damage.

But there was no way Laura could leave the girls alive. Courtney especially was like a loose thread. One little tug and everything would come unraveled.

As the vehicle coming up the road grew near, Laura looked around for a good spot to hide in wait to ambush whoever it was. She needed their vehicle and, one way or another, she planned to get it.

THEY WOULD HAVE TO SWIM soon. The water was rising faster now. Emma realized Laura must have closed off the main cistern tank. With the floodgates open, this tank was filling fast.

Creek water lapped at her waist. The three of them had moved to the edge of the tank closest to the door. They had tried to break down the door but to no avail.

Now they were just saving their energy for when they would have to swim.

"I'm so sorry," Courtney said, not for the first time. "When she contacted me I was just so glad to finally meet my birth mother."

"It doesn't matter now," Dakota said.

"We're going to die, aren't we?"

"No, we're not," Emma snapped. She wished Dakota's sister had her strength and courage. The young woman seemed to have been pampered much of her life. A little hardship and struggle seemed to hone a person for times like this. Courtney hadn't been tested and now, facing the biggest test of her life, was ill prepared.

"Do you hear something?" Courtney asked suddenly.

Over the sound of the water filling the tank, Emma listened. A vehicle.

Courtney brightened. "Someone is coming to save us, just like you said." She was all smiles now.

Emma shared a look with Dakota, who seemed to share her own worry. She hadn't heard Laura leave and now feared that whoever was coming was about to walk right into a trap.

ZANE SLOWED AS HE SAW the ranch pickup parked next to the well house. He'd pulled his shotgun down from the rack behind the pickup seat and had it and his pistol within reach.

Slowly, he pulled up behind the pickup and saw the flat tire. He killed the engine, listening through his open side window.

Where were they? More to the point, where was Laura Chisholm?

That's when he heard the water sloshing around in the old cistern tank. What the hell?

And in that instant, he knew. Jumping out of the truck, he ran to the door.

"Dakota? Emma?" he yelled. He could hear water running in from the creek and the faint sound of voices on the other side.

He tried the door, but it opened inward so the water in the tank would make it impossible to open.

There was only one option. He had to close the head-gates on the creek, divert the water back into the creek and drain the tank as quickly as possible.

He rushed around the side to the headgates. Someone had jammed a crowbar into them, locking the gates open. He was struggling to free the crowbar when he heard the first shot.

A bullet whizzed past his ear. The second shot splintered the wood next to him.

Diving for cover, he used the momentum and his weight to dislodge the crowbar. But the gate was still open, water still filling the tank, just not as quickly.

He peered out, trying to assess where the shots had come from. He didn't need to ask who had just tried to kill him.

Another bullet whizzed past. Laura had to be in the trees up on the side of the hill. He could still hear the water flowing into the tank. In order to drain the tank, he had to get from where he was across twenty yards without cover.

She'd fired three shots, but he didn't doubt she'd come with plenty of ammunition. Nor could he wait her out. The flow into the cistern had slowed almost to a trickle but he had to drain the tank. He didn't know how long Dakota and Emma could stay afloat in there. If they were even still alive.

The thought forced him to move. He pulled out his pistol and hoped he was right about Laura being in the trees on the hillside. It was a chance he had to take. Once he got the drain opened…

He got ready, then, firing as he ran, sprinted toward the cistern. If he could reach it and get on the far side…

DEPUTY HALLEY ROBINSON SAW the smoke and the men putting out the last of the grass fire as she raced down the road toward the Chisholm house.

She recognized her fiancé, Colton Chisholm, on the fire line but she didn't stop. Her orders were to get to the house as quickly as possible and arrest the woman she knew only as Mrs. Crowley.

Halley had to ask the dispatcher to repeat what she'd said.

"The housekeeper is believed to be Laura Chisholm."

Halley still couldn't believe it. She'd seen the cantankerous Mrs. Crowley on numerous occasions when she'd been out to the ranch house. Everyone gave her a wide berth. Halley wasn't sure she'd ever looked the woman in the eye or really studied her face.

Now, as she neared the house, her only thought was of Emma. She'd fallen in love with Colton's stepmother, everyone had. If this report was right, then Laura Chisholm was a killer hell-bent on killing Hoyt's fourth wife—as she had his other two.

Halley parked in front of the house, noticing that the pickup Mrs. Crowley drove wasn't anywhere around. But there was a ranch pickup out front.

Climbing out, she unsnapped her holster, her hand

on the butt of her weapon as she mounted the stairs, crossed the porch and knocked at the door. No answer.

She tried the knob. "Hello?" No answer again.

She made her way to the kitchen, Emma's domain. The house had an eerie feel to it that she didn't like. The moment she saw the cluttered kitchen she knew something was wrong.

Then she saw the note. Mrs. Crowley had written that they had gone into town. But that was marked out and below it was scrawled "Well house, Laura has Emma and Dakota." It was signed "Zane."

Fortunately Colton had taken Halley up to the old well house once on a horseback ride. She ran for her cruiser, called in her ETA and a request for backup she knew wouldn't be coming in time as she raced up the road toward the foothills.

McCALL GLANCED AT THE CLOCK on the wall and felt another hard contraction coming. "Check and see if there has been any word from Halley," she said, her voice strained.

She was worried. There'd been no word on what was going on out at the Chisholm ranch. More and more, she suspected that Hoyt had been right. The house-keeper *was* Laura Chisholm, and everyone knew what that woman was capable of.

"I checked a few minutes ago," Luke said. "Honey, there is nothing you can do but have this baby. Halley can handle herself. So can the Chisholm men."

McCall nodded and tried to breathe through the contraction. Luke was right. There was nothing she could do for Emma or anyone else. She was about to have their baby. She tried to concentrate on breathing.

Just think about your baby.

"Did you call my grandmother?" she asked as the contraction ended.

Luke laughed. "Of course. She'd made it clear she was to be notified the moment you went into labor, and I'm not about to cross Pepper Winchester. Or your mother. Ruby and Red are on their way. Hunt's driving your grandmother in from the ranch."

She smiled and looked into her husband's handsome face. She could feel their baby inside her, ready to come out into the world and make them a family. *This is your world, right here in this room,* she thought.

Another contraction hit. Dr. Carrey stuck his head in the door. He was wearing his Stetson but he'd changed into scrubs.

"Pepper called to tell me not to deliver the baby until she got here, but I've got a rodeo tonight so let's get this baby born," Doc joked as he took off his hat.

McCall saw Luke step outside the room to take a call. She caught his expression before the door closed and realized he was as worried as she was about what was happening at the Chisholm ranch.

"What?" she asked when he came back in.

"Halley, she called in. She's all right."

"And Laura?" McCall asked, her voice breaking as another contraction gripped her.

He shook his head. "They'll get her."

Chapter Sixteen

Zane sprinted toward the cistern, firing the pistol toward the trees as he ran. The air filled with the reports of shots, his and Laura's. He still couldn't tell where she was firing from and right now it didn't matter. As long as he reached the drain and could get it open…

He was ready to dive over the side of the hill to open the drain at the base of the cistern, when he felt the searing heat of a bullet. His left leg collapsed under him and he rolled, still firing. Fortunately, his momentum took him over the edge of the hill.

Rolling down the slope, he came to a stop at the bottom of the well house next to the drain. He knew he was hit; his leg felt on fire, but he was able to crawl over to the drain valve.

He didn't have much time. In order to open the drain he would have to use both hands. And even then he feared it wouldn't be enough. The valve wouldn't have been opened in years. His fear was that he wouldn't be strong enough without some sort of tool.

Blood soaked into the thigh of his jeans. He quickly laid down his pistol and grabbed the valve handle with both hands. It didn't budge. With a curse, he pulled himself up and put all his weight into it. The handle turned a few inches.

He heard the sound of footfalls on loose gravel. Laura was coming. Any moment, she would be down the hill and around the cistern.

Zane put everything he had into turning the handle.

LAURA KNEW SHE'D HIT HIM. She'd seen him go down. He'd been heading to the backside of the cistern where the drain was located. He'd managed to stop the flow of water into the tank. She couldn't hear the women. They would have to be swimming by now. The creek water was cold. They couldn't last long.

By now Courtney would have drowned. That thought gave her a moment's pause as she came off the hillside. Two to go—if she could stop Zane.

Laura smiled to herself. This would be over soon. She had just reached the road when she saw the dust and heard the roar of a vehicle engine. Company. Even from this distance she could make out a sheriff's department patrol SUV. McCall.

"Make my day," she said under her breath. This day was just getting better.

She could hear Zane trying to open the old drain. *Good luck with that,* she thought as the patrol car zoomed up the road. Laura crouched down in front of her pickup to wait. There was time. Even if Zane got the drain open, it would take a while for the water to drain enough to get the door open.

THE HANDLE TURNED. Zane heard a *clunk,* the sound of the lock released. He fell back, pulling the drain lid open. Water began to gush out. Inside the cistern, he heard the faint sound of women's voices. He couldn't make out the words but there were at least two women in there, still alive.

The water was rushing out quickly. If they could just stay afloat a little longer…

Picking up his gun, he knew he couldn't stay here. He would be a sitting duck. Actually, he was surprised Laura hadn't already found him. She would know where he'd been headed. So where was she?

He listened. That's when he heard the sound of a vehicle coming. But there was another noise as well. He looked up and saw a small plane headed in this direction.

DEPUTY HALLEY ROBINSON SLOWED as the well house came into view. Two pickups. The one Mrs. Crowley had been driving. The other must be Zane's.

She didn't see anyone as she pulled up behind Zane's truck. She cut her engine and opened the door, pulling her weapon as she did. Staying behind the driver's side door, she peered around the edge. She could hear water running.

"Zane!" she called. "Zane?"

He appeared at the lower edge of the cistern. She could see that his left leg was soaked with blood. He leaned against the stone structure, a gun in his hand, and motioned for her to stay back.

"Mrs. Crowley is Laura. She's got a gun!" he called.

Halley took in what she could see of the area. No sign of the housekeeper. Or anyone else.

She listened and heard running water. Closer, crickets chirped in the tall grass. The sun beat down. Nothing moved.

Halley never heard her. At the last minute, she sensed the woman behind her. She felt the hair rise on the back of her neck. As she started to swing around, she felt a viselike arm come around her neck. The barrel of a gun jabbed into her back. Her own weapon was wrenched out of her hand.

In the SUV's side mirror, Halley caught a glimpse of the woman she'd known as Mrs. Crowley. The scar was gone. So was the one white eye, the one dark eye. Two very blue eyes burned too brightly from a face that was surprisingly attractive.

She'd always wondered about the first Mrs. Chisholm and what it would be like coming face-to-face with a monster. Now she knew.

"Don't think for a moment that I won't kill you," Laura said.

Halley didn't. She'd almost been killed by someone much tamer than this woman when she worked on the West Coast.

"Zane!" Laura called. "I have Halley." She jabbed the deputy hard in the back.

Halley let out a cry.

Zane appeared at the bottom edge of the cistern again.

"I need you to throw down your gun," Laura said. "Then I need you to toss me your truck keys. If you don't, I will kill your future sister-in-law."

Zane hesitated only a moment. He tossed his gun away from him, then reached into his pocket and pulled out his keys. He threw them up on the road just a few yards from them.

Halley heard the airplane. It sounded as if it was going to land on them as it zoomed just over their heads.

"Today is your lucky day," Laura said, and gave Halley a shove that sent her over the edge of the road and rolling down the slope to the creek.

A moment later, Halley heard a pickup engine fire. Gravel pelted the patrol SUV as Laura spun the tires on the truck and took off down the road.

DAKOTA HEARD THE SOUND of someone trying to open the door. The water had drained down until they could stand, but the cold creek water still pooled around their ankles. They were weak from the exertion of swimming. The cold water had zapped all their strength and all three of them were shivering convulsively. She worried that if they didn't get out soon, they would die of hypothermia.

When the door swung open, the first thing Dakota saw was Zane's face in the bright sunlight that poured in.

She stumbled to him, only then seeing the bandana tied around his thigh, the blood-soaked jeans and the lack of color in his handsome face. He grabbed her, holding her tightly against him as Halley wrapped a blanket around Emma and Courtney and helped them out into the sunshine.

Dakota began to cry as she pulled back to look into Zane's face. She'd feared that she would die in the cistern and never get to see him again. She'd known he'd come for her, prayed that he would be safe.

"We have to get Zane to the hospital," Halley was saying. "He's lost a lot of blood."

As Courtney and Emma climbed into the patrol SUV, Halley helped Dakota get Zane into the back.

Halley gave her a blanket from the back and Zane held her. She couldn't stop shaking.

Halley slid in behind the wheel and took off toward Whitehorse.

"Laura?" Emma asked, her teeth chattering.

"She got away," Halley said.

"I don't think so," Zane said as he motioned out the side window. In the distance they could see the pickup barreling down the road, a cloud of dust boiling up as it went.

A small airplane was coming from the other direction. It was headed right for the pickup.

LAURA SAW THE PLANE COMING directly at her. Hoyt. So this was how it would end, she thought, and sped up. She just hoped she got a good look at his face before she died—and he got a good look at hers.

As the plane roared toward her, sun glinted off its windshield. She squinted, trying desperately to see the man behind the controls as she braced herself for impact.

She'd been so sure he would kill himself before he'd let her get away that she hadn't been paying attention to the road ahead.

At the last minute, the pilot pulled up. The plane's belly practically scraped the top of the pickup's cab—he'd called it that close. It happened so fast. All she could see was the plane out the pickup windshield, then it was gone and she was staring not at the road ahead but open, rugged country.

The road had turned and she hadn't even noticed. She hit the brakes but the pickup was going too fast. It began to skid and hit the edge of the road hard, slamming her against the door.

She fought to get control as the truck dropped down into the ditch. She could see the embankment coming up and braced herself as the pickup went airborne.

The truck plummeted over the embankment and nose-dived into the ground at the bottom. Her head snapped back hard. She saw stars, then darkness before the pickup came to a stop half-buried in dirt and sagebrush not two miles from the Chisholm ranch house she'd once called home.

When she opened her eyes, Hoyt was beside the pickup, staring at her through what was left of the shattered side window. He had a gun in his hand.

"You can't kill me," she said, sneering at him.

He raised the gun as she fumbled for her own weapon. Hadn't she always known this was the way it had to end?

She pulled out her gun, but never got to aim before he fired.

"WOULD YOU LIKE TO SEE your daughter?" The nurse brought the blanket-wrapped bundle over to her and put the infant into her arms.

McCall stared down at her daughter and felt tears rush to her eyes. "She's beautiful."

"Just like her mother," Luke said as he leaned over to look at his daughter.

All McCall could do was stare at the infant in awe. "We did this?"

Luke laughed. "Yes, honey, we did."

"I wondered how I would feel when I held my baby." She looked up at her husband. "There are no words."

"You're going to be a great mother. You know that now, don't you?"

McCall nodded, too choked up to speak. She didn't know if she would be great, but she did know she would give it everything she had. And, unlike her mother, she had Luke.

"They said I have a great-granddaughter," Pepper Winchester said as she stuck her head in the doorway.

McCall smiled at her grandmother and turned the bundle in her arms so Pepper could see her. Pepper's eyes filled at the sight of the infant. She reached for McCall's hand and squeezed it.

McCall fought her own tears at the sight of the grandmother she'd never known until recently crying over this new life. *Strange the twists and turns life takes,* she thought. Her daughter would know her great-grandmother. She would have more family than McCall would ever have been able to imagine. Dozens of cousins, loads of people who loved her.

As if on cue, her own mother came into the room. Ruby stopped a few feet away and seemed to be waiting for an invitation.

"Well, don't just stand there," Pepper snapped at the daughter-in-law she'd denied for twenty-seven years. "Come see your grandbaby."

Ruby smiled and came over to the bed. Her eyes widened. "It's a girl?"

McCall nodded.

"Have you chosen a name?" Pepper asked.

"Tracey, after my father," McCall said, and heard Pepper let out a sob. "Tracey Winchester Crawford." Pepper covered her mouth with her hand for a moment, tears spilling from her eyes, as if fighting to keep from bawling.

Her husband and the man Pepper had loved since she was sixteen came up behind her and put an arm around her. She turned to press her face into his broad chest. Hunt smiled at McCall over his wife's shoulder and mouthed, "Thank you."

"Is that all right with you?" McCall asked her mother.

Ruby nodded. "I know your father would have liked that."

Epilogue

Zane woke in the hospital room to find Dakota asleep in the chair next to his bed and Dr. Carrey standing nearby, writing something in his chart.

"She refused to leave here," Doc said of Dakota, keeping his voice down. "I got her into the only dry clothes we had."

Dakota was dressed in hospital scrubs. She couldn't have looked cuter.

"The bullet didn't hit any bone so I think it should heal nicely," Doc was saying. "You just won't be running any footraces for a while."

"Are Emma and Courtney all right?" he asked. He'd been surprised to see Courtney come out of the cistern, surprised and thankful. All charges against him would be dropped now.

"They're fine. Both were treated and released. You do have another visitor, though. He's been waiting for you to wake up."

Doc left. A moment later, Hoyt came in. He glanced at the sleeping Dakota and smiled. "How are you, son?"

"Doc says I'm going to be fine. Emma and Courtney are all right, too, he said."

His father nodded.

"Did Laura…"

"She's dead."

Zane studied his father's face. "I'm sorry."

Hoyt let out a sound like a cross between a laugh and a sob. "I'm not. I'm just sorry she put my family through so much."

"We're Chisholms. We're pretty resilient."

His father smiled. "Yes," he said. "We are. Well, I best get home. Emma's got the rest of the family building on to the dining room. She says the current one isn't going to be able to hold all of us." He glanced toward Dakota, who was starting to stir. "I suppose she's right about that."

DAKOTA OPENED HER EYES to see Zane grinning at her. She was reminded of the boy she'd known, that cocky rodeo cowboy who used to grin at her just like that.

"Hey, beautiful," he said as he reached for her hand.

She took it and let him pull her out of the chair and into his arms. "Easy, you're injured."

"Doc was just here. I'm fine and as soon as I get out of here…" His grin widened.

She shook her head, wanting to pinch herself. Hadn't this been her girlhood dream? She thought about the diary Courtney had taken, no longer caring if it came to light. She'd been afraid of her feelings for Zane, afraid that he could never feel the way she did for him.

Wasn't that what had made Laura so crazy? She'd believed that her love was greater than Hoyt's and it had driven her insane. If she wasn't half-crazy before that.

"There's something I need to ask you," Zane said, suddenly serious. "This isn't the way I planned it. All the way, racing up to the well house, I had this romantic plan how I was going to ask you to marry me." He shook his head. "But when I woke up to find you asleep in that chair next to my bed…"

"Your sanity came back?" she joked.

His gaze locked with hers. "I realized anywhere is the perfect place and I can't wait another moment. Dakota, marry me. I know this might feel sudden, but we've known each other since we were kids and—"

"Yes," she said, leaning down to kiss him.

He laughed and pulled her down for another kiss. "Easy, cowboy."

"I love you, Dakota. I've always loved you from the first time I saw you try to ride a sheep. You must have been five at the time. I'd never seen a little girl with so much grit." He laughed. "I was so impressed when that sheep stopped and you did a face-plant in the dirt, and got up and didn't even cry as you dusted yourself off and walked away."

"I went behind the rodeo stands and cried. Mostly I was mad at myself for not staying on longer." She touched his cheek. "I've always loved you. As a matter of fact, I kept a diary and in it I said that someday I was going to marry you."

"And now you are," he said, and started to kiss her again but was interrupted by a sound at the door.

They both turned to find Courtney standing there.

"I'm sorry to interrupt, but I wanted to say goodbye and how sorry I am for everything," her sister said.

"Where are you going?" Dakota asked.

"Back to Great Falls. My mother…" Her voice broke. "My *real* mother, Camilla, wants me to come stay with her awhile until I figure out what I want to do with my life."

"I'm going to walk Courtney out," Dakota said. Zane squeezed her hand.

"Again, I'm sorry, Zane."

He nodded. "Put it behind you, Courtney. We have."

Dakota walked her out. "How are you getting home?"

"I'm taking the bus." Courtney looked away. "Do you think things like this happen for a reason? I mean, that they can completely change your life?"

"I do."

Her sister raised her gaze. "Sometime, I'd like to know more about my father."

Dakota nodded. "We're sisters, Courtney. The same blood runs through our veins. When you're ready, come back. I've always wanted a sister." She stepped up to Courtney and hugged her. Her sister hugged her tight. "Be happy."

"You, too," Courtney said. "You and Zane belong together. Send me a wedding invitation," she said with a grin.

"I won't need to. You're going to be standing right next to me as my maid of honor."

EMMA LOOKED AROUND the large dining room table. *Glad I talked Hoyt into adding on,* she thought with a smile as she took in her family.

A little more than a year ago, she'd come here as a new bride to find she had six rambunctious and wild step-sons all in need of a woman to tame them. To think she'd thought she was the one to find them the perfect mates.

"What are you smiling about?" her father asked. Alonso had finally decided he'd better fly up from California and see how his daughter was doing.

"It's a long story," Emma said as she reached over and took his hand. "Isn't this all wonderful?"

He laughed softly. "God has blessed you."

"Yes." She couldn't have agreed more as she met her

husband's gaze at the opposite end of the table. She took in Halley and Colton, Billie Rae and Tanner, Jinx and Dawson, Alexa and Marshall, Blythe and Logan, and finally Dakota and Zane.

In the past year she'd come close to losing all of them. But the Chisholms had prevailed. They were a strong, determined bunch, just like those who had settled this part of Montana before them. They'd weathered rough storms and yet here they all were, laughing and talking all at once around this table.

Once they got through all the upcoming weddings, there would be grandchildren before long. Hoyt was already talking about getting some small saddles and gentle horses for them. She'd never seen her husband more happy. He'd faced his worst fear, and now here he was among the people who loved him.

Her eyes filled with tears and she had to hastily wipe them as Hoyt rose, tapped his glass to get everyone's attention and said, "I'd like to make a toast."

The room fell silent, all eyes on her handsome, wonderful husband.

"To my family," he said, his voice breaking with emotion. "The Chisholms and the future Chisholms. Long may they live on this ranch and prosper."

"And multiply," Colton said with a grin as he looked over at his wife. Halley blushed.

"Hear, hear," Emma said, and felt tears rush into her eyes. She couldn't wait to be a grandmother, and apparently she didn't have long to wait.

* * * * *

A sneaky peek at next month...

INTRIGUE...

BREATHTAKING ROMANTIC SUSPENSE

My wish list for next month's titles...

In stores from 20th July 2012:

❏ The Perfect Outsider – Loreth Anne White

& Baby Breakout – Lisa Childs

❏ Her Hero After Dark – Cindy Dees

& The Marine Next Door – Julie Miller

❏ Cavanaugh's Bodyguard – Marie Ferrarella

& Private Security – Mallory Kane

❏ Special Ops Bodyguard – Beth Cornelison

Available at WHSmith, Tesco, Asda, Eason, Amazon and Apple

Just can't wait?

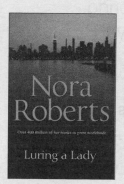

The World of Mills & Boon®

There's a Mills & Boon® series that's perfect for you. We publish ten series and, with new titles every month, you never have to wait long for your favourite to come along.

Blaze.
Scorching hot, sexy reads
4 new stories every month

By Request
Relive the romance with the best of the best
9 new stories every month

Cherish™
Romance to melt the heart every time
12 new stories every month

Desire™
Passionate and dramatic love stories
8 new stories every month

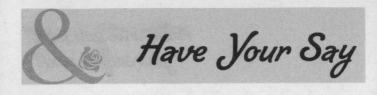